THE AUTUMN DEAD

Jack Dwyer used to be a cop. Now he's a rent-a-cop and part-time actor. Dwyer isn't complaining—not much anyway—he's got a  a little heavier, but what th woman who drove him cra s, Karen Lane, re-appears; st bewitching. She wants him to locate a missing suitcase. But Dwyer knows there's more to this than an elusive bag. And soon enough, he becomes enmeshed in his own past, tracking down old secrets, secrets that someone wants very much to remain buried—even if it takes murder to keep them there.

THE NIGHT REMEMBERS

Jack Walsh is a private detective with a past. He used to work for the sheriff's office, and that's when he helped send George Pennyfeather up for murder. But now George is out, and his wife Penny is asking Walsh to help prove his innocence. Walsh is naturally reluctant. He feels like he was right the first time. But he is drawn into the case when a young woman is murdered in the Pennyfeather's backyard. Is George being framed? And if so, is it just possible that he was framed twelve years ago as well? Walsh starts interviewing Pennyfeather's friends and former employer and in no time at all discovers that someone definitely doesn't want him on the case again.

THE AUTUMN DEAD
THE NIGHT REMEMBERS
Ed Gorman

STARK
HOUSE

Stark House Press • Eureka California

THE AUTUMN DEAD / THE NIGHT REMEMBERS

Published by Stark House Press
1315 H Street
Eureka, CA 95501, USA
griffinskye3@sbcglobal.net
www.starkhousepress.com

ISBN: 1-933586-60-5
ISBN-13: 978-1-933586-60-1

Cover design by JT Lindross
Book layout by Mark Shepard Graphic Design

First Stark House Press Edition: December 2014
FIRST EDITION

Reading Ed Gorman
by Benjamin Boulden

Ed Gorman is an unheralded writer of uncommon ability. He is a writer with a conscience—his characters reflect the world and he has an uncanny ability to make them sympathetic—but he is also an immensely entertaining storyteller. Mr. Gorman's work has ranged wide, but he is particularly good at the first person detective story and two of his best are collected in this omnibus: *The Autumn Dead* and *The Night Remembers*.

In 1985 Ed Gorman, in his second published novel, introduced his first private detective, Jack Dwyer. Dwyer is a former cop who got the acting bug after being cast in a local public safety commercial. He started acting lessons, quit his job, applied for his private investigator's license, and took a security job to keep the wolves away. Jack Dwyer appeared in five novels and *The Autumn Dead* is the fourth.

The Autumn Dead is the definitive Jack Dwyer novel. It fulfills the potential and promise of both Dwyer as a character and Ed Gorman as a writer. It is a richly detailed detective novel strong on story and scored with a thought provoking working class commentary. Jack Dwyer is the principal instigator of the novel's action, but he is also a spectator of the melancholy and hard world he inhabits. He is not a saint, and is unable to right many, if any, wrongs, but he notices the humanity around him. More importantly, he understands humanity in all its beauty, frailty and brutality. In an early scene from *The Autumn Dead*, Dwyer describes a housing development built in the 1950's:

> "They'd built the houses in the mid-fifties and though they weren't much bigger than garages, the contractors had been smart enough to paint them in pastels—yellow and lime and pink and puce, the colors of impossible flowers, the colors of high hard national hope—and they were where you strived to live in 1956 if you worked in a factory and wanted the good life promised by the Democrats and practiced by the Republicans."

It is a neighborhood forgotten by time and left to crumble and tarnish new generations with a hardscrabble existence. It is a place where dreams die, girls become hard and old before they reach maturity, and a place where the lowest rung of humanity struggles to survive. In the novel this hopelessness and poverty is juxtaposed with the comparatively well off. The professional classes and the downright wealthy. Dwyer is unable to claim membership in either class—he was raised in one and has never been able to fully gain access to the other. The conflict of class is personified by an old classmate and friend named Karen Lane.

Karen seemingly escaped her childhood poverty, but she gave herself away in the attempt. She is described much like Truman Capote's Holly Golightly. She is a woman-girl desperately trying to erase her own bitter world with her sex, and while her surroundings changed, for a time at least, she was never able to completely overcome the poverty of her childhood. A passage describing Karen's borrowed room in the home of a friend captures the rub between the dream of something more and reality.

> "The clothes—fawns and pinks and soft blues and yellows, silk and linen and organza and lame and velvet—did not belong in the chill rough basement of a working-class family. There was a sense of violation here, a beast holding trapped a fragile beauty."

There is a bitter melancholy in much of Ed Gorman's work and *The Autumn Dead* is no different. It is a narrative of loss and disappointment; the loss of time, the slow crawl to death, and the disappointment of failure.

> "You know what his problem is?"
> "What?"
> "He isn't a boy anymore."

In 1991, Ed Gorman introduced his second private eye, Jack Walsh, in *The Night Remembers*. Jack appeared in only one novel, and while he would have made a wonderful serial character, his story is seemingly complete in a single volume. Jack is 62, a World War II veteran who fought at Salerno, a retired cop—Linn County Sheriff's Department headquartered in Cedar Rapids, Iowa—and a live-in manager of a rundown apartment building in a decaying neighborhood. Jack operates a one man private investigation shop, smokes six cigarettes a day and has an on again off again relationship with a woman nearly half his age named Faith Hallahan.

Faith is a major player in both the novel and Jack's life. She is the mother of an 18-month old boy named Hoyt—she claims Jack is the father—and Faith is nearly certain she has breast cancer. Faith, like many of Mr. Gorman's female characters, has a gentle sadness, an almost broken quality, about her. She is described with an intimate fondness.

> "[R]egal, imposing, and, even at times such as these, a little arrogant. The hell of it is—for her sake anyway—she'd had one of those terrible

childhoods that robbed her of any self-confidence her looks might have given her. 'I'm only beautiful on the outside,' she's fond of saying in her dramatic way."

Amazingly Jack takes Faith's indecision about their relationship in stride. He truly loves Faith and Hoyt. There are several tender scenes between the three, which develops a visceral intimacy. Jack has an indistinct role in Faith's life. He is a mixture of father, priest and lover, which summarily describes his outsider role in society.

Jack's personal strife is a backdrop to the mystery, but it is an important and rewarding element because it focuses an understanding of his viewpoint, and it is Jack's view of the world that shimmers in the narrative. It is offhand references to real world people like Lyndon LaRouche, George McGovern and Jimmy Carter—"…Carter I never could stand. Maybe it was that psychotic smile."—and the sympathetic brush Mr. Gorman paints his characters with that pushes the novel beyond. He is particularly good at capturing a mood, a sorrow, an ill, in a few simple, sparse sentences.

"The little girl watched me as I started down the stairs. She looked sadder than any child her age ever should."

In another scene, a rambling bigot who justifies his hate with religion, is described with a keen sense of understanding—or maybe pity—without allowing for credibility or justification of the hate.

"In his plaid work shirt and baggy jeans and house slippers, he looked like the sort of melancholy psychotic you saw roaming the halls of state mental institutions just after electroshock treatment, the pain and sorrow only briefly dulled by riding the lightning."

Jack, like Dwyer, is an observer of a world he doesn't quite understand, but a world he has a wistful empathy for. A world filled with desperate, scared people behaving in ugly and malicious ways, but allowances are nearly always provided. Small understandings, if not always completely satisfactory, are conveyed in the narrative explaining the ugliness.

"She enjoyed making you despise her. I suppose she hoped that somebody would despise her almost as much as she despised herself."

The Night Remembers and *The Autumn Dead* are similar—first person narrative with a sentimental, intelligent, and watchman-like protagonist—but beneath the surface both are very different novels. *The Night Remembers* is a wistful, sentimental novel filled with betrayal and an exhausted weariness while *The Autumn Dead* is very near angry. The novels are both dark, but there is humor. Jack Dwyer is a self-deprecating wise-ass. There is a Jim Rockford moment in *The Autumn Dead* when a bartender wants five dollars to tell Dwyer where he can find a man.

"It worth five bucks to you?"
"That's only in the movies. Just call Chuck."
"I need some grease to do it because I got to walk all the way down the basement stairs. The intercom is on the blink."

Jack Walsh is less smart-alecky than Dwyer, but the humor pops up unexpectedly—the reference to Jimmy Carter's "psychotic smile" and an exchange between Walsh and the owner of the building he manages. A man he refers to as "young Mr. Banister." His description of Banister is one of the highlights.

"He was approximately thirty-five with a short earnest haircut, black earnest horn-rim glasses, an earnest white button-down shirt, an earnest blue five-button cardigan sweater, and a pair of earnest chinos that complemented his very earnest black and white saddle shoes. It was the wrong sissy touch, those shoes on a man his age, and told me more than I wanted to know about young Mr. Banister."

Jack Walsh also appeared in the 1990 short story "Friends," but he was disguised under the name Parnell. The primary backup players were there—Faith and Hoyt—and the story is worth finding. Jack Dwyer appeared in five novels, *New, Improved Murder* (1985), *Murder in the Wings* (1986), *Murder Straight Up* (1986), *The Autumn Dead* (1987), and *A Cry of Shadows* (1990), and three short stories, "Failed Prayers" (1987), "The Reason Why" (1988), which is the basis for *The Autumn Dead*, and "Eye of the Beholder" (1996).

—April 2014
Cottonwood Heights, UT

Benjamin Boulden is a crime fiction writer and editor of the renowned website, *Gravetapping* — gravetapping.blogspot.com.

Cruising the Literary Strip with Ed Gorman

by Rick Ollerman

The most durable thing in writing is style, and style is the most valuable investment a writer can make with his time. It pays off slowly, your agent will sneer at it, your publisher will misunderstand it, and it will take people you have never heard of to convince them by slow degrees that the writer who puts his individual mark on the way he writes will always pay off.

—Raymond Chandler

In the days after spinner racks and before the near-complete disappearance of books in grocery stores, I picked up a book on my way through the checkout line. It was Dick Francis's *Proof,* the first of his books I'd ever bought.

Anyway, I went home, read it, loved it, and became a lifelong Dick Francis fan. I gave the book to my father, who never had any patience for the comic books or science fiction of my youth, but was a strong reader himself.

When he was through and I asked him how he liked it, he nodded his head (a good sign, I thought) and said, "It was easy to read." I felt vaguely let down. "Easy to read" sounded like a gentle put-down, a sort of casual disappointment. How could he not like the book? An average sort of man going about his business of wine selling, suddenly facing the horrific actions of some Real Bad Men, made for a compelling contrast and shocking story.

"No," my dad said to clarify, "I liked it. 'Easy to read' is not a bad thing."

Oh, I said, and I thought about it some, and I still think about it every time I contemplate reading *Ulysses* (which hasn't happened so far).

Easy to read is not a bad thing for a book to be. It is actually a very good thing. It means the book has clear language and a good pace, it means it has interesting characters, and it means the single most important thing to the average reader: they want to keep turning those pages. 'Easy to read' is good.

Dick Francis is easy to read, all thirty plus books. Stephen King, like him or hate him, is clearly one of the most popular writers in history, is easy to read. Many other writers are as well. And so is Ed Gorman.

What I wrote above is personal, an example of what *reading* can mean to readers. Gorman's *writing* is often quite personal, infused with a well-defined sense of place, certain kinds of men and women who appear in his books, a definite love of music—and not the mellow, almost brooding Miles Davis or John Coltrane-type jazz that has become such a trend in the current market—all of which adds up to a healthy sense of the nostalgia of Gorman's youth.

A lot of what we get from Gorman's contemporary works is a sense of nostalgia. The under the covers activities from high school, not always positive, but images that evoke the sweet memories of that time: that first car, your first girl— or boyfriend, the songs that affected your younger emotions. Individual songs can be triggers to events and times in your life, and Gorman plays those notes like a master.

The obvious example is his Sam McCain series of novels, each named for a different song from a different time of McCain's—and Gorman's—life. A lot of Gorman seems to be in McCain, a not-too successful lawyer who makes his bread and butter by investigating cases for one of the town's richest citizens, who just happens to be a judge. Her family lost their preeminent position in local society almost to a fluke but the rampant nepotism, fueled by plenty of money, keeps the judge frequently at odds with the rest of the gentry. And by extension, McCain, who not only has to solve the crimes the judge becomes interested in, but is also welcome to embarrass the local sheriff, who often arrests the first and most obvious suspect he can find.

The McCain books show the character aging in something like real time and the first book, 1999's *The Day the Music Died*, a nod to the death of Buddy Holly in a plane crash near to the city where Gorman himself makes his home, takes place in 1959. The short, unpopular lawyer from the wrong side of the tracks is in love with Pamela who is in love with Stu. Mary, as well as Pamela, are both from the same poor side of the town as McCain. She is in love with McCain but is in turn loved herself by the local pharmacist.

Stu represents Pamela's ticket to the upper classes, despite the fact that he is married. She's also McCain's first love, and Gorman not only plucks that common heartstring, he knows just the way to do it. While Pamela is McCain's unrequited love, the equally beautiful Mary is just putting off her pharmacist boss in the hopes that McCain will come around. McCain loves her too, but he can't set aside whatever it is, that indefinable chain that connects us to our first true loves, long enough to do what he knows he should. Eventually Mary grows tired of waiting, as you would expect, and that only adds to the poignancy and small-scale human tragedies we all face when we find we can't get out of our own way. It's the reverse situation of the girls who go for the "bad boys"; in this case, no one involved can pull back enough to do what's right for each of them.

Pamela may let go of Stu, but that doesn't mean she'll turn to McCain. McCain may find a way to let go of Pamela, but that doesn't mean that Mary's the answer for him. In all of this, the person we perhaps most identify with is the character of Mary, who does nothing wrong and whose only sin is to love a man who doesn't love her back. Well, he does, but as I've just tried to point out, it's complicated....

This is back story, these are the things that inform us to who McCain really is; he's defined more by his personal life than by his professional one, the one in which he solves crimes for Judge Whitney, the beautiful but society-spurned socialite who takes juvenile pleasure in firing rubber bands at McCain to see if he can dodge quickly enough to keep from taking one in the face.

But there are crimes in these stories, nasty ones again stemming from the very disparate but real personalities that populate Black River Falls, Iowa. The local sheriff, Sikes, hates McCain not only for his background but for the woman he works for. Sikes is also from the wrong end of town, but a fortuitous change in his family's wealth helped to supplant the judge's family—but it also gave rise to a sheriff who is fond of handing out spontaneous beatings as he resents his own fallibility when McCain frequently proves the person Sikes has arrested is actually innocent.

Neither McCain's personal or professional life is an easy one, and only one aspect of that is his own fault.

In *The Day the Music Died*, Judge Whitney's son apparently murders his cheating wife and then commits suicide. Before he performs the final act, he confesses the shooting to McCain. But McCain doesn't believe him and that sets up the two upper class factions, the old regime and the new, in a high level war of words and politics that has the hapless yet capable McCain caught in the middle.

The mystery itself is fairly conventional, and it and its sub-plots are wrapped up fairly easily. The real appeal of this book is its full-press charm. No one in town seems to like McCain much but Mary, despite his success and ability to produce results that law enforcement can't. His relationships with his parents and friends make him very real, especially if you've ever lived in the kind of small-town filled with "big fish in small ponds" and the arbitrary politics of the rank and file. Gorman writes McCain as someone who the reader not only feels an affinity for, but an empathy for his social situation. Like Mary, we, the reader, like McCain quite well.

Throughout the entire series, it's McCain himself and how he handles the ever-evolving love triangle he's trapped himself in, as well as the personal changes he experiences as he ages that are the main attractions.

In *Will You Still Love Me Tomorrow* (2001) the charm of the series is enhanced through the portrayal of Gorman's late fifties Americana. From the cars to the music, from roller skating to drug store lunch counters, the atmosphere and the personalities of the characters overshadow the mystery here even more so than in the first book.

Richard Conners has been murdered and there's a "better dead than red" sentiment that is riding high. Why had Conners disappeared shortly before his death? Who were the two attractive out-of-towners, working for apparently different sides, but using the same techniques to get what they want? Bodies pile up and the reasons become more obscure, and that really is okay here because the more endearing plot line is the continuing triangle of McCain's love for the unattainable Pamela, Pamela's love for the wealthy but married Stu, and Mary's dedication to McCain.

For a moment, it looks like Pamela may end up with McCain but then he finds himself with somebody else. Ultimately there's no Pamela but Mary is back in the picture. And then she's gone again. The book ends with the mystery resolved, though frankly it doesn't have a lot of impact on the overall story of attorney/private investigator McCain. What isn't resolved is the status of any of the relationships that matter, and the "relationship cliffhanger" at the end will have you scrambling for the third book in the series. A note at the beginning of the book tells you the story actually takes place the year *before* the first book happens. So the cliffhanger continues....

The Sam McCain series is Gorman's ode to an idyllic time gone past; those fabulous fifties with the birth of rock and roll, cruising the streets with the top down, and unrequited first loves. Like walking down Main Street at Disney World with steam locomotives, barbershop quartets, sweets stores and the like. Yes, we all have to grow up sometime, but isn't it wonderful for a writer to be able to take us back to the rose-tinted old days and flash us back to that optimism of youth rather than wallow in the acquired cynicism of middle age? This isn't nihilistic noir where everyone's playing craps and shooting sevens, this is a shot of either real life, or what real life should have, pain. It hurts, but over time, we evolve and improve. In the meantime, there are enough behind closed doors scandals to keep it both real and interesting.

With the Sam McCain series, Gorman creates his tapestry of love letters to the golden times of his youth. The Depression is ended, the Greatest Generation has come home, and the Baby Boomers are growing up. Somewhere in the background is the Cold War and the background threat of nuclear war, but we also have the birth of rock and roll, the explosion of America's car culture, the innocent time as we fill the gap between war heroes and the counter-culture that came later in the sixties. We don't have drugs and rebellion in these books, we have the other side of *The Saturday Evening Post*, a celebration of American life colored through the longing glasses of a Time When Things Were Better.

These are crime stories, of course, but we don't necessarily care. In the town of Black River Falls, Iowa, the Sykes family had stumbled into enough money building government projects in the war that they've taken over, forcing out all but the last remaining Whitney, the judge that is Sam McCain's boss. This eccentric woman exemplifies the "good" in the town's upper class while McCain himself is much more comfortable among the great unwashed. He eats lunch at the Rexall counter, he reads science fiction magazines and Gold Medal paperbacks, and he mentions names like Harry Whittington, Peter Rabe, Charles Williams and David Goodis. The snobbish element in town looks down on him for this but others love him because he's real to them.

Another thing we hear from Sam McCain in every book is how he compares himself to screen actor Robert Ryan, one of Gorman's real life cinematic heroes.

No one played the flawed and wounded bad guy with such emotional range as Ryan. Never a breakout star, he appeared in such films as *The Wild Bunch, The Dirty Dozen, Odds Against Tomorrow* and other classic films in both the western and noir genres. Gorman's favorite Ryan movie appears to be *Bad Day at Black Rock*, where Ryan stands up to a one-armed Spencer Tracy while a town full of characters played by the likes of Ernest Borgnine, Anne Francis and Lee Marvin try to keep the secrets of their town's past buried and forgotten.

McCain may not be as tall or as good looking as the 6'4" Ryan, but it's his on-screen persona that McCain uses to bolster himself as Judge Whitney's investigator to help make up for his five-five height, hint of a babyface, and, according to him, lack of appeal to the woman he loves most.

The books are standalones as far as the crimes go, each one being a self-contained mystery story, but what keeps you coming back is McCain and his optimism, his appreciation of the pop culture exploding around him, and the current state of his complicated love life. No matter what they seem to do, McCain, Pamela and Mary all need each other, and McCain helps the women he loves however he can.

Despite all that happens to him, we get the feeling McCain himself doesn't really care. He's got his Ford ragtop, he's interesting enough to various women that he's not completely lonely, and he does a far better job at solving crimes at the judge's behest than Chief Cliffie Sykes, Jr., and it doesn't seem to matter that as a lawyer he's more or less at the bottom of the legal pecking order in town.

In the third McCain book, *Wake Up Little Susie* (2001), McCain gives us a bit of insight into his situation like this:

> I once asked my mom if our family had ever been hexed. You know, if somebody had a grudge against Mom and Dad and put a curse on their firstborn, which would be me. Condemn him to love a girl forever beyond his reach. I am twenty-three, a lawyer, and have what they call "prospects." And I have a '51 red Ford convertible with the custom skirts, the louvered hood, and the special weave top that most of the guys around here, even the cool ones, envy.
>
> That's my story. Hers is, she's been in love with Stu Grant since ninth grade, just the way I've been in love with her. He's big, good-looking, rich, and powerful. He's also married. Pamela's convinced he'll someday leave his wife and take his rightful place at her side. Right, just like Liz Taylor and Eddie Fisher'll break up someday too.

Despite Pamela's inaccessibility, he does find time to be seduced by a woman that may or may not be a Communist and may or may not be working subversively for the organization known as America First, but the story is a typical McCain mystery. We have him talking to various people in the town, some upper class, some lower class. Some of them like him, a lot of them scorn him. Here's a sample of dialogue between a girl he couldn't touch in high school and now is forced to talk to him because of his investigation:

> "I couldn't lift a person and throw her in a car trunk."
> "She probably didn't weigh a hundred pounds."
> "Oh, I see. I'm such a moose I could've done it, huh?"
> "Just about anybody could have done it, Amy."
> "You know what's funny?"
> "What?"
> "I was the one who got her on the cheerleading squad. I mean she was nobody. And I just thought it'd be neat if I, you know, sort of extended my hand. I was the captain of the squad so I figured I should set the example. The other girls didn't want her. They called her 'Jane' because she was always reading those Jane Austen novels. My mom said Jane Austen was a lesbian."
> "Well, if anybody would know about Jane Austen's sex life, it'd be your mom."
> "But I felt sorry for her. So I insisted. And ten years later she steals my husband. Small world, huh?"

This is life in Black River Falls. In high school we have cliques, in adult life we have class and social status. There seem to be a fortunate few, like Sam McCain, who can put on his Robert Ryan mask when he needs to and navigate the worlds of both.

In one of the books (*Everybody's Somebody's Fool*, 2004), the wife of a suspect asks McCain: "You ever wish we were kids again?"

"All the time," he answers.

You get the feeling so would Gorman.

Ed Gorman started out working in advertising, as some of his earlier settings suggest. His first book, *Rough Cut* (1985) is a fairly conventional murder mystery centered around an advertising agency with enough boozing, philandering and white collar crime to make the cast of *Mad Men* blush. When describing a sleazy PI, Gorman gives us lines like, "He wore a double-knit black sport coat with lapels wide enough to play shuffleboard on," and "A smirk parted his lips, revealing teeth the color of a urine specimen."

Before transitioning from short stories to longer works, Gorman had begun his professional career by working as a copywriter and other jobs in the advertising business, including work with three different ad agencies. Eventually he started his own firm in Cedar Rapids and produced television commercials. When he turned that business over to his partner he began writing political speeches. This helped inform his opinion on politics, which he appears to share with the character in his Dev Conrad series, which began with 2008's *Sleeping Dogs*.

Conrad is a political consultant, brought in to help candidates get elected and keep scandals at bay, or at least to minimize their effects. All too often, books about

Hollywood, sports and politics wind up pushing on us the same stereotypes we've grown up with in bad fiction and on television movies of the week. But here we don't get adjectives like "presidential" or comparisons to the charisma of Jack Kennedy. Gorman's candidates are just that: people running for office. Whether they win or not is less a matter of destiny than how well one party machine out-maneuvers the other. The biggest difference in all this is the realistic character of Conrad himself.

"Real" in a fictional character means he thinks and acts more or less like the rest of us. Dev Conrad is under no illusions about the political system. He doesn't be-lieve one candidate is better than another, or one party superior to all others. No, he has the cynicism bred into an age where Congress's public approval rating dwells consistently below the ten percent mark. Conrad knows this, but this is the work he does, often working at odds with, if not his actual candidates, family members and the people around them.

All of Gorman's political insights are here, without cliché, and he's not shy about dropping the names of a few past presidents into the mix as he labels the misuses of power in the course of these stories. What saves Conrad from being more than a cynical SOB and actually being a good man who is good at his job, is his belief that these candidates may be flawed, and they may commit many sins, but *most* of the time they manage to do things that match the greater good. The feelings of entitlement, the privilege, the power and prestige, can all be overlooked as long as Conrad believes this is really so. As, likely, do most of the rest of us, at least those of us past a certain age. We can vote for change but we'll never get it, Gorman seems to tell us, but if the individual good acts outweigh the bad, well, that's the system we have.

When the books give us blackmail and murder, Conrad suffers what may be the greatest sin of all: disillusionment.

As a political consultant, Conrad is a "fixer," the guy behind the scenes who is probably smarter than the candidates he works for, and also a man who would probably make a better candidate himself if he were just wired differently, enough to want to do that particular job.

Sleeping Dogs gives us all of this but regardless of the mayhem, Conrad works for a man he no longer respects, not only as a politician but as a man, and he has to navigate through the lies, the dirty tricks, and other crimes in order to see his man through. That is, if he survives himself.

The second book in the series, *Stranglehold* (2010), gives us much the same sort of mischief that goes on in *Sleeping Dogs*. Sometimes books in a series can seem repetitive but here we get a book that feels like slipping bare feet into broken-in woolen slippers. Despite the despicable deeds, we're comfortable as Gorman takes us further into the world of real world political machinations (as well as the crimes that make these books the mystery novels they are). If we like *Sleeping Dogs*, Gorman delivers to us more of what we want.

We get more of Conrad the man: slightly self-loathing, talented, lonely, and with a penchant for getting bounced on the head. Still supremely capable, he knows politics and he knows people, and clearly Gorman does, too. He gives us a book that manages to both play fair with the reader yet pull the rug out from under us with a clever twist. Or more.

Conrad delivers his cynicism as well as his optimism; he delivers the sort of self-referential remarks that let the reader know that what his side does to win a campaign is no different than what the other side does to win theirs–and they both play dirty. The reader rankles along with Conrad when he occasionally ruminates about wealth and privilege in Washington and how those things corrupt, along with the addictions of power.

The ones willing to burn in the flame are the ones willing to do almost anything else. These are the facets of human nature that Gorman captures so well and makes this series so compelling.

Several agents and a number of publishers rejected Gorman's first book, *Rough Cut*. By the time that book was finally published, Gorman had written and sold two more. His second, *New, Improved Murder* (1985) has the same basis as *Rough Cut* in that the characters' immoral or amoral acts give rise to the conflicts in the story, also concerning the shenanigans surrounding an ad agency. Instead of an amateur sleuth from the company, Gorman gives us his first series character, Jack Dwyer: part-time actor, former cop, and now private investigator. In many ways it's a similar book to the first one but the writing is clearly smoother and more confident. And we get more Chandler-esque quotes like:

> This specimen wore several rings, a toupee at least one size too small, and a chain around his neck that could get you through a snowstorm in winter. He stared at me with a mixture of contempt and fear. He must have sensed that I wouldn't mind smashing his face in.

1987's *The Autumn Dead* is another entry in the Jack Dwyer series and it shares very strong overtones with Gorman's Sam McCain series. Nostalgia is nearly always one of his themes–though not in his westerns–and this one gives us high school sweethearts, a school reunion, and a terrible secret from the past. There is an ex-crush of Dwyer's, a very unreliable woman, who taps him to track down a mysterious briefcase.

Dwyer knows she's not telling everything she knows, but then, no one else is, either. There are life-ruining secrets here, and the book strikes a wonderful balance of tragedy and tone. There's another tie to the ad game with Dwyer's girlfriend, Donna, more consumption of Pepsi (think James Lee Burke's love of Dr Pepper), more references to the movies and music of Gorman's youth, and above all the nostalgic sense that the present is informed by the past, a wellspring of melancholy that haunts these characters.

Does this make for a happy ending? Gorman shows us that just because a case is solved there is still an awful cost to people and their lives.

In this, the beginning of the series, Gorman seems to pattern Dwyer more or less after himself but as the years have gone by, the two have grown apart, with Gorman's political views, health, and personal habits all veering away from the trajectory that he had originally set to Jack Dwyer.

Eye of the Beholder (1996) is what Gorman calls the last Jack Dwyer story. In addition to being a prolific novelist (maybe a hundred books? Gorman himself doesn't know for sure) he's also turned out a prodigious number of short stories. This is a good one, about a beautiful young woman who has her face slashed one night, causing ruinous damage to her good looks. Really, though, what stands out here is Dwyer's emotional state: he's lonely, as we've all been at times in our lives, but almost desperately so as he searches for a woman that he can not only take to dinner but continue with a serious relationship.

He tries all the usual places; different bars, supermarkets, anywhere he happens to come across attractive women. He makes a few starts but they don't go anywhere. And worse, he knows they won't even as the relationship unfolds, but some mistakes are just too tempting to pass up.

In the story, Dwyer spends most of his time with the mother of the attacked girl, only to learn inadvertently that she had become romantically involved with another man. Dwyer is neither particularly surprised or particularly disappointed. It's as if the situation has met his sad and lonely expectations.

This is a serious and profound look at an aging character, a subtle glimpse into the nature of what it means to be alone and wishing it were otherwise. But wishing don't make it so, as they say, and all Dwyer can do is keep on with his life as he's made it. Will he ever find personal happiness? Will anyone? The answer may or may not be part of his personal equation.

The plot of *Eye of the Beholder* is a fairly straightforward PI story, where Dwyer identifies a number of suspects before eventually landing on the actual perpetrator, but even that turns out to be an elusive solution due to the deft way that Gorman compels the reader to a double take at the end.

In a way this is more than a fitting farewell to Jack Dwyer, not only for Gorman but for the world he once inhabited.

In addition to the hundreds of novels and short stories Gorman has produced, he has become one of this generations' most prolific anthologists. Ever a champion of the written word, he has compiled dozens of anthologies, often with collaborators such as Martin H. Greenberg, Larry Segriff, and others, including the two volume set *The Black Lizard Anthology of Crime Fiction* (1987 and 1988) which highlight that wonderful publisher's mission to bring back paperback era favorites such as Peter Rabe and Harry Whittington. He has also produced several "best of the year" anthologies, collections of western stories, pulp fiction, cat crimes, and an invaluable collection of non-fiction essays celebrating all things noir, *The Big Book of Noir* (1998) with Lee Server and Martin H. Greenberg.

Pulp Masters, from 2001, showcases short novels from the pulp to slick era featuring such writers as James M. Cain, Donald E. Westlake, Lawrence Block, John D. MacDonald, Micky Spillane and the "king of paperbacks," Harry Whittington. Gorman is more than just a writer himself, he's a fan, and a spectacular one, whose work as an anthologist has perhaps done as much to further interest in the forgotten culture of crime fiction than anyone.

In 1985 he and Robert Randisi started *Mystery Scene* magazine, a periodical about the crime writing world. He's won The Eye award for lifetime achievement from the Private Eye Writers of America, he's won the Shamus Award (also from the PWA), the Bram Stoker Award for his horror fiction from the Horror Writers Association, the Spur Award from the Western Writers of America, the Macavity Award, the Anthony, the Ellery Queen Award, and more. He is a writer and scholar of the field who believes in giving back. Many writers cite Gorman as helping them start their careers and as always being a welcoming source for help and support.

Gorman's standalone novels often come from places that are either personal or have a personal interest to him. In 1994's *Shadow Games* he takes on a subject that may very well be too close to home for many writers. In real life, Gorman had a cousin named Bobby Driscoll. Driscoll had been the Disney studio's first contract player, playing roles like Johnny in the controversial *Song of the South* (1946), Jim Hawkins in *Treasure Island* (1950) and was the voice of the original and classic animated story of *Peter Pan* (1953).

Bobby Driscoll was Hollywood gold, with the natural talent, the looks, the charm, everything the public could want. But he developed a heroin habit when he was seventeen and his too-brief career ended when his body was found in an abandoned East Village tenement by two children in 1968. He was just 31 years old.

In *Shadow Games* Gorman plays with conventional structure and, according to his introduction to the 1994 Cemetery Dance edition, wrote and discarded three drafts before selling the fourth. Then, with the help of a friend, he wrote yet another version, all the while wondering if the book's construction would make it difficult for it to find an audience. He needn't have worried as the book sold quickly in Europe and was very well received.

The book opens with a child Hollywood actor already getting into trouble, then jumps ahead to a point in time where he has apparently received treatment and reformed. Along the way we meet the people in his life, all with their own Hollywood secrets and back stories. Then a body turns up, horribly mutilated and posed for display. The actor goes on the run, and a PI steps into the frame, looking to help.

As the body count continues to rise, the reader is never sure who is behind the killings. Gorman gives us ample motive for any number of characters as one by one each of their own back stories is revealed, opening up the possibilities of motives not previously made clear. The actor may be the man on the run, but that doesn't mean he's the guilty party, and Gorman keeps us guessing as we're never sure who is actually guilty of what. That is the question that runs through the latter half of the book as the PI eventually catches up to the solution. Is it a successful

conclusion? Let's just say it's one we read about in Hollywood year after year.
This is a very interesting novel, one that keeps the reader off balance in the way that the best mystery novels do. Yes, there's a private investigator involved but the book isn't a PI book: it's a mystery that has a PI in it. The things the investigator actually does don't do a lot to alter the events in the book.

Less personal but keeping with the Hollywood theme is another standalone Gorman wrote, this one in 1995 and called *The Marilyn Tapes*. This is a first person novel written a decade into Gorman's book writing career and he gives us a highly detailed, complex thriller comprised of many rotating points of view. It's an effective technique and as the story moves along and the cast of characters shrinks (remember, this is a crime novel). How this develops is at least half the fun of the book. Most of the characters come straight from history: Marilyn Monroe, J. Edgar Hoover, Clyde Tolson, Louella Parsons, John F. Kennedy. There is a bibliography in the back of the book that shows the amount of research Gorman put into the crafting of this book.

Marilyn Monroe herself only appears in extracts from the tapes mentioned in the title, and the tapes themselves serve as the MacGuffin that has criminals, government officials, private eyes and psychopaths all on the hunt. The tragedy that was Marilyn Monroe is only hinted at, but that serves to make it all the more poignant. If the essence of the real Norma Jean Baker had been overlooked in real life, the essence of the real Marilyn Monroe is purposely overlooked here. Gorman's voice and sensibility are on display in passages like this:

> *Weird that Tully would fall in love with a girl who had an artificial leg. He had met her the previous fall, at an outdoor restaurant by the La Brea tar pits, where he was having a few drinks watching the sunset.*

Most of the characters in the novel have a high level of moral ambiguity but in different ways, ways that suit each individual. They can be motivated by greed or love or money or loyalty or revenge but no matter their standing, be it high or low, none of them are portrayed as all bad or all good. This is a book of people existing in the grey areas, and when measured against what we now know about many of the people involved in Ms. Monroe's death (as well as the still rumored existence of actual tapes), the story seems every bit as complicated as whatever it was that happened in "real life."

The rule in writing horror fiction is that once the monster is revealed, the horror is over. While trying to solve the mystery of the missing scientists, something is terrorizing the dwindling search party; this gives the reader or viewer suspense (or cheese). It's not until the giant, radiation-spawned crabs crawl out of the ocean that the source of the horror is revealed, simultaneously removing the tension from the *What is going on?* to *Okay, when is the next crab grabbing a clawful of man meat?* A form of suspense can still happen, but it's no longer the scary kind, the kind where the reader's fear stems largely from not knowing who, or what, is actually responsible. It's camera and editing tricks. There's the *imagined* horror and there's the *actual* horror, two very different things. This is why many horror books can scare the pants of you until... they don't, and you feel let down by the almost mundane ending.

Cage of Night (1996) is not exactly a horror book but it's not strictly a thriller, either. Rather than end the horror by finally revealing the truth behind the "monster," it turns out the monster may not be real at all. But someone's responsible for what's been happening to the people in town, and while the answer turns out to be much more mundane than an unseen alien monster delivered via meteorite crash to the bottom of an old well, it's actually even scarier when the solution turns out to be far more mundane. And because of that, it's all the more real.

Cage of Night actually gives us several kinds of horrors, all presented in the context of ordinary life in a small town. We have high school kids misbehaving and getting away with violence towards women and various other crimes in large part because they're jocks and their value to their teams outweighs their bad behavior. In fact, it fosters it. We have peer pressure, we have social outcasts, we have a taste of nerd culture and how that can affect a man later in life when he comes in to a position of authority over others. The largest terror in the book is centered on the girl who wants love, a beautiful girl who attracts the roughest of jocks as well as others who can use even more raw strength and brutality to satisfy her desires.

The story centers around what happens when one man, a youth just out of the Army and looking forward to beginning a stint at the local community college, falls in love with a girl after meeting her at a party. Nothing can keep him away. Not physical violence, not the threat of prison or of death, and ultimately, not even the girl's own rejection.

You can see how the older characters relate to their past lives in high school, their music, their cars, and how that keeps that classic Gorman thread of nostalgia alive in his characters. One way or another, everyone is trying to go back to something, and more often than not it was something they never had in the first place.

The book was evidently a hard sell to publishers who didn't know how to classify it: was it a suspense thriller, a horror book, fantasy? At times and in parts it is all three and Gorman is able to keep enough balls in the air to keep the reader guessing throughout. The end may be neatly worked out, but if he's worked his psychological magic on you just right, Gorman will still leave you squirming.

The book was based on a novelette Gorman wrote and dedicated to Stephen King called "The Brasher Girl" (1995). In *Cage of Night*, the personalities of almost all the characters are vastly different than in the novel, and the characters from "The Brasher Girl" do things that were later attributed to new characters in *Cage of Night*. In the end, there's still room for the reader to ask, *Was there or wasn't there?* and all the psychological ambiguities are still in play. Is there a malevolent force in the woods, or is a combination of sex, lust and shared psychotic disorder to blame for whatever it is that has taken hold of the town? In the end, the reader decides; Gorman does not beat us over the head with the solution. Assuming he knows....

Though Gorman has said that "being all over the map has seriously damaged my career," his willingness to not stick primarily to series–he actually prefers standalones, another publishing ding–helps him to write across multiple genres, often combining them to great affect. While he has written a great many series characters (including Sam McCain, Dev Conrad, Robert Payne, Jack Dwyer) he has also written both standalone westerns as well as series westerns, starring characters like Leo Guild, and "Calvary Man" Noah Ford. In many of these books we have strong elements of noir and westerns, or simply noir back in the frontier days.

So what is western fiction? The best of it is informed by the same themes of human involvement that can be found in any genre. Larry McMurtry's Pulitzer Prize-winning *Lonesome Dove* has cowboys and Indians in it, but it is not a white man vs. Indian story. It's about the struggle of a pair of middle-age men seeking to discover new purpose in a changing world following their time in the Civil War. Along with the western elements, the human stories are stronger, and some of the more poignant scenes are borrowed from the central African exploits of Dr. Livingstone. It is a gut-wrenching portrait of humanity and dedication between true friends. It's about the sacrifice that men make for each other.

More recently we have books like Scott Phillips' *Cottonwood*, which blends history (the "bloody Benders" of Kansas) with the all-too human story of a man trying to make his way and find a niche for the future. He is often sidetracked by his own vice-driven needs as a man and filled with bouts of failure and success. The book reads as if it were written in the 1890's but with modern structure and language.

Gorman's *Wolf Moon* (1993) is a slender volume of similar themes but on a smaller scale. Chase is a man who once acted on a lark and moved to the wrong side of the law. This ended poorly, with his brothers murdered and himself thrown in prison. Meanwhile, the power behind the crime, ostensibly a respectable man, enjoys the wealth and power of his reputation, free from all suspicion.

This is a story of revenge, hatred, self-perception, and above all a tragedy that takes place in the pre-Industrial Revolution West. There aren't any more guns and gunfights than you would find in many contemporary police procedurals. There are no showdowns at high noon, no cattle ranchers competing for water resources, no rustling or horse thieving. This is a western because this is the setting where the human drama takes place. Could it happen in modern day Detroit? No. There's no FBI, no telephones, no television. It's not legal for a private citizen to own a wolf as a pet. The same story couldn't play out in today's world.

These things allow the dramatic tension to stem from the powerful personalities Gorman imbues in his characters. There are noirish elements, there are criminous ones, but mostly there is the human drama of the sort that all of us can relate to today, which happens to be the same way, according to Gorman, that people living in the late 1800's would deal with issues and emotions of the very same sort.

In *Trouble Man* (1998) we have all the expected western characters—the wealthy rancher, the gunfighter, the stagecoach robbers, the whores—but it's what Gorman does with them that is special. The wealthy rancher isn't a robber-baron dominating the town and cheating other men of their land or water rights. He is a man grieving from a past disaster, trying to hold his family together. The gunfighter has his reputation, but he came by it after just a few accidental showdowns. The stagecoach robbers are the same as criminals in any time or any genre. The same goes for the prostitutes to a large degree, but here we have a half-breed woman facing limited choices in a white man's world.

Gorman also gives us a tale of vengeance and if this were an old Republic serial we'd have the gunfighter riding into town facing down anyone and everyone, no matter the odds. Ray Coyle rides into town after his son has been gunned down, but more than outright revenge he's seeking the truth. People are afraid of him and his reputation as a gunny, and he doesn't hide from it, but it's justice he's after, be it with the law or at the end of a gun. It doesn't matter which way it goes down, but if it has to be with his gun it will only be by necessity—it's never his plan. He's not Billy the Kid carving notches on his pistol grip.

Throughout the story we get the touches of humanity that Gorman brings to his westerns, like the quest for the gunfighter to try to get a sense of the lost son he'd never really known. There's the rancher's grief, the struggles of the half-breed prostitute to escape the life she sees forced upon her, the rivalries between petty bullies and criminals, and the reckoned costs of the mischief men got into in a time and place where guns and a certain amount of lawlessness were the norm.

Trouble Man is a western but perhaps it would be better to think of it as a frontier story with western characters. It is an all too human one. This is not a glorified projection of violence on the Wild West, but a tale of three different families: one disintegrated, one broken up, and one fighting to keep itself together. We can even count four if we include the one that never gets a chance to start. The novel goes far beyond an illustration of the man who's got the quickest draw. And in the end, the greatest tragedy of all is that none of the families is the better for the tragedies that take place. This is noir.

The year 2001 gives us *Ghost* Town and while this book reads like a story of the Old West, it actually takes place in a railroad town in Wisconsin. In a similar but more complex story than *Trouble Man*, Gorman takes us deeply into a world of law and order where the criminals are not always homicidal maniacs. There are plenty of bodies, and something of a mystery for Bryce Lamont to solve, but he's a lifelong con man, not a gunslinger or a stagecoach robber or a stick-up man at a bank. This is a story of standing loyalties and debt and what happens when an old comrade crosses the line. And keeps crossing it, over and over.

It's interesting that this book can be called nothing other than a western. With a few changes, it could have taken place on the frontier, but the violent acts typical of a western tale take on a new light when couched in a (relatively) more civilized setting. This is a story of maturity and what might happen if frontier crimes took place in a land well past its settler days. The railroad is established, there are other cities within easy train rides, there are doctors and a hospital. What could be a quiet picture of a modern-day equivalent suburbia turns into the setting for a variety of crimes, of revenge, misplaced loyalty, and people cheated of love they deserve.

Loyalty between comrades allows not only the crimes to continue and compound, but in a strange way also keeps Bryce Lamont alive. Loyalty between men and women also runs deep with some of the characters, but these relationships end darkly, and with tragedy.

Good men are bad and bad men are good. Gorman often takes the tropes of the genre and gives then a good twisting, building rich stories into the unfamiliar curves and arcs of his books.

Deadly malaria is spreading through town and pictures of citizens falling ill are interspersed with the misbehavings and criminal behavior of the rich and powerful. One of the strongest figures standing up to both is the very rare sort of western character, a woman doctor. Not only does this strong woman stand up for herself and her profession, her dedication to her job and to her loved ones plays a significant role in the story. This is even more remarkable because the story is told in the first person from the point of view of a man, one with even fewer scruples than Dr. Laura Westcott.

A woman doctor, love torn apart before it has a chance to bloom, a forced fight for vengeance: again, this is noir.

Four of the wealthiest men in town leave for the big city on a retreat that only money, privilege and secrecy can buy them. But what happens there goes terribly wrong and the four men that left are not the four that return. A dark and terrible secret is born, one they'll all have to pay for in the coming years.

This is the set up for the 2006 novel *Shoot First*. When one of the men receives a mysterious visitor, and then a letter, and later turns up dead, the town is thrown into confusion. One of the richest men around, a seemingly upright civic leader, is gone and no one knows why or who might have done it. The famous Pinkertons come to town and as the three remaining rich men meet in secret, panic among them begins to take hold.

This is a mystery story with a large cast of deeply realized characters. It takes place in an unnamed town in an unnamed location, but it is clearly of a time that is the Old West. The story could, however, take place today, which makes this a western that is again not dependent on western tropes or devices. It's a story of greed, hubris, vice, murder and mental illness. It's peopled by characters that could exist in any time, with a story structure that effortlessly shifts suspicion from suspect to suspect until at last, the truth is revealed.

The mystery here is stronger than the crimes—who is really behind the murders, and why?—and it's the personalities of the individual characters that make the book deeper and more than just a clever plot. As it turns out, wealth is about the only thing the four powerful men have in common; as individuals they are vastly different. Even the sheriff's deputies are painted with their own singular personalities, character types that are usually the most cardboard in crime fiction, especially westerns. This is not your grandfather's Zane Grey.

Gorman's women continue to be strong characters in their own right. There's mention of a woman doctor here, although she's not the character of Laura Westcott from *Ghost Town*. There's a single woman running her own candle-making business. And there are women not afraid to stick up for themselves, even at the cost of alienating their own husbands. Again, Gorman's women, in his "westerns", seem to purposely go against stereotype.

The first of Gorman's western series feature the world weary Leo Guild. The book *Guild* (1987) is a book about a bank president gone bad, not uncommon in the western world (or the savings and loan debacle in the 1980's or even the fiddling of Wall Street in the current millennium). Indeed, *Guild* seems deliberately set in a more genre-typified atmosphere. We still don't get high noon quickdraw shootouts in the streets, but we get frontier town shenanigans in another unspecified midwestern community.

Bounty hunter Leo Guild is good with his gun, better with his fists, and his past haunting of a mistaken killing has honed his moral compass to the point where the letter of the law be damned, he's going to do what's right. And while he quickly falls in love with a beautiful waif, the book doesn't come close to the "Longarm" style of "adult westerns." There's sex but it's not explicit. There are gunfights, fist fights, stagecoach robbers, embezzlers, and aging powerful men betrayed by their less intelligent or more indolent progeny.

Despite some pretty prose, as if it could have been influenced by a James Lee Burke novel, this is much more of a traditional western than many of Gorman's standalone westerns. Still though, these old West settings are almost incidental to the plot. Sure, it would be more difficult to have a shootout in a whorehouse above a saloon in most modern towns, and there's not much percentage in a quick getaway on the back of a horse, but the themes, or the human elements that drive the characters' actions, are universal and independent of setting.

Guild is a solid if not unsurprising start to the series. It seems as though Gorman was giving "western readers" more of what they'd expect.

Death Ground (1998) is the second in Gorman's Leo Guild series and it strikes a much darker tone than the first. In many ways Guild is just one of an ensemble cast that features a pair of brothers, one sadistic and domineering over the other; a straight-laced sheriff; a combination mountain man/commune founder/criminal with a sort of genius despite his limited IQ; a priest who isn't really a priest; and a host of smaller characters. Guild is fifty-four years old in this book, and he's feeling every minute of it. He's collecting bounties for a stake but he's lonely and looking for companionship. He's fey throughout the book but he's compassionate to everyone, even the worst characters, the ones least deserving of anyone's help.

Guild has been hired to protect a man who believes someone is trying to kill him. When both he and the young man Guild hired to help guard him are gunned down, the sheriff tries to recruit Guild to go after the man he believes is responsible. Already going are two of the sheriff's deputies and Guild tells the sheriff he's not interested. He's not sure what went wrong but doesn't feel responsible and doesn't feel he has enough skin in the game to do justice to the job. He changes his mind when his feelings of guilt take over after visiting his slain assistant's mother. Guild reluctantly agrees to ride off into the winter mountains.

There are still misgivings and he's soon caught up in a web of betrayals, sadism, deception and disaster as he works his way through a myriad of complications in the pursuit of what initially seemed a fairly straightforward job.

This is not an action or plot heavy book; instead Gorman delves deep into the personalities of the principals, and it's their own traits and actions that shape what goes on in those mountains. This is a noir Western and in the end, no one goes away happy, and the book ends on a sweetly sad and melancholic moment.

Another series of western novels Gorman gives us are the "Cavalry Man" books with Noah Ford, an investigator for the U.S. Army. In *Calvary Man: The Killing Machine* (2005), Ford is on the trail of an improved version of the Gatling gun, a deadly and coveted killing machine that could command almost any price on the open market. Ford is tracking down the gun with the objective of getting it back to Washington, where it belongs. The problem is, it's been stolen by Ford's brother, David.

The Army doesn't want Ford on the case because of the familial conflict, but Ford insists and they relent. When he finds and confronts his brother he sets up a later meeting, hoping against hope his brother, once a Confederate soldier while Ford fought for the Union, will surrender the gun. Noah may have his doubts but he's counting on, in the end, his brother will do what's right.

Instead, everything goes wrong. The two men Noah brings with him are killed, Ford himself is shot, and when it's all said and done, David Ford has been found with his throat cut, and the gun has gone missing.

Four men are in town waiting for their chance to bid on the gun when David Ford is killed. The four have a secret (similar to Gorman's 2001 book, *Ghost Town*) and are trying to keep it hidden from Ford, whose mission has now gone from not only recovering the gun but finding vengeance for his brother. David had had a girlfriend that is a lady nurse, as opposed to *Ghost Town* where the slain brother's girl is a lady doctor.

Despite these similarities, *The Killing Machine* gives us a mystery just as deep: who is systematically killing the four arms dealers? Who actually killed David Ford? Who keeps trying to kill Noah Ford?

Instead of a bad banker, we end up with a bad sheriff, but this is after we go through a bad deputy and a bad mortician. In the end it's shown that they've all been working together but it takes a lot of bodies piling up before Ford finally finds the gun–and the real killer.

The second book in the series, *Calvary Man: Powder Keg* (2006) is a complex story of old grudges, long standing prejudices, and the inevitable right vs. wrong. In Gorman's westerns, it's almost as though he feels he can let loose with more *story*, as though he finds the conventions of the western–as set in stone as they may be to other writers–less constricting than those of the modern thriller.

Like most of Gorman's westerns, this is far from the been there, done that, read one, read them all genre books. Federal investigator Noah Ford has a friend and fellow agent whose career has been severely damaged by false accusations of wrongdoing. He doesn't deal well with the scandal and takes to drink even though Ford does what he can to look after him.

Two other Federal men are involved, and they're as crooked as the people they're supposed to go after. Washington doesn't quite see this, though, and they become the target of Ford's friend, Tom Daly's alcohol-fueled anger. Connolly and Pepper don't like this, of course, and it's a bit of a toss up as to just who is going to make the first move.

While Ford is working a case in another town, Daly conspires to put himself and his two nemeses in the same place; Daly to look for the man who killed yet another Federal agent, and Connolly and Pepper ostensibly pursuing a local bank robber. This man is a Lothario who not only is good with the ladies (married or otherwise) but is playing Robin Hood by stealing from his former rival's banks and giving the money to local landowners so they can keep their drought-starved lands from foreclosure.

When Ford's case wraps up and Tom Daly's wife wires him that her husband and Connolly and Peppers are all in the same town, the *Powder* Keg of the title is clear and Ford knows there's trouble ahead for his friend. He has no choice. He has to go, as quickly as he can, to help save the life of his friend. He has no illusions as to the character of both Connolly and Peppers.

Those are the big pieces in play and when more bodies turn up, another bank is robbed, and the victimized banker makes a private arrangement with Connolly and Peppers, they're all in motion with Daly finding himself square in the sights of Connolly and Pepper despite Ford's attempt at warning them off. When the interested parties find themselves all going after the bank robber each in their own way–some to help him, others to kill him, and some even to save him–demons from the past arise and cause more death.

Who is really at fault for what's going on? When the main suspect conveniently commits suicide, can the case finally be put to rest? Or is there yet another secret Ford can discover?

With the case seemingly solved, corpses continue to fall as Ford finally comes face to face with the unlikely perpetrator behind most, but not all, of the mayhem.

This is a complicated book. It has enough plots for four books but Gorman transitions from one to another with seamless ease. It's almost like reading a four or five part serial between the same two covers, and this gives the story much more

body than most other books, westerns or not. I once described a plot of a different book to an editor who interrupted me when I got to a certain point and said,
"But that's where the book has to end. Once they get the girl back, it's over." It
wasn't, but she couldn't see her way past that. With this book, she'd have fainted
dead away with how many times she'd have had to stop herself and say, "But this
is where it has to end...."
    Not with Gorman's work.

Similar to Gorman's expanding his novelette, "The Brasher Girl," into the full
length novel *Cage of Night*, a short story from a chapbook called "Out There In
The Darkness" (2000) served to show, in Gorman's own words, "[...] people be-
have differently in groups than they do individually. A lynch mob is comprised
of cowards made brave by sheer number." It's also a case where Gorman says he
wrote about a real person, something he "despises," but that it gave the story not
only some of its best scenes but added fire to some scenes, as well.
    When he expanded the story to novel length in the *The Poker Club* (1999), he
was able to go deeper with the characters, four very different types of men who,
for various reasons, are often that most natural but unexplainable of contradictions, committed friends. They meet for their regular ritual, a poker game, and
what seems like a routine night turns into a nightmare of the worst kind.
    The game is being held in the home of Aaron Tyler, a man whose family is out
of town. Also in the group are a co-worker of Aaron's from the same law firm, Bill
the doctor, and Neil, the most-liked member of the foursome.
    Tyler lives in a gentrifying area, still on the border between good and bad neigh-
borhoods, but an up-and-coming address just the same. They play cards in the
attic and when one of the men goes down to the first floor to get some water, the
rest of them hear a ruckus and go down as a group to investigate.
    Someone else is in the house.
    The so-called poker club gets their hands on one of the burglars but then dis-
aster strikes. It's accidental and the men are left with many crucial decisions. Thus
begins the fracturing of the friendship between the four men as individuals, and
we see the beginnings—which continue throughout the book—of the ebb and flow
of the group dynamic, Gorman's "lynch mob" mentality.
    As a group, are they willing to risk their lives as they've come to be—their careers,
their reputations, their families—to do the "right" thing? Or can they go around
the system, put the pieces back together and go back to their normal lives? Up until now, the four friends have acted together, even to the point of being somewhat
proud of what they've done. But the fracturing begins here.
    Despite the inner disagreements, they think they can make a bad situation go
away by being smart about what they do with the captured burglar. For a while
this seems to work, but then things start to get worse. "Out There In The Darkness" is a tauter version, more succinct in the way that a novelette needs to be, and
it ends with a truly Hitchcockian twist that manages to surprise, shock, and leave
the reader wondering at what beginning, not end, this story has ahead for the four

card players.

The Poker Club takes this central premise and expands on it, keeping very true to the short story but centering even more on the personality and inner conflicts of Aaron Tyler, the home owner and poker host whose wife and two kids are out of town. The novel spends much more time on Tyler's family situation, fleshing out the character of Jan, his wife, as well as introduces a new actor, a Detective Patterson, a cop who can sense there's more to the goings on than Tyler or any of the others are willing to share. How can guilty men who are not criminals fool an experienced homicide detective? Clearly not well.

Complications continue to crop up and through all the suspense and widening cracks of friendship it isn't until the very end that you finally become convinced that the situation is really and truly beyond the means of the four men to control. Gorman's skill at drawing out what is actually a fairly simple question into a book-length examination of seemingly good decisions and their ensuing unforeseen complications is exceptional.

The groups come up with plan after plan, often needing to overcome the objections of two of the more morally inflicted friends. Some of the plans come close to working but ultimately failure is snatched from seeming victory and nothing they manage to do ever fully resolves the situation. In the end, it's the victims that need saving and when it's all over, a terrible price has been paid.

As for the differences between the novelette and the novel, the shorter piece makes Gorman's point quicker and the cliffhanger ending is perfect, allowing the story to linger in the mind. It has to be considered among the best of his hundreds of shorter pieces. The novel-length version may suffer a bit for all of the family-centered angst Tyler goes through (we don't see what may be going on with the other three poker club members' home lives), but Gorman stays true to the distinctive personalities he's given all four members of the poker club, all the way to the end. If you like your suspense stories fully resolved, read the book. If you want to see what can be done with a suspenseful short story with a truly satisfying cliffhanger ending, be sure to read "Out In The Darkness" first. Reading the novelette won't detract from the novel.

Both works do what Gorman intended: he wanted to explore what could happen when the middle class runs into both a ruthless criminal element as well as having to deal with or deflect the attentions of the police, that dichotomous agency that is friend to you as a victim, and relentless foe to you as a perpetrator of wrongdoing. And what if the truth lies somewhere in the middle? That's what Gorman strives to show us.

There is a third version of the story. This is the 2008 movie version adapted by Richard Chizmar and Jonathan Schaech (of *That Thing You Do!* fame). The movie changes some small things with the characters and addresses some of the minor plot issues or questions Gorman left open in both the novelette and the novel. Unfortunately, they take the ending not from Gorman's tragic but more complicated resolution but instead tidy it up with more of a short cut Hollywood-friendly ending. The situations wrap up perhaps a bit neater, but they stray further from that messiness that is part of Gorman's more "real life" portrayal. If the movie would have kept going in its original direction it might even have been an improvement on the story. Instead, it makes two serious deviations, and the story itself becomes a much different one. For all of its deviations, it is still a movie worth seeing, especially for Jonathan Schaech's understated performance as Aaron Tyler and the more manic Johnny Messner as his poker friend, Bill Doyle.

Read "Out There In The Darkness" first, then *The Poker Club*. Finally, see the movie and decide for yourself the sort of message Gorman was trying to send.

Similar to other Gorman protagonists, Jack Walsh is an ex-cop who now manages an apartment complex for a break in his monthly rent. He's also a licensed PI. In *The Night Remembers* (1991) Lisa Pennyfeather tries to hire him to clear her convicted and recently released from jail husband, George. Walsh declines. He had been the lead detective on the case and still believes that George Pennyfeather is a guilty man.

But when another body turns up, a woman from George's past, and when she's found in the Pennyfeather's gazebo, it's clearly going to be only a matter of time before George is charged with her murder, too.

This time George's daughter tries to hire Walsh, who reluctantly agrees–without optimism– and soon begins to find disturbing ties between the past and the present. And not only for the Pennyfeathers, but for their friends the Heckarts, which only deepens the mystery.

Later Walsh comes across some insidious evidence to an unrelated crime and his nascent suspicions begin to coalesce. What is the real connection between what Walsh has found and the Pennyfeather family?

Gorman lets us feel Walsh's contradictions: his original belief that he is working for a family to clear the name of a man he felt was guilty; his less than healthy financial situation; and his lady love, the less-than-faithful Faith, who is battling a health crisis and moves herself and her young son into Walsh's apartment. Despite her failings, he is a dedicated man and would do anything he could to help her. The sub-plots of Faith's health, her relationship to Walsh, his own grudging revision of his past opinions, make this one of the most absorbing of all of Gorman's novels.

The Night Remembers as a book dovetails with Gorman's notion of a contemporary PI novel. Many of his recurring elements are here: the strong sense of nostalgia, including the music; the cars; the sense of loss for the way things used to be. What really adds a deepened tone to this story is the pervasive loneliness, the defining solitude, of the character of Jack Walsh. Even when Faith moves in and tells him she's been seeing someone else, the loneliness is replaced by fear and an inability to make things better between them.

If this book doesn't break as much new ground as a novel like *The Poker Club*, it takes us to a deeper place on a much more human and identifiable level. We may not all have been Elvis fans like Walsh, but we've all known loneliness and confusion in love. All of this makes for a heady mix that makes this book one of Gorman's most compelling.

For many years, perhaps no modern writer has been as prolific as Ed Gorman as a novelist, a short story writer, and an anthologist. Many of today's writers cite Gorman as being a friend to the working writer, and indeed, his "coaching tree" continues to grow.

Perhaps his most serious challenger in the area of sheer volume is the aforementioned Stephen King, and as I said at the beginning of this essay, they both share a love of writing across genres, of writing fiction of all lengths, and again, employ a style of writing that is easy to read. Being easy to read makes understanding the work nearly effortless and allows the reader to simply enjoy the story. When Gorman explores more of his serious themes, he has the ability to make the reader feel them right along with the characters.

Why the strong sense of nostalgia present in many of his books? We all have it to one extent or another, when you hear that song on the radio or stumble across an old yearbook. Gorman himself went through some tough times in his early adulthood, and perhaps the past connects him to his present and future in a way even more significant than for many people. It's this vein that Gorman taps so very well to do the same for us: to bring back our own pleasant memories and set them down in the midst of reading a contemporarily published novel.

Is Ed Gorman easy to read? Absolutely. But is his work simple? In no way.

Read his works: his short stories, his novels; move across genres along with him. It's a trip you'll want to take and right away you'll know that you're in the presence of a real writer. He's not taking your hand and leading you along a garden path. He's showing you the desperation, the loneliness, the vices and self-loathing that most of us feel or have felt at times in our lives. But he confines these things to his characters and his skill is such that they serve to define his characters, not to remind us of ourselves. His characters' troubles don't become ours, they don't make us feel the same consequences as they do. Ultimately as readers we all become voyeurs into an author's world. It's up to him or her to make this connection with us, and to entertain, possibly inform, and perhaps most importantly, to identify with the very human characteristics of the people he or she writes about.

Good books and stories don't have to do this, really. They don't have to do any of it. Writers write for different reasons, and readers read the same way. The fact that Gorman can imbue so many complexities into his fictional universes and keep us almost effortlessly involved, is his gift.

Yes, he's easy to read. So there should be nothing stopping you. Appreciate that. It's much rarer than you think.

–October, 2014
Littleton, NH

The Autumn Dead
by Ed Gorman

For my wife Carol, abiding love.

Night, the shadow of light, And life, the shadow of death.

—ALGERNON CHARLES SWINBURNE

Chapter 1

I spent two hours that rainy Tuesday morning honoring my boss's request to explain to a chunky twenty-two-year-old Chicano kid named Diaz why he'd get canned if he ever again used the choke hold on anybody.

"He was shoplifting, man," Diaz said.

"Not exactly the same as shooting or raping somebody."

"He looked dangerous."

"He's forty-three years old and he gets early social security because he shakes so bad from injuries he picked up in Nam. I saw him, Diaz. The poor bastard's barely alive. He shoplifts because the boys in Washington cut vets' benefits. And in his present condition, he couldn't whip Madonna." I lost it then, just a bit. "We're rent-a-cops, Diaz. We're not mercenaries or whatever those guys are in those magazines you read. You understand?"

Diaz has an annoying habit of snuffling phlegm up in his throat, then expectorating it into his empty Styrofoam coffee cup. I have to wait a few hours afterward before I can even think about eating again. He did it now and he kept his eyes on me all the time he was doing it. "I ain't gonna get wasted because of some weirdo creep, man. The boss don't let us carry iron, then he shouldn't have no objections when we use some force."

Carry iron. Inside his head, Diaz, like too many other rent-a-cops who can't get jobs as real policemen, lives out scenes from grade-B action movies. Carry iron. How about just saying "go armed"? But Charles Bronson would never put it that way, now would he? "Sometimes you have to use force, but not on somebody who's barely alive, and not the choke hold. Unless it's life and death, and it's rarely life and death."

He wiped his hands on the front of his uniform shirt. The American Security uniform is light blue with dark blue epaulets and fine gold buttons. It makes us look like cops who moonlight as bus drivers.

"I put up with this shit for minimum wage, man," Diaz said. He might have been nice-looking if he lost twenty-five pounds and did something about his zits and smiled. I'd seen him smile only once in the three months he'd worked here. That was the time Hanrahan, another rent-a-cop, told about the time he'd busted a shoplifter's arm. Hanrahan and Diaz swapped issues of mercenary magazines. Diaz, inhaling a Winston, said now, "I should at least be able to have a little fun."

He knew he'd really get me going with that one and I was all ready to let go, but then the intercom started crackling in the small back room with the Pepsi machine and the sandwich machine and the trash barrel that gets emptied only when the well-fed cockroaches join hands and start dancing around it. Poker gets played a lot back there, and according to legend, a very beautiful rent-a-cop named Stephanie did it with a rent-a-cop named Ken right on the table. To me that tale sounds like something out of one of Diaz's magazines.

"Dwyer?" Bobby Lee said.

"Yes?"

"Somebody here to see you."

"Can he wait a bit?"

"It isn't a he. It's a she." She explained this with a modest hint of disapproval. She and Donna have become good friends, and when Donna's not around, Bobby Lee acts as her surrogate home-room monitor.

"She. She give her name?"

"Yes. Karen Lane."

So there you have it.

I'm standing here in my para-bus driver uniform, forty-four years of age, ten pounds overweight, spending part of my time cuffing shoplifters and the other picking up small bits as an actor of dubious talent, not exactly what you'd call the American success story, and Karen Lane comes back into my life.

Twenty-five years ago Karen Lane, who then bore an unnerving resemblance to Natalie Wood, had broken not only my heart but my bank account. Even though we were both from the same poor neighborhood, the Highlands, Karen had early on gotten used to the pleasures to be had merely by smiling. Rich boys had been lining up for her ever since she'd first strolled onto a playground; I had never been sure how I'd gotten in that line, even if it had been only for a few months.

The odd thing was that no matter how many years passed, the stray thought came back once or twice a year that someday I'd run into her again, though of course in a lurid soap-opera fashion. I'd be an established actor by then and Karen would be this smiled-out hag with six kids and a husband who beat her as often as he had the strength left over from his job in the coal mines.

So there you have it.

She doesn't have the grace to wait till you're living in Hollywood and hanging around with Jimmy Garner and Bob Redford, uh-uh, she comes back some rainy Tuesday morning when you're chewing out some fleshy bullyboy who enjoys choking some poor vet who has to resort to stealing because he's broke.

"You look weird, man," Diaz said.

"Huh?"

"Weird. Your face."

"Yeah?"

"Yeah." He nodded to the intercom. "This lady, this Karen Lane broad, she must be special, huh?"

"Not the way you mean."

"Bitch, huh?"

I shrugged. "Used to be. Maybe she's changed."

"I knew a bitch once." He made a fist. Showed it to me the way most men would show you pictures of their babies. "She answered to Papa." He always called his fist Papa.

"Diaz," I said, but what was the use?

"What?"

"I know your situation."

"What situation?"

"Your home situation, asshole."

"Oh, yeah."

"Your mother couldn't get by without your paycheck. And this would be the third job you've lost in six months. So cool it with the John Wayne crap, all right?"

I was starting to feel sorry for him—his life wasn't without frustration, he had six brothers and sisters still of school age, and a mother too haggard to work and a father who had died of heart disease three months ago—but it was dangerous to feel sorry for Diaz because he'd kill you with your pity. He'd put you to the wall with your pity.

I said, "You get the impulse to put the choke hold on somebody, try to think of your mother, okay?"

"What you think I am, man, some kind of fruit?"

I sighed and shook my head.

He picked up his Styrofoam coffee and snuffled some phlegm into it. Then he held the cup out to me. "You thirsty, man?"

On the way down the hall, Robbins, the boss, stopped me. He's a big man, six-five, and the proud possessor of the world's largest collection of clip-on neckties. "Holy moley, Dwyer." He still says that. Holy moley.

"What?"

"That babe."

"Oh, yeah."

He smiled. He'd just gotten a haircut and there were white wiry flecks of hair all over his shoulders. He smelled of the kind of sweet hair tonic my father's barber had always used on all the working guys. Sweet enough to kill a chocolate urge. "Oh, yeah." Real casual like. He jabbed at my chest with a plump finger. "Donna's gonna kick your ass when she finds out."

"Robbins, honest, I haven't seen this woman in twenty-five years."

"Right," he said and winked. He had a wink like my uncle Phil, whom I once saw trying to peek in the women's john at a family reunion. He winked because he likes me and considers us friends, and I like him fine and I consider him a friend, too, if only because we are the only people in the agency who've actually been real cops. "You should keep me filled in on this stuff, Dwyer." Then he put a Tiparillo in his mouth and strolled off down the hall to his office.

All his talk about how good-looking Karen Lane was caused me to lean into the john, grind a comb through hair getting steely with gray, and make sure my teeth didn't have samples of my breakfast still stuck in the cracks. I stood there and looked at myself and then shrugged. I wasn't magically going to get any better looking.

So I went out to the lobby where Robbins, for reasons I've never actually understood, has arrayed blown-up black-and-white photos of criminals ranging from Jesse James to a guy he calls Lefty Dalwoski, who, he claims, was such a despicable bastard that he not only shot a nun but shot her in the back. "Christ," he always said, "at least if he'd shot her in the front, she'd have had a chance." What chance? To draw her Magnum? What order of nuns go armed—the Sisters of the Holy Luger?

In addition to the rogues gallery, there is enough cheap furniture to fill a small house: two coffee tables, four overstuffed chairs (one of which is honest-to-God paisley), and a lime-green couch that looks as if a pyromaniac used to work it over with cigarettes right after the kitties got done using it as a litter box. Robbins used to be in the loan-collection business, and what he couldn't get in cash, he took in furniture. "You need anything," he always says, "let me know. I got this warehouse full of shit." And shit it was, too.

In the center of the reception area sits another one of Robbins' catches, a desk big enough to play Ping-Pong on. This he got from a banker who'd embezzled several hundred thousand for the sake of a nineteen-year-old teller who wore falsies on her breasts and braces on her teeth. Robbins got these details from the coroner. The banker, trapped, killed himself and the girl. The banker had owed a loan company money (go figure) and Robbins had been dispatched to collect it. As usual on debts he couldn't collect, he took furniture.

Anyway, the desk is usually occupied by a woman whose breasts have inspired as many hours of conversation as the sins of Richard Nixon. Her name is Bobby Lee, and she is maybe forty (who would dare ask?) and she is the kind of woman who breaks into tears at the mere mention of Elvis Presley's name. Indeed, once a year she and her 1965 beehive hairdo and her mother and father drive in their motorhome to Graceland where, Bobby Lee claims, she once heard Elvis himself speak to her From Beyond The Grave. When she told me this, I asked, with at least a tad of condescension, "What did he say to you?" And she'd looked generally shocked. "God, Dwyer, that's personal. All I'll say is that it made me feel much better." Anyway, Bobby Lee and I had not gotten along until the last year or so, mostly due to her previously having been the mistress of my former employer, an anal retentive who runs a security agency the way wardens run death rows. The man had dumped Bobby Lee and in so doing had sent her running back to her Baptist faith, which she now espoused with the fervor of Saint Paul in a debating contest. Having her heart broken had turned her not only religious but human, too, so when the guy fired her, I got her a job over here.

Now she sat in the reception area and answered the phones and smoked enough Kool filters to give an entire stadium lung cancer and dispatched American Security people with the curt competence of old George Patton sending men into battle.

But it wasn't Bobby Lee I was looking at now. It was this beautiful five-five woman with dazzling auburn hair touching the shoulders of her white cashmere sweater and her hands tucked gracefully into the pockets of her white pleated trousers. She was as tan as a travel poster and benumbing as the first moment you ever fell in love.

As she raised her clean blue gaze to mine, I realized that Karen Lane had managed the impossible. She not only looked as good as she had twenty-five years ago—she looked better.

"Hi, Jack."

"Hi."

"I'll bet you're surprised to see me."

"Not any more surprised than I'd be if the Pope called me for lunch."

She laughed. She had a wonderful laugh. I wanted to dive in it and drown. "Still a smart-ass."

Bobby Lee took the Kool from the corner of her mouth and said, "That's what his girlfriend Donna always says. What a smart-ass he is." She scowled at me.

"Oh, so he has a girlfriend?" Karen said, picking up on the point Bobby Lee had wanted to make. She didn't take her beautiful eyes from me. Not for a moment.

"Yes, he most certainly does."

"Do you think she'd mind if I asked Jack to lunch?"

And her eyes were still on mine.

"I wouldn't think a real lady would need to ask a question like that," Bobby Lee said and put her fake Fu Manchu fingernails to the keyboard, blocking us out with Zen mastery.

And then Karen laughed again and for the first time let her eyes fall on Bobby Lee. "I'm sorry. I probably am coming on a little strong, aren't I? I'm actually here to see Jack on business."

Bobby Lee of course said nothing. But she exhaled in such a way that you could see how each and every fiber in her T-shirt strained against the overabundance of her breasts. Her T-shirts always had pictures of country-music stars on them. Today Willy Nelson had the pleasure of being buoyed on her bust.

"So how about it, Jack?" Karen Lane said. "Some lunch? On me?"

I looked at Bobby Lee. "I better ask my mom here first."

"Very funny," Bobby Lee said, then turned around again and started tapping on her Wang keyboard.

So Karen Lane and I left the building and went down to the curb to get her car. It was new and it was dazzling white and it was every inch a Jaguar sedan.

Chapter 2

The nuns who'd taught us would not have been proud of her.

On the way to the Harcourt, a restaurant I could afford to eat at only if I'd recently stuck up a 7-Eleven, she gave me some sense of what she'd been doing during the twenty-five years since we'd graduated from St. Michael's.

There had been four husbands. She did not describe them in emotional terms—"great guy" or "wonderful lover" or "wife beater"—instead I got their occupations and some sense of their financial status.

Number One was an "internist who lost a lot when the market got soft in the early seventies." Two was an AFL linebacker who'd been "very content to take early retirement and start his own insurance agency in Decatur, Illinois." Three was curator of an art museum and he was "all inherited money the bulk of which he wouldn't come into until he turned fifty and he was only twenty-nine." Four was a communications magnate "who took a big gamble on buying up independent TV stations and then really lost big when cable came in."

Then there were the places she'd lived: Los Angeles ("I've never felt lonelier"); Ft. Lauderdale ("If you've got enough money, you can pretend it's sixteenth-century Florence"); Denver ("No matter how rich they are there, they've all got cow shit on their shoes"); Paris ("No matter what they say to the contrary, their noses are much bigger than their cocks, believe me"); and New York ("From my window I could look over Central Park and I felt just like Holly Golightly").

It was when she said the last that I stopped her. "Can I ask you a question?"

"Sure."

"Is this on tape?"

She laughed her wonderful laugh. "God, I really am talking a lot, aren't I?"

"Then can I ask you another question?"

"What?"

"Who is Holly Golightly?"

"Didn't you ever read *Breakfast at Tiffany's* by Truman Capote?"

"I read *In Cold Blood*. It was great."

She frowned. "I started it, but it was too depressing. But *Breakfast at Tiffany's*—you know, we were in high school when that came out and one Saturday I went downtown to the library to pick up a book and I chose that one because, frankly, I've never been much of a reader and because it was very thin and the type was very big and there was this really fascinating photograph of Capote on the back. And so I took it home and read it and it changed my life. It really did. I mean, it really inspired me. I wanted to be just like Holly Golightly. Then after graduation I took the two hundred dollars I'd saved from my summer job and went down to the bus depot and got a Greyhound and headed straight for New York. God, it was fantastic."

And I heard then what I should have heard—and understood—back when I was twenty and hoping my frail hopes that she'd somehow fall in love with me: that something central was missing in her—my old man would have called it horse sense—that she was as giddy and unlikely and impossible as any tale ever told in the pages of *Modern Screen*.

But where most women gave up such dreams under the press of eight-to-five jobs or infants who demanded tits and taters or husbands who made it their business to crush every little hope their wives ever had—Karen Lane had had the sheer beauty and the sheer deranged gall to pursue her particular muses.

That was why, even back in grade school, she'd scared me. She was some kind of combination of Audrey Hepburn and Benito Mussolini.

Then we were sitting at a stoplight, a laundry truck on one side of us, a school bus on the other, and she leaned over and before I knew what was happening, she threw her arms around me and put her tongue, with the precision of a surgical instrument, right inside my mouth.

I could tell when the light changed because the cars behind us started honking and the drivers yelling.

She was soft and tasted great and I was trembling and feeling one of those erections you're only supposed to get when you're sixteen and every bit as daffy, at least at the moment, as she was.

Then, bowing to the authority of horns and curses, she took herself away from me, and I felt as deserted as an orphan.

But before she went back to driving, she patted me on the knee in an oddly cool, almost matronly way and said, "I know you're going to help me, Jack. I just know it."

The east end of the Harcourt sits on a promontory over a lake lost that day in fog and rain. Somewhere in the distance big wooden workboats moved like massive prehistoric animals through haze that blanched everything of colors. Everything looked and felt gray on this March day.

On this side of the vast curved window a waiter who seemed to have watched an awful lot of Charles Boyer movies was making a fool of himself over Karen while trying to keep up a French accent that was falling down like socks that had lost their elastic.

"Ze braised fresh crab claws," he said and rolled his eyes the way he probably did during sex.

"They sound wonderful. Just wonderful." And then she smiled over at me. "Don't they sound wonderful, Jack?"

"'Wonderful' isn't the word for it," I said.

"And ze sautéed fresh prawns with shredded ham and vegetables." He rolled his eyes again. I had decided that if he managed to work "ooh-la-la" into the conversation, I was going to deck him.

While he finished flirting with Karen, I glanced around the Harcourt and knew again that my speed was Hardees. Here you sat on English walnut chairs and stared at paintings by Matisse (whom I happened to like in my uneducated way) and large blow-ups of Cartier-Bresson photographs (which I thought I could probably duplicate with my Polaroid) and ate with forks that weighed two and a half pounds and daubed goose-liver pâté off your lips with brilliant white napkins big enough to double as sheets.

When the waiter finally packed up his French accent and went away, Karen said, "You look uncomfortable."

I sighed. "Can I be honest?"

"Of course. Honesty is something I really value."

I tried not to be uncharitable, but I couldn't keep the hard cold trust-department way she'd assessed her husbands out of my mind. If that was her idea of honesty, then maybe I would have preferred her a bit dishonest.

"Your father," I said.

She looked perplexed. "What about him?"

"He lived in the Highlands, right?"

"Why, yes. Of course."

"The Highlands being the area in this city with the lowest per-capita income and the highest crime rate."

"What's the point, Jack?" Irritation had come into her voice.

"That's where your father was from and my father was from and that's where you're from and that's where I'm from."

"Would you please come to the point?"

"I'm ashamed of you, that's the point."

"What?" She sat back in her chair as if I'd just tried to slap her.

"You've bought into an awful lot of bullshit, you know that? New white Jaguars and measuring people by their bank accounts and indulging silly assholes like that waiter."

"Are you drunk?"

"No."

"Are you on drugs?"

"No."

"Then you have absolutely no right to speak to me that way."

"Sure I do. I've known you since you were six years old and we made our First Communion together and you were always full of shit, Karen, but you've never been *this* full of shit before."

So—what else?—she started crying.

There were approximately three hundred other people in the big restaurant, most of them men and most of them with gold American Express cards pulsating in their suits, and now nearly every one of them was staring at us.

If she was faking, she was good at it because she didn't go for any big sobs or anything like that, she just sat there and put her beautiful head into one beautiful hand and small tears rolled down her beautiful cheeks and touched her beautiful red glossy lips.

"I overdid it," I said.

She just kept her head down.

I looked out at the fog and the wooden workboats and the hint of birch-lined shore somewhere in the haze.

I said, "I said I overdid it."

She looked up. "Is that supposed to be an apology?"

"About half an apology."

"I want and deserve more than half an apology."

"Your old man worked with my old man in the same factory. They had Spam for lunch and they played pinochle every Friday night, and even if they weren't smart and they weren't important, they knew enough to hate bullshit. And that's all you seem to know, Karen. Bullshit."

"Well, thank you very much."

Our positions had shifted subtly here. Her tears had dried and I was angry again. "You're welcome."

So we sat in uncomfortable silence for a time.

"You're making a lot of assumptions about me, Jack."

"Sure."

"You are. How do you know that I haven't had a lot of pain in my life?"

"You mean in between having your accountant going through your husband's bank account so you can decide if he's worth keeping or not."

"There was a perfectly good reason for each divorce."

"Right."

"Incompatibility."

She said it so fecklessly that it had an odd endearing quality. "Incompatibility? That's legalese, Karen. More bullshit. It's meaningless."

"Well, whether you choose to believe it or not, I was incompatible with each and every one of my husbands for a very simple reason. Because I wanted to find myself and they didn't want me to."

"Finding yourself went out in the seventies, Karen, along with earth shoes."

For the first time, she sulked, beautiful, as always but looking a bit trapped now. "Anyway, Jack, two can play the honesty game."

"Meaning what?"

"Meaning that I know very well why you're being so mean."

"Why?"

"Because of that night I took your car."

Actually, of all her many betrayals, that had been one that had slipped my mind. Now, though, instead of inspiring pain, it caused me to laugh. It was that outrageous. "I forgot all about that. You said you needed to borrow my car so you could help your mother with grocery shopping because your family car was getting fixed. And then you took my goddamn car—that I'd worked my ass off to buy—and you took Larry Price to the drive-in in it."

She leaned forward and pursed her lips as if she was getting impatient with my misunderstanding of her. "Well, for your information, even if I did use your car to take Larry to the drive-in, it wasn't what you think. The drive-in was just a good place to talk."

"Right."

I sensed but could not define something shift in her gaze.

Ever since we'd started talking about Larry Price, her jaw had set and a strange anger was in her eyes.

But I was too concerned with my own anger to worry about hers. I was almost overwhelmed with the purity of my rage even though twenty-five years had passed. "Larry Price, Ted Forester, David Haskins—you knew how I hated them. And you know why, too. What they did to Malley and me that night."

Price, Forester, and Haskins had been seniors when we'd been juniors. One night they'd depantsed a wimpy kid everybody picked on with the casual cruelty of young people who constantly needed to reassure themselves they were normal and cool and slick. Then they'd beaten him and beaten him badly. And it so happened that when Malley and I heard about it, we got a six-pack and sat around and talked about it a lot, kind of working ourselves up, and then we went looking for them. And it was all supposed to go our way because we were righteous and we were poor, and poor kids were supposed to be tough, but when we found them, it didn't work out that way at all. Even though Price and Forester and Haskins had only come to St. Michael's in a redistricting of Catholic schools and did not socially fit in—they were the sons of very wealthy and successful people—they were at least one thing they were not supposed to be, and that was tough. My friend fought Forester and did not do well at all, and then I fought Price and did even less well. For weeks we tried to explain that to each other—"You know, if we hadn't been so drunk, man, there wouldn't have been nothing left of those guys"—but it was all bull and we hadn't been tough enough, and that remained, even today, a source of secret shame.

So five weeks later, my supposed girlfriend Karen Lane borrows my car and takes Larry Price to the drive-in. "Maybe it wasn't what you think, Jack."

"Sure."

I was about to say more, coasting on my anger now, when she pulled something up from her lap and set it on the table next to the fresh-cut rose in the slender vase.

A white envelope.

"Money," she said.

"For what?"

"That isn't the question you should be asking first."

"What question should I be asking first?"

"You should be more curious about how much there is than what it's for."

"So how much is there?"

"A thousand dollars."

"I'm impressed."

"You should be. I'm practically broke."

"Now I want to know what it's for."

"Because I want you to do me a favor."

"I've already got doubts."

"It's perfectly legal."

"Right."

"All it involves is you getting back something that belongs to me."

"And what would that be?"

"A suitcase."

"Where is it?"

"In a condo on the northeast edge of the city."

"And who lives in the condo?"

"A man named Evans. Glendon Evans."

"Glendon?"

"That's his full name. But everybody calls him Glen. Including his patients."

"Patients?"

"He's a psychiatrist."

"I see." I sipped some water. "Why can't you just call Glendon or Glen and ask him if you can have your suitcase?"

"I'm afraid he's angry with me."

"Ah."

"What does that mean?"

"It means that I sense *amore* is somehow involved. True?"

"We lived together nearly a year."

"But now you want out?"

"I am out and have been out for a month, but he won't give me my suitcase back."

"Where are you staying now?"

"Do you remember Susan Roberts?"

"Sure." Susan had been a slight but lovely girl, given, unlike most of us in the Highlands, to things of culture and beauty. You never found Susan at the drag strip on Sunday afternoons. She had also been, as I recalled, obsessive about a guy named Gary Roberts whose sole desire had been to be a writer.

"She married Gary. Did you know that?"

"Yes," I said.

"He's a teacher. A very good one." She smiled. "And he still writes. Every day. And someday, he'll get something published. You wait and see."

"You're apologizing for him. That's arrogant. He's probably a lot happier than these jack-offs you've been married to."

"Would you please just not be so angry?"

I sighed. "You're right. I'm being angry, and I'm being arrogant and now I'll apologize."

"I appreciate it."

"So you've been staying with the Robertses?"

"Yes. They were the ones who told me that you'd been a policeman and now were a private investigator."

"Mostly I bust shoplifters."

Now she sipped her water. "But certainly you have enough experience to get my suitcase back."

"What's so special about it?"

"It's just got a lot of sentimental things in it."

Which I didn't believe at all. She struck me about as sentimental as Charles Manson's sister. But I let it pass.

"And the suitcase is in the condo?"

"Yes."

"So if I went in there and got it for you, I'd be committing B and E."

"B and E?"

"Breaking and entering."

"Not really."

"Why not?"

"First, because the suitcase belongs to me, and second, because I have a key."

Which she produced with a distinct air of *voilà*. Even in the blanched light of the gray day, she still looked tan and overpoweringly lovely.

"Did you know there's a reunion dance tonight?" she said.

"I know. Number twenty-five. I'm not going."

"Why?"

"Because I feel old enough already. I don't need to confirm my suspicions by looking at people with bald heads and potbellies and wattles like turkeys. I've got all that stuff myself."

"Actually, Jack, you're still very handsome in your way."

"You always said that, that 'in my way' thing, and it always bothered me."

"Well, you're not Robert Redford, but you're appealing. You really are."

"So what about the reunion?"

"Well, I thought it would be fun if you just kind of popped over this afternoon and got my suitcase and then popped over to the reunion. Then we could have some fun together. And you could have the money."

"I like the way you kind of ran those together."

"What?"

"Popping into a B and E and then popping over to the reunion. Real fast. You're good at it."

"Don't be cynical, Jack. This is all very straightforward. It's Tuesday and Glen sees patients till ten. He won't be there to bother you."

"I have an obvious question to ask."

"What's that?"

"Why don't you just go get it yourself?"

"Vibes."

"Vibes?"

"The vibes were so bad between us there at the end. If I so much as set a foot back into the place, I'd be depressed for a week. Really."

"Vibes," I said.

She took out five one-hundred-dollar bills and laid them out green and crisp and dignified on the brilliant white tablecloth.

"You'll do it?" she said.

"You really want to get me mixed up in all this?"

"In all what, Jack? It's just getting my suitcase back."

"Why don't you have me do something else?"

"Such as what?"

"Mow your lawn or take out your garbage or something."

"Jack," she said.

And then she put her hand on mine and in a very different way said again, "Jack."

Chapter 3

The winding asphalt road got steep enough that I had to keep the Toyota in second gear most of the way.

The sun was out now and the hills of pine and spruce were like a wall closing me off from the city behind. At one point I saw a deer come to the edge of the road and watch me with its delicate and frightened beauty.

After a few miles, country-style mailboxes began appearing on the left-hand side of the macadam, and then, up in the trees that seemed to touch the clouds themselves, you could see the sharp jut of the white stone condos, their Frank Lloyd Wright expanse of glass flashing gold in the sunlight.

I rolled down the window and enjoyed the odors, sweet pine and the tang of reasonably fresh water from a nearby creek and wild ginger and ginseng in the forest to the right.

When I saw the box reading GLENDON EVANS, I pulled the Toyota over to the side and parked and got out. At first all I wanted to do was walk a few feet up the asphalt and take in some more of spring's birthing sights, new grass already vivid green and cardinals and blue jays soaring in the air. I looked behind me, at the ragged silhouette of the city in the valley. This was an aerie up here, and Glendon Evans should consider himself damn lucky.

To reach the condo you had to walk eighty-some stone steps set into a hill at about a sixty-degree angle so narrowly laid out that you could get slapped by overhanging spruce branches all the way up. A squirrel who apparently wanted to get himself adopted accompanied me from a three-foot distance all the way up.

The condo, as imposing as one of the gods of Easter Island, had been set into a piney hill and angled dramatically upward, so that no matter what angle you saw it from, you knew its owner was more powerful than you could ever be. There were three floors. Draperies were drawn on all the windows. The lower level was a two-stall garage. The doors were closed.

Spread across the flagstone patio in front of the place was a variety of lawn furniture, the good doctor apparently getting ready for summer. A redwood picnic table, several lawn chairs, and a gas grill big enough to handle the Bears looked ready for burgers and beer. Only the lonely wind, a bit chill and tart with pine, reminded me that it was still a little early for lawn furniture, and suddenly there was an air of desertion about the place, as if the people who lived here had fled for some mysterious and possibly terrible reason.

I took the key from my pocket again and tried the front door. No problem.

Then I walked into something not unlike a French country house, with raised oak paneling and a limestone fireplace and Persian rugs and built-in bookcases and a leather couch as elegant as a swan's neck. There was a Jim Dine print above the fireplace. The east wall was a fan-shaped window that looked over the winding creek below, still silver with the last of spring's frost. The west wall was a cathe-

dral window from which you could see an impenetrable forest that stretched all
the way to a line of ragged hills above which the white tracks of jets now slowly
disintegrated against the bright blue sky.

Looking around, I realized that I had made a mistake coming here. Maybe, after twenty-five years of living in places like this, Karen Lane could claim this
world as her own, but I couldn't. I was as out of place here as an atheist in a church.

At the last I hadn't even taken her money, just agreed to help her out of some
misguided sense that she needed my help. But the condo said very different things
to me—that where Karen Lane was concerned, I was the one who needed help,
and that it was unlikely that I was here to get anything half as innocent as a suitcase full of "sentimental" things.

I went to the right into a kitchen that kept up the motif of gorgeous capitalistic
excess.

Sunlight struck blond wood floors and bleached pine cabinets and a free-
standing range that dominated the room. Above the sink, situated to the left of
a white wall phone, was an outsize photograph of Karen, done in a mezzotint for
dramatic effect. The reverence of the shot told me all I needed to know about the
good doctor. He was hooked.

I went back to the living room and was just passing the winding metal staircase
where it wound its way to the second level when something splatted on my forehead like a fat warm drop of summer rain.

I reached up and touched a finger to the wet spot on my skin. I brought my finger away and looked at it. There was no doubt at all what it was.

Suddenly I looked around the condo and saw not beautiful furniture of dash-
ing design but all the places somebody with a gun could hide. The afternoon shadows seemed deep now, and I was self-conscious, as if I were being observed.

I took a few steps back and looked up to the second level. Lying even with the
border of the carpeted floor was the back of a man's head. He was close to falling
off the edge. His dark hair and the shape of his skull were all I could see. There
was a bloody knot in the center of his head and it was from this that the blood
dropped, tainting the soft gray carpet below.

I took a few deep breaths and wished I had brought my gun and then cursed myself for not bringing my gun and then cursed myself for cursing myself because
there had been absolutely no reason I *should* have brought my gun. I'd come here
to a psychiatrist's condo to retrieve a suitcase. Not exactly dangerous work.

I went up the winding steps for a closer look at the man. He wore a mono-
grammed blue silk dressing robe over a pair of lighter blue cotton pajamas. The
monogram read "GE." He wore expensive brown leather house slippers, new
enough that you could see the brand name imprinted on the soles. He was maybe
six feet and slender and his skin was the color of creamed coffee. But he was one
of those black men whose features are as white as Richard Chamberlain's. He was
probably my age, but there the similarity ended because he looked brighter and
handsomer and, even unconscious, a lot better prepared to put his personal
stamp on an impersonal world.

I glanced quickly around the second level. This was an open area with another fan-shaped window to my right and a huge Matisse to the left. You could see dust motes tumble golden in the sunlight. The carpeting was the same light gray as downstairs, and it ran down a long hall with three oak doors on each side.

I lifted up his hand. His pulse was strong. I leaned down and looked closer at his wound. It was open to reveal pink flesh. It would most likely require a few stitches.

I went in search of a bathroom, which proved to be the second door down to the right. On the way I passed a room with a Jacuzzi and a master bedroom laid out to resemble a den where people only occasionally slept.

In the john—or should you call something composed of marble with a sunken bathtub big enough to hold Olympic tryouts a john?—I soaked a towel in warm water and then found some Bactine and Johnson & Johnson Band-Aids and then I filled a paper cup with water about the right temperature to drink.

I was halfway out the bathroom door when I thought about the few times I'd been knocked out back in my police days. I'd forgotten one important thing. I went back to the medicine cabinet, which I noted held any number of brown prescription bottles with Karen Lane's name on them. Among many others, the medicine included Librium and Xanax. Somewhere amid the prescriptions, I found some plain old Tylenol. I thumbed off the lid and knocked three of the white capsules into my hand. When I managed to get him awake, he was going to have a headache and he was going to appreciate these.

I was halfway down the hall, hands loaded with the towel and the Bactine and the Band-Aids and the drinking water and the Tylenol, when he staggered toward me and said, "If you move, I'm going to kill you. Do you understand me?"

"Yes," I said. "Yes, I do understand that."

And I did. He looked to be in pain. He also looked frightened and slightly crazed.

He held in his slender tan hand a fancy silver-plated .45, and I had no doubt at all that he would, for the slightest reason, use it.

"Now," he said, "I want you to lead the way downstairs. We're going to go to the kitchen and sit in the nook and you're going to answer questions, and if you do anything at all that seems suspicious, I'll shoot you right in the belly. All right?"

I hadn't realized till then how badly he was hyperventilating. Nor had I realized that he had begun to sob, his whole torso lunging with cries that seemed half grief and half frenzy.

Then he pitched forward face first and collapsed on the carpet soft and gray as a pigeon's breast.

The gun fell from his hand.

I wondered if I'd underestimated the severity of the head wound.

I wondered if Dr. Glendon Evans hadn't just fallen down dead right in front of my eyes.

Chapter 4

In one of the kitchen cupboards I found a bottle of Wild Turkey. I poured a lot
of it into the coffee I'd made us. Then I carried the cups over to the nook, on the
wooden windowsill on which a jay sat, overcome with the soft breeze. Beyond
were the hills of pine and the sky of watercolor blue.

"You feeling any better?" I asked him. I sat there and blew on my coffee, having overdone the heat in the microwave, and then I sat about staring at him again.

Twenty-five minutes had passed since I'd helped him downstairs and sat him
up on one side of the breakfast-nook table. Twenty-five minutes and he had not
uttered a single word. At first I wondered if he wasn't in some kind of shock, but
his brown eyes registered all the appropriate emotions to my words, so shock was
unlikely. I'd said a few things to irritate him just to see how he would respond, and
he'd responded fine. Then I'd considered that maybe he thought I was the man
who'd knocked him out, but now he'd know differently. Most burglars didn't put
iodine and Band-Aids on the wounds they'd inflicted.

Glendon Evans sat there, a slender, handsome, successful-looking man who
even in these circumstances gave off a scent of arrogance. He wasn't talking to me
no matter what I said and I didn't know why.

I had some more coffee and then I said, "This is pretty ridiculous. Your not talking, I mean."

He sipped his coffee, set the delicate white china cup back down. Looked out
the window.

I said, "Did they want the suitcase?"

This time when he faced me there was more than a hint of anxiety in his eyes.

"So it was the suitcase. You know what was in it?"

He went back to looking out the window. From some distant hill, a red kite had
been sent up the air currents where it struggled with comic grace against the soft
and invisible tides of spring.

"She told me it had sentimental stuff in it." I paused. "She made it sound very
innocent."

I went over and got the bottle and gave us each some more bourbon.

"How's your head?"

He turned and looked and, almost against his will, raised his shoulders in a tiny
shrug.

I sat back down and said, "I wonder who's going to get pissed off first. You because you're sick of me talking or me because I'm sick of you not talking."

I congratulated myself on the cleverness of that line, feeling for sure this would
open his mouth and get him going magpie-style, but all it produced was a wince
and a touch of long fingers to the back of his head.

So I watched the kite for a while, how it angled left, then angled right, red against
the light blue sky. It made me recall how warm even March winds were when you

were ten and had your hand filled with kite string.

I said, "She did it to you, didn't she?" I knew he wasn't going to talk, so I just kept right on going. "She did it to me when I was twenty. I really thought I was going to marry her and all that stuff. At the time I was working in a supermarket for a dollar thirty-five an hour and spending a dollar twenty-seven on her. I bought myself a forty-nine Ford fastback and one night she gave me a crock about needing it to help her mother and you know what she did? She took a guy to the drive-in in it." My laugh, bitter even after all these years, cracked like a shot in the aerie.

I poured us some more Wild Turkey. His body language—he was leaning forward now and his eyes started studying me—indicated he was getting interested.

He said, "Was that a true story?"

"The drive-in?"

He nodded. He had a great and grave dignity. He certainly had the right demeanor for a shrink.

"True," I said.

Then I went back to staring out the window at the kite and the birds. The silence was back.

I went and found a bathroom and came back. When I slid into my place in the nook I found a new hot cup of coffee in my place. He was pouring Wild Turkey into it.

He said, "Three months ago she told me she desperately needed money for her mother. Some illness. She was very vague. I gave it to her, of course."

"There's something I should tell you."

"You don't need to. I looked through an old scrapbook of hers. Her mother died in nineteen-sixty-four."

"Right."

The pain in his eyes was not simply from the head wound. "I really thought we were going to be married." His lips thinned. "God, what a stupid bastard I was."

"Was she a patient of yours?"

For the first time, he smiled. "A patient? You think she'd ever seek help? Ever think she'd need help? Her version of things is that the world is here to serve her, and if she occasionally has to inconvenience or hurt somebody to be served, then she just hopes there will be no hard feelings; Holly Golightly."

"That's Karen."

"I met her at a party." Miserably, he said, "Her pattern is to have a new one ready to go before she notifies the old one that he's finished."

"You know who the new one is?"

"No. But I'm sure there is one and has been for some time now." His face tightened. "You can tell." He shook his head. "She got calls a few times from a man named Ted Forester. Somehow, I didn't get the impression it was romantic."

So I sat there and thought about Ted Forester and his money and his arrogance. Then I remembered something I hadn't thought about in a quarter century. All the time I'd been going out with Karen, Forester had been skulking in the background, calling her, buying her gifts, waiting me out. She'd admitted this to me one night, saying, "Ted doesn't know what to do with himself now that he's fallen in love with a girl from the Highlands." Which was true enough. It was hard to imagine his parents approving of such a match. Then I spent a moment or two thinking of how Malley and I had smashed out his car window.

Glendon Evans said, "I suppose she told you I hit her."

"No."

"I did. I actually hit her. Not hard. Just sort of a slap. It was something I never thought I could do. Ever."

"She seems to have survived."

"Would you like some more bourbon?"

"No, thanks. Just some more coffee." I was making instant Folgers with tap water and setting it in the microwave. "You want some more?"

"Please."

So I made us some and sat back down and said, "What's in the suitcase?"

"I don't know."

"Really?"

"Really. She kept it in her closet. It had a clasp lock on it. Several times, after things started going badly for us, I was tempted to open it and look inside, but I couldn't see any way to do that without her finding out."

"You never got a glimpse inside?"

"Not a glimpse."

I sipped my coffee. "You have any idea who hit you?"

"None."

"Tell me about it."

He shrugged lean shoulders beneath the expensive blue silk robe. "I came home early today. The flu. I got undressed and into my pajamas and robe and went into the den to lie on the couch and watch the news on cable and that's when somebody came up behind me."

"You remember anything about him?"

"Not really."

"He didn't say anything?"

"No."

"You remember any particular odors or sounds?"

"No."

"How long've you been out?"

"Maybe an hour."

"So he was in here, waiting?"

"Apparently."

"It doesn't sound as if he got the suitcase."

"I know he didn't."

"How do you know?"

"I looked for it yesterday. It was gone."

"You sure she left it behind when she left?"

He touched manicured fingers to his lips. Thought a moment. "That's it. Now I remember. She said she'd pick up the suitcase when Gary Roberts got her things."

"Did she get it then?"

"No. That's the strange thing. He asked for the suitcase, but when I looked for it, it was gone."

"What did Gary say?"

"Oh, he's always polite. He's a holdover from the sixties and he can't let himself consciously admit that it bothers him that she'd live with a black man. He doesn't mean to be a bigot. I feel sorry for him."

"He got all her other things?"

"Yes."

"And he just left without the suitcase?"

"Yes." He thought a moment. "I could be wrong, but I believe the day before Gary came, somebody jimmied one of my windows."

"And got in?"

"Possibly."

Now Karen's coming to me made sense. She had sent Gary over to get her things. When Glendon Evans said the suitcase was gone, she refused to believe him. So she looked me up, sent me in to get it.

"I don't know if I'll ever feel safe here again."

More to myself, I said, "What the hell could be in the suitcase that so many people are interested in it?"

He laughed. "It couldn't be money. Not the way she depended on my Visa and American Express cards." His laugh was as harsh as my own. Then, "The terrible thing is I'd take her back. How about you?"

"Oh, no. She's been out of my system for a long time."

"So why did you agree to help her?"

"We're from the Highlands."

"Oh, yes," he said. "The Highlands."

"So she talked about it?"

"Frequently. She even had nightmares about something that happened back there. Always the same thing. She'd be waking up screaming and bathed in sweat and—" He stared down at his coffee. "My father was a surgeon. I rode around in a Lincoln and went to private school. I almost feel guilty."

I was curious. "She never told you what the nightmares were about?"

"No. But she did always use the same word. Pierce."

"Was that somebody's name?"

"I don't know. I thought you might, being from the Highlands."

"No."

He put a hand to the back of his head. "I'm afraid I'm going to need stitches."

"I was wondering about that."

"Would you give me a ride? There's a trauma center not too far from here."

"Sure."

He stood up. He was still wobbly. He put his palms flat against the table as a precaution.

"You all right?"

He looked up. He looked pale beneath his light-brown skin. I pretended I didn't see the tears in his eyes. "She's never going to come back to me, is she?"

Soft as I could, I said, "I don't think that's her style. Coming back to people, I mean."

Chapter 5

From a drive-up phone I tried my service to check for calls, discovered I had a radio spot for tomorrow in a downtown studio—a local spot but one that promised decent residuals—and that the same woman had called three times but had not left her name.

Finished with my service, I called Donna Harris's apartment. It was publication time for *Ad World,* and I didn't really expect her to answer—she tended to a bunker mentality the day everything got put to bed, eating innumerable and exotic pieces of junk food (I'd once seen her mix Count Chocula and Trix into a kind of bridge mix)—but she surprised me by being home.

"Hi," she said. "I was hoping you wouldn't call because I'm so damn busy, but then I was hoping you would call because if you didn't, I'd feel neglected. You know?"

"I know."

"I wish we could go to a movie tonight."

"That would be nice, wouldn't it?"

"You finished working?"

"At Security I am. Actually, I'm working on something else."

I explained what that something else was.

Her voice got tight. "You've mentioned her before, haven't you?"

"Karen Lane?"

"Uh-huh."

"Yes, I suppose I have." I sighed. "Please don't do that."

"Do what?"

"Get jealous. There's nothing at all to get jealous about."

"I trust you, Dwyer."

"Really?"

"The rational part of me does, anyway."

"How about the irrational part?"

"How does she look after twenty-five years? God, that sounds like a long time."

"It is a long time, and she doesn't look all that sensational."

"In other words, she looks gorgeous."

"She looks all right."

"Now I know gorgeous for sure."

"It's a job. You seem to forget that little incidental fact. She's actually paying me money."

"Otherwise you probably wouldn't want to get involved with her at all, would you?"

"You probably won't believe this, but no, I wouldn't. She's a classic example of retarded adolescence. Nothing to her matters quite so much as her tan or her new sweater or how that cute guy at the health club looked her over. It's a seventh-grade mentality and we're headed toward fifty. The big five-oh. It's a pain in the ass."

"You figured out what's in the suitcase?"

"Obviously something valuable."

"You think she might have stolen something from somebody?"

It was then I saw it for the first time. The sleek black Honda motorcycle. Driven by a sleek black-leathered figure. Black leather head to toe, with a black helmet and black mask. Across the street. Just sitting there. I looked back from my rearview and said, "I'm assuming that's what it's all about. Some kind of theft. Otherwise Glendon Evans wouldn't have gotten beaten up."

She sounded a bit scared. "I'm sorry I was so pissy."

"It's all right. You know how I got the other night when that old actor friend of mine stopped by our booth and spent twenty minutes staring at you."

"God, why are we so jealous?"

"Insecure."

"But why are we so insecure? I mean, we're bright, we're attractive. We should have at least a little self-confidence."

"Probably our genes." I looked into the rearview again.

The black-clad rider still sat astride his black Honda.

"Your mind is drifting. I can tell over the phone."

"Sorry."

"Something wrong?"

"I don't think so. Just my usual paranoia." Then I said, "You could do me a favor."

"What?"

"On your way back to your office, you could stop by my place and pick up some clean clothes for me."

"In other words, you want to stay all night?"

"If you wouldn't mind."

"No, that'd be nice. Only I want the window up."

Donna is never so happy as when she's covered with goose bumps and sleeping soundly. "Can't we flip for it?"

"We flipped for it last time and you cheated."

"Oh, yeah."

"So if you stay, the window's going to be up. Clean fresh air."

"Okay. And I appreciate you stopping by my place. I have the feeling I'm going to be busy."

"Where you going?"

"Up near the Highlands. Little housing development there. Where Karen Lane claims to be staying."

"Claims?"

"Right now, I'm not sure I believe anything she tells me."

"Good." Donna laughed. "Stay that way."

They'd built the houses in the mid-fifties, and though they weren't much big-ger than garages, the contractors had been smart enough to paint them in pas-tels—yellow and lime and pink and puce, the colors of impossible flowers, the col-ors of high hard national hope—and they were where you strived to live in 1956 if you worked in a factory and wanted the good life as promised by the Democ-rats and practiced by the Republicans. There were maybe four hundred houses in all, interlocked in Chinese puzzle boxes of streets, thirty to a block, glowing in the sunlight, hickory-smoked with backyard barbecues and driveways filled with installment-plan Ford convertibles and DeSoto sedans. The housing de-velopment seemed the quintessence of everything our fathers had fought World War II for. My own father never made it there; we always stayed in the Highlands farther down in the valley. But on Sundays we'd drive in our fifteen-year-old Ply-mouth with its running boards and mud-flaps through the streets of the devel-opment while my parents discussed just which type of house they would buy—there being four basic models—when the money came in.

Now this part of the development was as forgotten as Dwight Eisenhower's golf scores. In the late-afternoon sunlight, the houses looked faded now, and scraped in places and smashed in others, tape running the length of some picture windows, and chain-link fences giving some of the tiny homes the air of fortresses, partic-ularly those with Day-Glow BEWARE OF DOG signs. Blacks and Chicanos were pushing up the valley now, taking the same route as these whites had twenty-five years earlier. But you saw a lot of Dixie-flag decals on the bumper stickers of the scrap-heap cars along the curb, and, you saw in the eyes of the ten- and eleven-year-old kids—already wheezing on cigarettes and walking with their arms possessively around girls every bit as tough as the boys—you saw the sum total of decades of hatred. Meals, at least steady ones, were something you had to fight for up here, and blacks, to feed their own families, meant by one way or another to take your meals. So you had the old lady sew an NRA decal on your work jacket, and you even—just for curiosity's sake—went to the Klan rally held out on an outlying farm. You wouldn't kill a black man personally, but you wouldn't condemn someone who had.

The Roberts home was freshly painted white, and a new white Chevrolet sedan sat in the drive. The place was so clean and neat, it must have made its neighbors want to come over and smear dirt on it out of sheer envy.

I parked behind the Chevrolet and got out. A collie came up. He was bathed and smelled clean when he put his front paws on my stomach and asked to be pet-ted. From this angle I could see into the backyard. There was a clothesline filled with white sheets and shirts and the kind of pink rayon uniform waitresses wear. Beneath the sheets flapping like schooner masts in the breeze, I saw a pair of jean-clad legs.

I went back to the clothesline, the collie keeping me eager and friendly company, and when I got there I said, "Susan?"

And then I saw the feet go up on tippy-toes and saw her head appear over the sheets.

"My God," she said.

She was older now but still pretty. There was only a little gray in the otherwise auburn hair, and as she came around the sheets, I saw that she'd put on just a few pounds—far fewer than I had—and looked trim in her white blouse and blue man's cardigan and pleasantly snug jeans. In high school she'd always been one of my favorite people—she'd had a kind of wisdom that I attributed to the early loss of her father; she knew what mattered and what did not—and just the way her brown eyes watched me now, with humor and curiosity, I knew she was still going to be one of my favorite people.

"I don't believe it," she said. Then she smiled. "It's really nice seeing you."

"It's really nice seeing you." I nodded to the clothes, the pink waitress uniform, the shirts, the sheets. "I didn't know people still hung wash out."

She laughed. "I do because it's the cleanest smell in the world. Here. Grab one of those sheets and smell it."

"You serious?"

"Of course I'm serious."

So I did and it smelled wonderful, clean as she'd promised. "I see you on TV. On commercials. You're a good actor."

"I'm learning."

"It must be exciting."

"Sometimes." I nodded to the house. "How's Gary?"

For the first time, her face tightened. "He's in there working."

"He sell anything yet?"

"Stories here and there."

"He'll make it. You can't lose faith."

"That's the funny thing. I haven't, but he has." She shook her head. "He's been writing stories since we were in high school, right? That's why he went into teaching high school English, so he could stay close to what he loved. Well, he finally got some real interest on a novel a few weeks ago—after nearly twenty years of trying—and he burns it."

"He burned the novel?"

"Yes. Said it wasn't good enough."

She shrugged, glanced down at her hands. She had always been pretty rather than beautiful, with an almost mournful grace. It was a grace that had only deepened as she got older. Then she smiled and I wanted to hold her, she gave me that much sense of tenderness. "I'll bet I know why you're here."

"She here?"

"No. But she called. Said she'd see us at the reunion dance tonight. You going?"

"I hadn't planned on it. But if it's the only way I can see her, I will."

She said, "You're not starting up with her again, are you?"

"Do I look crazy?"

"I shouldn't have said that. She's my friend."

"She can still be your friend and you can still tell the truth."

"She's pretty messed up. All those husbands." She reached out and took an edge of the sheet and brought it to her nose. "I always associate this smell with my mother. I always helped her hang out the wash and I loved to put my face against wet clothes and let them freeze my cheeks till my skin got numb." She inhaled the aroma. "Unfortunately, I can't convince either of my kids to help me. It's a different age." She put the sheet back down. "But I was talking about Karen, wasn't I? She's kind of a basket case."

"She also may be in some serious trouble."

"Why?"

I started to tell her, but then the back door opened and a small, slight man with thinning brown hair caught back in a ponytail and rimless eyeglasses came up. Gary.

"God," he said and put out his slender hand. We shook. He looked much older than Susan, and much wearier. He was still thin, but it was a beaten thin, and his clothes were redolent of the sixties, faded tie-dye shirt and bell-bottoms, like a hobo looking for the ghost of Jim Morrison. Gary and I had lived two blocks away from each other in the Highlands, and sometimes I'd gone to his parents' apartment, where we smoked Luckies and drank Pepsis all afternoon and listened to Elvis and Carl Perkins and Little Richard, dreaming of owning custom cars and having as our own the women Robert Mitchum always ended up with. But that was just one side of Gary. He'd had a battered bookcase filled with paperbacks reverently filed alphabetically, everything from Arthur C. Clarke to John O'Hara, from Allen Ginsberg to e.e. cummings (he'd gotten me into Jack Kerouac, an affection I've never lost), and the only time I'd ever seen him hit somebody was one afternoon when a kid drunk on 3.2 beer tripped into Gary's bookcase, knocking a brand-new Peter Rabe to the floor. Gary, not big, not known for his temper, slapped the kid across the face with the precision of a fabled pachuco opening up somebody's gullet with a shiv. Now we stood on either side of twenty-five years and he said, "God, look at you."

"Look at you."

"I mean, you look great, Jack. I look like a sixty-year-old man."

And I heard then what had always been in him—some generalized bitterness, half self-pity, half frustration with a world that had passed your old man by and was intent on doing the same thing to you—and I glanced over at Susan, who watched her husband with the same concern she'd always had for him. In ninth grade she'd simply adopted him in some curious way, part maternal and part sexual, and she had never let go of that impulse or of him down all these long years.

Gary said, "We see you on TV."

"Yeah." Then, "How about letting me read some of your stories?"

"Oh, they're not much. You know that."

"Really, I'd like to read some." And I wanted to, too. He had the early knack for telling stories, very good ones when he wrote in the vein of the magazines we both liked, *Manhunt* and *Ellery Queen*, less so when he affected the styles he found in the *New Yorker* and the *Atlantic*.

"Hubris," he said.

"Why?"

Gently, she said, "He wrote a perfectly good detective story three months ago but wouldn't send it off."

"Why not send it out?"

"I don't want to be a detective writer. I want to be a real writer."

And then I remembered how he'd shifted somewhere in college, telling me about it one night behind a couple of joints and some wine, how popular fiction had started to bore him, how it was "genius" or nothing. So now he had a tract home and graying hair in a ponytail and he took the efforts of his heart and mind and burned them. Much as I liked him, and felt sentimental watching him now, he seemed alien to me somehow, aggrieved in a way that he wanted to be literary but which came off as merely pathological.

One of those awkward silences fell between us, until Susan said, "Jack thinks Karen's in some trouble."

His head snapped up. His blue eyes looked agitated behind his rimless glasses. "What kind of trouble?"

"I'm not sure," I said. "Something to do with a missing suitcase. Do you know anything about it?"

"Nothing about a suitcase," Susan said.

"Gary?"

"No. Nothing." But his air of anxiety continued. He reminded me of how Glendon Evans had acted earlier that afternoon.

"Kids," Susan said.

"What?"

"That's her trouble. No children."

Gary said, "That isn't her trouble."

"No?" I asked.

"No. Her trouble is that people think she's one thing when she's another."

"What is she, then?"

He flushed, seeing how seriously I'd taken his statement.

Then he put on a big party smile. "You shouldn't pay any attention to a forty-two-year-old man who's gotten more than two hundred rejections in his time."

I wasn't going to let him go so easily—I wanted to press him on his remark—but Susan said, "I'm afraid you drove out here for nothing."

"Not for nothing. I got to see you."

"You should take a few pointers from Jack, Gary."

He put out his hand again. "Well, I'm going to try to squeeze in a few more pages before dinner. Hope you'll excuse me."

"I really would like to see some of your work."

"Sure, Jack." Then he sort of cuffed me on the arm and left.

We watched him go inside. When he was gone, Susan said, "He has a surprise coming."

"What?"

"The detective story he thought he burned. He set it on fire in the fireplace, but I got most of it out. It's only singed."

"You've read it?"

"Not yet. But I know it'll be good. I'll send it in even if he doesn't want me to. Am I being a bitch?"

I laughed. "Somehow, Susan, I can't imagine you ever being a bitch."

"You always idealized me."

"I guess it's your eyes and your hands. They were always exceptional."

"Well, I can't tell you how nice it is to hear things like that. If I didn't have to go get dinner, I'd ask you to keep right on talking."

I said, "So you don't know anything about a suitcase?"

"No. She's never mentioned anything."

"And nobody's tried to break into your place?"

She said, "My God, no. Now you've really got me scared."

"I'd just keep everything locked up tight."

She looked a bit older now, her brow tense with worry. "What's going on, Jack?"

"I don't know."

"She really is in trouble, isn't she?"

"Yes. But as usual, she only gives you half the facts, so you can't be sure what's going on."

"She's my friend, as I said, but she can be a very frustrating woman."

"Yeah, I seem to remember that."

"I felt so bad for you. You know, the way she treated you back then."

I smiled. "I appreciate that—but it was probably a good experience for me. Taught me about things."

"You know, I've never believed that. I think a part of you should stay naive and unhurt all your life. I've never understood why pain is supposed to be good for you."

I laughed. "Now that you mention it, neither do I. But you've been lucky. You've always had Gary, and he's always had you."

"I'm sure we've both been tempted. Even up here. Among all the unfashionable Highlands people—" saying this with just the slightest sardonic touch— "adultery is the favorite. Until AIDS came along, most of my best friends were always having affairs while their husbands were at the factories. But there was so much pain—" She shook her head. "I suppose it's exciting—"

"Take my word for it, you haven't missed anything."

"Somehow I believe you."

She'd picked up the sheet again; smelled it. Dusk was a gauzy haze in which you could hear the suppertime laughter of children and the stern voices of TV anchormen enumerating the terrors of the day. Setting the sheet back, she said, "I'm glad you finally found some excuse to come up here."

"Yeah, me, too."

"I always liked you. Is that okay to say?"

"That's wonderful to say."

Then the pain was back in her eyes. "We were going to the reunion tonight, but Gary backed out. The last few months...." She shook her head. "Maybe you could take him out for some beer some night. Cheer him up. I can't seem to do it."

"I'd like that," I said, and I would, though I knew I'd never do it. "I'd like that very much."

She stared at me then. "You've been lucky."

"Pretty much."

"You got out of the Highlands."

"It's not so bad."

"You know better." She frowned. "He should've let me work. I could've helped us find a house somewhere else. Living here—it does something to you. You know how it is here, Jack. I just keep thinking maybe he would really have turned out to be a writer if we hadn't lived here. You know?"

I kissed her on the cheek, caught the scent of the clean wash again, and left. "Maybe he'll be a writer yet."

She smiled. "You know what his problem is?"

"What?"

"He isn't a boy anymore."

"He's nearly forty-three. He shouldn't be a boy."

"But he should still have some fun. He never has any fun. He just writes stories and tears them up and says they're not good enough."

I let her lean into me and we stood a moment, the air fresh with her laundry and the smell of new grass, and hamburgers grilling on the back porch next door.

"Can you believe we're twenty-five years older?" she said. "Sometimes it's scary, isn't it?"

"That's the right word for it, Susan. Scary."

I hugged her and listened for a time to the children in the dusk, their laughter like pure water, and then I went and got into my car and started back through the maze of streets. I had one other person I wanted to talk to about Karen, somebody I was not looking forward to seeing at all.

I was halfway there when I happened to glance in my rearview and found that not all my paranoia is unjustified.

Somebody in black leather on a black Honda cycle was accompanying me.

Chapter 6

The Highlands has a shopping district of four blocks, stores that even back in the forties looked old, two-story brick jobs mostly, with the names of their original owners carved in fancy cursive somewhere near the roof, the names running to Czech and Irish, with the polysyllables of an occasional Italian name also being included. Growing up, I'd come here with my parents to shop for groceries or to buy something from the hardware store or the auto parts store or to get a shirt from the secondhand store (when you really had dough you went to Penney's), but shopping centers had killed all that off now—you drove out to one of five malls on this side of town that had taken the place of the merchants who had settled and helped build this area since as far back as 1849, when six thousand people migrated up here from the Virginias. Now you didn't have merchants, you had tavern-owners. That's all that was left now, bars advertising naked women and country-western music and big-screen Bears games, with a store that sold fancy cowboy clothes or a concrete lot filled with the sad hulks of used cars thrown in to serve the workingmen who bring their paychecks and their beaten hopes down here. When you come here at night, it's not so bad, with workers from the slaughterhouse a mile away and their Czech girlfriends wandering from tavern to tavern like people out of a John Steinbeck novel. But in the daylight you see how everything needs paint and how the walks are cracked, and you see all the names spray-painted on the sides of the taverns, lurid reds and blacks and green on whitewashed surfaces; KILL QUEERS! NIGGERS SUCK! MEXES STAY OUT!

I pulled my car into the half-empty lot of a place called The Nook (needless to say, regulars called it The Nookie), and walked behind a couple of men with black lunch pails through the front door, smelling the silty residue from the hog kill. The air smells and feels a certain way when cows are killed. Hog kills fill the air with textures and odors all their own.

The interior, long bar on the left wall, three bumper pool tables down the center, booths and pinball games to the left, got rid of the hog odor anyway, replacing it with beer, cigarette smoke, microwave pizza, sweat, and perfume. The perpetually turning BUDWEISER sign hanging over the cash register and the wide space-age-model Seeburg jukebox (drop in two quarters and it would take you to Pluto, and play you a couple of Hank Williams, Jr., tunes along the way) and the pinball games with their busty ladies and the discreet little red plastic electric candles in the booths gave the long, low, dark place most of its light. The mood was jovial now—the men buying paycheck rounds of shots-and-beer and the women treated with outsize courtesy—but by nine it would all change and there would be at least a few fistfights, savage ones. Back in my police days, I'd come into dozens of places like this one and seen enough blood to rival the killing floor where many of these men worked—eyes hooked out with thumbs, throats ripped open with broken beer bottles, noses smashed in with working-shoe heels, and women slapped so hard and so long that their faces were swollen beyond recognition. But it was the women who were the most curious of all, because when you tried to arrest the husbands or boyfriends who'd done this to them, the women would jump on you, physically try to stop you from dragging their men to the curb and the car. It was as if they understood how miserable the lives of their men were and therefore forgave them nearly any atrocity.

I ordered a shell and had some beer nuts and looked around to see if I could see Chuck Lane, and when I didn't see him said to the bartender, whose arms were so thick with tattoos they looked like some kind of shimmering snakeskin, "You seen Chuck?"

"So who wants to know?"

"Friend of his sister's."

He shot me a smirk. "His sister's got a lot of friends." He put a fat left finger to his right nostril and snuffled like a cokehead in need. He was short and meaty with sideburns of a length and width I hadn't seen since 1967. His teeth were dirty little stubs. He had a blue gaze that combined malice and stupidity with chilling ease. If Richard Speck had a brother, this guy was it. "Rich ones, too, from what I hear. And you don't look like no rich one."

I sighed. "I just want to see Chuck. It's important. So if he's here, I'd appreciate it if you'd let him know that Jack Dwyer wants to talk to him."

"It worth five to you?"

"That's only in movies. Just call Chuck."

"I need some grease to do it because I got to walk all the way down the basement stairs. The intercom's on the blink."

"Consider it good exercise."

"I got an inflamed prostate. It hurts to walk."

"Goddamn, are you serious? You're going to make me pay you five bucks to go get Chuck?"

"Yeah."

"Why don't I just go down there myself?"

"He won't let you in unless you know the password. He's got, you know, bill collectors and like that after him."

"So I have to give you five bucks to go get him?"

"I ain't kiddin' you about the prostate." And with that he produced a brown prescription bottle and rattled it at me like some voodoo icon. "This is a legit prescription right from the doc." He kind of grabbed his crotch and frowned. "It's like I got this baseball between my legs and it's real hard to move."

So I laid five on the bar.

"Tell you what. While you're waitin', you have another shell and it'll be on Kenny."

"Who's Kenny?"

"Me."

"Oh, yeah. Thanks."

So Kenny, whose very theatrical walk reminded me of Charles Laughton as the

Hunchback of Notre Dame, asked a biker-like guy two stools down from mine, "You watch the register for me, Mike?"

"Anybody touches that sumbitch," Mike said, showing a gloved fist the size of a baseball mitt, "he's dead meat."

I had to make sure to bring Donna here next time we kind of wanted to relax and enjoy a quiet evening.

"So you're looking for Karen."

"Right."

"Mind if I ask why?"

"Yeah, I do mind."

He shook his head. "You still don't like me, do you, Dwyer?"

I sighed. "It doesn't matter, Chuck."

"You think because I live down here, I don't have any pride?"

I looked around. His "apartment" was one big room with imitation knotty pine walls and the sort of furniture you find at garage sales. There was an aged Ziv black-and-white TV with enough aluminum foil on the rabbit ears to cook several steaks in. There was a multicolored throw rug, meant to resemble a hooked rug, and you could see stiff patches where somebody had spilled things or thrown up.

This was about where you would expect to find Chuck Lane twenty-five years later. "Luckless" was the word for him. He'd been born with a clubfoot, and when he walked the movement was so violent and awkward, you forgave him any sin because you could gauge the physical pain and humiliation he felt just trying to get down the street. But there was a lot to forgive him for. He was a thief—in eighth grade, he'd taken my baseball glove, and I had yet to forget it—and he'd always played on the fringes of real crime, doing favors for punks who enjoyed brief power with hot-car rings or shoplifting rings or by hiring out to smash up people who owed money or who were plugging their private parts into places they didn't belong. In the early sixties Chuck had distinguished himself by trying to give his girlfriend an abortion in the back seat of his car with a coat hanger and a great deal of stupidity. She'd bled to death all over the seat covers and the floor, Chuck frozen in fear that he'd go to the slammer for murder. He didn't. He went to the slammer for manslaughter. When he got out, he came to work here at the tavern, which was owned by another man who lived on the periphery of law. But by this time in his life, Chuck wasn't more than a part-time bartender and occasional petty thief. He played a lot of poker. He wasn't any better at it than he was at anything else. During the days I'd gone out with Karen, I'd learned how much she'd loved him but also how much of a burden he was, always in need of money or a place to hide or, simply, comfort, his mental stability never having been the best.

Now he was in his forties and heavyset and shaggy with a reddish beard and the kind of colorful Saturday-night clothes that had gone out with leisure suits.

"Why're you looking for Karen?"

I sighed. "Chuck, I'm asking you a straightforward question. Do you know where Karen is?" I wanted to see her for a simple reason. To tell her how Glendon Evans was knocked unconscious, to get a simple, honest answer as to what was really in the suitcase.

"I ain't seen her."

"Right."

"I'm telling you the truth."

He got up from his overstuffed chair and crossed the room to get at a carton of Camels. I had to look away. I'd always felt ashamed of myself around him, ashamed, I guess, that my limbs were intact. He didn't deserve to be born crippled. Nobody did.

He tore open a new pack and said, "She in some kind of trouble or something?"

"You know anything about a suitcase?"

His sister's eyes stared at me. "Suitcase?"

"Right."

"Uh-uh."

He moved across the floor again. I looked away. "Still embarrasses you, don't it?"

"What?"

"My foot."

I didn't say anything.

"You always was that way, Dwyer." He laughed then and I didn't know why he laughed; all I knew was that he'd just shown me teeth badly in need of a dentist.

I wanted out of there, then. The mildew smell, the beer smell, the sagging single bed, the shabby clothes. I wondered what he dreamed of, what could possibly keep him going in these circumstances. There was not even a window to look out of. Only a few years ago he'd been a teenager, when there was always the hope that the cards would run good, but the cards hadn't run good at all for him.

"How about this suitcase?" he said.

"What about it?"

"What's in it?"

"I'm not sure."

"Why you want it?"

"Because I was hired to find it."

"But you don't know what's in it?"

"That's right, Chuck. I don't know what's in it."

He smiled.

"What's funny?"

"It's Karen, isn't it?"

"Karen?"

"Sure. This sounds like some kind of deal she'd get you involved in. Having you look for something but not telling you what it is exactly."

I glanced around. He had a poster of Farrah Fawcett in a swimsuit and a RE-

ELECT REAGAN bumper sticker on the wall.

Sitting on a bureau was a travel brochure to sunny Arizona with an envelope that looked to contain an airline ticket.

"You ever think of moving out of this place?"

"It getting to you?"

"Sort of, I guess."

"Gets to me, too." He shrugged. "It's about all I can afford these days. After the Amway thing went to shit, I mean."

"You sold Amway?"

"Yeah. You ever go to any of their meetings?"

"Uh-uh."

"Man, they get you all het up. It's like going to one of them TV evangelists. One night I was watchin' the tube here and I was pretty gassed up on beer and this TV evangelist came on and I watched him, really watched him for the first time, and I'll be damned if I didn't stand up and pledge myself to Jesus, and I mean I had tears streamin' down my cheeks, and I wrote him out a check for one hundred dollars and staggered down to the post office and mailed it in. It was like this light was shining in my eyes, this real strong light, and for about an hour or so it was like I was on this high I'd never been on before, really whacked out, you know, better than drugs or sex or booze or anything." Then he stopped and sighed. "But then in the morning I got up and remembered what I'd done, sending the check in and all, and I remembered that I'd closed that account and that the check would bounce and—" He smoked some of his cigarette. "Anyway, Amway was like that for a while. I'd go to these meetings and get real psyched up, but then...."

He let it drift off, the way so much in his life had drifted off.

The room was getting oppressive again.

"She's getting it together."

"Karen?" I said.

"Yeah. She dumped that spook."

Which almost caused me to smile, never understanding why one set of outcasts wants to put down another set of outcasts. Didn't he see that the same people who dismissed him as a clubfoot probably dismissed Glendon Evans for being black?

"But you don't know where she is?"

"Not really, man. She calls sometimes. I'll tell her you're looking for her."

"So you don't know anything about a suitcase?"

"Why you keep asking? I already said no. Jesus, man." He stubbed out his cigarette. "It's because of the baseball glove, isn't it?"

"Nah."

"Bullshit."

"Well."

"I take a crummy baseball glove thirty years ago and you still blame me."

I felt myself flush.

"People change, you know, Dwyer."

"I know." He had me feeling guilty. He had me feeling the way he wanted me to feel.

"I don't know from no suitcase, all right?"

"All right."

"And the next time you come down here, try not to look like you just walked into a leper colony, all right? Like you're going to get contaminated or something?"

I stood up. Held out my hand. "Good to see you, Chuck."

He got up and getting up was an effort and I averted my eyes and he saw me avert my eyes and then he shook my hand and said, "Being a gimp isn't so bad, Dwyer. It's other people *thinking* it's so bad that really gets to you, you know?"

I babbled. "Take it easy, Chuck."

"Right. That's how I always take it. Easy. I've got the charmed life, you know."

Chapter 7

These days they have names like Dead Kennedys and The Sea Hags and The Virgin Prunes, and when my sixteen-year-old son plays them for me I try to remember that back in my sixteen-year-old days I drove my own parents crazy with some very offensive people named Little Richard and Howlin' Wolf and, not least, Elvis himself.

Now I stood outside a four-story brick building in the middle of the Highlands looking up at a sky filled with stars and a slice of quarter moon and tumbling clouds the color of ghosts. There was no sign of a black Honda.

From inside St. Michael's came a medley of songs, including "Don't Be Cruel" and "Sea of Love" and "Blue Jean Bop" and "Runaround Sue" and "Walkin' to New Orleans," all done with feverish amateurish fun. I wanted for the sake of my son to enjoy the music of the Dead Kennedys, but maybe it was my age or the calculated offensiveness of their name, but when he showed me their album cover I had an instant fantasy about putting them up against a wall and punching their faces in. I didn't say that to my son, of course. I just put my arm around him and said, "Whatever happened to that Dion and the Belmonts tape I gave you?"

"It was all right till I found out what he's doing these days."

"What's that?"

"Making religious albums."

"Really?"

"Yeah, Dad, and I just have a real hard time taking anybody seriously who makes religious albums. Like all those ministers on cable. You know?"

So Dion, once of rock 'n' roll leather and rock 'n' roll heat, was making a very different kind of album now and maybe even believing the too-sweet, too-easy hype of commercial religion, and who the hell was I to judge him anyway? And now here I was standing outside the school where nearly forty years ago I'd started kindergarten and where twenty-five years ago I'd graduated high school. I had a Bud in one hand and a cigarette in another (these days I don't smoke more than ten cigarettes a week, just enough to keep myself worried and guilty and coughing), and I heard music that should have lifted me back to other times when you measured success by the kind of car you drove or whom you hung out with or what base (first, second, or third) you'd gotten to the night before. But all I sensed now was how time cheated you, tricked you, and one day you were young and then one day you were not young. And then people you loved began dying so that one funeral service became very much like another, the grimace on the faces of those bearing the casket, the chill silver drops of holy water sprinkled on the newly turned earth, the sound of tears lost in the cold wind and the flapping sound of the canvas tent at graveside. And so you stood on nights like this, the stars washed across the endless sky, and just tried to make simple animal sense of it all. But you couldn't, of course, because ultimately it made sense to none of us, not the priest who whispered solace nor the hedonist who tried to deny it in the noisy illusion of his passion nor the puzzled six-year-old trapped in the confines of a white hospital bed he'd never leave. All you could understand was how many millions had stood on just such evenings down the time-stream thinking the same thoughts and coming to the same conclusion, which was really no conclusion at all, just the hope, even among the most cynical of men, that there really was a God or something very much like a God, and that all this did indeed have significance somehow in the relentless cosmic darkness.

"Say, there's a Shamrock!" cried a drunken male voice.

And like some berserk chorus line, three people came down the front steps of the school, doing some kicks and singing along to "Take Good Care of My Baby."

"He *is* a Shamrock!" cried both of the women on either side of the chubby man. He was bald and plump and wore a red dinner jacket and a cummerbund wide as a pillowcase and a wonderful boozy grin. The women were also plump and wore clever gowns that disguised their widening middles and pushed up voluptuously their fortyish cleavage. The way they did their kicks and sang the tune aloud, they were like an Ample Lady version of the Rockettes and they were exactly what I needed to pull me out of my hole.

"Yeah, I'm a Shamrock," I said, the word on my tongue as silly as it'd ever been. The public schools had always had names like Wilson Wolverines and Roosevelt Rough Riders. We'd gotten stuck with Shamrocks. I'd just always known that Bogart would never have let anybody call him a Shamrock. Not without hitting the guy, anyway.

"Take it from me," the drunk said, "spike your own punch. It's too weak otherwise."

"Georgie has his own bottle," explained one of the women in a loud proud voice.

The other woman giggled. "He also has his own wife. But we lost her a while back."

So they staggered on to the car and I went inside and the first thing I noticed was, that they still used the same kind of floor wax they had for the past uncountable decades, the smell of it making me feel like I was imprisoned in a time capsule: a ten-year-old on an autumn day sitting in a desk at the back ostensibly reading my history book with a Ray Bradbury paperback carefully tucked inside.

"Jack Dwyer."

She sat at one of the two long tables where you checked in and got your name tag.

I had to glimpse at hers quickly so I'd remember who she was. "Hi, Kathy." Kathy Malloy.

"You didn't answer our RSVP. We didn't expect you. Looks like you might have made up your mind at the last minute." She tried to put a laugh on the line but it didn't work. The way her eyes scanned my rumpled tweed jacket and white tieless button-down shirt and Levi's and five-o'clock shadow, I could see that she hadn't changed any. She was one of those people born to be a hall monitor, to watch very closely what you did and to disapprove the hell out of it. She had gray hair now, worn in one of those frothing things that seem to be white women's version of an Afro, and she wore a red silk dress that despite its festive color was redolent of nothing so much as blood. She said, "Helen Manner is supposed to be helping out at the table here." She leaned forward. "Between you and me, I think Helen's developed a drinking problem over the years. She runs inside to the punch bowl every chance she gets. Don't say anything to anybody, though, all right?"

Kathy Malloy had probably done everything but rent a sound truck to broadcast Helen Manner's drinking problem and here she was telling me not to tell anybody. Right.

I got through the rest of it as quickly as I could, signing some things, accepting my name tag, hearing some more gossip, and then I went into the gym, which was like a vast dark cave festooned with low-hanging crepe of green and white, with a stage at front prowled by chunky guys my own age in gold-lamé outfits who, despite their lack of talent, seemed to be having one hell of a good time. Above the stage was a banner that said WELCOME CLASS OF '63, and I realized then how '63 looked as ancient as '23 or '17. I recalled a time when I couldn't believe it was ever going to be 1970. Now we were facing down the gun barrel of 1990. What was going on here?

For the first twenty minutes, I mingled. I was looking for Karen Lane and not finding her and in the process I renewed a lot of acquaintances, some reluctantly, some gladly, learning all those things that somehow measure lifetimes these days—the one who was married three times, the one who was wealthy at least with money, the one who was battling cancer, the one who had turned out gay, the skinny one who had turned fat or the fat one who was now a beauty, the one who was a florid-faced alcoholic, the one who was the cuckold, the one who was the menopausal male with the woman half his age. The ones you'd envied and wished in your petty heart the worst for—they'd all seemed to do pretty well, Buick-comfortable and suburban-smug. And the ones you'd feared for—the ones with limps and lisps and those little spasms of intolerable anxiety or even madness—they stood now in a cluster of the twisted and forsaken, accepting the smiles and salutations of their betters with the same kind of sad gratitude they'd long ago gotten used to.

And I still didn't see Karen Lane, though, according to various people I asked, I was drawing close—she'd just been seen on the dance floor, or at the bar, or out the back door, where a few people stood by the garage where the monsignor had parked his infamous black '57 Dodge (the primo fantasy of the time having been making out with your girl in its back seat). Joints and wine were being passed around among people who seemed almost fanatical in their laughter and who seemed to remember details of twenty-five years ago that I'd forgotten entirely.

I asked a man I recognized as a lawyer if he'd seen Karen Lane. He said, "Seen her? Hell, man, she's so gorgeous, I fell in love with her." Then he nodded to the alley behind. "I think she went out there with Larry Price."

I stood there and stared at him and time was a trap of spider-webbing I couldn't escape. Even after a quarter century, her being with Larry Price had the power to enrage me.

I pushed past the partiers and on out to the alley where a block-long of sagging garages, probably new about the time Henry Ford was rolling his first Model T off the assembly line, stood like wooden gravestones in the moonlight. They smelled of old wood and car oil and moist earth.

I looked up and down the long shadows and saw nothing. I was about to turn around and go back to the party when I heard the unmistakable moan.

Two garages away.

My stomach became fiery with pain and I felt the blind, unreasoning impulse of jealousy.

I wanted to turn around and go back to the school, and as I started to move toward the monsignor's garage again, I heard the slap, sharp as a gunshot.

Then in the soft night I heard Karen say, "Leave, Larry. Please."

"I'm not finished."

"But I'm finished, Larry, and I have been for a long time."

"I'm sick of that goddamn tale of yours, Karen. You know that? It goddamn happened and it's goddamn over and nothing can goddamn be done about it."

"Please, Larry."

"Bitch."

Then he slapped her a clean slap, probably more harmful emotionally than physically. "Bitch."

He came out of one of the garages down in the shadows and looked around as if an assassin might be waiting for him. He had changed very little—six feet, blond, attentive to his tan and his teeth. He sold BMW's and Volvos, mostly during long lunches at the Reynolds Country Club.

He was drunk enough that he leaned perilously forward as he moved. He almost bumped into me before he saw me. "Hey—"

And I dropped him. For a variety of reasons, only one even remotely noble— because he'd slapped her. The second was because he'd beaten me in high school, and the third because I was frustrated with the lies Karen had been telling me and I'd had just enough vodka-laced punch to work up a mean floating edge.

"God," he said, feeling his jaw and shaking his head.

By now, she was out in the moon shadows, staring down at him. "What happened?"

"He slapped you, didn't he?"

She glanced sharply at me. "What are you doing here, Jack?"

"Looking for you."

"Did you get the suitcase?"

"We need to talk about that, Karen. We need to talk very long and very hard about that."

If she hadn't screamed, I might not have seen him lunge at me.

I got him a hard clean shot in the stomach and then clubbed his temple with the side of my fist. He dropped to his knees and started vomiting.

"I can't watch this," she said, starting to pace in hysterical little circles. In her blue jersey jumper and white beads, she resembled a society woman who has just been informed that the entire family fortune has been embezzled.

Then, gathering herself, she went over to him and said, "Are you all right, Larry?"

"What the hell you doing with him?"

"He's helping me find something."

"What?"

"It needn't concern you." She sounded as prim as a schoolmarm. "I merely asked if you were all right."

But now he didn't pay any attention to her. He struggled to his feet, leaning back a bit from the booze. He was more sober now. Losing some blood and throwing up can occasionally work wonders.

"You think you're going to get away with this, Dwyer, you're really crazy. Really crazy." Then he turned on her and said, "You too, bitch. You too."

He left.

He walked bowlegged the way Oliver Hardy had in *Way Out West*. He wanted to walk mean because he was a basically mean guy and booze only enhanced his anger. But right now all he could do was look like Oliver Hardy and it didn't scare me and it didn't impress me and I'd already decided that if he came back, I was going to put a few more fists into him.

"That wasn't necessary."

"Sure it was," I said.

"You don't understand the situation here."

"I understand that Larry Price is a jerk and always has been."

"But that's all you understand."

"I met Dr. Evans."

Her eyes narrowed. "He was there when you went into the apartment?"

"He was there all right. Unconscious."

"What?"

"And bleeding."

She sighed. Shook her head. "So he did try?"

"Try what?"

"Suicide."

"Sorry."

"What?"

"Somebody hit him across the back of the head. Very hard. And several times. Guess what they were looking for."

"His money, probably. Some junkie or something."

"God, you're just going to keep it up, aren't you?"

"Keep what up? What are you talking about?"

"Keep up this guise that there's something very innocent in the suitcase and that you just kind of want it back for old times' sake. Are you dealing drugs?"

"My God, what kind of person do you think I am?"

"Did you do some jewelry salesman out of his ruby collection?"

"I don't want to hear any more."

"Somebody wants whatever's in that suitcase badly enough to risk B and E and assault with a deadly weapon. Those are heavy raps." I grabbed her by the shoulder—thinking that Glendon Evans had told me he'd hit her—and I dug my thumb and forefinger into her gentle and wonderful flesh. "You owe it to me, Karen."

"What?"

"The truth."

She laughed without seeming at all amused. "Oh, I wish I knew the truth, Jack. How I wish I knew the truth."

But I was in no mood for philosophy. "What's in the suitcase?"

"Would you make me a promise?"

"What?"

"If we went back into the gym and danced the slow dance medley, would you promise not to step on my feet?"

"Don't try to buy me off, Karen. I want to know what the hell's going on. You're in trouble, whether you know it or not."

"You used to be a terrible dancer, Jack, and for some reason I suspect you still are." She leaned up and kissed my cheek and I felt blessed and cursed at the same time. "But then you're cute and you're sincere, and sometimes those things are even more important than the social graces."

"Have you always been this superficial?"

"No," she said, and there was an almost startling melancholy in her voice. "No, Jack, I've had to work at it. I really have."

Then she took my arm and led me back inside the gym where in tenth grade she'd given me a lingering public kiss right there on the dance floor. Robert Mitchum had nothing on me.

So we started dancing, a little formally at first, as the band went through some Connie Francis numbers and then some Johnny Mathis numbers and then some Teddy Bear numbers, and I started looking around the shadows of the gym at the joke being played out before me.

Here were the kids I'd made my First Communion with and played baseball with and walked home from school with along the railroad tracks that smelled of grease and swapped comics with (Batman was always worth two of anything else) and watched change from little girls into big girls with powers both wonderful and terrible over me and little boys into half-men with a hatred that could only come from growing up in the Highlands—but whatever else we'd been, we'd been young and it had all been ahead of us—the great promise of money and achievement and sex, God yes, sex. But these people were trying to trick me now, they'd gone to some theatrical costume shop and gotten gray for their hair and padding for their bellies and rubber to create jowls, these very same people in my First Communion photo.

"You scared?" she said.

But I'd been lost in my thoughts and all I could give her was a dumb expression. "What?"

"Are you afraid?"

"Of what?"

"Look around."

"That's what I'm doing."

"In twenty years a lot of these people will be dead. Maybe even us."

"I know."

"It went so fast."

I was getting one of those seventh-grade erections, the kind you get but don't really want because it's embarrassing and you don't really know what to do with it. I was getting a seventh-grade erection there dancing in the darkness of our middle age.

"Why don't we go back to your apartment and go to bed?" she said. Her voice was curiously slowed. I wanted to attribute this to the incredible sexual sway I held over women but somehow I didn't think so.

I said, "You're drunk."

"No, I'm not. I only had two drinks tonight."

"Something pretty potent?"

"No, one of the pink ladies fixed me a Scotch and soda is all."

"Pink ladies?"

"Waitresses."

"Ah." And true enough, I had seen waitresses buzzing around. "They must have had some kind of incredible effect on you."

"Why?"

"You sound groggy."

"That's what's funny."

"What?"

"I sort of feel groggy, too."

"You want to sit down?"

"No, just hold me a little closer, will you?"

I sighed, pulled her closer. "Karen, I want you to tell me about the suitcase."

"Not now, all right?"

And she put her face into my shoulder and we danced as I once dreamed we would dance, eyes closed, even the tinny music melodic and romantic, and I felt her eminent sexual presence but also her odd vulnerability, and I held her for the girl she'd been and the woman she was, and I let my lips find her cheek and felt her finger tender on the back of my neck.

And for a time, moving just like that in the Shamrock gym, in unison with all the people in our First Communion picture, I forgot all about Dr. Evans and how he'd been knocked out and forgot all about a curious figure in black on a black Honda motorcycle and all about a suitcase that nobody seemed to possess but that somebody seemed to want very, very badly.

I wasn't thinking of anything at all really, just floating on her perfume and the darkness and the music, and at first I was scarcely aware of how she began to slip from my arms to the floor.

"Karen?" I said. "Karen?"

People around us were looking and a few giggling, making the assumption she was drunk, but I didn't think so.

She was dead weight in my arms. And that was exactly what I thought: *dead weight.*

And then one of those quick bursts of panic, some sort of concussion, went off inside me and I heard myself shouting for lights up and for people to clear space and I knelt paramedic-style next to her feeling for pulse in neck and wrist, touching the tepid, sweaty skin of her body.

I found no pulse.

A priest and a fat man in a dinner jacket whom I recognized as our class president came running up and said, "What's wrong here?"

"Ambulance," was all I could say, scarcely able to speak at all.

The overhead lights were on now and the magic was gone; you could see how old the floor was, and how beaten up the bleachers, and how cracked the tall windows. It was not the Stairway to the Stars of countless proms, after all. It was just a gym in a school more than half a century old and now in ill repair because the diocese saw no future in the Highlands. Nobody ever had.

She looked comic herself now, fake, the way the dancers had, fake gray tint in their hair, fake bellies, fake wrinkles and jowls and rheumy eyes, but what she was putting on was even more alarming because she was imitating death itself, like some phantom beauty from a Poe poem, but without the flutter of an eyelid or warm breath in her nostrils, not the faintest flicker in wrist or neck.

"Ambulance!" I shouted again, and this time I heard how ragged and desperate my voice had become and saw in the eyes of those encircling me a modicum of pity and a modicum of fear—both of her death and of the potential rage in my voice.

The priest, young as a rookie ballplayer, yet shorn of the grace that comes with age, knelt down beside me and said, "Maybe I'd best say some prayers with her." He didn't say "Last rites." He didn't need to. He produced a black rosary and began saying a "Hail Mary" and an "Our Father" and then a woman somewhere sobbed and for the first time I realized that the music had stopped, and that in the gym now there was just the rush and roar of time itself and nothing more, nothing more at all.

Chapter 8

"You were the man dancing with her?"

"Yes."

"Can we talk a minute?"

"Sure."

Forty-five minutes had passed since the dance had ground to a nightmare halt, all motion seeming to be slowed down for a time, faces ripped open with tears and fear and the bafflement only death can inspire.

A white box of an ambulance sat with its doors open near the west entrance. The three people from the coroner's office had finished with her now, and two attendants in white, both with potbellies and hippie beards and eyes that had gazed on death perhaps too many times, had put her inside a black body bag, which was in turn put on a gurney that was now being loaded inside the well-lit confines.

Fanned around the ambulance were three hundred people from the dance. Many of the women had their husbands' coats draped over their shoulders. While the women were given to tears and occasional whispers, the men seemed doomed to an odd silence, gazing at the ambulance as if it explained some long-sought answer to a puzzle. There was a great deal of booze, punch from the bowl, Scotch in pint bottles, gin and vodka in flasks, beer in cans and big clear plastic cups. They'd been ready for a night when alcohol would set them free; now all alcohol could do was tranquilize them. Technically, there was a city ordinance against drinking out here, but none of the cops in the three white squad cars said anything. They just moved through the chill night, the stars clear and white in the dark blue sky, the scent of fir and pine and new grass contrasting with the smell of medicine and mortality coming from the ambulance.

"You're Dwyer, right?"

"Right."

"Used to be on the force?"

"Right."

"Thought so." He offered me a Camel filter. I shook my head. "I'm Bill Lynott, Benny McGuane's cousin."

"Oh. Right."

Benny McGuane was a sergeant in the fourth precinct and we'd been buddies back in our first years of directing traffic and chastising husbands who kept wanting to break the bones of their cowering little wives. In those days, that was all the law would let you do, chastise them. Maybe that's why Benny drank so much and maybe that's why he'd had such fragile success with AA, on and off the program every few months or so.

"How's he doing?" I said.

"Much better."

"Good."

"Think it's really going to work for him this time."

"He's a good man."

"He is that." He had some of his Camel filter, standing there next to me, his face like a psychedelic phantasm of the sixties, alternately red and blue in the whipping lights of emergency vehicles. He exhaled. "Shitty thing to happen at a reunion."

"Yes."

"You know her?"

"For a long time."

"You have any reason to think there was any foul play involved?"

"I don't think so."

He looked at me carefully. He had one those fleshy Irish faces you associate with monsignors whose secret passion is chocolate cake. "You don't sound sure."

There was the matter of the suitcase she'd wanted me to find. The matter of Dr. Glendon Evans being beaten up. The matter of her argument with Larry Price in the alley. The matter of somebody on a black Honda motorcycle following me around. "I guess I can't be sure."

"Any particular reason?"

"She was a woman who had a lot of friends and a lot of enemies."

"I just got a quick look at her. Damn good looking woman."

"She was that, all right."

"You think I should call for a plainclothes unit?"

I thought about that one, too, and then I said, "I guess all we can do now is wait for the autopsy."

"That's twenty-four hours minimum."

"I know."

"If anything did happen here, aside from natural causes, I mean, that's a damn long wait. You familiar with poisoning victims?"

This kid was good. He must be taking all the night school courses available. That's one way you can divide cops these days. The men and women who put in their nighttime at the community colleges know a lot more than my generation of beat-pounders ever did.

"Somewhat."

"She look like she might have been poisoned?"

"You familiar with aneurysms?"

I shrugged. "Not really."

"Did she just slip into unconsciousness?"

"I guess. I'm not really sure. I mean, at first I thought she was just getting drunk."

"It might have been a stroke."

"Or a heart attack."

He sighed. "My old man always said not to count on anything and he was right." He snapped his fingers. "You can go just like that."

I was listening to him, sharing in his sense of how fragile our hold on living was, when out near the alley, next to a long silver Mercedes-Benz sedan, I saw Larry Price grab a short, fleshy man and shake a fist at him. A tall, white-haired man with a Saint-Tropez tan and an arrogance that was probably radioactive stood nearby, watching. His name was Ted Forester. He was the man Glendon Evans had told me Karen was having an affair with. The man getting pushed around was a forlorn little guy named David Haskins. In high school the trio had been inseparable, though Haskins had always been little more than an adjunct, an early version of a gopher. Then, abruptly, Forester opened up the rear door of the Mercedes and Price pushed Haskins inside. A lot of people were watching all this, including Benny McGuane's cousin.

"What do you suppose that's all about?"

"I don't know," I said.

"Think I'll go find out."

By this time, Forester was in the car and behind the wheel. The headlights came on like eyes and the car surged forward. Bill Lynott put himself in front of the silver car, daring it to run him over.

He went over to the driver's side. I edged closer, so I could hear.

"What's the trouble here?"

"No trouble." Ted Forester was obviously not used to answering the questions of some cop, of the uniformed variety yet.

"Why did you push that man into the car?"

"To be exact, Officer, *I* didn't push him into the car. My friend Larry Price pushed him into the car. And he did so because David Haskins, the man who is now snoring soundly in the back seat, got very drunk and obnoxious tonight. If, that is, it's any of your business."

"I'd like to see your license, please."

"What?"

Whatever powers the Supreme Court takes away from the police, a cop can always irritate you with his authority by asking to see your license.

"Your license, please."

"Why?"

"Because I have the legal authority to ask to see it and because I *am* asking to see it."

It was at this point that Ted Forester's eyes fell on mine and he frowned immediately. He glanced over at Larry Price, who nodded to him. I wondered if they were going to come after me in their big silver Mercedes. Then I wondered why they'd want to come after me in their big silver Mercedes.

Forester, tall, trim, handsome in the way of a bank president from central casting, took out a long slender wallet and opened it up like a diplomat presenting his credentials.

Billy Lynott, playing it out, took the wallet and shone his flash on the license and studied it as if he were going to be given a pop quiz on it.

Then he handed it back.

"All right, Mr. Forester," he said. "Just be sure to drive carefully."

Forester glowered at him and then at me again and then the Mercedes pulled out of the lot, Larry Price's eyes on me like lasers in the gloom.

"Asshole," Bill Lynott said when he came back to me.

"He always was."

"Maybe I should have made him walk the line."

"He probably would have sued you."

"Yeah, he's the kind all right."

The ambulance attendants were closing the back doors and coming around to get in the cab.

For a moment I felt her in my arms again, the warmth of her flesh, the lovely smell of her hair, the unknowable mysteries of her gaze. I'd loved her and hated her and been afraid of her, but after it all, she'd still been the little girl I'd first met in kindergarten, shared a nap-time blanket with, watched grow into the beauty among the weeds and screams of the Highlands. Then I thought of the suitcase again. What was in it she'd wanted so badly? What was in it that somebody would beat up Glendon Evans for?

"Maybe you should get out of here," Billy Lynott said.

"Yeah. Maybe I should."

"I mean, if downtown wants to get a hold of you, they'll just give you a call."

"Right."

He put a hand on my shoulder. "I'll say 'hi' to Benny for you."

Suddenly, ridiculously, I wanted to see Benny again, have a beer or four with him, shoot some pool, speculate on women and the Cubs and why Democrats just always seemed better than Republicans. I didn't want to be nearing forty-five.

"Yeah," I said, "if downtown wants me, they can give me a call tomorrow."

I went and got in my Toyota and got out of there.

Chapter 9

Donna wasn't there.

She has an apartment building you can get into only if someone inside buzzes you in. I buzzed several times. Nothing.

I walked out to the parking lot and watched the moon and thought about Karen Lane, alternating between absolute certainty that what had happened to her had been coincidental—stroke, aneurysm, as Bill Lynott had suggested—and knowing with equal certainty that she'd somehow been murdered.

"Hello," said a couple walking past me from their car. They were both stockbrokers and both wore gray flannel suits, and both drove Datsun Zs and smoked Merits and belonged to health clubs and vacationed in Aspen and subscribed to the Book-of-the-Month Club. I knew all this because Donna had profiled them for *Ad World* as typical age-thirty-five consumers. The odd thing was, they even looked alike in a certain way, blond and blue-eyed, friendly in an almost ingenuous way. Their name was Burkett and I sort of liked them.

"Hello," I said. Then, "Say, would you let me into the building?"

"Sure," Todd Burkett said. "Is everything all right?"

"I think maybe Donna's just taking a shower or something. I was supposed to meet her here but there's no answer."

"Come on," Mary Anne Burkett said.

So we went up to one of the nine dark brick buildings piled against small mountains of pine and fine green grass that stretched along a river made silver by moonlight. As *Ad World* became more successful, Donna's apartments became fancier.

"We're having some stir-fry and white wine," Mary Anne said as we walked up the wide dramatic staircase leading to the second level. "Would you care to join us?"

"Then we're going to watch *Cape Fear* on the VHS. Have you ever seen it?"

"Yes," I said.

"Isn't Gregory Peck wonderful?" Mary Anne said.

Then I realized that no matter how much I liked them, there was some spiritual demarcation line that would always divide us. The picture belonged—cigars, boxer shorts, cheap straw fedora and all—to Robert Mitchum. Peck is in fact a cypher, little more than a symbol of all that is right with Suburbia. Ethically, he's admirable as hell. Dramatically, he's as bland as an eighth-grade history teacher at a Fourth of July ceremony.

"No, thanks. But maybe some other time."

"Peck is really fantastic."

"Yeah, I know."

So they went to their woks and their Water Piks and their copy of *Cape Fear* and I went down to Donna's and knocked on the door.

I put my ear to the door the way private investigators who specialize in adultery always do. I heard all the sounds an apartment is supposed to make, the vague electronic buzz and crackle and hum that signify that all appliances are alive and doing well. But I heard nothing else.

Then down the hall I heard conversation and turned to see the Burketts talking to Candy James, a TV weather woman who lived in the apartment at the end of the hall. Candy was trying to get herself going in theater, too, and so we'd always just naturally gotten along. "Hi, Jack."

"Hi."

"I saw Donna leave a few hours ago. She said she was going over to your place."

But then she was supposed to come back here. "You didn't hear her come back?"

Candy, who is small and cute, with a curly cap of black hair and a smile that can melt metal, said, "No, I don't think so, anyway. You think something's wrong?"

"Probably not. I'm just kind of curious is all."

"Well, I've got a key. We swap keys in case we get locked out. You want it?"

"Great."

A minute later I had the key and went in and looked around and found nothing. As usual, the place was a tribute to work but not to tidiness, there being enough books and magazines stacked on the floors and on tables and on chairs to open a branch library. Unfortunately buried beneath all the *Ad World* research material were such gems as a drop-leaf harvest table with matching bird-cage Windsor chairs and a cast-iron mantel that she'd found in the city dump.

Her bed hadn't been made, there was yellow egg crust on the face of a green plate next to the microwave, the Crest tube in the bathroom looked as if it had been thrown into a trash compactor, then somehow lifted back out again (she has these killer moments of frugality).

Something was wrong. She is prompt, neurotically so, and if she said she'd meet me here, then she'd be here.

But she wasn't.

I went to the phone and stared out of the window at the silhouettes of the pines jagged against the night sky, their tips white in the moonlight. I let the phone ring at my place at least twenty times. Then I tried the offices of *Ad World* and got nothing and then I tried the number of her assistant, Jill, and got nothing there, either.

One thing about being paranoid is that you keep playing all these alternate scenarios out in your mind. The What-If game. I could reasonably assume she'd gone to my place. But that's all I could reasonably assume. Had she left there? If she hadn't, why wasn't she answering the phone? And that's when my paranoia kicked in and formed mental images of somebody on a black motorcycle, a Honda it was, and God alone knew what this person wanted. Or was capable of. I thought of Karen and how she had looked there at the last and then Karen's face became Donna's and something hard formed in the bottom of my stomach and I had one of those twitching spasms I used to get on the force just before I had to do something that scared me.

A rusted-out five-year-old Toyota is not necessarily built for speed, but I did a very slick job of setting a few Indy records on the way to my apartment.

Chapter 10

You find my place in the inner part of the inner city, on a block where every house has stucco siding and a fair majority of the people you pass on the cracked sidewalks are probably armed. Donna, determined to make my efficiency apartment more "livable," had come over one day armed with draperies and slipcovers she'd bought at Sears, bright and nubby materials they'd been too, but after half an hour she'd dropped to the floor in a kind of semi-yoga position and said, "There just isn't any way to decorate around water stains on the wall, Dwyer. There just isn't."

The vestibule smelled of bleach, marijuana, beer, and Chinese food (there's a take-out place a block away).

I went up the stairs two at a time, now having worked myself into one of those states of stress the magazines always say give you at the least hemorrhoids and at the worst cancer, and then I pushed my key into the gold Yale dead bolt (the only thing in the house that's less than eighty years old). And then, groping for the wall switch, I stared deep into shadow.

"Come in and close the door, okay?"

The table lamp, the one with the beer-stained lamp shade, clicked on and there she sat.

Donna. Editor of *Ad World*. Sitting in the corner of a couch with a white bath towel pushed up against her head.

The towel was soaked with blood.

"God," I said. And for a moment that's all I could do. Just stand there and say over and over, "God." Half the time it was a prayer, the other half it was a curse.

"So you opened the door and then what?"

"So I opened the door and came in."

"And?"

"And nothing. I turned on the light and looked around and I thought, Boy, Dwyer's really got to get out of this place. I mean, I saw cockroaches again tonight. The size of Shetlands, Dwyer."

"Forget the cockroaches. What happened next?"

"I picked out a shirt and jacket and pair of pants from your closet."

"And then?"

"And then I went and used the biffy. Have you ever heard of Tidi Bowl, Dwyer?"

"Donna, are you going to tell me or what?"

"How I got hit on the head?"

"Right."

"Well."

"Why are you hesitating?"

"Because now that I think about it, I'm not sure I remember exactly." She touched a hand to the back of her head, the way Glendon Evans had earlier today. She wore a white blouse and gray tweed jacket and designer jeans. She has red hair and green eyes, one of which strays to a small degree, like Karen Black's (though I never mention Karen Black to her, Donna not thinking much of her acting), and she's one of those women who is very erotic in an almost offhanded way.

(The only time she ever tried to be overtly sexy was when she got a baby-doll nightie, and I sort of spoiled it for her because her debut in the nightie coincided with Larry Holmes's title defense against Michael Spinks. She'd walked back and forth in front of the TV set about fifty times, so often I wondered if she wasn't doing some kind of aerobics, and finally she said, "Notice anything, Dwyer?" And all I'd said was, "Yeah, Larry looks old as shit." And then she'd walked out of the room and come back in and said, "Notice anything now, Dwyer?" She was completely naked.)

"You came out of the biffy," I said, leading her on like a prosecuting attorney.

"I came out of the biffy."

"And then he hit you."

She closed her eyes and thought a moment. "No."

"No?"

"No. I came out of the biffy and then...."

"And then?"

"Then I...." She thought a moment longer. "Then I leaned down to pick up your clothes where I'd rested them over the chair over there with just the one leg and then somehow she came up from behind me and hit...."

"Wait a minute."

"What?"

"You said she."

"Yes."

"She?"

"Perfume. Very sweet perfume. So I assume it was a she."

"God."

"What?"

"A woman."

"Equal opportunity, Dwyer. No reason there can't be female thugs."

"All right. Anything else?"

"Just a weird sound."

"What kind of weird sound?"

"A kind of—creaking."

"Creaking? Like an old house?"

"No—creaking like...."

Then another paranoid image formed. "Creaking the way leather creaks?"

"Yes. Exactly. That's very good." She was getting excited.

The guy on the motorcycle with the black leather. It's a woman.

"Did she say anything?"

"No."

"God."

"What?"

"She wants the suitcase."

"What suitcase?"

"You hungry?"

"Was that an answer?"

"I just mean why don't we have a close look at your head and then if you seem to be all right, go have something to eat and then I'll tell you all about the suitcase."

"Dwyer."

"Yes."

"You haven't kissed me."

"I didn't want to hurt your head."

"You won't hurt my head. I mean I don't want a big lip lock or anything but just a nice discreet little kiss that says I care for you very much."

I took her hand. "How about if I tell you that I care for you very much and then I kiss you and kind of reinforce the message?"

"That would be nice."

So that's what I did. That's exactly what I did.

Chapter 11

Most recording studios are designed to resemble expensive bomb shelters, tight as cocoons. Not only are the floors carpeted, so are most of the walls. Not only do the doors close tight, they are sealed along the edges. The baffling used to make the studios soundproof combines with somber indirect lighting to give the impression that even if Armageddon did come along, you'd never know about it inside here. You work in shadows, and the studio people seem to think this is just ducky, state of the art.

On the other side of a huge slab of glass, at a control panel the folks at *Star Trek* would envy, sat a very sleek guy with razor-cut hair and a mean black gaze and the kind of colorful, casual clothes that pass for southern Californian out here. He said, "Jack, I don't believe it. I mean, you're not coming across, you know?" He would take my six-second bit and mix it into the rest of the spot. Once he got me to read the way he wanted me to, anyway.

"Huh?"

"Look at the script, okay?"

I looked at the script.

"What does it say?"

"It says: 'If it wasn't for the home-equity loan I got at First National, I wouldn't have been able to send Timmy to college.'"

"Well, you've got to sound grateful."

"Right. Sorry."

"You all right this morning?"

"Long night."

He grinned. "Chicks?"

"Nah."

"You know Betsy our receptionist?"

"Yeah."

"She thinks you're cute."

"Great."

"Really." He whispered over the intercom. "Take it from me, Jack. This chick knows things that'll make you blush. And take a gander at those gazongas. *Playboy* material or what?"

Steve, his name was, and at least the way he told it, he'd slept with no less than 50.7 percent of the women under age ninety-six in the city. But he had an annoying habit of never giving them any attributes but sexual ones. They were never smart or dumb or even pretty or ugly, they were always described only by the size of their breasts or various exotic tricks they seemed to know that nobody else had even heard of. (Over beers one night he'd mentioned a "Mexican sleeve job, you know, like in that 200 European Sexual Positions," and I had been left to ponder what that could mean—why Mexican? And what in hell could a "sleeve job" be?)

"You should try her," he said.

"Actually, I've got a friend."

"Oh, yeah. That ad chick. Man, nice-looking."

I guess I should have mentioned earlier that Steve is fifty-seven years old and a tribute to Grecian Formula. He works out not once, not twice, but three times a day, and confided to me once that he attributes his self-described "amazing virility" to massive doses of bee pollen ("I don't have to tell you about bees, do I, Jack?") He is also, for all his unctuous gonadic style, the best recording engineer and director outside of L.A. He takes advertising copy very, very seriously, knows how to make even the most unlikely lines play well, and the agencies are only too happy to send to his place, on a regular basis, big trucks loaded with green Yankee cash.

"You know how I see Jim—this guy you're playing?" he said.

"Uh-uh."

"Close your eyes. I'm going to paint you a picture."

"All right." I closed my eyes.

"He's forty-three years old. He lives in one of the suburbs. He's twenty pounds overweight, and no matter how hard he tries to diet, around eleven o'clock every night he sneaks down to the refrigerator where his wife has got this big sign that reads THINK BEFORE YOU EAT. Only he's so ravenous, he nearly rips the door off and then he just pigs out. Preferably on sweet stuff, but at this point he'll go for anything. He's disgusting to watch. You getting a picture?"

"I'm getting a picture."

"He goes to a Methodist church every Sunday but he nods off during the sermon. He wears Hush Puppies. During the sixties he got a college deferment so he didn't have to go to Nam but he didn't necessarily agree with all the people in the streets. But now this is the tricky part. He works for this corporation where their people are always getting fired. His boss is a real tyrant. Jim uses Valium and Maalox and Tums because inside he's a mess. He's losing his hair, and his erections aren't what they used to be, and even sending his only child to a state university is killing him financially. He's not shit, you seeing it?"

"I'm seeing it." And I was. "He eats because he's secretly depressed, right?" It was like acting class, fun, exhilarating, and only faintly embarrassing.

"Right."

"And maybe he and his wife don't really communicate much anymore, right?"

"Now you're flying, Jack."

"And he always feels that his back is to the wall, and that even the wall's going to cave in on him, right?"

"Exactly. And so, when First National gives him a home-equity loan, it's much more than just a loan—symbolically. Here's this fat guy in Hush Puppies who's this absolute piece of dust with his wife and with his boss—it's First National saying to this guy, Hey, we're your friend, pal. Other people may piss on you and spit on you and revile you with every dirty name imaginable—but not us, we're your *friend*, can you dig that—your friend? So what do we hear in his voice when he says, 'If it wasn't for that home-equity loan I got from First National, I wouldn't have been able to send Timmy to college'? What are we hearing, Jack?"

The bastard nearly had me in tears. "We're hearing gratitude because somebody finally gives a damn about this poor sad son of a bitch."

"That's exactly what we hear, Jack, and that's exactly what we want to hear from you. Gratitude. Because First National's your pal, your compadre, your best bud."

We got it in one take.

After the session, I went down the hall to the john and on the way I glanced out one of the few windows in the two-story facility to the parking lot where spring was struggling to paint everything green and crocus purple and crocus yellow and apple-blossom pink.

She was at the back of the lot, between a Pizza 2-U van and a large blue Buick. She just sat there and I wondered if she ever got hot inside those black leathers and that inscrutable black helmet, and then I wondered if she wore them for reasons of safety or because she liked the melodramatic edge they gave her.

But now it was time I found out not only who she was but what she wanted, so I went to the west end of the building and down the FIRE EXIT stairs and out the door. Being a cop got me in the habit of always carrying a ballpoint and a tablet that fit in the back pocket of my pants. I didn't need a gun right now. I needed the tablet.

The outdoor smelled of sunlight and diesel fuel and flowers. I wanted to be fishing. I worked my way along a line of cars in the lot until I came even with where she was, six cars over. There was an old woman apparently waiting for somebody in the doctor's office next door. She observed the way I sort of crouched down as I moved. She frowned at me, not frightened in the least, but angry. She was probably going to turn me in.

I came up from behind the Pizza 2-U van and stood four feet from the motorcycle.

And then she turned, obviously sensing me somehow. She'd had her engine running, so it was no trouble to do a fairly exotic wheelie and get out of there. The bike reared like a bronc, the long and curving lines of the woman in leathers as one with the metal itself, and then it came screeching and roaring down in contact with the pavement again and shot off in between a maze of parked cars.

There was no way I could catch her and I didn't intend to try.

But now I had her license number, and for now that was the only thing in the world I needed.

Chapter 12

The fourth precinct was built back in the 1930s, when the then-Mayor had an architect for a son-in-law. A bad architect for a son-in-law. Which explains why Number Four looks like a cheesy papier-mâché set for a film set in mythical Baghdad. Built of concrete, it seems to be all minarets and spires and gargoyles—fanciful touches indeed for people named Mike O'Reilly and Milo Czmchek and Rufus Washington.

The interior of the Fourth resembles a big metro newspaper; desks butted up against each other, people running up and down the corridors between the desks, machines for coffee, sandwiches, pop, cigarettes, and newspapers lining the walls of the corridor leading to the rest rooms and the holding cells. Oh, yes, I should mention the para-bookmaking activities, too. At any given time, half the people in the Fourth, men and women alike, are laying down money on events of various descriptions, from the Cubs, Sox, Bears, to which local pols are finally going to get busted for (a) graft, (b) bestiality, or (c) general stupidity.

Somewhere in the welter of all this—the windows open wide to the spring and the cops daydreaming like fourth graders anxious to be outdoors—sat six-two Martin Edelman, my best friend and former partner. Today he was modeling one of his four Sears suits, the blue number, and one of the white shirts whose collar was blood-spattered from his shave this morning. (Even with a safety razor, he can commit atrocities Jack the Ripper could not have even conceived.) He has the sad blue eyes of a rabbi who has seen far too much of the world's nonsense and pettiness and cruelty, but then there is his smile, which is curiously innocent and open, if only occasionally on view. His brown toupee was on slightly crooked, but I saw no point in telling him. It is always on crooked.

A cop named Manning leaned in just as I started to put my hand on Edelman's shoulder. "You in for the Cubs?"

"How much?" Edelman said.

"Ten."

"Jeeze."

"Ten, Edelman. You won twenty last week. Maybe you'll win forty this week.

Edelman, taking out his wallet, said, "The way you hustle people, Manning, you should be an insurance salesman."

Manning said, "You forget, Martin. I *was* an insurance salesman."

"Oh, yeah."

"You got the Cubbies and two points," Manning said, and vanished.

Edelman started to go back to his typewriter—he does very well with two fingers, very well—when I said, "Someday one of the TV stations is going to do a story on all the betting cops do."

He turned around and showed me his smile. He always manages to make me feel as if seeing me is the most special thing that's happened to him in a week. And

I always hope it is.

"Dwyer, hey."

"Hey, Martin."

We shook hands and I just looked at him. In some odd way he's my brother, and I knew this the day we first met years ago back at the Academy when neither of us could shinny up a rope worth a damn. These days, we even share the same problems—we both need to do exactly the same things: lose ten to fifteen pounds, use a few more quarts of Visine a week, and try to convince ourselves that the sky is not going to fall in within the next twenty minutes.

"You hear Manning? I won forty last week." He sounded young saying it and it made me feel good.

"So what did you do with it?"

"You really want to know?"

"Yeah."

"Bought Parkhurst from Number Three a lunch I've owed him for a while, got some new Odor Eaters, bought a new band for my Timex, and then gave the rest of it to my son for a ball glove."

"Nothing's changed."

"Huh?"

"All the excitement."

He laughed. "Asshole." Then he picked up a pink phone slip and said, "I got a note this morning that you were going to be calling me about an autopsy."

"Right."

"Well, I've got some preliminary results." His fingers searched through several layers of paper and then he came up with it. "This is just what I took over the phone. You read my writing okay?"

"I'll try." Edelman's handwriting is a form of communication that would stump even the people who translate cuneiform.

So I looked at it and said, "Natural causes?"

"Yeah. You think it was going to be something else."

"I had some suspicions along those lines."

"Sorry."

"Librium and alcohol."

"Kills a lot of people."

"They going to rule it a suicide?"

He shrugged. "You know how it goes. Most of the time they try to spare the families and just say 'natural causes.' From what I gather, there was no note and the officer's report said you didn't find her particularly upset or depressed."

"I guess not."

"Sorry."

"Yeah."

"You don't believe it?"

"I'm not sure yet." Then I remembered the tablet in my back pocket. "How about running a number for me?"

"This got anything to do with Karen Lane?"

"Probably."

"Probably." He smiled. "Probably." He held out his hand and tore off the sheet of paper with the number on it and then turned around and picked up the phone.

While we were waiting, he said, "I assume if there's anything of interest in this for the police, you'll let us know right away."

"Of course."

"Why don't I believe you?" he said and started doodling on a lined pad. The phone still cupped to his ear, he said, "You and Donna set a date yet?"

"Not yet."

"I read this article on stress the other day. In the paper."

"I read it, too." Edelman wants me to get married.

"Married people have less stress," he said. And then into the phone, "Okay, ready."

He wrote it down, name and address, and then hung up and handed me the paper. "So how about it?"

"How about what?"

"She's a wonderful woman and I can tell just by looking at her that she wants to get married."

I straightened his toupee for him and said, "We'll call you the minute we decide, Edelman. The minute."

I turned to leave and he said, "That license number I ran through for you. You into anything I should know about?"

"Not yet, Martin. Not yet."

Then I left the station and went to look up a Mrs. Patti Slater.

Chapter 13

You might mistake the Windmere home for one of those piss-elegant motels all gussied up to resemble a seventeenth-century manor house. It isn't, of course, it's an old folks' home, or whatever it is we're calling people over seventy these days. The grounds revealed a great deal of brick and concrete and very little foliage or trees or grass. The east windows looked out on a parking lot and the west on the brick face of a natural-wood doctor's complex and the north windows on a vacant lot with a big FOR SALE sign. Grim, when you considered that many of the people herein had come here to die. Probably even daytime television was preferable to staring out a window that only revealed either other buildings or dinosaur-like semis chugging up the broad avenue outside.

The reception area continued the motel motif, a long waist-high counter running across most of a big, carpeted room that contained enough fake wood furniture and Starving Artist paintings to send the owners of Holiday Inn into sinful ecstasy.

Seated in one of the chairs was a palsied old lady whose twisted hands rested on a black cane and whose aged eyes stared mournfully at the death the chipper people who'd brought her here were trying cheerfully to deny to her. She wore a prim dark suit with a large brooch at the throat of her prim white blouse.

"She'll love it here," said a plump woman with hair tinted a color God had never invented. She wore a white nurse's uniform and smiled with formidable dentures.

"Did you hear that, Mother?" shouted a thin man with rimless glasses and a bald head. He wore a blue jogging suit and white Reeboks. The woman with him, presumably his wife, was dressed similarly. Were they going to head right for the track, as soon as they'd dumped the old lady off?

"We believe in keeping people active, that's one thing that makes Windmere so special," said the nurse, sounding like a living brochure. "We have a Jacuzzi and we play bingo four nights a week, and the community theater sends singers over several afternoons a month."

But the old lady wasn't going to be kidded. She clung to her cane as if it were life itself and stared down the hole they were about to push her in. I wanted to go over and sit next to her and put my arm around her and say something comforting, but what would I say when it came right down to it? That I was sorry she was pushing off, that I didn't want her to push off, that I hoped her son and daughter-in-law tripped all over their Reeboks?

"I'll get Ken," the nurse said.

Ken proved to look like a member of the Chicago Bears blitz circa mid-sixties. He wore a white T-shirt and white ducks and white socks and white canvas shoes and his gray hair was burr-cut and he'd shaved his fleshy face so smoothly it was as pink as a baby's. He had eyes like lasers and biceps you could rest refrigerators on. He also surprised the hell out of me by making the old lady not only look up for the first time but actually smile. He extended his arm and said, "Is this my date for the evening?"

"Don't I wish," the old lady said, and her voice cracked in real laughter.

So Ken led her off. Son and daughter-in-law signed some papers and started to leave and then the daughter-in-law turned back once to the hall where the old lady had disappeared on Ken's arm and then looked around and said, "You really think this is the right thing, David?"

"Honey, we have to be realistic."

Then she nodded and glanced down at her Reeboks and then they were gone, leaving his mother to the dubious balm of amateur entertainers and bingo.

I went over to the nurse. "I'd like to see Mrs. Slater, please."

She was now behind the counter and doing some very deft things with a computer keyboard.

She looked at me. "It's Wednesday."

"Yes, isn't it?"

"Visiting afternoons are Monday, and Friday."

So I went into one of my routines. I put out my hand and she didn't really have any choice but to take it and I said, "I'm Frank Evans and I'm her nephew from Omaha. I sell plumbing supplies and I was just driving through the city, so I thought I'd stop and say hi to her."

Not that I understood any of this, of course, why a black Honda motorcycle that could do maybe 150 miles per hour flat-out would be registered to a woman in a nursing home.

"Gosh," the woman said.

"What?"

"It'd really be a hassle."

"Really?"

"Yes. I mean, well, people aren't always ready to be shown at the drop of a hat."

"Shown" being the operative word here. I had the impression that they lined them up in their wheelchairs and hosed them off to get rid of the stench, then brought in an industrial waxer to shine pallor and wheelchair alike. Then they shot them up with enough Thorazine to make Charles Manson mellow for the rest of his life. And then they brought in the guests and moved them along quickly, the way you got moved along quickly in an art gallery where an especially popular artist was being shown, and the visitors got to see how clean and shiny and docile their parents looked and so the most wonderful thing of all happened. They could jump back in their Volvos, throw in some Barry Manilow tapes, and drive back to suburbia without feeling even 1.4 percent guilty.

"Gosh," she said. "I'm afraid it's impossible. You know, we really do try to be accommodating here at Windmere, but—" She was too plump and wore too much makeup, but still you could see the erotic twenty-year-old she'd probably been, the full lips especially knowing. But she ruined any real human heat with the living brochure monotone of her voice. She shrugged and her breasts raised slightly against the fabric of her bra and the bra in turn against the fabric of her white uniform and it was one of those odd moments—sunlight on linoleum, the smell of floor wax, a robin on a window ledge—when the thought of sex should not have occurred at all but it did. Oh yes, it did. But her green eyes held no promise, and so my erection slunk away.

"Has my cousin been here?"

"Cousin?" she said.

I smiled my glad-hander smile. "I imagine you'd know my cousin. Rides a motorcycle."

Now she smiled, too. "Oh, Evelyn Dain."

"That's right. Evelyn Dain."

"No, she comes Mondays and Fridays." The green eyes were haughty a moment. "The hours everyone else does."

"I *should* talk to her, I guess. About Patti. See how things are going." Here I had to be careful. Careful and casual. "You wouldn't know where she works, would you? I seem to recall she changed jobs a while back."

The phone rang, helping me. If the nurse had any doubts about me, about who I might really be and what I might really be doing there, they were forgotten in the rush of answering the phone. "Damiano's Aerobics over on Third Avenue."

"Thanks," I said. "And say hi to Patti for me."

She smiled with those wonderful erotic lips—you imagined them the kind of lips sixteenth-century kings demanded in their whores—and then waved me off to take her phone call. After answering, she said, "I'll be glad to tell you about Windmere." She was back to being a brochure.

Chapter 14

"How's your head?" I asked Donna.

"Pretty good. As long as I don't move too fast. She really hit me. Where're you?"

"Phone booth across the street from an aerobics place out on Third Avenue."

"You're joining an aerobics class?"

"No, the woman who hit you. It's where she works."

"God," she said. "That's neat."

"What's that?"

"That you've found her already. I mean, you really are a good detective."

"All I did was run down a couple of things."

"But that's what's so neat, Dwyer. You run down a couple of things and bingo, you've got it."

"That's just the problem."

"What?"

"I don't know what I've got."

"How come?"

"Well, the motorcycle is registered to a Mrs. Slater who resides at the Windmere nursing home. I don't know what relation she has to this Evelyn Dain or why Evelyn Dain is following me or what any of this has to do with the suitcase that Karen Lane hired me to find."

"Yeah, God, it really is confusing, isn't it?"

"Yeah."

"So why're you doing it? I mean, why not just tell Edelman?"

"Because right now the police are saying that Karen Lane's death was an accident resulting from mixing alcohol and barbiturates. Which means they won't be pursuing things. Which means it's left to me, I guess."

"I wouldn't mind if you, you know, sort of paid her back for me."

"Who?"

"Evelyn Dain."

"Paid her back?"

"You know."

"You mean hit her?"

"Not hit her, exactly."

"What's 'exactly' mean?"

"You, know, sort of trip her or something."

"Trip her?"

"That wouldn't be so bad. She wouldn't get hurt but she'd get the point."

I laughed. "It would be a lot easier if you'd just look her up and hit her yourself."

Now she laughed. "Be serious. I've never hit anybody before, Dwyer, except my older sister Ellen, and the one time I did it my mother grounded me for the weekend and I had to miss the Herman's Hermits concert."

"You liked Herman's Hermits?"

"I admit he couldn't sing but he was cute."

"If I get half a chance, I'll trip her."

"But not hard, all right? Just kind of a, uh, regular trip, you know?"

"Right. One regular trip coming up."

"I miss you."

"I miss you, too."

So then I went into the Hardees across the street from the small concrete building with the three storefront windows, one of which belonged to a Penny Saver shopper, one to an appliance store, and the third to the aerobics place. Inside that window you could see maybe twenty women doing exercises as grueling as anything I'd ever done at the Academy.

Knowing what was ahead of me—a stakeout and a long one—I self-pitied myself into justifying a double-decker hamburger, fries, and a vanilla shake. Stakeouts demand a lot of energy.

Loaded down with a white bag smudgy with grease, I went back to my Toyota, turned on the FM to a call-in show where people were arguing about whether condom advertising should be permitted on the air (AIDS was rearranging the American way of life), and proceeded to sit there for the next four and a half hours, watching both the storefront and the gleaming black Honda motorcycle in the adjacent parking lot.

This was a neighborhood in transition. In my boyhood days this had been the best section of town you could live in if your parents were working class, Irish, Italian, and Czech mostly, and every day on the sunny walks proud men in dungarees strolled to work, black lunch pails smelling of bologna sandwiches dangling from one hand, and a local newspaper they loved to curse in the other. You dreamed Plymouth dreams in those days (it had been one of my old man's fondest fantasies to pull up in front of the family house in a new 1955 baby blue Plymouth) as you moved away from the Highlands down here and as you gradually began to realize that, thanks to government loans and your parents' frugality, you were going to be the first generation that got to go to college.

But I didn't know what kind of dreams they dreamed here now. Sixteen-year-old girls pushed strollers past my car now, and your first impression was that they were the infants' sisters but in fact they were the infants' mothers. Scruffy boys in black leather jackets with tattoos on their knuckles and a cigarette hack bothering their throats already came by, too, and old men who gave the air of just wandering. Old women clutching small bags of groceries hurried on looking scared. And bored cops, tired of all the bullshit—and, man, you just don't know how much bullshit beat cops get laid on them day in, day out—watched it all, just wanting to get back to their tract homes and watch the Cubbies or watch their kids or watch their wives or watch any goddamn thing except this neighborhood get even meaner.

Dusk came and I had to take the risk of running into the Hardees can and emptying my bladder and running back out. I had a splotch on my crotch where, in my haste putting it back in, I'd dribbled. But the motorcycle was still there. The lurid neons at the Triple-X Theater down the street came on and then all the taverns lit up and this big annoying mechanical bear on top of a car wash started waving like King Kong to passing motorists. Several of them had the good sense to flip him the finger.

I watched the ladies and tried to figure out if the somewhat angular blonde leading the class was the woman I wanted. Possibly. But just as possibly she could be the manager, out of sight in some back office. My car stank of fried food. I wanted, in order, to talk to my seventeen-year-old son (who had started missing school lately, going through some kind of teenage funk), Donna, Glendon Evans (to question him more carefully about some of the things Karen Lane had said to him during their time of cohabitation), and Thomas Merton, the Trappist monk-poet whose books I'd been reading lately, to find out just how he'd managed to deal with all the craziness.

Then, around eight o'clock, my bottom very tired, my eyelids getting heavy, the women started filing out of the aerobics center. Their chatter was like bright birds on the soft night air and I liked listening to it. It was happy and human and hopeful, proud as they were of their workout and the good way they felt about themselves at this moment.

Then the lights inside the aerobic center went out.

I sat up straight and turned on my engine.

Then I sat there for twenty minutes, wasting a couple dollars' worth of gas.

Being a paranoid, I began to wonder if she had seen my car and simply gone out the back door, leaving her bike so I'd sit here all night like a very stupid rent-a-cop watching it.

Around eight thirty-five, she came out.

I still couldn't get a good look at her because she was back in her leathers again. She even had the helmet on. She looked like a super-heroine in a comic book.

Without looking around, without hesitating, she went over to the parking lot, mounted the bike with a physical economy that spoke of the condition she was in, and then, moments later, took off.

I took off after her, having no idea whatsoever where she was going.

Chapter 15

The old money built their homes east, on hills that formed a ragged timberline back when the only certain means of transportation other than walking had been the Conestoga wagon. They built east and they built big and they built conservative, brick and stone and wood, hammered and chiseled and curved to imitate the Victorian style. It was through this section of hills she led me, dips steep as roller coasters, peaks from which you could see the electric sprawl of the city beneath. Occasionally a timid deer came to the edge of the road, then disappeared, frightened, back into the pine and hardwood acres posted NO HUNTING. There were gates in the gloom, big iron gates, usually painted black, beyond which lay curving asphalt roads and then the houses themselves. Forty-five minutes had gone by. The temperature had dropped ten degrees, from early spring to late winter. The one thing the Toyota did well, besides rusting, I mean, was kick out heat. I was snug as a baby in the womb. I just didn't know where the hell she was taking me. Two thoughts kept crisscrossing: Was she aware of me and simply driving me around and around or did she just like to go for rides after work, the way I sometimes did?

Then she veered southeast, and we came into the section new money had built, lying below us in grassy foothills. From up here you could see down into their backyards with their inevitable swimming pools and inevitable tennis courts and inevitable sprawling flagstone patios. The style of the houses changed from Victorian to everything from French Provincial to Colonial to Mediterranean. In the night now they seemed to glow with prosperity, gods perched above the moaning masses below. You could hear dogs bark in the darkness and you knew they would not be pretty collies or cute Scotties. They'd be Dobermans or maybe even (this was the fashion this season) pit bulls. These days, with people standing in cheese lines two blocks down from where factories stood unused, these days the gods had damned well better get themselves some protection.

I kept a city block behind her, but even so she pulled off the road so abruptly, I nearly had to put the car into the ditch. I cut the lights. Waited.

She'd cut her own lights. For a time I couldn't pick her out in the starry blackness.

I felt awkward, foolish, trapped. Apparently she'd been on to me all along and was now waiting for me to make my own move. Turn around and go back the other way? Stroll up to her and ask her just who the hell she was and why she'd knocked out my girlfriend and most likely a shrink named Evans?

At first I couldn't tell if my eyes were only playing tricks or if she had actually just done what she'd seemed to.

Left her black Honda and started walking down the road.

I reached up and popped the lid off the dome light and then thumbed out the bulb. I didn't want my car to light up when I eased out of it.

I put one foot down on the road and smelled the chill piney night and then put a second foot down and watched the way rolling cumulus clouds covered the quarter moon. She was ahead of me somewhere, walking. But where? And why?

I went after her, keeping to the side of the road, where even the gods had to put up with empty beer cans and Hershey wrappers and Merit packages soggy with dew.

On my right the pines were solid, broken only occasionally by small clearings of grass, still dead and brown. The left held two homes set very far back, little more than lights glimpsed through the hardwoods. Hearing a car behind me, I turned my head to the left so the driver couldn't see my face. He turned into the opposite drive, a chunky silhouette in a red BMW.

Then I saw her.

She was crawling up the face of two steep iron gates with the acumen of a monkey showing off for Sunday-afternoon visitors. She was so good at it, I just stood and watched her, forgetting for a moment why I was here in the first place. In her black leathers, she was hard to see. Then she dropped down on the other side of the gate, her body making a small sound as it touched the asphalt, and then she vanished.

I walked the rest of the way over to the iron gates. The estate was surrounded by a large stone wall. Schlepping up the gates was probably easier than going over the stone wall. Just behind me was a country-style mailbox. I went over and hauled out my flash and looked to see the name.

I stood there a moment and contemplated what the hell it could mean. Things had come abruptly together here. Yet, at the same time, nothing had come together at all.

The name on the mail box was LARRY PRICE, the same Larry Price who had been my high school classmate, the same Larry Price I'd gotten into a fight with during senior year, and the same Larry Price who had mysteriously been arguing with Karen Lane out in the alley the night she'd died.

Why would the woman in black leathers be coming to see Larry Price?

Another car swept past. I jumped into brush on the side of the intricately patterned iron gates. It hurtled on into the gloom.

I put my hand to the rough surface of stone. In movies, guys are always vaulting over walls like this one—it couldn't have been much higher than seven feet—or shinnying up them with rope ladders. But unfortunately, I had never been able to list vaulting or shinnying among my useful skills.

Hoping for blind luck, I went over to the gate and put my fingers through the bars and tried to see if they might not magically come apart and let me just sort of amble right on in. But there would be no ambling.

There would be only vaulting or shinnying.

So I put my right foot in the gate and proceeded to climb. I just hoped nobody was watching, especially the woman in black leathers. I had this image of her sitting somewhere in the bushes inside the estate laughing her shapely ass off.

It couldn't have taken longer than two or three hours to get over the gate and land—as in crash-landing—on the other side. All the way, between sweating, groaning, and cursing, I kept promising to enroll myself in some sort of mercenary school and learn how to do stuff like this. As a cop, the most strenuous thing I'd ever had to do was chase a car thief two blocks. He had done me the favor of being at least fifty pounds overweight.

I stood on the other side breathless and soaked, panting and cursing still. And then I looked around at the estate fanning out before me. The asphalt road wound up past steep copses of pines and then wound back again to grounds that displayed a gazebo almost luminescent in the moonlight and a tennis court canvas-covered for the cold months and a small hothouse appearing almost secretive, tucked as it was into a stand of hardwoods.

The house, not as big as you might expect, was a garrison-style Colonial, two-stories, an off-yellow. To the west was a three-stall garage. All the doors were open. There were no cars. I glanced back at the house. Darkness. Stillness. Nobody home.

But she was in there somewhere. My motorcycle rider.

Taking a deep breath, hefting my flashlight as a weapon the way cops do, I started toward the house. If she'd found a way in, I'd find a way in. And then I'd confront her and find out all the things I needed to know, and maybe then I'd stumble onto the suitcase Karen Lane had hired me to find.

I was halfway to the house when she hit me. She got me from behind and she got me clean and I don't think I even had time for one good obscenity before the back of my head seemed to crack open and before I automatically put my hands out to soften my collision with the ground.

Chapter 16

The back of my head hurt and the front of my head hurt and the side of my head hurt. There was a terrible taste in my throat and I needed to pee. Badly. The way you do when you wake at 2 a.m. from a night's drinking. I lay in a cluster of dead leaves over which a sheen of frost sparkled silver in the moonlight. My hand, for no reason I could understand, clutched a brittle brown pine cone.

I began the careful process of getting up, trying to gauge if I'd been hit hard enough to suffer a concussion, and wondering vaguely where the closest emergency hospital was.

The first thing I did was take care of my bladder. I leaned my left hand against a hardwood for support and then let go, the yellow stream raising steam and making a hard constant noise on the last of autumn's leaves. Then I took out my handkerchief and began daubing it against the back of my head. There was only a small smudge of blood on the white fabric when I held it out for appraisal. Despite a headache, I did not seem to be hurt badly. My watch said nine-fifteen. I'd been out less than fifteen minutes.

In the west wing of the house, on the second floor, I saw the arc of a flashlight splash across a pinkish wall, and then go dark. She was inside now. Busy. I wasn't going to let her get off easily. Not at all. I thought of Donna's joke—couldn't I trip the lady in leather just a little bit? I was going to trip her a whole lot.

I moved awkwardly at first, staggering a bit like a stereotypical drunk, but gradually I got used to the headache and moved with a little less trouble. When I reached the front yard, which was defined by severe flattop hedges on both east and west ends, I went up to the oak front door and tried the knob.

Locked.

I put my ear to the door. Faintly I heard the hum and thrum of a house at rest but nothing else.

I went around to the rear, to the area between the garage and back door. It was cold and my head still hurt, but I was angry with her now and I was damn well going to get to express my anger.

I tried the knob on the back door. It turned easily. I went inside, up three steps covered with a rubber runner, and into one of those open kitchens with a huge butcher-block table like a sacrificial altar in the center, and pots and pans hanging from a suspension above. They gleamed in the moonlight falling golden through the mullioned windows. I smelled paprika and cocoa and coffee. I smelled thyme and mustard seed and basil. They were feminine smells and pleasant and I wanted to stand there for hours and float on them the way I used to float on marijuana. Contact high is the term I wanted, I think.

Upstairs she bumped a piece of furniture and it was loud as a truck overturning. She was searching for something, apparently, and apparently searching desperately.

I wrapped my hand around my flashlight and proceeded through a house with accents of bricks and brass, with beams over the living room, and crown moldings everywhere. The furnishings ran to Early American but I don't mean the stuff you see in suburban furniture stores. I'm talking, among others things, two items of special note: fan-back Windsor chairs and a Chippendale mahogany slant-top desk, items antique hunter Donna would get goofy about. I'd always known that Larry Price had come from a wealthy family; I just hadn't known how wealthy.

A sweeping staircase curved up into the darkness at the top of which two long narrow windows let in light.

I moved as quietly as I could up the stairs. At the top I smelled perfume from the master bedroom that lay thirty feet away. An eighteenth-century walnut longcase clock tocked the time. I looked down the hall. Light from her flash shone in a room at the end of the hall, between door and jamb.

The clock covered any noise my tiptoe steps might have made. I was going to go in fast and make no concessions just because she was female. I was going to trip the hell out of her.

The door was open maybe three inches. I raised my foot to kick it in.

But I didn't have to. She yanked it open for me.

And then stood there with a very fancy silver-plated .45 in her hand and said, "You bastard. I should kill you right here."

Chapter 17

Five minutes later, me sitting on a couch in a den filled with the sort of leather-bound classics nobody ever actually read and enough leather furniture to please the richest lawyer in the land, she threw my wallet back at me.

"Who the hell are you?" I said.

She just shook her head and went over and sat very efficiently on a broad leather ottoman. Her bottle-blond hair was almost white against the black leather of her riding suit. For the first time, her helmet gone, I could see her face, the broad, lopsided mouth, the earnest blue eyes, the freckles that somehow made her seem younger than the lines around her mouth and eyes indicated she was.

She put her head down, like an athlete who has just finished a long run, but the one time I squirmed to lift weight off one buttock and put it on the other, her head snapped up and she pointed the .45 in the approximate vicinity of my forehead.

Then she put her head back down again and it was then I sensed it, that certain but special air the insane exude. I'd experienced it once while visiting a cop friend on a psych ward, felt it in the vivid stares that followed me with both fear and ferocity, in the curious inexplicable smiles some odd gesture would suddenly evoke. You feel sorry for them but they scare you, too—like a sick dog you come upon, wanting to help him, but fearful he might be rabid.

She raised her head and said, "He killed Sonny. He was one of them, anyway."

"What?"

She spoke with the kind of fragile gentleness you associate with poor but honorable spinsters. "Isn't my English clear, Mr. Dwyer?"

"What I guess you said is, 'He killed Sonny.'"

"That is in fact what I said, Mr. Dwyer."

"Well, I've got a couple of questions about that."

"Which are?"

"First of all, who is the 'he' you're referring to, and second, who is Sonny?"

The blue eyes grew grave. She sat there looking old suddenly, and tender too, and something like a chill worked down my back, and I felt afraid of her. It wasn't the gun, it was her simple flat connection to some truth I did not understand, the ageless mad truth of the fanatic.

"You know who 'he' is, Mr. Dwyer, and you certainly know who Sonny is. That's why you want the suitcase. So you can sell it to the men who killed him."

Then she very carefully got up and, even sensing what she was going to do, all I could do was sit and watch, fascinated as much as frightened.

She got me just once, but it was a good clean hit with the butt of the .45 right on the edge of my jaw. The headache, which had waned, came back instantly. It was now joined by something very much like a toothache.

I started to move, my male arrogance instinctively believing that I could simply grab her fragile wrist and throw her to the floor, but she had other ideas.

She put the cold, oil-smelling weapon right to my temple and said, "I'm going to make you a deal, Mr. Dwyer."

"What deal?" I wanted to sound hard, even harsh, giving her the impression that even though I had a mouth full of blood and the world's biggest ice cream headache, I was still in charge here. I was a man, and dammit, men were always in charge of women, right? Even women with guns. Right?

"I won't kill your girlfriend if you get the suitcase and bring it to me at ten o'-clock tomorrow night. I'll phone you where I want you to bring it. Do you understand me?"

I started to snarl something about what I'd do if she so much as looked at Donna again, but for the second time that night, the tall, slender woman in the black motorcycle leathers caught me fast and cracking sharp across the back of the head.

This time I fell into the darkness with something like relief. My head was starting to ache intolerably and I was tired and confused and at least a little bit afraid of what I saw in her blue eyes, the same thing I'd seen one night ten years earlier when a young mother had put an ice pick through the eyes of her infant and then waited patiently for the policeman she'd summoned. I had been that policeman.

Chapter 18

The next morning I woke with Donna sitting on the edge of my bed in a royal blue belted robe and her beautiful wild red hair fresh from the shower. I was in her bed in her apartment, where I'd come in a stupor not unlike drunkenness after leaving Larry Price's house, where the woman in black had knocked me out not once but twice.

"How're you feeling?"

"Better than I should, probably," I said.

"This should help."

I sat up in bed like an invalid and she set the tray across my lap. There were two lovely eggs over easy on a pink plate. And two lovely pieces of delicately buttered toast. And three lovely orange slices. And a lovely steaming cup of coffee. And two round little white tablets that unfortunately were not half as lovely as the other things on the plate.

"Aspirin," she said. "I figured you'd need them." She bent over and gave me a soft kiss and I just held her there momentarily, knowing her for the prize she was.

"Thanks," I said.

Her bedroom was a woman's room, with yellow walls and canopied bed, and outsize stuffed animals, one I like especially, a plump bear with oddly forlorn eyes and a little red cap. He sat in the corner, his arms forever spread in greeting, watching me eat, which I did with boot-camp hunger.

"Man," I said.

"Taste good?"

"Tastes great."

"Boy, I love to watch you eat."

"I thought you said I needed to lose ten pounds."

"You do. But I still love to watch you eat. It just makes me feel—secure somehow."

She leaned over and gave me a kiss again and then she said, "May I tell you something?"

"Sure," I said, wiping up egg yolk with the last piece of toast. I let my gaze lie on the windows, blue with cloudless spring sky. A jay flitted past the window and perched on a branch just blooming. The window was partly opened. I thought of how fresh laundry smelled in the breeze.

"That woman's threats last night?"

"Yes."

"I'm scared, Dwyer."

I put my hand out and brought her over to me. She sat on the edge of the bed. She smelled of perfume, bath soap, and clean skin. She smelled wonderful.

"I want you to go to Joanna's for a few days," I said.

"What?"

"Please."

"Joanna? You think I could handle it for a few days? All those heartbreak stories?"

Joanna was a news writer at a TV station, a woman gifted not only with talent but great looks that did not seem to do her much good with men. She was perpetually heartbroken.

"I really wish you'd call her," I said.

"What about you?"

"I'll stay at my place. I'll be all right."

She touched my head. "Dwyer, she's mean. So far she's knocked out three people, and from what you say, she's not hinged quite right."

"I know." Then I smiled. "All the more reason for you to stay at Joanna's. You've got the magazine done for the month. You can just sort of hole up. What I'd like you to do is pack a bag now and leave. And watch your rearview very carefully."

"Make sure nobody is following?"

"Right."

"God, people really do do that, don't they? I mean, it's not just in detective movies, is it?"

"No, it isn't."

"What're you going to do?"

"Check the calls on my answering service. Then I'm not sure."

She picked up the tray. "Did you really like it?" She's very insecure about her cooking, probably because her former husband Chad was always criticizing her for her lack of culinary imagination and, by implication, her lack of culinary skills.

"Honey, it was great, and it was sweet. It was very sweet."

"Thanks for saying that."

"It's the truth."

Water ran in the kitchen sink; then the bathroom door closed; then the hair drier erupted. I phoned my service. This was my day off at American Security, so my first dread was that there'd be a message saying somebody hadn't shown up so would I please come in. Fortunately, no. The only message came from a Dr. Allan Cummings. I wrote his number down and thanked the woman picking up the calls this morning. Just before we hung up, she said, "I saw one of your commercials on the tube last night. You did a good job."

"Thanks."

"Oh, that doctor who called?"

"Yes."

"He sounded real—uptight or something."

"Thanks."

"Sure."

We hung up. I dialed Dr. Cummings' number. These days, getting through directly to a doctor is nearly as unlikely as winning a lottery. So I was surprised when a baritone male voice said, "Dr. Cummings here." He must have given me a direct number.

"Doctor, my name is Jack Dwyer."

"Oh yes, Mr. Dwyer, thanks for returning my call." He sounded nervous. Then he stopped talking. I sensed hesitation.

"What can I do for you, Doctor?"

"Well, I was wondering if we might talk a few minutes."

"Of course."

"What I have reference to, Mr. Dwyer, is the story in the newspaper this morning."

"I see."

"The one about Karen Lane dying of an accidental overdose of Librium and alcohol."

"Yes."

"Well, the story said that you were with her at the time of her death and that you were a former policeman, so I thought I would tell you something that might be pertinent."

"What's that, Doctor?"

"Karen Lane was my patient for several years. I'm a medical doctor, not a psychiatrist, but for some of my patients who tend to get depressed or overanxious, I prescribe various kinds of tranquilizers or antidepressants."

"I see."

"The point I'm trying to make here, Mr. Dwyer, is that I once prescribed Librium for her."

"And?"

"And she had an allergic reaction to it. Welts appeared on her tongue and her throat got very red and sore."

I threw my feet over the side of the bed. It was one of the moments I wanted a cigarette. "So what are you saying?"

"I'm not sure what I'm saying, Mr. Dwyer. I wish I could say absolutely that Karen Lane would never take Librium, but sometimes, as we get older, our allergies change. We begin to tolerate things we once couldn't tolerate—and vice versa."

"When was the last time you saw her, Doctor?"

"Oh, five or six years ago. She moved from the city, and when she came back she apparently found another doctor."

"So the sensible thing for me to do would be to find who her doctor is currently and to see what sort of medication he was prescribing for her, right?"

"That seems sensible to me."

But I knew who her current doctor was. And I also knew the vested interest he had in keeping Karen Lane his own. For the first time I started considering Dr. Glendon Evans a murder suspect.

"I really appreciate this, Doctor."

"Of course." A pause again. "Karen was a very striking woman."

"Yes, she was."

"I—" He stopped talking again and in his silence I could hear that he'd been smitten, too. "We went out a few times."

"I see."

"I'm afraid I was married and I'm afraid it got messy for everybody concerned."

This was the part where circumstances forced me to be a surrogate priest. I never much cared for the role. "I was afraid that if I went to the police with this, I'd get dragged into the papers myself and it would bring up some bad memories for my wife."

"I see."

"So if my name could be left out—"

"Of course."

"My wife and I have a much better marriage now." I made careful note of the fact that he didn't say "good marriage." Only "much better." His sadness got to me and I wanted to say the right soothing thing, but I didn't know what that would be.

"It was very good of you to call."

"I felt I owed it to Karen."

"Thank you, Doctor."

As I was hanging up, Donna appeared, leaning model-fashion against the doorjamb, imposing in a dark blue cashmere sweater, designer jeans, and short leather boots, her red hair wild as mountain water down her shoulders.

"Well, I guess I'm ready." She sounded like a little girl who was being sent off, much against her will, to a summer camp run by bona fide ogres.

"You ready?"

"I guess," she said. "But you're not." Then she smiled. "God, Dwyer, I really think we should start sort of a kitty so you can get yourself some new underwear and socks."

"Thanks."

"You're nearly forty-five."

"Gee, don't I like being reminded of that."

"And all your underwear and socks have holes in them. Like a kid."

"They're clean, though."

"That's true. They are clean. But—"

So I went over and grabbed her and yanked her back to the bed and she said, "I just got dressed."

And I said, "I think we should have some general underwear inspection here. I just want to make sure that you're not being hypocritical. How do I know your underwear isn't in rags?"

"Dwyer, you really are nuts, you know that?"

But she relented and let me inspect her underwear anyway.

Chapter 19

"The name Sonny mean anything to you?"

"It's the name of a song."

"Yeah," I said.

"There was Sonny Liston."

"Right."

"And Sonny and Cher."

"Uh-huh."

"And Sonny James."

"Who?"

"Country-western singer."

"Oh."

"Don't give me your crap about country-western singers."

"All right."

It was one-thirty in the afternoon in Malley's Tavern on the Eighth Avenue side of the Highlands. The place smelled of beer, disinfectant, and peanuts. Strong warm sunlight brightened the aged wooden floor. Bob Malley, paunchy, bearded, wrapped around with the spotless white apron that is his pride, stood behind the bar he owned and idly flipped a quarter, checking heads or tails every time it came down. I imagine he does this as often as five hundred times a day. Some people find this the kind of minor social irritation that can turn nuns into psychopaths. But I'm used to it. Though he was a grade ahead of me, Malley and I have been friends since, respectively, first and second grade. I've seen him flip quarters probably twenty million times by now.

Ordinarily I come in three afternoons a week. Today I had two reasons to be there. To say hello and to ask for information. Malley remembers our school days with the reverence of Thornton Wilder recalling an autumn afternoon in New England.

"Sonny Tufts," I said.

"Oh. Yeah. Sonny Tufts. You want another shell?"

"Nah."

He grinned. "Donna's a good influence on you, Dwyer. You've cut your drinking in half since you met her. So when's the date?"

"We fornicate without benefit of clergy, Malley. We have no plans to get married. We're not ashamed. She's not even Catholic."

"That's my only reservation about her."

"Right."

"So what's with this Sonny jazz?"

I told him about the woman in the black leather and how she'd mentioned Sonny.

"And you were in Larry Price's house?"

"Yeah," I said.

"Then she probably meant Sonny Howard."

"Who?"

"Sonny Howard. Summer of our senior year. Remember we went to summer school so we could take a lighter load during the regular year?"

"Yeah."

"Well, he went to summer school, too. Except he hung around with Price and Forester and Haskins. Then he killed himself."

He tossed it away so casually it almost went right by me, like doing a bad double-take shtick. Then, "What?"

"He killed himself. Don't you remember? He jumped off Pierce Point."

"Give me another shell."

"I thought you didn't want one." He smiled and got me another shell.

"Tell me some more about him."

"Don't know much more about him," Malley said, setting down my beer.

"Why don't I remember him?"

"Probably tried to forget him."

"Why?"

"He sort of hung around Karen Lane. That's when you were chasing rich chicks and trying to forget all about her."

"He knew Karen Lane?"

"I don't think they were getting it on or anything—I mean, I don't think she put out very much when you came right down to it—but I remember toward the end of the summer they were together a lot."

"Why were people so sure he killed himself? I mean, Pierce Point, you could fall off real easy."

"There was a witness."

"Who?"

"You're being a cop again. Ease off, okay? I'm not especially fond of cops."

"So you've told me."

"Witness, I don't know, seems it was David Haskins."

"You're kidding?"

"You asked me. Why would I kid you?"

"David Haskins was the witness?"

"David Haskins was the witness."

I drained half my shell and set it down and watched white foam slide down into the yellow beer. I liked taverns, hearing the crack of cards as men played pinochle, and the clatter of pool and the sound of workingmen loud at the end of a workday. At four I used to sit in union taverns and eat salted hard-boiled eggs and sip my old man's beer and learn all the reasons why you should never trust Republicans.

"Killed himself," I said. "Killed himself."

"I take it you don't believe that."

I looked right at him and said, "No, Malley, I don't. Not in the least damn bit at all."

Chapter 20

Mrs. Haskins was reluctant to tell me where her husband was employed. "If you're a friend of his, then you should know where he works," she said on the other end of the phone.

"I didn't say I was a friend, exactly, Mrs. Haskins. I said I was a classmate."

"Oh. I see. At the university?"

"No. High school."

"Oh."

"I really would like to speak with him."

"It's urgent or something?"

Years of police work had taught me that politeness is almost always more effective than belligerence. "I'm trying to locate someone, Mrs. Haskins. It's not a big deal, but I believe David could help me."

"You don't know him very well, do you?"

"Ma'am?"

"He's 'Dave.' He hates David. That's what his father always called him, and to be honest, he never cared much for his father."

"I see."

She sighed. "I suppose I sound terribly unfriendly, don't I?"

"Not at all. You're protective of your husband. That's an admirable trait."

"Yes, I suppose so, especially with the divorce rate these days." She paused and then said, as if with some effort, "He works at Smythe and Brothers. It's a brokerage downtown."

"Thank you, Mrs. Haskins."

"I just hope I've done the right thing."

"Thanks again."

I called Smythe and Brothers. An icy female voice told me that Mr. Haskins was out and would not be back until three-thirty. I thanked her, then phoned the tavern where Chuck Lane worked. He was out, too, I was informed, and wasn't expected back until probably six or so, when he started working. From him I'd wanted some more discussion on the subject of Karen's senior summer. Then I phoned Dr. Glendon Evans' office and was told he was with a patient and would I mind sharing with her (that's what she said, the verbal equivalent of earth tones, sharing with her), but I just said no, I'd call back. I'd do my sharing alone.

I sat in the Toyota flush with the pull-up phone listening to a radio report live from the Cubs training camp. Oh, it could be one hell of a year, the third-base coach allowed, that is, if the X-rays on their leading pitcher's arm came out okay, and if their best base stealer didn't take advantage of his free-agent potential and go play for the Dodgers, and if those unfortunate drug charges against their leading hitter got dropped. Oh, it could be one hell of a year.

I dropped in another quarter. The number I wanted was busy. I wasn't that far away. I decided, keeping the window down and the radio up, to drive out there, the summer-like seventy degrees making me feel younger than I had any right to. This time there weren't any sheets blowing on the clothesline like sails on racing sloops. In fact, the small tract home looked battened down, garage door closed, curtains drawn. I parked in the drive and went up to the door and knocked and got exactly the response I'd figured on. Nothing.

I stood looking at the scruffy brown lawn and then at the endless row of similar houses stretching to the vanishing point. This was the step up from our fathers we'd been promised. All it showed was how far down our fathers had been in the first place. Uselessly, I knocked again.

Then the door opened abruptly and there stood Susan Roberts pretty as always. She wore a man's blue work shirt and jeans and her hair was pulled back in a soft chignon whose luster could be seen even in the shadows of the doorway. She had been crying, and very recently and very hard.

"Hello, Jack," she said.

"I'm sorry. I seem to have come at a bad time."

"No... it's just... you know, the thing with Karen and all."

"That's what I wanted to talk to you about."

She seemed surprised. "Karen?"

"If you wouldn't mind."

"Did something new happen?"

"I'm not sure."

She smiled a bit. "You always did like being mysterious. Come on in."

Five minutes later we sat at a Formica-topped kitchen table and looked out on a brown backyard and at the redwood veranda of the house on the opposite end of the backyard.

She had made us instant coffee in a small microwave. She set down gray pewter mugs and then sat down across from me. She sipped her coffee and I watched the beautiful life in her hazel eyes, the intelligence of them, the compassion of them. Then she said, "I'm just being selfish."

"How so?"

"I'm not really thinking of Karen. I mean, that's not why I was crying when you came to the door."

"Oh?"

"There's an old Irish saying that the person you really mourn at a funeral is yourself. That's what I was doing. Mourning myself." She had some more coffee and said, "Do you think about dying very often?"

"To the point of being morbid."

"Me, too." She sighed, knitted hands chafed from work but still long and beautiful in form. "Our kids are in high school. Gary still hasn't ever finished a novel. And every day I look in the mirror, I see this odd old lady taking my place there." She stared out the window again. "Karen wasn't so hard to understand, really. She just wanted to be young and beautiful forever." The lopsided smile again, the warm tears still on her perfect cheeks. "Is that too much for a woman to ask?"

I said, "Did you ever know her to hang around anybody named Sonny?"

"Sure. Sonny Howard."

"Right. Sonny Howard. Can you tell me anything about him?"

She narrowed her eyes. "Why bring up Sonny Howard after all these years?"

"It could be important."

"Why?"

"Maybe Karen didn't die of an accidental overdose after all."

"I knew it."

"You did."

"Sure." She snapped her fingers. "That's exactly what I told Gary."

"That she didn't kill herself?"

"Yes. She really didn't have it in her. I mean she tried that once and—"

"What?"

"Yes. Didn't you know that?"

"No."

"It was the summer she hung around with Sonny Howard, as a matter of fact."

"Did you ever know why?"

"Not exactly."

"She didn't give you any hint?"

"Just something happened. In July I went away for a week's vacation with my folks. When I left she was fine. But when I came back she'd gotten into these terrible crying jags. I thought maybe it was over Sonny. She'd been hanging around him a few months, but then I remembered her telling me he was just a friend, so...." She sighed. "None of it ever made much sense to me."

"Do you ever remember her saying anything about Ted Forester or Larry Price or David Haskins?"

"Just that she was afraid of them."

"You mean physically?"

She shrugged. "I'm not sure. One time we were at a party and they came in and she ran out the back door. Literally ran. But that was the strange thing, too."

"What was strange?"

"I can still remember their faces when they came in and saw her there at the party."

"What about it?"

"They looked just as afraid of her as she was of them."

"Where did Sonny fit in all this?"

"He hung around with Forester and the others. He was just here for summer school. Actually he went to St. Matthew's, but they didn't offer the courses he needed, so he came over here. He was just their friend, I guess."

"But she wasn't afraid of Sonny?"

"She never said so." She shook her head. "Doesn't it all seem so long ago, like some old movie?"

I finished my coffee. "I wonder if you'd do me a favor."

"Sure, Jack."

"Let me see the room downstairs where she stayed."

"Of course."

"Thanks."

The basement, like the rest of the house, was furnished in odds and ends, styles and colors that should have clashed, but that Susan's hand had brought together in an uneasy harmony. The basement was five degrees cooler than upstairs. It had red-and-white-tiled flooring, imitation knotty-pine walls, a low white ceiling. There was a furnace to the left, a small bathroom whose open door revealed sink-shower-stool, an overstuffed couch facing a massive relic of other days—a Buddha-like black-and-white 21-inch Motorola console—and finally a new but unpainted door that creaked back to show me a room with a severe little single bed, a bureau covered with expensive perfumes and bottles and jars and vials and vessels of makeup, and then a sturdy piece of rope used as a hanger for more clothes than most department stores would have to offer. The clothes—fawns and pinks and soft blues and yellows, silk and linen and organza and lamé and velvet—did not belong in the chill rough basement of a working-class family. There was a sense of violation here, a beast holding trapped a fragile beauty.

On the bed lay an old hardback copy of *Breakfast at Tiffany's*. I went over and picked it up, its burnt-orange cover bright even after all these years, the pen-and-ink sketch of Capote on the back just as calculated now as it was then. I opened the front cover: Karen Lane's name was written in perfect penmanship, but when I flipped to the back I saw that it was a library book checked out the last time on May 3, 1959.

Susan laughed. "I think it was the only book she ever read. She loved it. She'd never give it back."

"Really?"

"They'd send her notices all the time. Virtually threaten her. But she wanted to keep the copy she'd first read. No other copy would do. Finally, she just paid them for it and kept it."

"Mind if I take it?"

"Be my guest."

I looked around. "She was here one month?"

"Just about. But actually she'd been staying overnight here for the past six months." Her mouth tightened. "I suppose if I raise any question about Dr. Evans, I'll sound like a bigot."

"Not to me, you won't."

"Well, I met him twice at lunch with Karen. He has this very calm, polished exterior, but he also has a terrible temper. She came here several times with bruises he'd given her."

I planned to see Dr. Evans tonight. I was fascinated by how easy it would be for a shrink to "accidentally" overdose somebody he lived with.

I studied the front of the book again, as if it were going to tell me something.

She said, "So did I miss anything the other night? I really wish I could have gone."

"You know how you feel about looking in the mirror and seeing this strange old lady there? That's how I felt at the reunion. We're getting to be geezers, Susan. Geezers."

She poked me on the arm girlishly and said, "Speak for yourself, Jack."

Then she walked me up and we exchanged a chaste kiss and I liked the hell out of her all over again the way I had back there in grade school.

Chapter 21

The receptionist wore a gray suit with wide lapels and a frilly white blouse. Her nails appeared to be her pride, they were as red as manicuring and lacquering could make them. Perhaps they were compensation for the fact that she was one of those women who are almost attractive but not quite, a bit too fleshy, a bit too inexplicably sour, a bit too self-conscious that all the time you're watching her you're saying to yourself that she is not quite attractive. She gave the impression that clothes probably interested her more than people. She touched at long hair that had been carefully tipped with a color not unlike silver.

"David Haskins," I said, going up to her desk.

Smythe and Brothers occupied its own floor in a new and grotesquely designed downtown office building. It was all leather and wood and forest-green flocked wallpaper. It exuded the aura of a men's club where the average member is over age seventy-five.

"You have an appointment?"

She knew by looking at my blue windbreaker and open white button-down shirt and faded jeans that it was unlikely I had an appointment.

"I'm afraid I don't."

"May I ask what this is about?"

"Personal matter."

She assessed me once more. She was not impressed. "May I have your name, please?"

"Jack Dwyer."

She stood up. She was taller than I'd thought and her extra pounds were surprisingly attractive. But she wasn't any nicer. She pointed like a grumpy eighth-grade teacher to a leather couch the size of a life raft and said, "Would you take a seat, please?"

So I took a seat and proceeded to look through a stack of magazines, each reverential in different ways about the subject of money.

He came out fifteen minutes later and he didn't look so good. He didn't come all the way over to me. He sort of let her lead the way and he sort of stood behind her and peeked out around the padded shoulders of her jacket.

"Hello," he said, leaning out.

He was maybe five seven and twenty pounds overweight and wearing one of those double-breasted suits only Adolphe Menjou could get away with. He was losing his auburn hair so fast you could almost hear the follicles falling off. He was also slick with sweat and gulping. He gulped, and I mean big comic gulps, as if he could not get enough air, every few seconds.

"Hello," I said.

"How may I help you?"

"Do you remember me?"

"Uh, sure."

"Jack Dwyer."

"Of course." He looked at the receptionist the way a very young boy looks at his mother. For help.

"I saw you at the reunion dance the other night, Dave."

"Right."

She said, "He's very busy."

He said, "She's right, Jack, I am." He gulped. "Very busy."

So I decided to jackpot. I wasn't going to get past his receptionist here if I didn't roll some dice. "I was wondering if you'd tell me why Ted Forester and Larry Price were pushing you into the car the other night."

"What?"

"You seemed to be having a fight with them. I wondered why."

This time his glance at the receptionist was desperate. This time he looked as if he were going to faint. "I don't know what you're talking about."

"Aw, Dave." I decided maybe a little folksiness would help.

"Please, Jack, I'm—"

"He's very busy," the receptionist said. She took him by the shoulders and turned him back in the direction of his office. The corridor was lined with stern black-and-white photographs of dour men who'd devoted their lives to money. They'd probably grown up reading Scrooge McDuck comic books and taking them literally.

Then she gave him a shove, as if pushing a boat out to sea on choppy waters.

"Nice to see you, Dave," I called after him.

She snapped her not unappealing body around and said, "Exactly what the hell do you think you're doing?"

"What I was supposed to be doing was talking to Dave Haskins. But you wouldn't let me."

"Get out of here."

"You must get paid a lot of money."

"You heard me."

"You like working around all this money?"

"Get out."

I got out.

I didn't go far. I went down in the parking lot and found a drive-up phone where I could keep watch on the parking ramp exit where I hoped Dave Haskins would be appearing soon.

I decided to call Dr. Glendon Evans. But first I prepared myself. I'd done *Cuckoo's Nest* in dinner theater, so I tried to get back in that character—I had played one of the garden-variety loonies—and I did a good enough job that by the time I actually dialed his number, I sounded as if I were standing on a bridge and about to jump off. The nurse put me right through to Dr. Evans.

"Yes?" he said, concern tightening his deep voice.

"It's Dwyer."

"What?" He went from concern to anger. "I just stepped out of session because my nurse told me—"

"Forget what your nurse told you. You and I need to talk."

"I'm sorry for what happened to Karen."

"Not good enough."

"Exactly what does that mean, Mr. Dwyer?"

"It means that she died of an overdose of Librium."

"And so?"

"And so I'll bet you have a lot of Librium on hand."

"You're implying that I killed Karen?"

"It's a possibility."

"I loved Karen."

"That doesn't mean you wouldn't kill her."

"People don't ordinarily kill people they love, Mr. Dwyer."

"Of course they do. Spend a week in a squad car. You see it all the time."

"I didn't kill her."

"Did you ever treat Karen as a patient?"

"No."

"Be very careful here, Doctor."

"Are you threatening me?"

"Yes. Because if I think you're lying to me, I'm going to call the police and tell them I think I've put it all together. At the very least, the publicity won't do your practice a lot of good."

He sighed. "I'm not sure what you mean by 'treat.'"

"Psychoanalyzed her."

"That's an occupational hazard, Mr. Dwyer."

"Don't be coy, Doctor. You know what I mean."

A pause. "We were both lovers and friends, Mr. Dwyer. It was only natural that she tell me things about herself and her past."

"Did you ever give her any kind of medication that might loosen her inhibitions?"

"I don't know if I want to answer that question."

"I assume, then, that that means yes."

"I was trying to help her. As her friend."

What a powerful grip psychiatrists can have on people. Particularly people they might love. In the name of helping them, they can enslave them through deceit and manipulation and drugs forever.

"You knew you couldn't keep her otherwise, didn't you?"

"That's very damned insulting. Both professionally and personally."

"I'm going to be at your condo at six. I expect you to be there and I expect you to talk. I'm going to ask you some questions, and if I'm not happy with the answers, I'm going straight to the police."

I didn't say good-bye. I just hung up.

Two minutes later Dave Haskins came flying out of the parking ramp in a new blue Oldsmobile. Three minutes after that, I found a nice snug place a quarter mile behind him on the expressway and decided to settle in and find out where he was taking us.

Chapter 22

From bluffs of oak and birch you look down into a deep valley where the river runs wide and green and deep in the springtime. Every few years you see sand-bag crews work around the clock to minimize the flood damage. During flood years the river itself becomes a political issue and has defeated at least two candidates in recent memory.

The marina was busy today. People were hammering, painting, scraping, washing boats of all sizes. Music from fifty radios clashed, and shouts loud as boyhood boasts floated on the soft air and then fell away like birds vanishing. Sunlight and water and sails caught the breeze. More than enough to make most reasonable people happy.

I parked up in the bluffs and got out, taking my binoculars with me. Haskins had pulled into the marina's private parking lot. Without a card to open the automatic device, I was never going to get in there.

I brought the 'nocs into focus and began following him from his car, down along the pier, past several clusters of chittering houseboat owners, to a small leg of pier where a splendid white yacht overwhelmed everything within sight.

Two men stood on the prow of the yacht. Ted Forester, tan, trim, silver-haired, wearing the sort of casual Western getup you associate with very rich Texans. And Larry Price, smoking one of those 100-mm cigarettes, blue windbreaker contrasting with his movie-star blond hair and his weary sneer. By age forty-three he had to be tired of hating people as much as he did. He had to.

It happened very quickly.

Dave Haskins had not quite gotten aboard when Larry Price reached out and slapped him. He hit him hard enough that Haskins fell back into Forester's arms. Then Forester grabbed Haskins and shoved him against the cabin. All this was in pantomime. It was not unlike a silent movie. Everything looked very broad and theatrical.

I had no idea what was happening here, but I felt certain it had something to do with a missing suitcase and with an accidental overdose that wasn't accidental at all and with the mysterious mission of a crazed woman on a black Honda motorcycle.

I got back in the Toyota and drove the rest of the way down the hills, swerving once to avoid a squirrel who sat by the roadside looking much cuter than any rodent had a right to, and then easing on into the traffic flow, flanked on one side by a BMW and on the other by a Porsche. These guys probably thought I was here to clean out some houseboat toilets that had gotten plugged up over the years.

I parked just outside the private gate. From the glove compartment I took the Smith & Wesson .38 I'd used back in my days on the force, pushed it down inside my belt, and then set off over the gravel to the yacht a quarter mile away.

The people I passed were as festive as carnival goers, smiling, laughing, saying hi though they didn't know me, standing atop houseboats watching speedboats cutting through the long miles of river lying east. There had been paddle wheelers here as recently as a hundred years ago, and now the smell of fish and the scent of mud and the white flash of birch made you want to be a boy of that era and see one of the big wheelers come sidling into the cove half a mile downriver.

When I got to the leg of the pier where the yacht sat, I touched the .38 as if for luck. They were below deck now, the vast white boat empty up top, its three red mast pennants flapping with the force of gunshots in the wind.

When I got abreast of the yacht, I moved quickly, jumping aboard without pause. Then I stood there, waiting to find out if they'd heard me. If they had, they'd come up through the small oak cabin doors. And they would not be happy.

From what I could see, the yacht had a large aft deck, an upper salon and lounge, and carried decals that designated twin Cummins main engines. There was a lower dining salon, and it was there I assumed the three of them had gone.

Everything was given over to the wind here, the cold clear force of it, and the scent of water. I heard nothing from below.

Then a voice said, "You planning a party tonight?"

When I turned to him, I saw that he was a dapper elderly man in a Hawaiian shirt and white ducks and baby blue deck shoes. Liver spots like tattoos decorated his hairy white forearms. When he saw who I was he frowned, obviously disappointed.

"Oh, I thought you were one of the Forester party." His tone implied that I owed him an explanation for not being such.

Damn, I thought. My idea had been to get as close to the cabin as possible and hear what was going on. Standing here talking was bound to get them up from below deck. I wouldn't learn anything at all.

But then I got lucky.

A woman of similar age called to the man from down the dock. He waved to her.

"I'm with maintenance," I said quickly.

"Oh," he said, "maintenance." He said it as if he knew exactly what I was talking about. I was glad he did. Then, "My wife. She wants me to help her paint the walls. On our houseboat."

I wished he weren't talking so loudly. I wished he would leave.

She called again and he shrugged, as if embarrassed a woman would have such power over a man, and then he left. I stood there counting minutes on my Timex again, waiting for them to burst through the cabin doors and demand to know what I was doing there.

Another three, four minutes went by. And nothing.

I touched my .38 for luck again, then crept over to the far side of the cabin and knelt down and pressed my ear very hard against the thin white wall.

I hoped the next few minutes would prove I would be well rewarded for all my trouble of the past hour or so.

Chapter 23

I knelt to the left of two windows that looked down into the dining area. A single glimpse had shown me that Forester and Price stood over a chair in which Dave Haskins sat, hands in lap, head down, miserable.

Forester said, "There's one thing the three of us need to do. And that's keep calm."

"Calm, right," Price said. "With this little bastard thinking of going to the police."

In a voice that was almost a sob, Haskins said, "Larry, honest to God, I didn't say I was going to the police, I only said maybe we should."

"Maybe we should? You little candy-ass. Don't you know that would ruin us? Every goddamn one of us."

"Maybe they wouldn't prosecute," Haskins said. He sounded painfully young and naive.

"Right," Price said. "Maybe that fat-ass mayor of ours would give us a medal."

Forester said, "That's enough, Price."

A sullen silence ensued. There was the sound of wind, the aroma of meat cooking on a grill somewhere nearby, laughter warm as the sunlight.

Forester said, "I got another letter today. Just reminding us to be there tomorrow night at ten at Pierce Point."

Another silence. Once, Haskins moaned. Price swore continuously.

"I'll take care of this son of a bitch," Price said.

"You'll calm down and shut your mouth," Forester said. He had one of those tempers you could push a long way but then suddenly no further.

"Two hundred thousand dollars," Price said. "We can't afford it."

"Do we have any choice?" Forester said.

"Oh yes," Price said. "I forgot all about your political ambitions. It'd be worth two hundred thousand to you to ensure that you got a shot at congress next time, wouldn't it?"

Haskins said, "We could go to the police. Tell them what happened. Tell them—"

Forester said, as if to a child, "Dave, try to understand something, will you?"

"All right, Ted."

"It's not so much a question of legal culpability here. It's a question of what would happen to our reputations once it got out. Think it through, Dave. Think of how your wife would feel, or your children, your friends at the office, the people you know at church. Think of how they'd look at you. In their eyes, you'd never be the same again. Every time they saw you, they'd think about it. They might not even mean to. But they would."

Another silence.

Dave Haskins said softly, "You're right, Ted. I wasn't thinking clearly."

"If that goddamn Dwyer hadn't come along the other night at the reunion, I would have beaten it out of her," Price said. "Who she was working with, I mean."

"You sure she was involved in this?" Haskins said. "Somehow—"

Price laughed. All his cynicism was in the sound. "Somehow you don't think she was the kind to get involved in shaking somebody down for money?"

"She wasn't cruel," Haskins said.

"No, she was the next thing to a saint."

"Be quiet," Forester said. "We have to decide what we're going to do about tomorrow night." He paused. "Does everybody have his share ready?"

"I do," Haskins said. He seemed like a good little boy doing just what the teacher wanted him to.

"I don't want to pay it," Price said.

"That wasn't what I asked you, Larry," Forester snapped.

"I asked you if you had your share ready."

Price said, "Yes."

"Then please hand it over."

"What? Why to you?"

"Because I'm the one who'll take it tomorrow night."

"Bullshit."

"Then let's take it to a vote. All right?"

"A vote would be fine with me," Haskins said. He seemed to be in shock.

"All in favor of me taking the money, raise their hands."

"You bastard," Price said. "You know you can bully this little pecker around."

"Do you vote for me?" Forester said.

"Of course I do, Ted."

"Thank you, Dave."

"Assholes."

"I'd like your money," Forester said. "I'd like it now."

A pause. Then Price said, "I don't like this. I don't like this at all and I want to go on record as saying I don't like it." The wind had come up and I was starting to lean in closer, maybe dangerously close, to the window when a voice floated over to me on the air currents.

"Say, are you sure you're with maintenance?"

It was my elderly friend. He was down on the pier. I realized quickly enough that I probably appeared, kneeling down as I was, to be burglarizing the boat. He looked suspicious, angry.

He didn't give me time to respond, "Ted! Ted, are you down there! You'd better get up here!" he called.

I got to my feet, knees cracking and stiff from kneeling, and began hobbling across the deck.

Seeing me move toward him, he took the broom in his hand and held it crosswise, like a martial arts weapon.

"I'm not going to hurt you," I said. "Just relax, all right?"

I jumped back on the pier, trying to get to my feet as I reached the wood.

Behind me, I heard Larry Price shout, "Hey! Stop!"

The old man put his broom toward me, but I just gently pushed it away. "Just relax and enjoy the day, all right? Don't get mixed up in this."

Price surprised me by doing a dash across the boat and clearing the water and landing on my back. He smelled of sweat and hair spray and heat. He was still strong in the sinewy way of high school days.

"Atta boy!" the old man shouted, as Price threw me to the pier.

Price got his arm around my neck and started to choke me. I hadn't been in this kind of street fight in thirty years. At first I had no idea what to do. He took my hair and slammed my head against the pier once. The old man said, "Kick his butt, Larry! Kick his butt!" And then Price did something foolish, he tried to turn my face toward his so he could hit me dead-on. I surprised him. I got him one clean shot with my elbow in the teeth, and it was enough to make him fall away, and for his open mouth to fill up immediately with thick red blood. I got to my feet and he started to get to his. I kicked him once very hard in the abdomen. He went over backward and sprawled on the pier.

"Hey, that's not fair!" the old man said. To him I was the Mad Russian in some goofy pro wrestling match.

Forester and Haskins were on the deck now and running toward me.

I took off down the pier, running as best I could given knees that were none too good to begin with.

The pier was still packed and it was easy to lose myself among the crowd and find my car and get out of there.

Chapter 24

At the time we'd agreed to meet, Dr. Glendon Evans opened the door of his condo. I started across the threshold, the pines surrounding his aerie sweet on the dying day. Then I stopped. He had a gun, some kind of Mauser, and he wanted to make sure I saw it.

"Not exactly your style, is it?"

He wore an open white shirt and blue trousers with a brown leather belt and penny loafers without socks. He looked angry and he smelled faintly of bourbon.

"I'm not going to take any of your shit, Mr. Dwyer. I'm warning you."

"You really think that's going to help?"

"I've done a little checking on you."

"I'm impressed."

"You used to be a cop."

"I would have been more than happy to tell you that myself."

"Cops have ways of getting people to confess to things they didn't do."

"And you're saying you didn't kill her."

"That's exactly what I'm saying."

"Then there's no reason for the gun."

"Does it make you nervous, Mr. Dwyer?"

"Of course it makes me nervous, Dr. Evans. You're an amateur. Amateurs terrify me."

He glanced down at the weapon in his hand as if it were a growth slowly eating its way up his arm. "I don't suppose I am very good at this sort of thing."

"No," I said, reaching out and gently taking the gun from his hand, "I don't suppose you are."

"I violated half the ethics I'm supposed to believe in."

"You want me to call you names?"

"Maybe I'd feel better if you did, Mr. Dwyer."

This was half an hour later. We sat in the breakfast nook. We were sipping some of his Wild Turkey again. The night sky was purple and starry. Jets rumbled in the gloom above like gods displeased.

"Tell me what happened."

"Drugs," he said. "I gave her drugs."

"How many times?"

"Twice."

I had some more whiskey and just stared at my fists.

"I—I thought it was the only way I could keep her." He shook his head as if it hurt to do so. "I'd never had to deal with anything like it before." He had some whiskey himself. "You know how I told you I rode around in Lincolns growing up?"

I nodded.

"Well, it was the same with women. Never any problem. My color rarely seemed to matter. I just naturally seemed to be attractive to women and I always took that for granted." More whiskey. A sigh half anger, half remorse. "I was a good lover. I know I was. I don't mean in bed necessarily, though even there I always tried to make sure that they had their satisfaction before I took mine." He waved a hand. "I mean I was a good lover in the sense that I tried to be as attentive and sensitive as possible. When things ended, it was always me who ended them, but even then I tried to make it as easy as possible. And it wasn't because I was bored, it was just—I knew there were more things I needed to learn from women. They're the great teachers, you know, women; the best ones are, at any rate."

I laughed. "It's true. But let's not let them know that."

He smiled. "I'm afraid some of them do." Then he went back to frowning. "I'd never had anybody treat me the way Karen did."

"As good and as bad."

"Exactly."

"But it's the bad things you remember, isn't it?"

"That's what's so odd. I know we must have had hundreds of good times—but now I can barely remember any of them."

I was just letting him talk, easing him into his confession. He was eager to give it and I was eager to hear it. We both just kind of had to be in the right emotional spot. I poured him more whiskey.

He said, "For two decades I've been telling men and women alike that the idea of sexual enslavement is largely a myth. Now I know better."

I said, "You must have been getting pretty desperate when you started with the Pentothal."

He surprised me by laughing. "In other words, you want me to tell you what I found out."

I shrugged. "There's no easy way to say this, Doctor, but it's not a case of you violating your ethics because you didn't have any ethics to begin with."

"I wish I could get indignant and argue with you."

"So what did you learn?"

"Nothing."

"What?"

"Contrary to popular belief, drugs don't always dislodge memories, at least not the kind I could give Karen without her being aware of them. If I could have strapped her down to an electro-shock table and given her Pentothal... but I had to do this on the sly, of course, over the course of long weekends up here."

"And you didn't find out anything at all?"

"I found out only one thing for sure." He hesitated.

"Yes?"

"The odd thing is, I still feel very protective of her. Even after all she put me through."

I poured more whiskey.

"Go ahead," I said.

"She may have killed somebody."

I did a double take Jackie Gleason would have been proud of.

He nodded. "The boy's name was Sonny Howard."

"Christ."

"Something happened the summer of her senior year. She had repressed it to the point that she couldn't talk about it even under the influence of the drugs. But she did begin talking about this Sonny Howard, and then she just broke down, sobbing and saying 'I killed Sonny, I killed Sonny' over and over again. I had to use a different drug to calm her down."

"You mind if I open this?"

"What's wrong?"

"I'm getting claustrophobic."

So I leaned over and opened the window and smelled the fresh pine and listened to birds and crickets and dogs. Evans started to say something, but I waved off his words.

"It getting to you?" he said after a time.

"You really think she could have killed somebody?"

He did not hesitate. "Yes."

"And you think she really might have killed Sonny Howard?"

"Yes."

"It would explain a lot, wouldn't it?"

"It would indeed, Mr. Dwyer. Her inability to make a commitment of any kind, her living in a sort of soap-opera fantasy world half the time, the sense she always gave you of somehow being afraid of virtually everything."

I closed my eyes and leaned my head back. I was beginning to realize there was one person I needed to talk to. The woman on the black Honda motorcycle.

"You're leaving?"

I was on my feet. I put out my hand.

"Are you going to report this?" he asked.

"Don't see any reason to."

"I'm a good doctor, Mr. Dwyer. Despite the way I behaved."

"I guess I'm going to have to take your word for that, aren't I?"

He tried to smile. It wasn't especially convincing. "Yes," he said, "yes, I guess you are."

Chapter 25

The aerobics class was going on —women in expensive exercise suits doing boot-camp jumping jacks now—but the Honda was not in the parking lot to the left of the shopper.

The disco music was overpowering when I walked inside. I moved along the right-hand corridor, trying to keep my eyes from all the breasts and thighs and buttocks my gaze gravitated to so naturally. The women were as curious about me as I was about them. A few even smiled in my direction, not in the inviting way women do at private investigators in books, but just because this was a female domain and there was something vaguely naughty about my being there and that made them curious.

The west wall was all mirrors to make the place look bigger; the carpet was cheap indoor-outdoor stuff hopelessly worn; the stereo speakers could have sufficed at Yankee stadium. (At least the owners had great taste in music, the Crusaders working their asses off on a killer number called "Sometimes You Can Take It or Leave It," the pure unremitting jazz of it as exhilarating as any exercise you could do.) The place smelled of perfume and sweat. Lined up along the back were a rowing machine, a ballet bar, a stationary bicycle, and a Coke machine where, with two quarters, you could put back all the calories you'd worked off.

On the other side of a glass wall, a chunky woman with a bad red dye job and arms as thick as a fullback's sat working over books. Occasionally she poked a fat finger at a calculator so hard you wondered if she had something against it.

I knocked on the window. When she glanced up and saw me, she did not look happy.

I pantomimed Can I Come In, the music too loud for me to be heard otherwise. She didn't pantomime. She just made a face.

I went over to the door and opened it up and went inside.

She said, "We don't get a lot of men here."

"So I see."

She picked up a package of Winston Lights, tamped one out, got it going, exhaled a long blue stream of smoke, and said, "So how can I help you?" She looked like Ethel Merman with a bad hangover. Her nametag said HI, I'M IRENE.

"There's a woman who works here."

The flesh around her eyes grew tight and her mouth got unpleasant again. "Yeah. So?"

"So she drives a black Honda motorcycle and so I'd like to know who she is."

"Why?"

"Is that really any of your business?"

"As a matter of fact, it is."

"Now why would that be?"

"Because she happens to be my best friend."

"I see."

"And I protect her."

"From my few experiences with her, I'd say she doesn't need a hell of a lot of protection."

She had some more cigarette. "She's high-strung."

"At least."

She glared at me. "What's that supposed to mean?"

"It means I think she's probably clinical."

She sighed. "She's had some problems, I'll admit. But now that her aunt's in the nursing home—" She allowed herself several cigarette hacks, then said, "Evelyn has spent some time in mental hospitals."

"I see."

"That doesn't mean she's crazy."

"No," I said and meant it. "No, it doesn't."

"Her aunt raised her; Evelyn's own mother died when she was six. And then there's what happened with Sonny. That's when all the trouble started."

"What trouble?"

She jammed out one cigarette in a round red metal ashtray and promptly lit another. "You want a Coke?"

"Sure. I'll get it for us. You want regular or Diet?"

Given her weight problem, I figured she'd say Diet Coke.

For the first time she smiled. "You want to learn something today?"

"What?"

"There are reports that show that people who drink diet pop actually gain weight instead of lose it."

"So you want regular Coke."

"Right," she said, "regular."

So I went and got her a regular and me a Diet and could not help but look at least briefly at the wondrous backside of the little black woman conducting the class, and then I went back into the tiny office gray with smoke.

"So what's with her aunt?"

"Sonny dies," she said, slipping into present tense. "Her aunt doesn't believe anything the police say. She starts becoming obsessed."

"What did the police say?"

"Suicide."

"They said he jumped off Pierce Point?"

She looked surprised that I knew about Pierce Point.

"Right."

"Was there a note found?"

"Suicide note?" Irene said.

"Right."

"No."

"Then why did the police assume it was suicide?"

She shrugged. "They said he was despondent."

"Did they say about what?"

"No. But they said they checked with his teachers and the teachers all said he was despondent. Even the aunt had to admit that. He was usually an A student. He went to summer school between his junior and senior year so he could graduate early. But then he screwed it up."

"Screwed up his grades?"

"Yeah. He got Ds. In summer school you have to get at least Cs."

"So how does Evelyn fit into all this?" Now I was talking in the present tense, too.

"Evelyn is five years younger, right, a very pretty but very high-strung kid. Always had problems. Manic depression, actually. Well, when Sonny buys it, the aunt puts everything on Evelyn. She expects Evelyn not only to share the grief but to spend the rest of her life with her, too. The aunt has money, right, so the aunt builds Evelyn her own wing on the house and Evelyn is expected to stay there the rest of her life, right, and to get caught up in all her obsessions—her hypochondria (this woman has sent a dozen doctors screaming into the sunset), her paranoia about her investments (I mean most of the stockbrokers in this town would rather have gasoline enemas than deal with her), and with proving that Sonny was actually pushed off Pierce Point by persons unknown. So Evelyn, being none too stable herself, does in fact get caught up in all this. Very caught up. And in the process becomes sort of a half-ass detective, really going into Sonny's life and particularly into Sonny's life the summer between his junior and senior year." She stopped.

"And?"

"And to be honest, I don't know so much about lately."

"Lately?"

"The past few weeks."

"You haven't seen her?"

"Oh, I see her. But she's in one of her—moods." Her voice was an odd mixture of anger and sorrow. I liked her. She was tough in the way good people are tough. "I mean, I don't think we've split up or anything. She just gets—"

"Kind of crazy."

"Yeah, I guess it wouldn't be unfair to put it that way. Kind of crazy."

I thought of how she'd said 'split up.' Obviously she wanted me to know they were lovers.

"I wonder if you'd give me her address."

"You gotta know I'm going to ask you why?"

"Because I may be able to help her."

"True blue?"

"True blue. I may have a lead of sorts on Sonny."

"Everything's in her aunt's name."

"Huh?"

"House, credit cards, even her Honda."

"I see."

"Just look up her aunt's name in the phone book and you'll have the address."

"Thanks."

"She was supposed to be here tonight but she didn't show up. Didn't phone or anything. That's why I had to pull Mimsy in."

Now I wanted to leave and she still wanted to talk.

She said, "I guess there's one thing I should tell you."

"What's that?"

"She can get kind of violent."

I thought of what she'd done to Donna and to Glendon Evans. Not to mention me. I said, "Yeah, I've heard rumors to that effect."

"But even if she did hurt you, she wouldn't mean to."

I smiled. "I'm sure that would make me feel a lot better."

She laughed and went into another cigarette hack and said, "She's great at apologies. I guess that's what I'm really trying to say. She does these terrible things— anybody else I would have left years ago—but she's got this fantastic way of apologizing. You ever know anybody like that?"

In fact, I had.

Her name had been Karen Lane.

I thanked Irene and left.

Chapter 26

I called American Security to see if they'd need me tonight (supposedly we work four nights on, three off, like firemen in some cities). They didn't. Next I called Donna, told her about my last three conversations.

"So this Sonny Howard was a friend of Forester and Price and Haskins and you think there's a possibility that Karen Lane killed him."

"A few people seem to think so."

"But why would she have killed him?"

"That's why I'm going to look up Evelyn."

"Then who killed Karen Lane?"

"If I knew, I'd call Edelman."

She sighed. "Boy, Dwyer."

"Come on."

"What?"

"You're trying to make me feel guilty about not taking you along."

"Am I succeeding?"

"No, because Evelyn is somewhere on the loose and she's not quite hinged properly."

"So I noticed."

"So what are you and Joanna doing?"

"Well, *Bringing Up Baby* is on PBS, so I guess we're going to watch that."

"You don't like Katharine Hepburn."

"I just can't get past all her mannerisms."

"Then concentrate on Cary Grant."

"I'd rather concentrate on you."

"You can't go."

"Boy, that's pretty cynical, Dwyer. Thinking I'd only compare you to Cary Grant because I wanted to go along."

"Right."

"It's a good thing I'm not sensitive."

"Bye, hon."

"Please, can't I?"

"Bye."

"Please?"

The three-story gabled house sat on a shelf of land dense with elm, maple, and spruce. A gravel road led up to it. A ring-necked pheasant ambled in front of my headlights and gave me a dirty look. I hit the brakes, the Toyota nearly doing a wheelie. The pheasant did not seem impressed. He didn't speed up at all. He just continued walking his way across the gravel drive and into the night.

I sat there, B.B. King loud suddenly on the FM jazz station I was tuned to, wailing very lonely there on the spring night, a night cold enough for a winter coat. I was still mad at the pheasant, or whatever feeling is supposed to be appropriate to a pheasant who has pissed you off (I guess I wanted to have a talk with him about traffic safety, you know—about looking both directions before you cross any thoroughfare, gravel drives included), and it was while I sat there kind of scanning the underbrush in the wash of my headlights that I saw the black glint.

At first it registered as nothing more ominous than something black and something metal and something shiny glimpsed through the dead brown spring weeds.

But after a few seconds I knew what it would be. What it was.

A black Honda motorcycle.

I clicked off the radio and suddenly the night silence was a roar of distant dogs and trains.

I got out, but at first I didn't go anywhere. I took a piece of Doublemint out of my pocket and folded it over and put it in my mouth and I stared up at the big house. It was exactly the kind of place my old man always had dreamed of, here on several acres of its own land, enough maybe to plant some corn and tomatoes and carrots and green beans on a plot in the back to convince yourself you were really still a farmer the way all the Dwyers only two generations ago had been, and say "screw it" to all the burdens of city life. But watching the house now, I recalled how it hadn't worked out for him, not at all, how he'd ended up owing $700 on a six-year-old Pontiac whose transmission had never worked right, and how the closest he ever came to the country was the cemetery where he got planted.

I heard a moan.

I had put it off as long as I could, and now I couldn't put it off any longer. I had to go over there and see what I'd find.

This had happened to me a few times on the force, when I'd let somebody else have first peek at somebody badly injured or dead. But now first peek belonged to me.

When I saw her I thought again of Karen and how she'd looked there at the last in my arms and I thought of my father there in his hospital bed and I thought of a wino I'd seen beaten by a couple teenagers, I just remembered the eyes and the fear that gave way to a curious kind of peace, some secret they knew just before pushing off, some secret you only got to understand when you were once and for all going to push off.

I knelt down next to her there in the weeds. She wore, as always, her leathers. Now the torso part was sticky with red. Somebody had shot her in the chest. The blood was like a bad kitchen spill, splotchy and gooey. It was warm and smelled. I got my hand under her blond hair the color and texture of straw. Her blue eyes watched me all this time. The fear was giving way, fast. In a couple of minutes she was going to know the secret everybody from St. Thomas Aquinas to Howard Hughes had wanted to know.

"Evelyn, I need you to answer one question."

Just watching me.

"You've been following Karen, trying to get some proof that she killed Sonny."

Faintly, a nod.

"Did you kill Karen?"

Shaking her head. Then blood began bubbling in the corner of her mouth. I closed my eyes.

Then she cried out, "Sonny!" And now it was my turn to watch her, watch the secret come into her eyes, and feel her start to go easy in my grasp.

I said an "Our Father" for her, not knowing exactly what else to do, just an "Our Father" silent to myself, as a train rattled through the night in the pass above, and a dog barked at a passing car somewhere down the road.

I checked her neck, her wrist, and then put my head to that part of her chest not soaked in blood. She had pushed off, no doubt about it. I took her hand and stared at her face there, lit by my flashlight, at the freckles, the forlorn mouth; and for the first time I was curious about her—what her favorite foods had been, what sort of music she'd liked, what her laugh might have sounded like on a summer afternoon. There is an Indian sect that believes you can see a person's soul leaving the body if you watch out of the corner of your eye. I watched out of the corner of my eye, but I didn't see anything. Maybe it was gone already; or maybe it was just waiting for me to leave before it rose, shimmering and transcendent; or maybe, the worst thought of all, there is no soul—maybe the body I stared down at was no different from the body of a rabbit or cat you saw on a dusty roadside, filthy in death and useful only to those who relish the taste of carrion. Maybe that was the secret, and if it was, I didn't want to know. I didn't want to know it at all.

I turned out my light and left her there in the weeds and went on up the sloping gravel drive to the dark house.

I tried my American Express card and when that didn't work I went over into the garage and got a screwdriver and tried that and that didn't work either, so I did what the real novice criminal does; I took off my jacket and wrapped it around my fist and then pushed my fist through the back-door window, the noise of smashing glass almost obscene in the stillness, and then I took the jacket off my hand and slid it back over my body and simply reached in through the broken window and undid the lock.

Inside, I went through a back porch that smelled of apple cider and lawn fertilizer. Then I went through a kitchen that smelled of the sort of food you fix in a wok. Then I went through a dining room big enough to give a major restaurant some problems. Moonlight shone softly through a line of long, narrow windows onto the ghostly white cloth covering the formal dining table and the built-in buffet. The living room had a soaring ceiling, a real Palladian window, and a fireplace above which hung a McKnight print. Evelyn may have suffered from mental problems; she certainly hadn't suffered from poverty.

I went up the stairs to my right, the sound of my footsteps lost in the deep-pile carpeting and the noise of the wind outside.

The second floor was every bit as impressive as the first. There was a master bedroom Tut would have envied, complete with a sunken bathtub big enough to hold swim tryouts in, and a den filled with forty years of Book-of-the-Month Club selections, all those oddments from curios like Jack Paar to the real stuff like William Faulkner.

The room where the boy had lived was easy enough to identify. There were a single bed, a bookcase with twenty-five cent paperbacks of Robert Heinlein, Jerry Sohl, Mickey Spillane, and several of the Dobie Gillis books. The closet contained chinos with little belt buckles in back, the kind that had been popular at the time he'd died in 1962, and the bureau drawers orderly stacks of white socks and jockey shorts. On the walls were posters of the Beach Boys (Brian looked to weigh about 100 pounds in those days) and Elvis with his sneer.

In other words, nothing useful.

Two doors down the hall my luck changed. What appeared to be nothing more than Evelyn's room with its Wedgwood blue curtains and matching bedspread and stuffed animals (a duck's eyes seemed to sparkle with intelligence, watching me) proved otherwise once I sat down at her desk.

Next to a Wang computer was a large reel-to-reel tape recorder that was patched into a phone system sitting next to it. I wondered what this was all about. I turned on the recorder, tiny amber lights haunting the darkness, and sat down and listened.

"You know who this is, don't you?" This was Evelyn's voice.

"I'm getting very goddamn tired of this."

"You're protecting that woman. It's time you came forward."

"I have to go now." Not until then had I realized whose voice it was. Ted Forester's.

"If you go, I'll phone the police."

A sigh. "How much money do you want?"

"You should know me better than that by now, Mr. Forester."

"I—I'm in no position to go to the police."

"You know she killed him."

"I really need to—"

"Why are you protecting her?" Anger had begun to edge into her voice.

"I'm not protecting her."

"Of course you are. All three of you are. And I won't let you anymore. I won't let you. You'll see." By now she was in tears, her own kind of dark psych-ward tears. There was rage but there was no power, she was drifting off into her madness and so she did the only thing she could. She hung up.

I let the tape roll and sat there in her room and felt sorry for her again, thinking of her freckles and her crazed eyes. She was one of those born truly luckless; not even money could put her life back together again.

The next conversation was with Larry Price. Predictably, he was not as diplomatic as Forester had been. He cursed her a lot and threatened her a lot and it was he, not she, who hung up.

Then came Dave Haskins. From the beginning, he sounded miserable. Over and over he said, "You don't understand what's going on here. We're not—" Then he stopped.

"You're not what?"

"I can't say. Ted and Larry would—"

"Hurt you?"

"Yes, God, don't you understand that? That's exactly what they'd do. They'd hurt me."

"She killed Sonny. And I'm taping all these conversations to turn over to the police. And—"

"If you want to talk to somebody, don't talk to me, all right? Ted and Larry are the ones—"

"I followed you the other day."

"What?"

"I followed you."

"Why?"

"I follow all of you. I follow everybody." She paused. "You almost went to the police, didn't you?"

He said nothing.

"Didn't you?"

Very softly: "Yes."

"You're getting tired of it, aren't you?"

"Yes."

"You're the only good one of the three. And I'm not just saying that. I've followed all of you and I've talked to you on the phone and I know that you're the only good one of the three. I know that." She was going off again, and the rest of the conversation consisted mostly of her telling him how good he was and wouldn't he please go to the police. But all he said at the end, and obviously without any conviction, was "Give me a few days to think about it, all right? Please give me a few more days."

The next call was the real shocker and as soon as I heard who it was I thought of what Dr. Evans had said, that Karen's pattern was to have a new lover waiting in the wings before she got rid of the old one. And Evans had sensed that there was, in fact, a man in her life at the time Karen had been withdrawing from him.

I sat there in the prim pleasantness of the dead woman's bedroom and listened to the voice, an old-familiar voice, and didn't know what to think or say or do; I just thought of all the people involved, and all the people betrayed.

After a time, I turned off the player and just sat there, listening to the night wind and lonely creaking of a house where anything like real life had stopped in the summer of 1962.

Then I got angry and it was what I needed just then, real anger, and I went down the stairs and out of the house and down the gravel road past where Evelyn lay sprawled in her leathers like some piece of trendy violent sculpture, and I got in my Toyota.

Ten minutes later I was at a drive-up phone.

"You can go home now."

"Really?" Donna said. "You're not worried about that woman anymore?"

"She's dead."

Pause. "You don't sound so good, Dwyer."

"I don't feel so good."

"Why don't you meet me at my apartment in an hour or so."

"There's something I've got to do."

"It doesn't sound like something that's going to make you very happy."

So I thought about it and then I talked about it and then I felt much better than I should have, much better than I would have keeping silent. Donna does that for me.

Chapter 27

"Jack."

"Hi. Gary home?" I tried sounding as if it were Christmas and I were dropping off presents for the kids and I were wearing a red Santa cap and a glow from toddies, but I knew better and she knew better, too.

"What's wrong?"

"Nothing."

"Jack, come on. I've known you a long time. Something's up."

"It's probably nothing. I just need to see Gary."

"He's at school."

"At this time?"

"He teaches a course in creative writing at night. Adult ed."

"I see." I stared past her into the house. It was inevitably tidy, tidy as she was, with the same kind of poor but resolute dignity. "I'm going to ask you something, and I wouldn't blame you if you'd ask me to leave."

"God, Jack." She put her hands to her face. "You're scaring me."

"I'm sorry."

"Oh, Jack."

And then she came up to me and slid her arms around me and I held her, sexless as a sibling in the soiled light of her living room there, and I permitted myself only certain pleasures in her embrace, the clean smell of her hair, the faintest shape of her small breasts against my chest, the ageless sense of the maternal that bound me up when I finally relaxed and let her begin stroking the back of my head. I was the one who had frightened her, yet she was calming me down. I thought of Glendon Evans' remark that women were the great teachers. And so they were.

"Mom?"

The boy's word said many things, all of them shocked, all of them scared.

She eased away from me and said, "It's just Jack, honey. He's just—sort of upset about something. Jack, I don't believe you've met Gary Junior."

"No," I said, trying to find my voice like a freshman who's been caught kissing a girl in the sudden presence of her father. "No. I haven't."

So I made a big beer-commercial thing of shaking the kid's hand and cuffing him on the shoulder and standing back as if he were a car and I were appraising him and I said, "He's got your looks, Susan." He was a chunky kid with his old man's shaggy brown hair and that odd gaze of belligerent intelligence, as if he knew something vital but would be damned if he ever told you what it was.

She smiled. "And Gary's brains."

He was seventeen or so and he just wanted out of there. "Can I take the Pontiac?"

"I just finish telling you how smart he is and he says 'Can I take the Pontiac?'

Honey, it's 'May I take the Pontiac?'"

"May I, then?"

"You know where the keys are. And tell Jack that you were glad to meet him."

But I was the guy he'd just seen in some kind of curious embrace with his mother and he didn't feel much like saying that he was glad he'd met me. And I didn't blame him at all.

After he was gone, she looked at me levelly and said, "You were going to ask me something that might cause me to ask you to leave."

"Right."

"Well."

"Does Gary have a writing room?"

"As a matter of fact, he does. The attic."

"I wonder if I could see it."

"You want to see Gary's writing room?" For the first time irritation could be heard in her tone. "Why?"

"It's not anything I can explain."

"Jack, please tell me what's going on. I don't want to be angry with you. I don't want to ask you to leave, but I need you to tell me the truth."

I thought about that, about telling her the truth, but it would be too complicated and would only hurt her more. And at this point, I wasn't sure of what the truth was exactly, anyway.

I said, "I think Karen gave him something."

"Karen?"

"Yes."

"Gave him what?"

"I'm not sure."

"Jack, this is all so crazy."

"She may have given him something that will shed some light on her death."

"Well, you don't think Gary had anything to do with it, do you?"

I said it very quickly. "No."

She sighed and broke out in a grin that was accompanied by tears of relief. This time she hugged me hard enough to hurt my back.

"You had me so scared," she said. "I didn't know what was going on." Then she took my hand and said, "I'm going to take you to the steps leading to the attic now, Jack, and you take all the time you want."

It was about what you might expect, an unfinished attic filled with bookcases containing hundreds of paperbacks, everything from Thomas Mann to Leonard Cohen, from e.e. cummings to Gregory Corso.

What I wanted I found with almost no difficulty. I only had to rattle open and rifle through a few file drawers, jerk back and sort through a few desk drawers.

And there it was.

I slid it inside my shirt and went back downstairs.

She must have heard me coming down the steps because she called from the kitchen, "Come on out here."

When I got there, she said, "You know what I made tonight? Gingersnaps. Real ones. Here. Have one."

So I had one and then I had two and all the while we made quick talk of weather and gingersnaps and teenagers these days, and then she said, "Well, find anything?"

"'Fraid not."

"Oh, I'm sorry, Jack."

"It's all right."

She said, "You want another one?"

"No, thanks." I had my hand on the back door. I wondered if she knew. The thing I'd shoved down inside my shirt seemed to be glowing. She had to see. Had to know.

"You sure?"

"I'm sure."

She laughed. "Well, I hope the next time I see you, it's on a happier note."

"It will be, Susan. It will be."

Then I was gone.

Chapter 28

Ft. Wilson had been built during the final economic boom of the sixties, when so many dead young Americans over in Nam meant so many live jobs over here, and it had been designed, by an architect who was too tricky by half, with a waterfall between the two main sections of the rambling two-story brick structure, a comic imitation of Frank Lloyd Wright.

It was nearly ten-thirty and people were drifting out to their cars in the lot. They were middle-aged with middle-aged flesh and an air of middle-aged dreams. At forty you don't take night school courses because you've got an eye on glory; all you've got an eye on is the next rung up in some vast drab institution somewhere. Level Six, as the people in Personnel might say, the exception being classes such as Creative Writing, where glory is still possible, even if said glory does only come in the form of a fifteen-dollar check for your first professional sale to a magazine promoting the likelihood of an imminent alien invasion or the possibility that Liberace has joined James Dean and John Kennedy on an island in the Pacific known only to an ancient race of henna-skinned religious cannibals.

The inside of the high school was almost lurid with fluorescent light and the odor of cleaning solvent. The main hall was jammed with people heading for cars. I asked one of them for directions to Mr. Roberts' room and she told me.

When I got there, he was sitting on the edge of his desk, smoking a cigarette and talking earnestly to a plump woman in a yellow pantsuit that had gone out of style with Jimmy Carter. She was smoking, too.

Watching him, I had the sense that he must be a good teacher, taking everybody just as seriously as he took himself, looking for the same talent in his students he sought in himself, and probably finding it in neither.

He stuck out a Diet Pepsi can for the woman to push her cigarette in and then he said, "All you need to remember, Mary, is that it's better to put in the things about your childhood later on, after you've got the reader hooked on the story line itself. I'd start out right off with the ambulance scene. It's really gripping."

The way she smiled, she might just have discovered the real meaning of life.

"Oh, Gary," she said, "I just love taking your class."

"You're doing very well, Mary. Very well."

She pulled a purse big enough to hold a Japanese car over her wide shoulder, picked up a pile of schoolbooks, nodded good-bye, and left the room. On her way out, she saw me and smiled. "He's wonderful, isn't he?" And he was—patient, caring, taking pleasure in her pleasure.

I smiled at her and her enthusiasm. She was my age maybe, and she radiated a high, uncomplicated passion for life. And that's something I've always only been able to envy, that kind of simple and beautiful enthusiasm for things. I'm always too busy worrying about what can go wrong or wondering what the guy *really* meant.

Gary still hadn't seen me. He was busy pushing papers and books into a brief-case as scuffed as his shoes always were. I watched him there amid all the empty desks, like lifeboats on a mean vast ocean, his graying hair pulled back into a pony-tail, his jeans still bell-bottomed, his eyeglasses rimless. He was the last of the species *hippie*. At his funeral somebody would probably read something from one of the Doors' songs.

I said, "How long were you having an affair with Karen, Gary?"

He didn't look up. He knew exactly what had been said and he knew exactly who'd said it.

I came into the room. He still hadn't looked up.

I put the manuscript on the desk. The room was painted the dull green of most institutions. It seemed to hush us with its terrible powers to disintegrate person-alities. Finally, I said, "I didn't get a chance to read it all. But I read enough of it."

All he said was, "Susan know about this?"

I shook my head.

"Jesus," he said. "I really have fucked things up, haven't I?"

"Yeah, I guess you have."

"The only other time I was unfaithful was back in the sixties. At some kind of English teachers' seminar. This woman with a face that reminded me of Cherie Conners. You remember Cherie Conners?"

"Sure."

"I always wanted to screw her. That's sort of what I was doing with this woman at the English teachers' convention. Closing my eyes and pretending she was Cherie. You know she died of an aneurysm a few years ago? Cherie, I mean?"

"I heard that. She was a nice woman."

"It's all crazy bullshit, isn't it, Dwyer?"

"Yeah, it is."

"You going to tell Susan?"

I kept staring at him. He was treating this as if I'd caught him in nothing more than a simple case of adultery. But Karen had been murdered, and so, earlier tonight, had a sad woman named Evelyn.

"What time did your class start?"

"Eight o'clock."

"Little late for night school, isn't it?"

"We took a vote the first night of class. Everybody wanted eight o'clock." He took out his cigarettes. Lit one. "You gave 'em up, huh?"

"Yeah, almost."

He coughed, as if for emphasis. "Wish I could."

"You know a woman named Evelyn Dain?"

For the first time I could see that he was lying. He just sort of shrugged.

"She was killed tonight. Murdered."

"I'm sorry to hear about that. She a friend of yours?"

"She was obsessed with the idea that Karen Lane killed a boy named Sonny Howard. This was the summer we were going into senior year."

He talked with smoke coming out of his mouth. "Well, that's bullshit."

I picked up the twenty-page manuscript. It was sloppily typed, with many strikeovers, many words written in the margins with pencil. *"The Autumn Dead.* It's about Karen, isn't it?"

"In ways. It's my version of Holly Golightly, too. Very selfish but very fetching. A woman you need to get rid of but can't. She had a story of her own, her own True Life Tale, as she called it. She said we could turn it into a good novel if we collaborated. She said all it needed was a good second draft. She never got around to showing it to me, though."

"Karen tell you everything that happened to her?"

"She told me some of the things."

"Such as?"

"Oh, about her brother. Things like that."

"What about her brother?"

"He's kind of a bastard. She's always tried to help him but it hasn't helped much."

"She ever mention anything about blackmailing anybody?"

He laughed. "God, Dwyer, being a cop really screwed up your mind, didn't it? We're talking about Karen Lane here. She was a cheerleader, she liked to go shopping, she got very sentimental over Barry Manilow records—" He shook his ponytail, trying to rid his eyes of tears. They were big and silver, the way his wife's had been earlier.

I didn't say anything for a time.

He turned away from me and sometimes he snuffled and sometimes he smoked but mostly he just kept shaking his head, his ponytail bobbing, as if to awaken himself from a terrible dream.

I said, softly, "It started when she moved in, you and her, I mean?"

"No. A few months before."

"How'd you keep it from Susan?"

"We just sneaked around a lot. Motels, I guess. Karen had credit cards." He turned back to me. "I knew she was keeping something from me."

"Any idea what it was?"

"No. It was—almost as if it was the central part of her personality. You know, like missing the one vital clue in a mystery. If you knew what she was holding back, then you could understand her. But...." He shrugged. "She had nightmares a lot."

"She ever talk much about Ted Forester or Larry Price or Dave Haskins?"

"Price came to see her one night."

"What?"

"Yes. He came to the door and asked if she would come out to the car with him."

"She went?"

He nodded. "When she came back, I could see a welt on her cheek. As if he'd slapped her."

I said, "Was this about the time you started hearing from Evelyn?"

This time he sighed, acknowledged he knew her. "Yes. She started calling me and said she wanted me to help her prove that Karen had killed a boy named Sonny Howard. She scared me, this Evelyn. Really a crazy woman."

"You didn't go to the reunion?"

"No, I didn't. Why?"

"Curious."

"Jesus, you think I had something to do with Karen's death?"

"Possibly."

"Christ, Dwyer."

I touched the manuscript again. The parts I'd read detailed how a middle-aged man falls miserably in love with a beautiful woman from his past and pleads with her to run away with him. "You were in love with her."

"Yes. In a very positive way." He exhaled blue smoke. "We were going to go away together."

He said it so easily, so confidently, that it wasn't half as funny as it should have been. She'd been with many men, good and bad, but they'd had one thing in common, and that was the power of their money to protect her from her demons.

She and Gary Roberts would have lasted maybe three months.

"You don't believe me?"

"I believe you," I said.

"I gave Karen things nobody else ever had."

"Tell me more about Larry Price."

"What about him?"

"He ever come around again?"

"No. But he called."

"When?"

"A few weeks after he came over. She was very upset, sobbing, when she hung up. Then she went out to see her brother."

"She didn't say why?"

"No."

"I need to say something here and I'm going to come off sanctimonious," I said. He looked at me with his middle-aged eyes and said, "I know."

"You've got a fine wife."

He nodded. "Don't you think I feel like shit?" Then, "So you're not going to tell her?"

"Of course not."

"Thanks."

"You can still patch it up."

"I want to. It's just—" He shrugged. "It was like being a teenager again. It really was. I mean, we made love everywhere possible. Wrote notes—" His laugh was sour. "While all the time Susan was at home being a good wife."

I set my hand on his shoulder and thought of us as young boys playing ball one summer, and how I could never have predicted that thirty-five years later we'd be standing here having this conversation. We were part of the same generation, falling away now, some of us, to be joined later by the rest of us, our moment on

the planet vanished, the sunlight on baseball grass shining for different generations.

I felt sorry for him and angry with him and even half-afraid for him, a marriage
being not so easy to put back together again, and at last I said, "You're a goddamn
good teacher, you know that?"

"Really?"

"Yeah. I stood in the doorway watching you with that last woman. You're really good."

"Well, thanks. I mean, I'm not sure I'm ever going to sell anything as a writer.
But as a teacher—"

I said, "Why don't you go home and take her out somewhere nice."

"Tonight?"

"Hell, yes, tonight."

"Why will I tell her we're going?"

"Tell her because you just realized all over again how much you love her."

He laughed. "You should write sappy greeting cards, Dwyer. That's a great
idea."

"Nobody's ever accused me of that before."

"What?"

"Having great ideas."

Chapter 29

"So who has the suitcase and what's in it?"

"That's the trouble."

"What?"

"I don't know."

We had been in bed for close to an hour now. My shoes were off but that was it. Donna was in her blue thigh-length football jersey with the big 00 on the front. She looked attractively mussed and I wondered what she saw in me anyway.

"You want a back rub?" she said.

"No, thanks."

"You want some underwear inspection?"

"I wish I did."

"You want some herbal tea?"

"Sorry."

"You going to let me help you?"

"I guess not."

"Is it okay if I turn on the tube then?"

"Sure."

"Will you at least take off your clothes?"

So I got out of my clothes and got under the fancy blue-and-white grid work comforter and tried to watch David Letterman.

"He's such an ass," Donna said.

"I know. So why are we watching him?"

"Nothing else on."

"You pay fifty-one dollars a month so you can have thirty-eight cable channels and you say there's nothing else on?"

"You want to argue? Will that make you feel better?"

"Apparently."

"All right," she said. She picked up the remote dial and clicked off Letterman and then sat up Indian-legged with her container of Dannon banana yogurt in one hand and her handful of raisins in the other. A white plastic Dairy Queen spoon stuck out of the Dannon. She always kept her Dairy Queen spoons and she went to the Dairy Queen a lot. "All right," she said.

"All right what?"

"All right your face is sort of messed up from somebody hitting you. And all right your high-school girlfriend is dead, presumably murdered. And all right a crazy, sad woman named Evelyn got blown over her motorcycle by somebody probably equally crazy. So, all right, start talking."

"About what?"

"About how you're feeling."

"I'm feeling like shit."

"So tell me about feeling like shit, Dwyer. Tell me all about it because I can't stand it when you get quiet like this. You just sit there and suffer and it's terrible. For both of us."

"I feel like shit is all. Doesn't that sort of say it?"

"Are you feeling like shit because maybe you sort of got a crush on Karen Lane again?"

"I knew that's what you were thinking. And the answer is no."

"Are you feeling like shit because you don't know what's in the suitcase?"

"Partly."

"What are you guessing is in the suitcase?"

"Something that will explain what really happened to Sonny Howard and will also explain why Forester and Price and Haskins are willing to pay so much for it."

"And who are you guessing has the suitcase?"

"That I don't know yet. That's why I'm going to the park—" I glanced at my Timex. It was well after midnight. "Tonight."

She dropped some raisins into her yogurt and said, "You're kind of menopausal, you know that? I mean the way you deal with things."

"Gee, thanks."

"No. You really are. You kind of go through these hot flashes and do irrational things."

"Such as what?"

"Such as going to the park."

"That's irrational?"

"Of course it is. That's the kind of thing you should call Edelman about. If there's going to be an exchange of the suitcase for money, then the police should be there, not you."

"This is different."

"No, it's not. It's menopausal."

She clicked David Letterman back on. He was being coy as usual because the topic was sex, a subject he seemed to find disgusting.

I lost it then. It all came down on me and I lost it and I grabbed the remote bar and thumbed through several other channels and as the channels flipped by— pro wrestling, an Alan Ladd movie, William Bendix, a severely hair-sprayed man discussing Wall Street—as the channels flipped by, she moved over to her side of the bed and put her face in the pillow.

It took me two or three long minutes to say it. "I'm sorry."

"Right." She started to cry softly.

I leaned over and kind of kissed her arm. "I don't mean to take it out on you."

She kept facing the wall. "I get so damn discouraged about us when you push me away like that. You've been doing it since you walked through the door."

"I want to ask you something."

"What?" Sniffling now.

"I want to know if you'll let me inspect your underwear."

"You bastard," she said.

But she laughed. Or at least she sort of did.

Several times the next morning I thought of calling Edelman. Once I even got into a phone booth. Dialed. Waited while they put me on hold. Ready to tell him what I knew. But then I hung up and got back in my car.

In the afternoon I went into the American Security offices to pick up my paycheck.

Bobby Lee gave me some fudge that she'd made for Donna, and Diaz, the kid who'd put the choke hold on the Nam vet, gave me some grief.

In the back room, Diaz said, "You ever seen these?"

His smirk said it all. He was going to pull something out of his windbreaker pocket that was going to irritate the hell out of me and he was going to love it.

"Diaz, I'm really not up to it today. All right?"

"Here," he said.

He brought his hand out. Over his knuckles were the metal ridges of brass knuckles.

"No more choke holds, man." He looked proud of himself. "Just these babies."

I put my hand out, palm up.

"Give them to me."

"What?"

"I want them, Diaz, and right now."

"Bullshit. They're mine. I paid for them with my own money."

I didn't say anything more. Just went over to the intercom phone and picked it up.

"Hey, what're you doing?"

"I'm going to fire you, Diaz."

"Hey asshole."

"Don't call me asshole, Diaz. You understand?" I punched a button. "Bobby Lee. Is he in?"

Diaz grabbed my shoulder. "Jesus, all right, here they are."

"Never mind, Bobby Lee," I said.

Diaz threw the knucks down on the table. They clanged.

"Enough people are getting hurt and dying these days, Diaz. We don't need to help it along."

I heard it in my voice and so did he. The same tone I'd heard in Evelyn Dain's voice. A kind of keening madness.

Diaz surprised me. He said, "You okay, man?"

"Why don't you just get out of here?" I sensed tears in my voice.

But Diaz, bully-proud in his bus driver's uniform, just stood there and said, "Man, listen, we have our arguments, but they don't mean jack shit. I mean, you're a decent guy. You know?"

I sighed. "Thanks, Diaz. For saying that."

"You let shit get to you all the time. You shouldn't. I worry about you. Everybody here does, man. The way it gets to you."

He came over and patted me on the back. "Can I tell you something?"

"All right."

"You look wasted. You got the flu or something?"

"No."

"Bad night?"

"I'll be all right, Diaz. I appreciate your concern."

But it hadn't been concern at all because as he pushed between me and the table, I saw his right hand go behind his back and lift the knucks and start to slip them into his back pocket.

I brought my fingers up and got him hard by the throat, hard enough that he couldn't talk.

"You got ten seconds to get out of here, Diaz, you understand?"

He nodded.

"And if I find you're using any weapons, including knucks or choke holds on the job, you're out. You understand?" He nodded again.

When I let go, he said, "You need some nooky, man. Or something. You need something, man, and you need it fast."

He said this in a raspy voice. I'd dug into his throat pretty hard.

When he got to the door, he said, "Some night, Dwyer, you and me are going to face it off. You know that?"

But I didn't say anything to Diaz. He was young and hot and worried about his honor. I was thinking of Karen Lane and Dr. Evans and Gary Roberts and wondering if there was any honor left that was even worth worrying about.

Chapter 30

In my apartment I clean and oiled my .38, checked the snap on the shiv I'd once lifted off an extremely successful pimp, and then slid on Diaz's knucks just to see how they felt. They felt good. They really did, and I knew I wanted to use them, in just the same eager bone-smashing way Diaz wanted to use them.

It was five o'clock then and I watched "Andy Griffith" on cable and wished there were a real Mayberry and Aunt Bee and Opie and Floyd the barber and Ange and Barney because I'd go down there and see them all and maybe stay a year or two. And then it was six o'clock and the news came on, AIDS and teenage suicide and crooked local politicians, and I started staring out the window at the spring rain, chill and silver on the window, and the whipping night trees beyond. And then it was seven and cable ran a "Three Stooges" episode before the ball game started, and I just sat there staring at Shemp's face, a face that even as a kid had made me sad, the gravity of the eyes, the frantic deals he tried to make with a world that needed to make no deals at all with his kind. Then I picked up Karen Lane's copy of *Breakfast at Tiffany's* and looked through it for the fifth time, hoping to find something enlightening in it. But it was nothing more than it seemed to be—the favorite book of a girl from the Highlands who saw in Holly Golightly the perfect escape, the one person who seemed to do exactly what she wanted—lie, cheat, steal, care about no one but herself—and be loved for it. Holly might be fine for gentle little books and arch romantic movies, but I'd known a few Hollys in my days and they weren't forgiven or indulged forever. They were punched or even killed or they just moved on, and by age thirty-five the things in them that had been cute or fetching just looked silly and empty, and a meanness overtook them then. Go into half the bars in this town and you'll see women who used to be Holly Golightly. Now they're just drunks with evil mouths and sour memories. "She ought to be protected against herself," said a character on page 104, and I thought about that, about how Karen had needed that. And then I started wondering about the suitcase again and what was in it and thinking that maybe she was trying to protect herself with whatever it held. Then it was eight o'clock and I put a bowl of Hormel chili on the hot plate and crunched up about ten saltines in it. Then it was eight-thirty and I had two cold generic beers and went back to checking my .38 and my shiv and my knucks and knowing I was ready, knowing I needed this. Then it was nine and I went down and got in my Toyota and drove out to Pierce Point.

Chapter 31

The small scarred houses of the Highlands were dark in the rain as I followed the street leading to Pierce Park. The business district came next, and even in the rain glow of neon and wet pavement it looked shabby, the windows with beer signs and the porno shops with long posters of fat strippers promising the least redeeming of pleasures.

Two blocks later I was up in the hills, driving on a two-lane asphalt road that cut through deep hardwoods. The trees looked slick with rain, as if they'd been varnished. On my right, in a clearing, I saw playground equipment yellow in the sudden jut of my headlights, and then a park pavilion with all its benches and tables piled up for winter. Nearby, I cut my lights and pulled off the side of the road, into a grove of timber, so that my car could not be seen from the asphalt. The radio was off. No kind of music could soothe me now. The rain banged on the metal roof. The windows steamed over immediately. Somewhere on the far side of the woods I could see the sprawling lights of downtown, a radio tower with soft blue lights as warning for airplanes a watercolor against the gloom. I checked everything in the big flap pockets of my green rubber rain jacket. Shiv. My .38. Diaz's brass knucks. From the flask in the glove compartment I took a long drink of Jim Beam. It felt hot in my throat but it felt good, and by the time it reached my stomach it felt wonderful. I put up the hood on my jacket and took another quick drink, not so deep this time, and got out of the car.

Where I wanted to go was a quarter mile away. I kept to the timber. The night smelled of dead wet leaves and a skunk that had been killed within half a mile or so. I could see my silver breath. The most real sound was my breathing. I carried just enough extra weight that moving through undergrowth winded me. Twice more I took hits from the flask. To keep me warm, I told myself. A dog came up, some kind of collie whose coloration I couldn't tell because he was soaked. He looked me over and apparently didn't think I was worth bothering with. He went right, deep into the timber, and disappeared. A few times I glanced up at the quarter moon behind gray clouds promising a continuation of the rain. It was a very bright moon, luminous enough to cast long shadows here in the timber. My heavy work shoes crunched pop bottles, beer cans, the plastic odds and ends left here by children playing on sunny days. Then I came to the edge of the timber and stopped, making sure to keep behind the cover of the trees. Here was Pierce Point.

Lovers had moved on to other places these days, but back in the fifties, this was the preferred spot for making out. If you were a male you came to show off your girl, and if you were a rich male you came here to show off both your girl and your car, some of the fancier ones running to chopped and channeled black '49 Mercurys, the kind James Dean drove in *Rebel Without a Cause*, or red street rods with white leather interiors and soft white dice hanging from their rearviews, or customized '55 Chevys with glass-pack mufflers that turned motor sounds into symphonies of power and prowess. The times I'd come up here with Karen Lane, we'd come in my '49 Ford fastback, and once or twice I'd had the impression that she was vaguely embarrassed by the car, as if it marked us—which it did, I suppose—as being from the Highlands, when obviously the rest of the kids were from the better areas of the city.

On the northeast corner of the Point was the edge of a cliff that was a straight quarter-mile drop to pavement below, a road used mostly by heavy trucks on their way to the power plant that squatted like a shining electric icon from a terrifying future. This was where Sonny Howard had dropped to his death.

I held my Timex up to the moonlight. In ten minutes the exchange was to take place. I had no idea how it was supposed to happen, just that it was. I sat in the cold and rain of the timber and waited. In a few minutes I'd meet Karen Lane's killer.

They came in Forester's new Mercedes.

They came right up the muddy road to the middle of the clearing and stopped, leaving their headlights on.

I got out my .38.

The rain was heavier now, almost cutting with ferocity, and in the yellow headlights it was the color of mercury.

The Mercedes just sat there for several minutes. I could see the shapes of three silhouettes through the steamy windows.

Then the driver's door opened up and Ted Forester got out. He wore a London Fog raincoat and a golf hat. In his black-gloved hands, he carried a black briefcase.

In the downpour, he walked to the center of the Point, where a formidable smooth boulder lay, a vestige of the Ice Age, and a perfect surface on which to write the name of the girl you loved. By now thousands of names must have been put on that rock.

Forester walked over to it and looked around as if he knew very well he was being observed, and then he set the black briefcase on top of the boulder that was maybe three feet wide and two feet tall.

Finally, I started to see what was going on here.

Forester looked around some more, hunching under the battering rain, and walked back to the Mercedes.

He got inside and slammed the door.

The Mercedes was put into reverse almost at once. It swept magnificently back onto the muddy road and then proceeded to back all the way out of the Point to the asphalt road, taking the warm civilized illumination of its headlights with it.

Then it was dark again, the quarter moon gone entirely behind clouds now, and there was just the rain and the smell of cold dead leaves. I took out my flask and had another belt. Not a big one or one that was going to impair me. But one I needed.

I didn't, of course, take my eyes from the boulder or the black briefcase resting on top of it.

Ten minutes passed, which surprised me.

Most money drops depend for success on speed. You get in fast and get the loot and leave.

The black briefcase was just sitting here and I wondered why.

But then when the man appeared from the east side of the timber where he'd been hiding, I knew exactly why this had taken so long.

Because he was not a man given to courage. Because he was not a man given to cunning. Because he was not a man given to success in any kind of venture, not even one like this, where he had something that other people wanted very badly.

He came moving awkwardly out of the woods on his clubfoot. He wore one of those disposable plastic raincoats you can buy for a dollar. On his head was a Cubs baseball cap and in his hand was a baby blue suitcase covered with travel stickers.

Halfway to the boulder, he tripped on something and started to fall, arms pushing out to make the fall easier, but then he righted himself and continued on.

He had no trouble making the exchange. He took the black briefcase down and opened it up and looked inside. I thought I saw him smile but I couldn't be sure. Then he closed the black briefcase and set it on the ground next to him and he took the baby blue suitcase and set it up on the rock, and then he turned and started away.

And that's when I moved.

"Stop!" I said.

Terrified, he started moving away. I called, "I've got a thirty-eight sighted right on your back. One more step and you're dead. You understand me?"

That was all it took, that was all it ever took with somebody like him.

I walked across the soggy ground. The rain was relentless. When I reached the boulder, I grabbed the baby blue suitcase. For a moment, it felt strange in my hand—so many people wanted this, it held the secret to so much. Then I hefted it and walked over to him.

I put the .38 right against his forehead and pulled off the safety.

"What the hell you going to do?" Chuck Lane said.

"I want to kill you."

"Jesus, Dwyer. Please. Please."

"She was your own goddamn sister."

"Dwyer, listen."

"Your own goddamn sister." I was getting crazy. I really did want to kill him.

"Whenever she needed money, Dwyer, she'd tap them. I was just going to tap them once myself. The same thing. No different from her." He was gibbering.

"Why would they pay her?"

"Because of something that happened."

"How'd you get the suitcase?"

"I went over to that spade's condo. No sweat." He sounded proud of himself.

"Why is Forester willing to pay for it?"

"You really don't know?" His spaniel eyes looked perplexed.

He had just started to speak when I heard a car come roaring down the muddy road, and before I could even turn around to confirm that it was Forester's Mercedes, the shotgun started firing.

In front of me, Lane's left shoulder exploded into blood and shattered bone. But what was amazing was his gaze. Perfect and complete bafflement, as if this was something he could not fathom. He stared at the large red hole where his shoulder had been and then glanced up at me as if I could explain it.

I pushed him behind the boulder as the Mercedes started its circle. All they had to do was keep circling, firing from a moving car, cutting us both down.

They started on their first pass. I dropped to one knee, grabbed one wrist, steadied the gun and myself, and let go.

I got Dave Haskins, who had been leaning out the back window with a shotgun, right in the face.

For a moment, the car veered toward the trees, lights spraying over the sodden black night. All I could hear was screaming—the sounds Haskins made as he was dying, the sounds Forester and Price made at the terrible prospect of his dying.

Chuck Lane was in a pile against the boulder, unconscious. He smelled now of blood and vomit and his own feces. I reached into his belt and found a .45. I jammed it into my pocket.

The Mercedes started to back up.

I shot out both rear tires. The back end of the car sank abruptly lower.

Inside the car you could still hear Haskins screaming. That and the rain were the only sounds. After thirty seconds or so, Forester cut the headlights. I heard Price say, "Shut up, Dave! Shut up, Dave!" I had to agree with him, the dying sounds were getting unbearable. I wished I'd hit him cleaner. Then I heard the crunch: something heavy against bone. Price had shut him up, apparently crushing what was left of his skull.

Then there was just the sound of the rain and the occasional low moan of Chuck Lane.

A few minutes later the sound of the far back door opening impressed itself on the gloom even above the noise of the rain.

I didn't know which of them it was but it was obvious what they were going to do.

I got Lane by the collar and dragged him to the other side of the boulder.

Then the firing started again. It was impressive. The bullets kept coming for three or four minutes without stop and all the time the only thing I could do was hunch down and say prayers because I was so afraid. I could barely swallow and my stomach was burning all the way up my windpipe. He had an automatic rifle, maybe more than one of them. I did not want to die. I thought of Donna's advice about involving Edelman. I should have.

"They're going to get us, aren't they?"

Lane was awake again, and crying.

"Shut up," I said.

"You're scared, just like me."

"Shut up," I said again.

The gunfire had abated. I tried to listen through the rain. The leaves betrayed him and so did a furtive glimpse of moonlight.

Larry Price was circling to the east of the boulder, fanning out wide, setting himself up for some easy target practice. I shot him once in the face and twice in the chest.

He made no sound other than falling into the leaves. A moist, final sound.

Forester called out, "Larry? Larry?" He was still in the car, sticking his head through the window.

"He's dead," I shouted back.

He had an automatic weapon too. He opened up with it and he kept up with it for two full minutes. Next to me, coming awake, Chuck started to scream. Then I started screaming, too. I was tired of being afraid of dying. I thought of the old number about the man who was so afraid to die, he committed suicide. Only I wasn't going to give Forester that satisfaction.

I put my final two bullets into the gas tank of the Mercedes and watched it go up.

It was impressive against the night—for a moment it was hot and bright as a July noon—and you almost couldn't hear him scream and then you couldn't hear him at all, there was just the beautiful white noise of the explosion itself.

I was watching it all when I felt something bump the back of my head, and I knew that Chuck Lane was even more of a loser than I'd imagined.

"I always carry a spare, man. I'm not a dummy."

"Right, Chuck. You're not a dummy."

"I don't give a shit what you think of me, Dwyer."

He kept punching the gun into my head. It hurt. From inside my jacket I took the shiv. I eased it into my hand. Ready.

"You killed her, your own sister, man," I said.

"Bullshit. I didn't kill her. No way. I stiffed that crazy broad, Evelyn, because if she went to the cops, then the whole blackmail number would be ruined. But not my sister, man. Whatever else, she was blood."

He jammed the gun into my head again. His breath was coming in heaves that were almost sobs. "You're gonna help me to my car, man."

"Sure, Chuck."

"You're gonna help me or I'm gonna kill you."

All it took was ducking a little to the right. He got a shot off but it went wild. Just what you'd expect from a sad, desperate man like Chuck Lane.

I got him up clean, just under the sternum, and I put it all the way in and I twisted it twice, liking the sound of his surprise, and the sound of death.

"Jesus," he said.

And then I saw his face and I had to look away.

"Jesus," he said again. But he wasn't cursing. He was praying.

"You gotta help me, Dwyer," he said.

"There's nothing I can do, Chuck." I still couldn't look at him. All I could do was shake my head.

He started to cry and then he started to vomit and then he started to scream and then he just went silent. Like that, silence.

I knelt there, my back to him, soaked now, listening to the night, the rattle of rain against the trees, a factory whistle announcing a change in shifts.

The fire that had been the Mercedes was burning lower.

I got up then and walked around and stared at each one of them.

In the distance I could hear sirens.

I went back to doomed Chuck Lane, the screw-up. He was still piled up against the boulder. His eyes were open. I got down on my haunches and closed them for him and then I put my hand on his shoulder and said a prayer, a long one, and it was only partly for the men who'd died here tonight. A lot of it was for me, a whole lot of it, and what might be happening to me, the way I hadn't minded taking off Haskins' face, the way the shiv felt right and good jamming up inside Chuck Lane.

The sirens got closer.

Chapter 32

"So they raped her?" Edelman asked me two hours later.

We sat in Malley's. Dolly Parton was on the jukebox. The pool balls were clacking. The rain ran like mercury down the front window. It just wasn't going to stop.

"Forester and Haskins and Price and Sonny Howard," I said. "She hung around them because she was trying to move up the social ladder, get out of the Highlands any way she could, and so she went to their parties and dated Forester sometimes and dated Price others. And then one night they all got drunk and they took her up to Pierce Point and they showed her what poor girls were really worth."

By the end I was making fists.

"You don't sound real sorry they're dead," Edelman said softly.

"I'm trying real hard," I said and without irony. "But I don't know if I'm going to make it."

He nodded to my shell. "How about another one?"

"How about six more?"

"Six more is fine by me."

So we started our way through six more, having shots brought along. "What the hell," Edelman said. "I always secretly wanted to be blue collar anyway." So he knocked back the bourbon and made a terrible face and said, "That was great."

"Right."

He sipped at his beer. "So this Evelyn thought that Karen Lane killed her cousin Sonny?"

"Right."

"Did she?"

"No. After the rape, Sonny started hanging around Karen, and he fell in love with her. He was very guilty about being involved in her rape. So guilty that Forester and the other two were afraid he was going to go to the police and confess. They were the ones who pushed him off Pierce Point. They killed him."

"You ready for another?"

"You're going to?"

"Why not?"

"I'm sure glad you got the other boys to spell you tonight."

"Let them clean things up for once. I usually get the shit detail, anyway." He signaled to Malley for another round.

I thought of what Pierce Point must look like by now. Ten emergency vehicles, red and blue lights startling in the gloom, the dead bodies.

He knocked this one back too, except he coughed. "Christ," he said. Then he smiled. "Being blue collar isn't as easy as it looks."

"Wait till you have to get up some morning and go punch in at some factory.

Staring at stiffs sounds like fun all of a sudden."

He took a handful of peanuts from the red plastic bowl in front of him and said, "So she blackmailed them?"

"She and her brother. Over the years. Never for a lot, a few thousand here, a few thousand there. Then her brother got greedy."

"He took the suitcase. From Doctor Evans?"

"Right."

He paused. "You going to let me see it?"

"I don't think so."

He sighed. Put his hand on my shoulder. "Its evidence."

I put my head down and thought about what I'd found in the suitcase. The story for one thing, the story she told Gary Roberts she wanted him to "touch up" for her, the story that laid it all out. Terrible writing. Confession magazine stuff crossed with the worst sort of Holly Golightly daydreams. But it told it all—the rape, the blackmail, the brother she'd helped drag through life.

But it wasn't the story I'd remember.

It was the clothes. In the Highlands there was a tradition, brought over from the old country, and officially frowned on by the priests, of being buried with any limbs of yours that you might have had amputated during your life. I knew of an old Highlands Irishman who kept the bones of his cancer-riddled leg for forty years till he died, then he instructed his son to throw it into the casket with him.

What Karen Lane had done was not unlike that.

She'd kept the clothes she'd worn the night of the rape. All these long years later the blood soaks were almost black and the torn cotton material faded. She'd even kept her underpants. They'd been in shreds. I'd never know now if she wanted them as evidence or if she wanted to be buried with them, the way some Highlanders would want to be. I'd never know now what to think of her. She would always remain just on the outer edge of understanding, unknowable.

"I better go call my old lady," Edelman said.

I laughed.

"Just wanted to see if you were paying attention."

"Wait till I tell your wife you referred to her as your 'old lady.'"

"I'm just talking the same way everybody else here does." I noticed he swayed slightly walking to the pay phone. I went back to my beer. I stared at all the stuff Malley sold behind the counter, combs, razor blades, breath spray, aspirin, potato chips, decongestants. He was turning the place into a 7-Eleven. Then I noticed his new hand-painted sign listing the prices for his most popular drinks, including 7 and 7s, wine coolers, pink ladies, and shell-and-shot. ("I get tired of being a frigging human menu," Malley always said.)

Then Edelman came back. "I told her I called her my 'old lady.'"

"She laugh?"

"Nope."

"You got problems, my friend."

"I told her you said it first."

"Thanks a lot."

He had some more beer and said, "One more thing bothers me."

"What?"

"Why did Karen hire you to get the suitcase?"

"Because she wanted to stop her brother from really putting the big arm on Forester and the other two. She planned to leave for Brazil next year and she wanted to put the last huge shot on them herself."

"Why Brazil?"

"It's where Holly went."

"Who's Holly?"

"Somebody who never existed, or shouldn't have, anyway."

"You're getting drunk," he said, wiggling a finger at me.

I smiled. "So's your old lady."

I spent the night at Donna's. We had popcorn and then we had underwear inspection and then we watched an "Early Bird" movie called *Curse of the Vampire*, which was actually sort of scary, and then it was dawn and we slept, one of those rare times when she let me sleep touching her (she likes me to have my side of the bed and her to have hers), and then we woke up because she had to go in to the office early and so I sat in bed while she took a shower and kind of scratched myself in various places and picked at myself in others and all the time something kept bothering me, really bothering me, but I couldn't think of what it was. And then I remembered Malley's sign from last night, the one listing all the drinks and prices, the one including pink ladies, and then I recalled what Karen Lane had said right before she died: "One of the pink ladies brought me my drink." And then I remembered something else, too, so I got up and found the phone book and looked up the name of the woman who'd been checking off names at the reunion dance that night, and we had a few words of this and that and then I asked her my question and she said, "Boy, that's a weird one," but she answered it nonetheless and I said thank you and hung up fast.

Donna was still in the shower as I washed my face and brushed my teeth.

She peeked out through the curtain and said, "God, Dwyer, you're going someplace without taking a shower?"

"I figure the world can take it if I can."

"Seriously, Dwyer, you look real intense."

I sighed. "Yeah. I guess I am."

"You going to tell me?"

"Tonight. Over dinner."

She started to yell at me but she was naked and in the shower and there wasn't much she could do.

I went down and got in my Toyota.

Chapter 33

It was a watercolor day, china blue sky, plump white clouds, grass greener than grass had any right to be.

I pulled in the drive and got out of the car and saw she was in back. There was laundry hanging on the line.

"Gosh, hi, Jack," she said.

"Hi."

"You probably came back for another whiff, didn't you?" She laughed. "You're getting addicted."

And I probably was. The laundry in the soft wind smelled fine and clean and made me want to be a little boy with my whole life ahead of me.

She said, "Gary was very relieved when he got home the night before. He said that everything was all right between you two." She wore a clean man's work shirt and jeans and her hair was pulled back in a soft chignon. She was everything I liked about working-class women.

"Everything's fine," I said.

She watched me and I watched her back. We both knew what I was going to say. I looked at her brown eyes and remembered that in her First Communion photograph her hair had been done in perfect little ringlets. She was female in a way as soft and seductive as the smell of fresh laundry, in just that exact way, and I wanted to hold her as I'd held her the night before, when her son had walked in on us.

She started putting clothespins on a pink blouse. She had one clothespin in her fingers and one clothespin between her teeth.

"You not going to hang your pink waitress uniform?"

She stared at me. She took the clothespin from her mouth. "You figured it out." She sounded betrayed.

"Shit," I said. The waitresses that night had worn blue. Karen Lane had mentioned a "pink lady," meaning a waitress in pink. Susan sneaking in to poison her drink.

She said, "You know the funny thing?"

"What?"

"I still liked her." She smiled, and precisely that moment her eyes went silver-blue with tears. "I probably even loved her." She put her hands out to me and I took them and felt the dampness and the roughness of laundry soap and then I slid my fingers further up to where the skin was soft and the down blond and the bones fragile as a poem.

And then I took her in my arms and let her cry and I thought of all the years I was holding here, pigtails and the mysteries of menstruation and prom gowns and hot crazed first sex and life that had borne life and the sad, silent wife she had become when Karen took away gray, failed Gary. And finally I thought of the frail frightened woman here now and I cupped the back of her head in my hand, the chignon coming softly apart, and I lifted her mouth to mine with what I hoped was reverence, and kissed her softly as I had never kissed her as boy or man, kissed her with a curious innocence as I'd always wanted to kiss her, her tears warm and salty now on lips teeth had nibbled on nervously, and I said, "You have a savings account?"

She said, "I've always wondered what it would be like to kiss you. When we used to square dance in sixth grade, I used to kiss my pillow every night and pretend it was you."

I smiled. "Did I kiss well?"

She laughed. "That's the nice thing about being in sixth grade. Everything's perfect."

I said, "I don't have to tell anybody."

"Oh, Jack. Of course you do."

"No, I don't. My friend Edelman the cop thinks that Chuck Lane killed his sister."

"But you'd know."

"I could live with it."

"No, you couldn't." She took my hand and put it to her face. Her tears were as tender as my little boy's hands when he was a baby. She smiled. "You're too much of a guilty Catholic, and so am I."

"You won't like prison."

"No, I don't suppose I will."

"So let's give it a try, all right? A secret just between us?"

She sighed and reached out and touched the laundry and brought it to her nose like a bouquet. "She would have dumped him, of course. Probably after a month or so. If even that long." She started crying again. "He's all I have, Jack. He's all I have."

I took her shoulder. Turned her around. "Susan, listen. I really won't tell anybody. I really won't."

Then I saw the line of her gaze raise slightly as somebody came up behind me. It was her son. The one who'd caught us embracing.

He saw his mother's tears. His hands became fists. He was a Highlands boy, same as me. "He hurting you, Ma?"

"No, honey," she said. "He isn't hurting me." Then she put out her hands for him to take. "Why don't you wait here with me while Jack goes inside to make a call?"

The kid started toward us.

"You sure?" I said.

She nodded. "I'm sure, Jack."

The kid went past me, hands still fists, sneer on his uncertain mouth, taking his mother's hands gently as I had.

"You got a great mom there, kid, you know that?"

He managed to grin a little bit and said, "Yeah, that's what I heard."

I looked at her a long time, the girl of her and the woman of her, and I said, "I'm going to write you a whole lot of letters and tell you a whole lot of things."

"I sure hope you're not kidding."

I had to clear my throat because I was getting bad. I said, "I'd never kid a woman like you, Susan. Never."

Then I went in and did it. Picked up a yellow wall phone in the kitchen and dialed the fourth precinct and asked for Edelman and after I'd told him he said, "It never turns out for shit, does it, kiddo?"

Chapter 34

That afternoon, getting ready for work at the Security company, I went to the back room and found Diaz dropping peanuts into his Pepsi, one of the more arcane rituals he practices, and tossed his knucks on the table to him.

"This some kind of trick?" he said.

"No." A few days ago I'd felt superior to Diaz and his appetites. Now I wasn't so sure.

I turned and started toward the front of the building. "Hey," he said. "I heard all about you on the radio. Shit, man, you wasted those guys."

I didn't say anything. There was nothing to say.

Diaz grinned. "You're a hero, man. You know that?"

"Yeah," I said, "that's what I am, Diaz. A hero."

Then I went back up front and talked to Bobby Lee and asked her if she would please tell me what Elvis had whispered to her on her recent trip to Graceland, the thing that had made her feel a whole lot better.

Because that was just what I needed this soft spring afternoon. I needed to feel a whole lot better.

THE END

The Night Remembers
by Ed Gormam

Thanks to Ruth Ashby for her considerable
contributions to this book.

"The Child"
Without meaning to they stand watching
while it plays; occasionally the round
living face emerges from the profile,
clear and whole like some ripened hour
that rises and chimes unto its end.
But the others don't keep track of the strokes,
dim from toil and sluggish from life;
and they don't even notice how it bears—,
how it bears everything, even then, still,
when wearily in its small clothes dressed up
beside them as if in the waiting room
it sits and keeps on waiting for its time.
—Rainer Maria Rilke

Chapter 1

"Hello."

"Is Faith there?" I said.

"Not right now. I'm Marcia."

"Marcia?"

"The babysitter. I live in the building. I work the night shift at Rockwell. On the line. That's why I can babysit this morning."

"Oh. Where's Faith?"

"I'm not sure."

"She didn't say?"

"Not exactly."

"Marcia."

"Yes."

"I'd like to ask you a question."

"All right."

"Is there something you're not telling me?"

"Is this Mr. Walsh?"

"Yes. Why?"

"She said you'd probably be calling."

"Oh. Did she say anything else?"

Hesitation. "Just that I wasn't, uh, supposed to say anything."

"Say anything about what?"

Hesitation. "Well, you know, the way she left and all."

"What about the way she left?"

Hesitation. "She'll get mad. You know her temper."

"I know her temper."

"So maybe I shouldn't say anything."

"I'm right across the street, Marcia. I can walk over there easily enough."

Sigh. "God, you make it sound like a threat or something."

That, anyway, had been my intention. "So what about how she left?"

"Well."

"Marcia, we're wasting time."

"Well, she was crying."

"Do you know about what?"

Hesitation. "I'm not sure."

"Sure you're sure. Now tell me."

"Well, she found something."

"Found something?"

Hesitation. "It probably isn't anything. I mean, I've got a cousin named Rosie and she found the same thing and the doctor told her it wasn't anything to worry about at all. She has to go back and get it checked every six months or so, but she's fine. Just fine."

"What did she find?"

"I really don't think I should say any more, Mr. Walsh."

"Did Faith tell you how much I care about her?"

"Huh-uh."

"Well, I care about her a lot."

"She said you're a nice man."

"Well, Marcia, put yourself in my place."

"Huh?"

"You call up and a stranger answers and she says she's babysitting and that Faith is gone."

"Oh. Right."

"And furthermore, she tells you that Faith has 'found something' and then she mentions something about a doctor and a cousin named Rosie who has to go back every six months for a checkup. Do you think that would scare you, Marcia?"

"I guess, sure."

"Then you'll tell me?"

"It's just a lump. I really don't think it's a big deal at all."

"A lump?"

"Yeah. On one of her breasts. That's what she found this morning. You know how she gets. Sort of hysterical. I'm not putting her down or anything, but she does kind of overreact sometimes."

"I suppose she does, yes. So where did she go?"

"To her doctor's office. She took a cab."

"Oh."

"So I'm watching Hoyt."

Hoyt is a year-and-a-half. His favorite food is from Dairy Queen. His favorite TV show is *Sesame Street*. Faith insists I am Hoyt's father. I am not convinced of that as yet. "Did she say when she'd be back?"

"Probably two hours or so."

"And she left when?"

"About an hour ago."

"I'd like you to do me a favor."

"Sure."

"I'd like you to leave her a note that says to call me as soon as possible. I'll be at my office."

"All right, Mr. Walsh. I'll write it out right now before I forget it."

I said thank you and hung up.

Chapter 2

That was how Wednesday morning began. With Faith Hallahan, a thirty-two-year-old woman thirty-two years my junior, finding a lump on her breast and rushing off to the doctor's.

After talking with Marcia I went out to the parking lot of the apartment house I manage and got into my blue 1978 Pontiac Firebird. I was stunned enough by the news about Faith that I just sat behind the wheel for a time. I had a cigarette, one of the six a day I was allowing myself of late, and I watched Mr. Fredericks, an aged black man who always seemed to be wearing the same gray cardigan, the same denim work shirt buttoned tight at the top, and the same gray wrinkled work pants. He used to be a postman. He retired when he was fifty-seven and lived for two years in Florida until he found out his Miami daughter was a prostitute. An angry man and a religious man, he found himself incapable of forgiving her and moved back here to Cedar Rapids. He told me all this one Christmas Eve when neither of us had anything better to do than become friends of a vague but necessary sort. Now, he pulled the lid off a garbage can and slammed a greasy grocery sack inside the can with exceptionally violent grace. After putting the lid back, he became aware of my gaze, looked up, and stared at me. He shook his head as if he'd caught me doing something despicable and then went back inside the three-story brick apartment house called The Alma. Rather than have another tenant get suspicious about me sitting out in my car (What would they think? Suicide? Masturbation? Some sort of stroke?), I worked the gas pedal carefully—you couldn't give her too much or too little—and left the parking lot.

"You look surprised to see me," Irma said.

"Not at all."

"I shouldn't be here?"

"Of course you should be here."

"I realize I'm not a licensed private investigator, but I've picked up a few things over the years."

"I'm sure you have."

"You want some coffee?"

"God, that would be great."

"Then why don't you go get us some down at the Big Boy? I'd like cream in mine if you don't mind."

"My pleasure," I said, and left.

Ozmanski and I were members of the Linn County Sheriff's Office a total of sixty-one years—thirty for me and thirty-one for him. Both detectives. We'd met over in Salerno during World War II, just as things were turning the right way for the Yanks. We bowled, fished, drank, played shuffleboard, and, after retirement, opened up a small investigative agency in downtown Cedar Rapids, in one of those gray four-story stone buildings that are falling, one by one, to urban renewal. Mostly our shop does two types of work—trial backgrounds for defense attorneys and background checks for employers. We were in business two years before Ozmanski ran his new Dodge Dart into the rear end of a bread truck out on 149. And died. Everybody assumed he was drinking. Being his partner, I had to defend him and say *hey bullshit you knew Don better than that.* But I assumed he was drinking, too.

Three weeks ago, four months after Don's death, his widow, Irma, started showing up. Not every day. Just once in a while. "To pick up," she'd say. So she'd dust or sweep or ask me if I had any typing that needed doing. The hell of it was, Irma and I had never much gotten along. My dead wife, Sharon, always called Irma a gossip and a troublemaker, and she'd been absolutely right. Every time Sharon and I had any sort of spat, Irma would start the story, under the guise of great sorrow, that we were on the verge of a divorce. She didn't single us out. She spread such stories about everybody. So now when I was nice to her I felt I was being disloyal to Sharon. That probably didn't make a hell of a lot of sense, but when you think about it, very little does.

I got two big paper containers of coffee and walked back to the office. The temperature was fifty-seven and downtown Cedar Rapids was beautiful in the Indian summer day, morning sunlight golden off the windows of the brokerage houses, the breeze soft and warm off the Cedar River two blocks away. At my age, though, you keep flashing back to the way things used to be. I could still taste the strawberry malts Woolworth used to serve at their lunch counter, and the tang of the pickles on their cheeseburgers. Up the street from Woolworth had been the Palace Theater, a second-run place just right for a cop and his family. They'd played a lot of James Cagney and Humphrey Bogart movies for Sharon and me and a lot of Francis the Talking Mule films for the kids. There is absolutely no evidence of Woolworth's or the theater's existence now. They might have belonged to a lost race. Today the downtown is largely a business and financial center unexpected and impressive in a small city like this one, with BMWs and Mercedes-Benzes wheeling around the streets. I still miss the Palace and eating at Tony's next door with my family and listening to Jo Stafford and Nat "King" Cole on the jukebox.

"Visitor?"

"Huh?"

"You got a visitor."

"Oh."

"You won't believe who she is."

I sat her coffee down on the desk and leaned forward to her. Irma is twenty-five pounds overweight, always wears a little-girl blue ribbon in her iron-gray hair (sort of like Petunia Pig, actually), and tends to flowered housedresses that she obviously feels hide her bulk. "Sound carries in this place." I put a finger to my lips. "If I've got a visitor in there, then she probably heard every word you said."

"Oh. I'm sorry."

"No problem, Irma. You just have to whisper is all."

She splayed her hands. "So I'll whisper from now on." She sounded defensive and maybe even irritated.

"Good."

The outer office where Irma sat doubles as the reception area and the working office. You can't work for long in the other office. Too hot. In the winter the steam heat gets overwhelming. In the summer direct sunlight broils the place. About all you can do is have brief conferences with clients and then get out of there. That's why you'll find the reception area packed with two desks, two upright manual typewriters, two phones, and three filing cabinets. And a lot of dust. In a building this old—in stone just above our window is a piece of fancy carving that reads In God We Trust 1888—dust settles slowly but without mercy. It's a perpetual process and God help you if you've got bad sinuses.

"You got any typing or anything?" Irma said. Now she sounded hurt.

"Irma, it's great having you here. I'm sorry I kind of snapped at you."

"It really is? Great having me here?"

Why had I lied? It was terrible having her here. Maybe if I'd kept up the mean stuff she'd have taken the hint and done what she was always threatening to do, go live with her oldest boy up near Green Bay, Wisconsin, the professor who was always in trouble because he was the only supporter of Lyndon LaRouche on the entire faculty. (I'd always voted Democratic, even for McGovern though that had been a pretty tough lever to pull, and that had always bugged the hell out of Ozmanski.)

"This coffee is delightful," Irma said. "You got just the right amount of cream."

I heard all the loneliness and grieving in her voice then and felt, as I usually do, like a total slug. I remembered the way she'd sobbed in spasms at graveside when they'd lowered Don into the ground in his coffin, the sound of that first thrumming shovel of dirt throwing her back in her seat as if she'd been shot. A total slug I was.

I raised my paper cup and saluted her. "Nice to have you here."

Then I went into the other office.

She sat in a perfect blue suit in perfect blue pumps with a perfect blue leather bag on her lap. She had once been beautiful, but even with a few laugh lines at mouth and eyes, even with a little loose flesh on the neck, she was still damn near perfect, one of those prim, trim women who never quite lose their appeal no matter how old they get. Her, I put at forty-five to fifty.

As I closed the door behind me, I noticed how the sunlight made a nimbus of her frosted hair. "Hello," I said.

"You don't remember me, do you?"

I walked into the room. It contained a couch and two wing chairs the building manager had found in the basement. His guess was that they'd belonged to two women who'd run an interior decorating service. Over in the corner was a dead 19" Motorola black and white TV set. It hadn't worked since the Cubs had started using lights at the ballpark. Maybe the set was protesting.

I looked at her more carefully, which was certainly a pleasure, but still I saw nothing familiar about her.

Then I remembered what Irma had said: "You won't believe who she is."

I sat down in the facing wing chair. "I'm sorry if I sound rude."

"Then you don't remember?"

"I'm afraid I don't."

"Pennyfeather. George Pennyfeather."

Then I remembered. Of course. "And you're—"

"Mrs. Pennyfeather. Lisa."

"That's right."

"How is—" I stopped myself. I'd been about to ask, *How is he doing these days?* But that probably isn't the right kind of casual social question to ask about somebody you helped put in prison.

"He's out. Just last week."

"I'm happy for you."

"It's been a long twelve years."

"I'm sure it has." I realized now why Irma had been so amused at the presence of this woman in our office. Most ex-convicts don't send their wives to see the detective who conducted the investigation that ultimately landed them in the slammer.

"He's still innocent, Mr. Walsh. He was when you put him in prison, and he is to this day."

"I see."

"I'm embarrassing you, aren't I?"

"A little, I suppose."

"I don't mean to. I'm speaking without recrimination. I'm simply stating the facts."

"Oh."

"We don't even blame you for thinking he was guilty."

"He was guilty, Mrs. Pennyfeather. He really was."

She waved a sweet little hand dismissively. She even had a perfectly sad little smile for me. "I know you hear this all the time. How this man or that was framed. Over the past twelve years I've gotten to know a number of women whose husbands are in prison. Almost all of them believe their husbands are innocent."

"That's a natural defense mechanism. It's how you deal with that particular kind of grief is all."

"You're awfully philosophical for a policeman."

"Ex-policeman. And not all of us move our lips when we read."

"I've embarrassed you again."

"I'm just not really fond of stereotypes."

Something I said seemed to amuse her. "How about the stereotype of the meek little accountant who couldn't deal with his wife's infidelity in any other way but to kill her lover? That's been a cliché ever since I was a girl, anyway." She opened her blue leather bag, which even from here looked expensive, and took out something that almost shocked me: a package of Lucky Strikes. Women of her generation still smoked—despite all the Surgeon General's reports and rough TV advertising to the contrary—but probably not many of them smoked Luckies. She tamped a cigarette against the pack and then put it between red lips that parted perfectly to receive it. She clicked on a tiny gold lighter and got her cigarette going and then threw her head back and let a long blue stream of smoke escape her mouth. With a delicate fingertip, she daubed a minuscule fleck of tobacco from one of her gorgeous lips.

"First of all, he was never my lover."

"Karl Jankov, you mean?"

"Yes. Karl Jankov. That's not to say that I didn't consider it. At the time, George was having a few—problems, and my life was fairly miserable." She blew out some more smoke and then looked at me with a gaze that managed to be both harsh and seductive. "George and I came from very different backgrounds."

"Your father was a prominent state senator, correct?"

"Yes. He even served a term in Washington, but he was thrown out during the Goldwater debacle. I've always resented that. My father was a very moderate Republican. It's terrible how people blame you for things you didn't do." She stopped herself. A tint of red was in her cheeks. "I wasn't making a reference to George."

"I know."

"I suppose I've grown into this victim attitude. All the years waiting for him to be set free."

"I'd like to ask you a question."

"I'm sure I know what it is." She sighed. Her small hands fidgeted on the surface of her purse. "Why did I come here to see you?"

I nodded.

She put her head down. I looked over at the Merchants Bank building. It filled most of the westerly window.

She raised her head. There was an angry dignity in her eyes now. I would pay for trifling with her, her gaze said.

"I want to hire you."

"I see."

"You hide your shock well."

"Years of practice."

"It makes sense when you think about it."

"What makes sense?"

"My hiring you to prove that George is innocent."

"What?"

"That time it showed. Your nostrils flared a little bit and your eyes narrowed. But why else would I be hiring you, Mr. Walsh?"

"I'm the man who arrested him."

"Believe me, I'm quite aware of that. As is my entire family. At Christmastime Carolyn, my youngest child, used to work herself into a frenzy thinking about her father sitting in prison and you home enjoying yourself. Oh, believe me, Mr.

Walsh, I'm quite well aware of what you've done."

"And you still want to hire me?"

"Who knows the case better?"

"It's been a long time."

"But you'll have access to all the records. Spend an afternoon with them and you'll be caught up to date in no time. I've hired several detectives over the years, and they got nowhere."

I said, "I'm not sure I'll be taking any cases anyway. Not for the foreseeable future."

"Oh? Is something wrong?" She leaned forward in the wing chair like an animal that had suddenly sensed something amiss.

"A friend of mine may be ill. I just can't make any commitments." I tried to picture Faith in the doctor's waiting room. She'd be biting her fingernails and solemnly shaking her head, convinced that the worst possible fate awaited her.

"That is it, then."

"What is?"

"Your slight air of being distracted."

"You're observant."

"I haven't had much else to be the past twelve years. There were friends who thought I should get divorced and friends who thought I should run away and friends who thought I should date. I did none of those things. I sat in our very large house and looked out our very large window and sometimes it would snow and sometimes it would rain and sometimes the sun would be shining and then one day I looked at my son, David, and he was a twenty-five-year-old graduating law school and getting married. And Carolyn was in college. And I was alone. That's when I became observant, Mr. Walsh. Loneliness does that to you—it's a survival technique, I think. You become very aware of deceit and dishonesty on the part of those around you."

"I'm sorry for the life you've had."

"So you don't see any chance that you were wrong?"

"There's always that possibility."

"How diplomatic."

"But I don't think I was. Not as I remember things, anyway."

"If I wasn't Karl's lover, then George would have had no reason to kill him."

"Actually consummating the relationship is irrelevant. People get threatened over things as small as glances and smiles. If your husband was having 'problems,' as you describe them, he was probably predisposed to anger anyway."

She looked at me not with dislike but a certain pity. "How easy life must be for you, Mr. Walsh."

"It's not easy at all."

"To be so certain of yourself and all your perceptions. So certain."

"I think you can see why it's probably not a good idea I work for you."

She stood up. She exhaled the last of her Lucky, blue smoke against the golden stream of sunlight. She put out a slight hand and I shook it. For the first time I saw some sign of what this visit must have cost her. Her mouth had begun to quiver, and her eyes were wet with tears.

"I'm sorry for my sake that you're not more open-minded, Mr. Walsh," she said.

I started to open the door for her, but she stopped me with an upraised hand. She opened the door for herself and went out. She shut the door very quietly. If she'd slammed it, I could have just dismissed her as another crank. But the quiet way reminded me of her lovely sad eyes and the disappointment I had put in them. I would remember those eyes far longer than I would a slamming door.

Chapter 3

"Hi."

"Hi," I said.

"Help you?"

"Oh. You don't know who I am."

"Gee, no, I don't."

"I'm Walsh."

"Oh, Mr. *Walsh*. C'mon in."

"I can hear Hoyt."

"Yeah. He's got some kind of rash. Nothing serious but—Why're we standing out here? C'mon in. I'm Marcia Ramey, by the way. The babysitter you talked to on the phone."

"Right."

"Anyways, I'm Marcia and she isn't back yet."

"Oh."

"Shouldn't be long though."

The apartment was, as always, impeccable, filled with rattan furnishings and hanging plants and huge abstract paintings done in earth tones and signifying nothing. The modular couch was white, as was the daybed pushed against the wall. The floors had been stripped to bare, beautiful wood and polished with painstaking and neurotic love. It was one of the few places I'd ever been that looked *better* than magazine layouts.

"You like some coffee?"

"No thanks, Marcia."

"You want me to get Hoyt?"

"If you wouldn't mind."

"Like I said, he's kind of crabby."

She went and got Hoyt. He wore clean blue pajamas with feet in them. He smelled wonderfully of baby oil and baby powder. She put him on my knee.

"Don't let him sit too square on his bottom," she said. "That's where the rash is."

"Uh-huh."

So we played, Hoyt and I, and I forgot all about Marcia Ramey. I goo-gooed with him, I tickled his chin, I combed his soft blond hair with my fingers, I made silly faces that he took in with his somber blue eyes, and I gave him my comb and let him comb my hair, something he never tires of doing. Hoyt is one of those infants you just know is going to be a linebacker somebody. If you saw him eat, you'd know why.

"He went number two."

"Huh?" I said.

"Number two. The poop shoot. He went."

"Hoyt did?"

"Sure, Hoyt. Who else?"

"I guess that's a good question."

"Anyway, he made lump-lump."

"How can you tell from across the room? I can't tell and he's sitting in my lap."

"I'm the oldest of six brothers and sisters. Mom had arthritis so I took care of all of them. You just develop a nose for that kind of thing, no pun intended."

For the first time, I really looked at Marcia Ramey. She gave the impression of being capable, even athletic, big but in no way fat, attractive if not quite pretty, and filled with the kind of durable good spirits that make you envious. She wore a man's work shirt and blue jeans and white socks and white Reeboks. She came over and snatched up Hoyt and took him into the bedroom and did what she had to. About halfway through the procedure, she got him laughing, something I hadn't been able to do.

I decided on the coffee. I was just raising the cup when I heard the key in the doorway.

She came in and said, "Oh. You're here."

I knew this wasn't the time for a joke. I just nodded.

She came in even farther and went over to the couch and sat herself down with a great deal of decorum. Ordinarily, she sort of flings herself onto it.

"How'd it go?"

"Not sure yet."

"Oh."

"Wish I was."

"I'll bet."

"I'd just as soon not talk about it while Marcia's here."

"I understand."

"Oh, Walsh, the hell with you. You never act like this and you know it."

"Like what?"

"Kissing my ass and being so polite."

"Tell me what you want me to do and I'll do it."

"Get lost. That's what I'd like you to do."

She sat there then and really started crying. Her whole body shook.

I went up to the bedroom door and said to Marcia, "You think it'd be all right if I closed this?"

"Faith come in?"

"Right."

We just sort of stared at each other.

She pantomimed, "Is she all right?" and kept pointing to her mouth as she did so, as if she needed to direct my eyesight as well as my hearing.

I grimaced and shook my head. I closed the door and went back and sat across from Faith.

Today she wore, from the feet up, penny loafers and argyle socks and designer jeans and a mint-green sweater that brought out the green of her eyes. She's red-haired with freckles. But don't think of the pug-nosed variety. No, hers is classical beauty—regal, imposing, and, even at times such as these, just a little arrogant. The hell of it is—for her sake anyway—she'd had one of those terrible childhoods that robbed her of any self-confidence her looks might have given her. "I'm only beautiful on the outside," she's fond of saying in her dramatic way.

"I'd like you to tell me what the doctor said."

"He didn't say anything."

"He didn't examine you?"

She kept right on crying. "Yes, he examined me."

"He didn't draw some conclusion?"

"Yes, he drew a conclusion."

"Well, that's the part I'm interested in. The conclusion part."

"He said he wasn't sure."

"Sure about what?"

"Wasn't sure if it was cancer or not."

"Oh."

So there you had it. The most dreaded word in our vocabulary. Sitting there in this really fine room with rattan and plants and fancy if incomprehensible paintings—and sitting there with a hauntingly good-looking woman—and then the whole thing got spoiled with one little word.

I started trembling. I wanted to cry. If Marcia hadn't been in the other room, I probably would have.

"I'm sure it's going to be all right."

"Please don't say stuff like that."

"I'm sorry."

"Do you know how infuriating shit like that is?"

"I know and I'm sorry and I won't say anything like it."

"Why don't you just slap me? I'm being such a bitch."

"You're perfectly fine."

"Any other time I was acting like this, you'd at least think of slapping me."

I decided to be honest. "Kiddo," I said, "this isn't any other time."

I went over and sat down beside her. I took her hand. It was very cold. I had a terrible image that it would feel like this when she died. I hated myself for thinking it.

"Why don't I fix you some lunch?"

"I'm not hungry."

"I'll bet you didn't have breakfast."

"No, I didn't."

"Then at least let me fix you some soup. You don't even have to drink it. You can just sip it. Like tea or coffee."

"You're a pretty decent guy, Walsh, you know that? Even if you won't admit Hoyt's your son."

"You still got all that tomato soup I bought you on sale that time?"

For the first time, she smiled, sniffling as she did so. "You bought me so much of that crap, Walsh, there'll be soup up there after I'm dead."

Then she realized what she'd said and started crying again.

Chapter 4

Ordinarily, young Master Banister comes on Saturday morning, which is when the BMWs and the Porsches and the Volvos invade our neighborhood. These are the lawyers and CPAs and doctors who own the apartment buildings that have bloomed in the wake of the old Victorian houses that once made Third Avenue so spectacular on sunny Sunday drives. "Rental property" is the correct term. Fill up the apartments and you not only get your bank payment made for you, you also make enough net income to invest in other rental property. Pretty soon you can afford to *hire* somebody like me as your live-in manager.

Anyway, young Master Banister arrived late that Wednesday afternoon, just as the skies turned black and a chill rain began to fall. He and his wife were, he said, headed for Chicago, some sort of Northwestern class reunion, and he needed to check things out with me now since he wouldn't be here Saturday. He hoped, he said, I didn't mind that he'd forgotten to call me in advance.

He brought, as usual, his checklist in the form of a single page of a small leatherbound notebook that he flipped through after carefully wetting the tip of one finger. He was approximately thirty-five with a short earnest haircut, black earnest horn-rim eyeglasses, an earnest white button-down shirt, an earnest blue five-button cardigan sweater, and a pair of earnest chinos that complemented his very earnest black and white saddle shoes. It was the wrong sissy touch, those shoes on a man his age, and it told me more than I wanted to know about young Master Banister.

"Why don't I run it down apartment by apartment?"

"Fine," I said.

"Mrs. Knapp in A?"

"Still complaining that her faucet leaks and keeps her awake."

"We checked it. It doesn't leak any more than all the others."

"All right."

"Mrs. Hester in B?"

"Nothing going on there."

"She still has the cat?"

"Yes."

"She get it declawed yet?"

"Yes."

"Good."

"I told her otherwise you'd evict her."

"You really want to make me the bad guy here, don't you? Is it my fault she's legally blind?"

"She just didn't want to hurt the cat. She said it would be like somebody ripping off her fingernails."

"Hardly."

"You want to ask me about C?"

"Is Mr. Wylie still playing that country western music so loud?"

"Yes, but Mrs. Gamble says she doesn't mind any more. She said she's gotten used to it."

"Fine. D?"

"I still don't think she's a hooker."

"You ever take a close look at her?"

"Of course I have. She's an attractive young woman."

"I still say she's a hooker. When Cindy and I pulled in here a few weeks ago, I saw a man walking her out to the sidewalk and he gave her money."

"Maybe it was her boyfriend."

"Does she have a boyfriend?"

"Not that I know of. But then I don't know everything."

"Implying I do, Mr. Walsh?"

"You want to know about E?"

"Is this the woman who made that remark about me?"

"Yes. Mrs. Kramer."

"She had no right to say what she did."

"You broke in while she was on the toilet."

"I hardly 'broke in.' I own this place. Plus, I didn't know anybody was there."

"Well, she hasn't made any other remarks about you."

"These people have just got to learn some respect." The way he said "these people," you knew he was talking about more than just the residents of The Alma. He meant all people who didn't drive BMWs and who didn't wear earnest black horn-rims and sissy saddle shoes.

"F?"

"F allegedly had the cockroaches?"

"Not allegedly. I saw them too."

"Winter should be here soon enough."

"And?"

"And winter usually takes care of cockroaches."

"Not these cockroaches."

He sighed. He wrote something in his little notebook. "I'll have the Orkin man come out here and have a look. How about G?"

"No problems there. Mrs. Fetzer is very happy now that you put in a new window."

"I didn't break it in the first place."

"I know. But neither did Mrs. Fetzer."

"These people are going to learn someday that I can't fix everything the vandals destroy."

"It got pretty drafty without her window."

"I suppose. H?"

"Mr. Odell says his hot water heater doesn't work."

"He's nuts."

"I know he's nuts, but that's a separate issue."

"Meaning what?"

"Meaning (a) he probably is legally insane. Meaning (b) that his hot water heater doesn't work."

"Do you know how much those cost these days?"

"Do you know how much a hassle it is taking a shower in cold water especially when you're in your eighties?"

"Just ducky. They don't want me to make any money in this place, do they?"

"Would you like to know about I?"

He sighed again. "I suppose they need a roof or something."

"I is fine."

"Really?"

"Really."

"How about J?"

"J is the Randalls and they've still got the same old complaint."

"They're the ones with the dishwasher."

"Right. The dishwasher that doesn't work," I said.

"Just tell them to give me a little time."

"Mr. Banister, they've been waiting a year and a half."

"These people just have no conception of what things cost."

"Right," I said.

"What about K? Still empty?"

"Afraid so. I'm talking to a nurse from St. Luke's Hospital. Just split from her husband and needs a place fast. She seemed to like what she saw, except all the hanging doorknobs sort of scare her a little."

"I told you to fix those."

"I'm not a handyman, Mr. Banister. I told you that when I took the job."

"Then what do I pay you for?"

"You don't pay me. You give me half my rent free for handling all the complaints and making sure that everybody stays reasonably pacified. In a way, it's a glorified security job."

"There are plenty of people who would like this position if you don't."

"Not when they add up the number of muggings, stabbings, and break-ins that go on in this neighborhood in a single month."

"Yes, and it's people just like these tenants of mine who are committing all those crimes, too."

"Mr. Banister, the average tenant here is sixty-five years old. You don't find many muggers that age."

"Well, no matter how old they are they manage to scare the hell out of my wife. She was telling these friends of ours the other night that everybody who lives here looks like one of the living dead."

"Tell her I thank her for the kind words."

He flushed. "Not you, Mr. Walsh. Not you. The others."

I sighed and stood up. "You're running late, no use keeping you."

He smiled, trying to ease some of the anger. "They just have no conception of what I have to spend on this place. No conception at all." He clucked and moved to the door. "You're doing a good job, Mr. Walsh. I didn't mean to imply that you're not. I like having an ex-detective managing my place. Makes me sleep better at night. And I should tell you that goes for Cindy, too. She was telling some of her friends at the country club all about you the other night. What a dependable man you are."

"I appreciate that."

"I'm sorry we got a little testy today."

"We get a little testy every day," I said.

"I suppose it's part of the job."

"I suppose."

Two minutes later he was in his red BMW and headed off to where people who wore saddle shoes preferred to live. He'd forgotten to ask about the other apartments, but there hadn't been anything to report anyway.

I turned back from the parking lot just in time to see the bald, eighty-one-year-old Mr. Odell standing on his second-floor balcony giving the finger in the general direction of the departing BMW. "He's a sissy bastard," he called down to me.

"You get back inside, Mr. Odell. You forgot to put your shirt on and it's thirty-six degrees." In typical Iowa fashion, what had been an Indian summer day was now gray and cold.

"He's a sissy bastard," Mr. Odell repeated and went back inside. He had not only forgotten his shirt, he had also forgotten his dentures, thus somewhat spoiling the effect of his wrath.

Chapter 5

Dinner that evening was a can of Campbell's chicken noodle, three Saltines, and a glass of Hamm's. In the living room I watched *The Andy Griffith Show* first on Channel 9 and then a second episode on Channel 3 from Chicago. It was one of Sharon's favorite shows and now it's mine. I'd like to get up some morning and walk down a sunny street and stop in at the barber shop and have Floyd cut my hair while Barney regaled me with tales of how he conquered reluctant women and bold criminals. Then maybe Andy, in that calm way of his, could tell me why I spent so much time feeling anxious and depressed. If Andy didn't know, who the hell would?

The phone rang three or four times, but it was never Faith. Twice it was people trying to sell me things and once or twice it was tenants with questions. But no Faith.

At nine on the American Movie Classics station a Gregory Peck movie called *The Gunfighter* came on. I was glad I was alone. This particular movie has always had the embarrassing ability to make me cry. I remember the first time I saw it back in the fifties when my two boys were young. There I sat in the Palace Theater with the lights coming up and tears in my eyes. The boys both looked at me and then at each other, and for the next two days it was all they talked about. How Dad was sort of sniffling at the end of the movie. Gregory Peck gets killed at the end by the western equivalent of a snotty young bastard who wears saddle shoes.

At ten the phone rang. There was something urgent and important in the way it rang and I got it right away, assuming it was going to be Faith and I was going to go over there and we were finally going to have our talk about what she'd learned at the doctor's.

"Hello."

"Mr. Walsh?"

"Yes."

"This is Mrs. Pennyfeather."

"Oh. Hello."

"I'm sorry to be calling so late."

"That's fine."

"I'm afraid something's come up."

"I see."

"I wondered, in fact, if you could come out here."

"Out to your house?"

"Yes."

I hesitated. "Mrs. Pennyfeather, I just don't think it would be a good idea."

She hesitated. "Circumstances have changed, Mr. Walsh. I really don't know whom else to turn to."

"Did something happen?"

"Nothing I'd care to go into on the phone. Nothing I can go into on the phone."

"Where do you live, Mrs. Pennyfeather?"

"Out near Bever Park. Off Grande." She gave me the address. "You're coming, then?"

"I'm still not sure this is a good idea."

"This afternoon, when I met you again after all these years, I sensed you were a decent man."

"Thank you."

"I'm sorry I left so abruptly."

"That's all right."

"It's just been such a trying time for me."

"I'm sure it has, Mrs. Pennyfeather."

"I'm really rather desperate, Mr. Walsh."

I sighed. "I suppose I could come out there for a little while."

It was an odd time for it but she started crying then. Very softly. "I'm sorry, Mr. Walsh, I just feel so alone."

"That's all right, Mrs. Pennyfeather."

"You know how to get here, then?"

"Yes. I'll need half an hour."

"Fine. I'll see you then. And thank you. Thank you so much."

In the bathroom I brushed my teeth and shaved and took quick stock of my six-one, one-ninety body. All my life my baby face had been something to joke about and something that had kept me from feeling as rough and tough as I'd wanted to. Rough and tough guys just didn't have baby faces. Now, at my age, the face was something to be thankful for. When I kept my weight down, as now, I looked ten years younger than I should have. In the bedroom I put on a pair of red argyles, a white shirt, black slacks, cordovan penny loafers, and a gray wool sport coat. I went back into the bathroom and ran a comb through my soft white hair. I kept it short, almost in a crew cut, which seemed to make it for some reason seem less old-mannish. The final touch was the Old Spice, which I slapped on with a certain ferocity. I hadn't forgotten that Mrs. Pennyfeather was a damn good-looking woman.

In the living room, just under the framed portrait of JFK that Sharon had bought on a trip to New York the year she'd died of a heart attack, I lifted the receiver and dialed Faith's number. Finally, I had an excuse to call her. I would be going out and just wanted to check in with her.

The phone rang ten times before she picked it up. "I know it's you, Walsh." She hadn't said hello or anything.

"I just wanted to see how you were doing," I said.

"It's just easier right now if I'm alone."

"All right."

"I know I'm overreacting."

"You have to handle it the way you handle it, Faith. There's not any right or wrong way."

"Thanks for saying that."

"It's the truth."

"Maybe we could have breakfast tomorrow morning at Country Kitchen."

"I'd like that."

She paused. "I called my mother tonight."

"How'd it go?"

"She was drunk."

"Oh. I'm sorry."

"When I told her she started crying and carrying on. Just what I was afraid she'd do."

"Maybe you shouldn't have called her."

"She's my mother."

"She's also the woman who ran off and left you before you were fifteen years old."

"She's always been an alcoholic. She couldn't help it."

"I guess."

"You've never liked her, have you?"

"Not much."

"She can be very sweet when she's sober."

I had long ago tired of the subject of her mother. "I have to go out. That's why I was calling."

"Out?"

"A case. Sort of, anyway."

"At this hour?"

"I know."

"When will you be back?"

"Few hours, probably."

"God, I didn't realize how secure I felt."

"About what?"

"About knowing you were just sitting there by the phone. Waiting for me to call. It was really something I depended on."

"It's not like I'm going to Des Moines."

"Still."

I laughed. "Maybe I could get a walkie-talkie."

She laughed, too. "You should've seen Hoyt tonight. He let Sam get up in his lap and they sat there for a long time and watched the Road Runner." Sam was their tabby cat.

"I should be back here around midnight or so."

"I'm sorry. I just have to work through this stuff."

"I know."

"Maybe I'll call you around midnight."

"I'd like that."

"Take care of yourself, Walsh."

"Right. See you."

Chapter 6

The Pennyfeather house was up Grande near Bever Park. Even in the sullen, rainy darkness it looked like a pleasant and prosperous home for pleasant and prosperous people, one of those huge, old amiable white houses with green shutters and gables and even a captain's walk. Easy enough to imagine shiny black Model T's parked out front and the clink of horseshoes being pitched out back.

Three cars were parked in the driveway: a new Cadillac, a Lincoln Town Car, and a blue Volvo. I thought of how anxious Mrs. Pennyfeather had sounded on the phone. Had she panicked and called in other people to help her, too?

I pulled up under bare elm branches dripping silver rain and went up to the door.

The laughter drifting out from the living room startled me. I don't know what I'd been expecting exactly, but certainly not laughter.

I glanced around a chinaberry bush into a living room dominated by a huge fireplace with a sculpted mahogany mantel, fawn-colored matching couches that faced each other across a mahogany drop-leaf coffee table, and three different walls of French doors. Three people sat on each couch. Between them on the coffee table was a cake with innumerable glowing candles, all the more effective because the rheostatic lights had been turned low. The fireplace glowed, too, with a treated log that pulsed slow blue flame.

I wondered if I had come to the wrong place. Perhaps next door.... But just then Mrs. Pennyfeather came through one of the French doors bearing a bottle of champagne. Her smile matched those of the others, and her own soft laugh gathered with theirs.

I knocked.

She did the following in pantomime: she glanced to the right, where the front door was, she made a dramatic gift of the champagne to a beautiful girl in a blue dress who could only be her daughter, she leaned over and kissed the slender man who was her husband, and then she waved a delicate hand in excuse as she moved backward to the front door.

It was still several seconds before she reached it. I inhaled the fresh cold air, then exhaled, watching my white breath in front of me. A neighbor's dog sounded lonely in the long night.

The door came open with a quick *whoosh* and there she was, looking younger than she had earlier today. Perhaps it was the dark strapless cocktail dress or the way her hair was swept up on the side with a small rhinestone comb caught perfectly in the sweep of it.

She surprised me for the second time tonight. Instead of inviting me in, she came out onto the small porch and said, "Thanks for coming."

"You sounded pretty scared on the phone." I nodded inside. "But you're having a party."

"I don't suppose this is anything I should admit, Mr. Walsh, but I'm very good at hiding my feelings. I had to learn that, all those years George was—away."

I shrugged. "That seems fair enough, Mrs. Pennyfeather. I'm just not sure why you wanted me here."

In the shadowy porch light, her expression changed abruptly. She rubbed naked shoulders cold in the dark wintry chill. "Would you follow me please?"

"All right."

We went to our right, so we wouldn't have to walk past the front window. The grass was soggy from the rain, the night scented with dog droppings. "Those darn dogs in this neighborhood," she said. "We don't even have one and yet we have a yard full of—" She let the sentence drop.

The house was more massive than I'd realized, an imposing structure with an overhang roof and a vast screened-in porch on the back where you could imagine Japanese lanterns and fireflies suspended in the velvety night air.

In the back was a two-car garage recently repainted and re-roofed, the shingles gray and shiny in the gloom. Mrs. Pennyfeather may have wanted for companionship and dignity while her husband had been away, but she had obviously not wanted for money.

There was also a gazebo, one of those small but fastidious replicas of band-concert gazebos you used to see in the back yards of the wealthy. Like the garage, the gazebo was many decades old, but it had been kept up with paint and shingles and what appeared to be new latticework. It floated like a dream on the sloping back lawn.

As I approached the gazebo, curious, she put a small gentle hand on my arm. "I'm going to have to do something here I may regret."

"What's that, Mrs. Pennyfeather?"

She looked up at me. "I'm going to have to trust you, Mr. Walsh."

Now I was not only curious but vaguely apprehensive, too. My stomach tightened. "I'm afraid I can't agree to anything unless I know what we're talking about, Mrs. Pennyfeather."

"Just take a look first. Then we'll talk. All right?"

I sighed, thinking better of what I was about to do. She lifted a frail arm and pointed to the gazebo.

I walked through wet grass down the sloping curve of earth to the structure. Ground fog played at my ankles. A quarter moon was beginning to emerge behind the drizzle and the puffy gray-black clouds. The lonesome dog three or four houses away still sounded lonesome.

In shadow, I stepped up into the white gazebo, bringing enough weight to bear that the old wood creaked and let off a scent of damp rotting boards that no amount of paint could disguise. In the cold wind and rain it gave off the aura of summer dying in autumn.

It was then I saw the woman.

She was easily enough found, a heavyset, dark-haired woman in a cheap tan trench coat, hosed thick ankles in cheap black pumps. Next to her an imitation black patent leather purse had sprayed its contents of lipsticks and powder case and cigarettes and used Kleenex like a cornucopia smashed against a wall. She appeared to have been flung into the swing of the gazebo, a blooming rose of sopping red blood discoloring the matronly heave of her chest.

From the jacket pocket of my sport coat I took the small flashlight I always carry with me and put the light on her face.

She had used too much makeup, her face the puffy texture of an aged doll, the lips too red, the eyebrows too black, the eyes hard blue and drained of life, like diamonds from which the color had somehow been sucked.

From habit, I bent down and began playing the flash to the left and right of her, looking for any of the obvious things you hope to find at a murder scene. Later, when the people from the laboratory got here, they would search for those minuscule clues that cheer overworked county attorneys. For now, I wanted the blind-luck items, the cigarette of foreign make, the footprint left perfect in the mud, the murder weapon itself.

Nothing; nothing.

I didn't hear Mrs. Pennyfeather come up behind me. She said, "I don't know who she is."

"Was," I said. "Who she was."

"Oh, yes. Was."

"When did you find her?"

"About an hour ago."

"She was out here?"

"Yes. Just where you see her."

"What were you doing out here?"

"I had gone to the store for some extra ice cream." She pointed to the garage. "On the way back, I cut through here to the back door. I thought it would save some time."

"You're freezing," I said.

She had begun rubbing her shoulders again, hunching into herself.

"Why don't you go inside and get a jacket?"

"Then they'd know something was wrong."

"They're going to know anyway."

"I wanted to talk to you first. The thing I'm least worried about right now, Mr. Walsh, is catching a cold."

I took off my sport coat and draped it over her shoulders.

Her flesh felt distractingly good, even covered with rough little goose bumps like the surface of a cat's tongue.

I put the light back in the face of the dead woman.

"Wouldn't it be horrible?"

"To be murdered?"

"To be murdered—and to have two people standing above you. Not even knowing who you are. It's so—impersonal. At least her loved ones would be crying and mourning her. We don't even care about her, really. She's just a nuisance, not much else."

"Nuisance?"

"Of course. Whom do you think the police will suspect, Mr. Walsh?"

I paused. "I see what you mean."

"They'll go right to George. He was convicted of murder once. It wouldn't be all that difficult to convict him of murder again."

"I suppose you're right. But there's a reason she's here."

"Oh?"

"It's unlikely the murderer killed her in your back yard by coincidence."

"You're ruling out coincidence? My father was a big fan of Stephen Crane's. Have you ever read Crane?"

"Some."

"He believed in a completely random universe. Everything was chance and accident. No God. Just the randomness and the blackness."

I turned off my light. I didn't want the dead woman's face to burn itself into my vision the way a drowning victim's once had. She'd been ten and pig-tailed and a rotted purple by the time two fishermen found her. For weeks after I would sit in my sons' room just watching them sleep in the darkness, trying to protect them, though against what exactly I hadn't been sure.

"How many people are inside?"

She thought a moment. "Seven including myself."

"How long have they been here?"

"Let's see—the first arrived about six o'clock; the last one about seven-thirty, I suppose. Why?"

"Because it's at least a possibility that one of them killed her."

For the first time, she let me see her considerable anger. "You happen to be talking about my husband, my two children; my husband's former boss and his wife and his brother. Hardly the type."

"That isn't what the police are going to say."

"You're alluding, I suppose, to my husband."

"I'm just telling you how the police are going to view it."

"The same way they viewed it the first time—that you viewed it the first time, Mr. Walsh—that George was guilty?"

Before I had a chance to say anything, a vague yellow yard light cut through the darkness collected here beneath the bare maples and elms of the back yard. A confident young man's voice said, "Mother? Mother, are you out there?"

"Over here, dear." To me, she whispered. "My son, David."

He came down from the screened-in porch, a tall, young man in a tan sweater and well-pressed dark slacks. He was clean-cut in the way of a stockbroker, and except for his eyes he seemed open and friendly. Even in the shadows you could detect some troubled quality in his gaze. He carried a bottle of Heineken in his right hand and a single potato chip in the other. He came across the wet grass in an amiable stride that faltered only when I stepped down from the gazebo and he saw that his mother had a companion.

"Hello, David," she said. "This is Mr. Walsh."

He did not like me and did not particularly try to hide that fact. "In case you've forgotten, Mother, there's a party inside for Father."

"Oh, I haven't forgotten," his mother said. "It's just—"

"Why don't you go back inside and I'll talk to Mr. Walsh. I'd like to know what he's doing here."

"We seem to have a problem," I said, already tired of his attitude.

"Oh," he said, "and just what would that be?"

If he had been a little less arrogant, I might have spared him the shock tactics. But he wasn't and I didn't.

I raised the flash and turned it on the dead woman's face.

"My God," David Pennyfeather said there in the cold darkness near the gazebo. "My God."

Chapter 7

"Do you have a family lawyer?" I asked Mrs. Pennyfeather.

"Yes."

"I'd call him after I call the police."

The son was still visibly disturbed. "You know what the police are going to think, don't you?"

"I know," I said. "But the longer we put off calling the police, the worse it's going to look for him."

"Would you—go inside with me?" Mrs. Pennyfeather asked me. "Perhaps you would call the police for us?"

"Of course."

David said, "Do you want me to stay out here—with her?"

"I don't think it would be a bad idea," I said, taking his mother by the elbow. "Thank you, David."

"It's all right. I understand." Those were his first civil words to me.

We went back across the wet, moonlit lawn, the neighbor's dog starting in once again, the wheels of a car splashing through the street out front, romantic music playing low, as background, coming from inside. Just as we reached the back door, she paused and took off my sport coat and handed it back to me. "George has always been the jealous type." She tried to smile but couldn't quite.

We went in through a big shadowy kitchen that smelled of spices and out into a wide dining room. A long formal dining table with a silver candelabrum in the center glistened from scrupulous polishing over the years. The lighted candles cast a soft tan glow in the room.

At the table sat three people, a prosperous-looking man and woman who were dressed up properly, he in an expensive blue double-breasted suit, she in a black evening gown with a gigantic diamond brooch riding her bosom. Lisa Pennyfeather said, "Nedra and Paul Heckart, I'd like you to meet Mr. Walsh."

The couple looked puzzled. Who was I? What was I doing here? Every one of their social instincts said I didn't belong here. I put out my hand. Heckart, who had to be in his early sixties, grabbed on with an almost painful clasp, one that said despite white hair, a bit of jowliness, and a certain air of country-club indolence, he was still a strong and purposeful man.

Mrs. Heckart took my hand, too, though it was a brief social touch and nothing more, nothing to prove in it. Despite the twenty extra pounds that encased her, you could see that in her time she'd been a good-looking woman, bright of gaze and teasing in a pleasant womanly way of rich, full mouth.

The third person was a younger, trimmer version of Paul Heckart. He spoke with a certain secretiveness into a mobile phone. The way he squirmed in the chair, the fist he clenched and unclenched on the table, spoke of a deep anxiety. I wondered if it could have anything to do with a dead woman in the gazebo swing.

He glanced up at me with frank resentment. I was an intruder. The Heckart brothers ran a locally prominent interior design studio for the carriage trade. They were just as snotty as you'd expect them to be.

He said, "Well, Donna, he's your husband. If you don't feel he needs to go into detox for treatment, then I guess I won't bother trying to help anymore." He spoke not in anger but instead with a certain weariness. "I'd better be going now," he said into the phone. He clicked off the connection by pushing his thumb into a button. Shaking his head, he said, "Office problems. They never end.

"It's no use, Paul," he said to the man across from him. "We've done all we can now. About all that's left to do is let him go, I'm afraid."

"God, I hate to do that," Paul Heckart said, sounding genuinely sorry.

Lisa Pennyfeather leaned forward, putting a hand on the man's shoulder. "Richard, this is Mr. Walsh."

"Nice to meet you," he said, not sounding happy at all. He didn't offer his hand. He sat there in an open-necked white shirt and blue blazer looking something like a clothing ad. His silver hair lent him a sophistication his rough blue gaze denied. He was one of those seemingly pampered men whose violence always surprised you. I'd had to arrest my share of rich drunks over the years and while the majority tried to bully you with their connections, there was still a good number who were every bit as given to biting, kicking, and punching as the lowest derelict.

"I have to tell you something," Lisa said.

They sensed the urgency of her tone right away. They watched her carefully.

"I'm afraid the night's been rather ruined."

She couldn't find the words.

I leaned in and said, "Mrs. Pennyfeather found a dead woman in the gazebo out back."

"My God," said Paul Heckart.

"A dead woman?" asked Richard Heckart, trying to absorb what I'd said.

"Poor George," Mrs. Heckart said.

"We're going to have to call the police, of course," Mrs. Pennyfeather said.

"Of course," Nedra Heckart said.

"Would you mind staying here a minute or so? I'm going into the front room and speak with George and Carolyn."

"Of course," Paul Heckart said.

We went into the living room. On one of the fawn-colored couches, seated as close as lovers, sat George Pennyfeather and his daughter, Carolyn. In a blue frock with white lace at top and wrists, she was most obviously her mother's daughter, fetching and gentle in the flickering reddish flames of the fireplace.

Her first impulse was to cock her head curiously, something her mother did quite often, and say, with the soft earnestness of someone far younger, "Hello, Mother. Father was just telling me about your first date."

Her mother offered a sad smile. "Oh, that was a disaster. I'm surprised he even wants to talk about it. I was so prim."

"A goody-goody," Carolyn said, laughing. "And you still are."

My eyes moved to the small man next to her. You see them all the time, the mismatched couples: the man drab, the woman beautiful, and you wonder how and why they ever got together. George and Lisa Pennyfeather were like that, George being short, slender, with thinning gray hair, wire-rimmed eyeglasses, a baggy cardigan sweater, a dull red shirt beneath, and the slightly distracted air of a man who is more alive to internal demons than anything he sees in the material world. He sat slightly slumped, prison-ashen of pallor, offering little smiles that attached to nothing, just a nervous habit, probably, from surviving the wiles of the penitentiary. Seeing him now, I remembered spending three months on the investigation twelve years ago. He'd been like that then—quiet, pained, apologetic. One night, following two hours of intense questioning, he'd said, "I suppose all this is as much a burden on you as it is on me." He'd seemed concerned about me in some way and I'd never forgotten it, the oddness of such a reaction to a man who was trying to arrest you for murder.

"Hello, Mr. Walsh," he said now.

"Hello."

At mention of my name, Carolyn Pennyfeather turned toward me, her eyes filling instantly with anger. "Mr. Walsh?" she said. "What are you doing here?"

I didn't know what to say.

"He's going to help us," Lisa Pennyfeather said gently.

"Help us? Help us with what?" Carolyn Pennyfeather asked. "Help us ruin our evening with Father?"

Now that she was standing, I saw that she, like her brother, stood at least a foot over her parents. She had her mother's good looks, but she also had an assertiveness new to the Pennyfeather lineage.

"I don't want him here, Mother. I don't want him here at all." I put her age at a few years younger than her brother. She was probably twenty-four or twenty-three.

"I'm not trying to ruin your night," I said.

"I—I asked him here," Lisa Pennyfeather said.

"What, Mother? You invited him here?"

"Something's happened."

George Pennyfeather put his palms flat on the cushions of the couch and pushed himself to his feet. Prison had made him old. He took Carolyn's arm. "Honey, Mr. Walsh was only doing his job when he arrested me. Why don't we listen to what your mother has to say?"

I wanted him to be angry, to hate me for all I represented. It would have made a lot more sense to me, and it would have made me feel a lot less guilty. The longer I looked at this forlorn little man, the more difficult it became to imagine him a killer. Then or now.

"There's a woman in the gazebo," Lisa Pennyfeather said.

"A woman?" Carolyn asked. "What woman?"

"We don't know. That's why I asked Mr. Walsh out here. To help us figure out how to handle it."

"Handle what?"

"She's dead, Carolyn. Stabbed."

"What?"

George Pennyfeather's eyes turned ever more inward. He sat back down on the couch, slowly, as if it might be the last act of his life. He looked up at me. "It's starting all over again, Mr. Walsh."

I had to say something for everybody's sake. I could no longer be detached in the way I wanted to be. I said, "I'm going to help you find out what happened here tonight, George." I glanced at Lisa Pennyfeather. "But now I'd better call the police."

"They're going to arrest me, aren't they?" George Pennyfeather said in a dazed voice from the couch.

The strength I'd attributed to Carolyn Pennyfeather went quickly enough. As Lisa showed me to the phone, I saw Carolyn go over to a plump armchair, sit on the edge, and break without inhibition into little-girl tears.

Chapter 8

"So you came out here because she asked you to?"

"Right," I said to the detective named Gaute.

"Kind of strange, don't you think?"

"Me coming out here?"

"Sure. You put her husband away."

I shrugged. "I suppose."

"You mind going over it one more time?"

"Nope."

He turned on a battery-operated recorder he carried in his pocket. He put it close enough to kiss, identified who he was and who I was and what we were talking about, and then said, "You want me to read you your rights?"

I shook my head.

"Go ahead."

"Lisa Pennyfeather called me earlier this evening."

"What time would that be?"

"Approximately ten."

"All right."

"She said something had happened."

"You know Mrs. Pennyfeather?"

"Somewhat. When I was a detective I worked on a case involving her husband."

"A case?"

"A murder case."

"I see. Continue."

"Plus which, she came to my office earlier today."

"Do you mind telling me why?"

"She wanted to hire me."

"Hire you for what?"

"To prove that her husband was innocent."

"Of the murder you arrested him for?"

"Right."

"So what did you do?"

"I declined."

"Why?"

"I felt uncomfortable. Plus I still believe he was guilty of the murder."

"Tell me about tonight."

"I arrived here about ten-thirty. Mrs. Pennyfeather came out on the front porch and led me around to the gazebo."

"How did she seem?"

"Her mood, you mean?"

"Yeah."

"Very calm. I mean, given what she was going to tell me."

"So you saw the woman on the swing?"

"Yes."

"Did Mrs. Pennyfeather know the woman?"

"She said not."

"How did Mrs. Pennyfeather explain finding the body in the first place?"

"She said she'd gone out for ice cream and put the car in the garage when she got back and had to pass the gazebo. That's when she saw the woman."

"Why didn't she see the woman on the way out to the garage?"

"That's a good point."

"You can't answer it, though?"

"No. You'd have to ask Mrs. Pennyfeather."

"How did the people inside react?"

"About the way you'd expect. Shock. Disbelief. Carolyn, the daughter, seemed to take it hardest of all."

"How about Mr. Pennyfeather?"

"He's afraid you're going to blame him for the woman's death."

"Did he say why he thought he'd be implicated?"

"Well, he's only recently been released from prison for one murder. He gets home and a few days later an unidentified woman is found in his back yard. Dead. Anybody would get nervous."

"So nobody inside the house said or did anything that might lead you to think they had something to do with the murder?"

"No."

He shut off the recorder. He was a tall, chunky man in a tan all-weather coat and a snappy gray fedora spattered with raindrops. He smoked a cigarillo with a white plastic tip, and he smelled of Aqua Velva. He was probably fifty. "You got any thoughts on it at all?"

"Not really."

"You don't find it strange she called you?"

I thought about it. "I find it strange, yes. But I don't think she set me up or anything."

"You base that on anything in particular?"

"No," I said. "I think she found the woman and got scared."

"So why did she come to your office this morning?"

I saw what he meant. It did seem awfully coincidental. I looked out at the back yard. It blazed white with lights from the county men doing the medical exam and the lights from Channels 2, 7, and 9. Down some of the white latticework on the gazebo you could see a few lurid splotches of red blood.

"I guess I should talk to Mrs. Pennyfeather a little more," Gaute said.

He put the recorder back into his coat pocket. In profile, his silhouette against the lights in the back yard looked broken and tough. "It all looks pretty strange right now. By morning things should be a lot clearer."

"There's a positive mental attitude."

He smiled. "They gave you that crap, too, when you were working for the county?"

"Sure. They had these psychologists come in every year or so and try to pump us up."

"You see a kid get run over, you just got to keep it in perspective. That kind of stuff."

"You got it."

"What a crock that stuff is."

I laughed. "It doesn't help you a lot when you're really down, that's for sure."

He tipped his hat toward me, starting to make his move to the back yard. "Those shrinks?"

"Yeah?"

"They're crazy. Every one of them."

He went down the steps and into the explosion of light that had made the ground soggy brown, the trees flat black, and the gazebo the drab gray color of all things that die in winter.

Chapter 9

I sat in a room filled with a Baldwin baby grand and several bookcases packed with the book club editions of the past decade's bestsellers. A floor lamp, burning low, made everything shadowy and melancholy.

This was another half hour past the time I'd spoken to Detective Gaute. Through louvered windows, I could see where the police had roped off the front of the lawn to keep onlookers out. The ambulance gone, the crowd was beginning to thin. In the rain the onlookers had the soaked fervid air of religious zealots awaiting a miracle. It was unlikely the dead woman was going to come back from the grave.

I had wanted to say goodbye to Lisa Pennyfeather. Now, seeing that my watch read past midnight, I wanted only to get home. I'd tried Faith's number. The line was busy. I knew what that meant. Whenever she was upset, she took the receiver off the hook. I'd tried the operator just in case. She checked the number and said that there was apparently a problem with the line. She said she'd report it. I said not to bother.

So I sat now with a slick magazine called *Country Home*, staring at pictures of a rambling rustic home Sharon would have loved, leaning into the soft glowing warmth of lamplight and letting my eyes close every few seconds in drowsy bliss. Not unlike Faith, I sometimes dealt with problems by sleeping through them. Unfortunately, I had learned this trick only a few years ago. Before then I'd been given to pacing and cigarettes and coffee liberally laced with whiskey.

In the back yard you could hear the wind in the darkness and then the police and officials moving around in the light-blasted night. Every once in a while there would be a laugh, and in the silence of this small, handsome room the sound seemed vulgar and out of place.

I must have dozed. I heard my name called softly. When I got my eyes opened I saw that the door had been closed, and before it stood the beautiful daughter Carolyn.

"Mr. Walsh?"

I sat up, setting the magazine back on the stand.

"This is sort of embarrassing," I said. "I must have been asleep."

"I'm the one who's embarrassed."

"Oh?"

"For treating you the way I did."

I smiled. "Believe it or not, I've been treated much worse."

She came from the shadows in the circle of light. She was her mother thirty years ago, floating on the generational tide. "I've hated you for so many years now, I'm shaking." As evidence, she showed me a small, well-turned hand. It trembled.

"I would have hated me, too."

"But you were only doing your job. Somehow I didn't realize that until tonight."

"If a man had helped put my father in prison, I would have hated him, too."

She came closer into the soft shadowy light, an anxious animal. Until now, she'd kept her left hand behind her back. Now, she brought it around. It held a white envelope. She leaned forward and gave it to me.

"I'd like you to take this," she said.

"What is it?"

"A check for five hundred dollars."

"For what?"

"I want to hire you."

I slumped back in the seat, unreasonably tired and already hating myself because I knew what was coming, and because I was going to refuse her. "As I said to your mother this morning, I just don't think it's a good idea."

"He knew her."

"I beg your pardon?"

"He knew her. My father knew the dead woman."

"Oh."

"You heard what he told the police?"

"No."

"He told them that he'd never seen her before and had absolutely no idea who she was."

"That wasn't smart. They can check."

"They can and will. That's why I need to hire you."

"Your mother wanted me to prove your father was innocent of the first murder. Now you want me to prove that he's innocent of the second as well?"

She put her hands primly in front of her. The Pennyfeather women had a way of making primness most erotic. "They're connected."

"The first murder and the second?"

"Of course."

"You know that for a fact?"

She shook her head. "But common sense would say so."

"Common sense doesn't get you very far with the law. Not unless you have some sort of evidence to back it up with."

"Think about it. He hasn't been out of prison a week and here a woman is murdered in his back yard. Somebody decided he would be the best candidate for a—well, a frame-up, as melodramatic as that sounds."

"He was framed for the first murder and now he's been framed for a second?"

"Don't scoff."

"I'm not scoffing. I'm merely being properly skeptical. It's something to be skeptical about, don't you think?"

"You know my father. Do you really think he could kill anyone?"

"Sometimes the meekest of people become the most savage of killers."

"Well, that may be so. But not my father."

"I don't see how I can help."

"Check on the woman. Find out whom she knew and what she had to gain from my father."

"Why are you so sure he knew her?"

"Because I saw them together yesterday at Ellis Park."

"You did?"

She nodded. "Yes. I was following him."

"Your father?"

She stared at me with her huge luminous eyes. "It sounds terrible, I know. But each afternoon since he came back he'd go off somewhere by himself, and when he'd come back he'd seem very upset. I asked him about this but he wouldn't say anything. He said he just liked to drive around and enjoy his freedom. But I knew better."

"You didn't hear anything they said?"

"No, I wasn't that close. But I did look in her car and copy down her name and address. They're in the envelope." She looked off into the gloom of a darkened corner. "He's so sweet. So gentle. He has been all our lives. He—Well, you can see how beautiful my mother is. I don't suppose you'd expect her to marry a man like my father. She was obviously pursued by so many more handsome men. But they didn't have any of my father's quiet charm or his dedication to being a husband and a father." She turned back to me, her eyes shiny with tears. I saw her mother again in her face and heard the whisper-soft sorrow in her voice. "There's nobody else I can turn to, Mr. Walsh. Nobody else."

I got up and put my arm around her and she came into my embrace and I held her while she cried. She moved with soft frenzy as she pressed against me. The door opened, and her mother came in and saw us. "Carolyn!" she said. "Honey, what's the matter?"

Carolyn turned from me and started to compose herself.

I said, "She just hired me, Mrs. Pennyfeather."

"Hired you?" Lisa Pennyfeather asked. "But I thought—"

I laughed. "Nobody could resist two Pennyfeather women. Nobody."

"Well, at least looks still count for something in this world," Lisa Pennyfeather said. At another time it would have been a wry observation; now it just sounded forlorn, particularly since it was accompanied by thunder rumbling across the midnight sky.

I said goodbye and was pulling away from the curb in less than a minute and a half.

Chapter 10

On the way home there were a few snow flurries. They made the night seem darker and more endless, and inside my car, the heater roaring, I felt isolated, as if I were trekking along across an infinite and unknown prairie. Drunks from taverns weaved home on foot, angled against the bitter wind and flurries. The closer I got to my apartment house the more patrol cars became evident, a teenage driver stopped here, an aged black man with empty eyes and a shabby topcoat stopped there.

The Alma's parking lot was filled. My spot, clearly marked Manager, was empty. Sometimes I'd come home late, find something there, decide against hassling the residents to find out whose car it was, and park three blocks away, the closest parking area.

Lights shone in only two of the fifteen units as I made my way up the sidewalk to my apartment. The flurries were becoming real snow now. I stood outside my door letting the snow hit my face and melt. I even stuck my tongue out so a few flakes would land there. The first snow always makes me revert to childhood; over on 10th Street S.W. I was the first kid on the block out with my Western Auto sled, even if only a few flurries had been spotted. I smiled at the memory. So many decades ago. It seemed impossible—and even more impossible that the boy of that memory had anything to do with the man who stood here now, all these long years later. There were going to be a lot of different me's crowding that coffin when the time came.

With the door only halfway opened, the first thing I noticed was the smell, the unmistakably pleasant odor of eggs, hash browns, toast, and coffee.

When I got in and closed the door, she came out of the kitchen, an apron tied around the waist of her forest-green shortie robe, a spatula in one hand and a glass of clear liquid in the other. The liquid would be vodka. She liked to drink it straight and warm. She was one of those people who got mildly drunk on two stiff drinks and then coasted on the buzz the rest of the evening.

"You want to go in and kiss Hoyt?"

"Sure."

I went into the bedroom. In the moonlight I could see Hoyt in his blue jammies with the feet. She had him carefully propped between two pillows so he wouldn't roll off the double bed. I went over and bent down and kissed him. His face was warm with sleep. He breathed as if he were slightly plugged up with a cold. Sometimes, like now, I just closed my eyes and held him tight. At these moments I knew he was mine and knew that however thorny my relationship with Faith, she'd given me my life's last important gift. I touched his plump, warm little cheek with my fingers and pulled the covers up to his chest again (Hoyt was a hell of a kicker and could strip his bed in twenty minutes just by rolling around). I plumped his pillows, making sure they'd keep him from falling off.

In the kitchen, she said, "I should get him baptized."

"I'm not pushing."

"You're a Catholic. You know you want him baptized."

"I tried to call you earlier."

"Had the phone off the hook."

"How you doing?"

She looked at me. Her red hair slightly mussed, her green eyes red from crying earlier, she said, "Fair."

"You must be doing better than fair."

"Why?"

I grinned. "The food. Looks like you're going to feed a baseball team."

"Oh. Right." She sounded slightly dazed. "I woke up in my apartment. It was real dark and funny."

"Funny?"

She nodded. "You know how you wake up and you always hear cars going by on Second Avenue?"

"Uh-huh."

"Well, I woke up and I didn't hear anything. It was as if—as if I'd died. It was very dark and there wasn't any sound at all."

I took two steps toward her. I was tall enough to tuck her into my arms. I held her just that way for a long time, closing my eyes as I had with Hoyt. I'd always assumed that because of my age, the first death we'd have to face together would be my own. All that was changed now—at least potentially.

"The bacon," she said.

"The hell with the bacon."

She started crying. "At least turn it off, would you?"

"Sure."

I went over and turned it off, then took out the eight strips and laid them on the double fold of paper towel she'd laid on the counter. I daubed the excess grease off with the towels and then put the strips on a white china plate.

I went back to her and put my arms out but she said, "I guess I just don't feel like being held anymore." She looked at me and kind of shrugged. "I'm sorry." She glanced at the eggs and the bacon and the toast popped up in the silver four-slice. "We should eat."

"You really feel like eating?"

"I don't want to waste the food. It's your food."

"I'm not worried about the food."

"I could try to eat."

"I wish you would."

She ate three eggs, four strips of bacon, and two pieces of toast that threatened to disintegrate under the weight of all the Kraft grape jelly.

"I'd hate to see what you'd do if you ever really got hungry," I said.

She stuck her tongue out. "Very funny."

We sat at the drop-leaf dining room table in the living room, the table I'd bought

Sharon right after World War II, the table at which my boys had eaten while growing up. They were fathers themselves now, one in California and one in New
Hampshire. I'd turned on the small light on top of the TV and opened the blinds
so we could see the snow. It was coming hard and big and fluffy now, and it was
going to stick. If it had been just any other night when Faith and I were getting
along, it would have been wonderful to sit here and feel animal-snug and animal-
warm sheltered from the cold and snow.

She said, "They've scheduled me for a mammogram the day after tomorrow.
You know what that is?"

"Yes. Where?"

"Mercy."

I sipped coffee. "You didn't tell me what the doctor said. At least not exactly."

"I'm sorry about this morning. I was pretty freaked out." Then she smiled.
"God, 'freaked out.' I haven't said that since 1968."

"That's all right. I still say 'scram.' I don't believe anybody's said that since
1939."

"'Scram'?"

"Ummmm."

"I had an uncle who used to say that."

"He probably wasn't your favorite uncle, though."

She smiled. "I guess he wasn't."

"So what did the doctor say?"

"He said that eighty percent of the lumps found in women's breasts are non-
cancerous. They're filled with fluid and called cyst-asperate. A lot of these the
doctor can check right in his office. By touching the lump, he can generally tell
how well defined the edge is, how close to the surface it is." She had a quick hit
of her vodka. "I wasn't that lucky. About him being able to tell right in his office.
He said he just couldn't be sure."

"That isn't necessarily bad news."

"I know. I'm just scared."

"Does breast cancer run in your family?"

"Two aunts. One survived it, one didn't."

"This could all be about nothing."

"I know."

"Your babysitter Marcia said her cousin Rosie turned out to be all right."

"Isn't she great? Marcia, I mean." She was never more enthusiastic than when
she was describing a woman she liked.

She'd had problems with men all her life—too beautiful for some, not beautiful enough for others, though I found that unimaginable—and as a consequence
she spoke with pure delight about women and with great guarded skepticism
about men. Then, "You mind if I stay here for a while?"

I grinned again. "Honey, I've been asking you to move in with me for a year.
Why would I object now?"

"I guess I didn't figure you would."

"Anything you need, you just tell me."

"All right." She paused and looked at me. "There's something I should tell you."

She used a certain tone whenever she was about to tell me something that would hurt me. She used that tone now. "I've been seeing somebody."

"All right."

"Kind of seriously, I mean."

I nodded.

"Seriously for me, anyway. He's the usual rotten jerk. He even hit me once. He gets real jealous and—I don't know what to do."

I could feel my jaw start working.

"You know how I told you once that sometimes I need you to be my lover and sometimes I need you to be my father?"

I cleared my throat. "I remember."

"Well, for a while anyway, I need you to be my father. Do you mind?"

"No, I don't mind."

"I mean, I'm not going to see this guy. I really want it to be over with."

"All right."

"But I don't feel like—well, you know, making love or anything. Can you handle that?"

"Sure."

"And I'm really scared so I'm probably going to be kind of bitchy to be around. Will that be okay?"

I laughed. "Yeah, I sure haven't ever seen you bitchy before."

She reached across the table and put her hand on mine.

"God, I really do love you. You know that?"

I slept on the side of the bed with the nightstand in case the phone rang. I had a tough time getting to sleep. Hoyt rolled over against me and I just held him small and warm against me and looked out the window at the snow in the yard light. Faith went to sleep pretty fast, snoring softly and wetly in the darkness. Just as I started to drift off, Hoyt's considerable little fist bonked me on the nose hard enough to make me tear up. Then I teared up for real and lay there cold and scared. I said a Hail Mary for Faith. I hoped Hail Marys still applied in the modern world.

Chapter 11

"Do you remember it?" I asked.

"Sort of. Pennyfeather?"

"George Pennyfeather."

"Right. Gimme a minute."

The clerk at the sheriff's office had been there for at least twenty years. As a consequence he remembered me, and there was at least a chance that he remembered the Pennyfeather case. I needed to look through the files before I got anything serious accomplished, which was why, twenty minutes after breakfast with Faith and Hoyt, I'd come down to Mays Island, where you find the new Linn County sheriff's building, the Linn County courthouse, and, on the far end of the island, the Cedar Rapids municipal building. The island divides the city in half. Early in Cedar Rapids history the island provided a home for various types of reprobates, including horse thieves and the homegrown version of pirates. Now things are a little more respectable, though I've known some lawyers who hang out at the courthouse who are not necessarily any better than the reprobates of a century and a half ago.

At dawn the snow had stopped, leaving an inch of powdery whiteness that a strong southeasterly wind was blowing away from car windshields and roadways. The sky, framed in the window of the office where I sat, was low and gray. The day's drabness hadn't helped Faith any. She's one of those people who live at the mercy of weather.

While I waited, I smoked a cigarette and looked around at the orderly row of filing cabinets, the General Electric clock radio with the minute hand that no longer swept, and the clean glass ashtray I was about to violate.

He came back in, crisp in his tan uniform and his narrow bald head, sat down behind his desk and said, "Oh, yeah. Right. George Pennyfeather." He skimmed through the pages and said, "He killed this Jankov because he thought Jankov was sleeping with his wife."

"Right."

"And you were the detective in charge of the case?"

"Right."

"How come the Cedar Rapids boys didn't get involved?"

"The killing took place in a fishing cabin out near Ely. County matter. Though they assisted."

"Oh. Right." He looked through a few more papers. "Murder weapon was a .38, never found."

"Mmm-hmmm."

"Witness put Pennyfeather at the cabin fifteen minutes before the shooting." Riffling through additional papers.

"Never pleaded guilty to a lesser charge."

"Apparently he thought he could beat it."

"Or knew he was innocent."

"Thanks for the vote of confidence."

He looked up and smiled, revealing a gold-capped tooth.

"Sensitive bastard, aren't you?"

"I suppose."

"He's back in the news."

"Yeah."

"Dead woman in his back yard."

"Yup."

"I assume he's under suspicion."

"I would think so."

"You going to read this file here?"

"Right."

"I can't let you make copies or anything."

"I understand."

"And all the offices are filled at the moment so you'll have to sit right here."

"Okay."

"I usually walk over to that bakery across the bridge and get a roll. Takes about fifteen minutes in all. Wife makes me because of my weight."

"Yeah, and having that roll probably helps your weight out."

"It isn't a big roll."

"Now who's being sensitive? I was making a joke."

"Cigarettes."

"Huh?"

"I gave up the cigarettes and I put on twenty pounds in the first three months and I still can't get rid of them."

"Maybe that's why I don't quit."

"Well, I'd rather have a gut than lung cancer."

"I guess you've got a point there."

"Also a hint."

"Huh?"

"I wish you wouldn't smoke while you read the file."

"Oh. Right."

"Stuff just hangs in the air and gets into my hair and into my uniforms. Can't stand the smell of it anymore."

He pushed the manila file at me and stood up. "Well, time for my walk." He went over and got a green parka that was part of the uniform. "Good luck."

"Appreciate it."

"You want me to bring you a roll back?"

"I had a good breakfast."

"That's the hell of it."

"What is?"

He zipped up the parka. The noise was louder than you might think here in the quiet of this back office. "I had a good breakfast, too. Now I'm going out after another one."

He gave me something that resembled a salute and left.

Chapter 12

They were never rich or fancy houses, the ones that stretch out Ellis Boulevard along the river, but after the war and well into the Sixties they were the kind of sturdy middle-class homes people I knew wanted to live in. I'm not sure when it changed, when the new Chevrolets and new Fords and the occasional sparkling Pontiac became rusted-out metal beasts that seemed to be dying of some disease... but change it did. The people with good factory jobs moved out, up into the hills, or out into the dense housing development along O Avenue, or over near Edgewood Road where young doctors and other professional people were starting to give the west side a good reputation again. Leaving Ellis Boulevard to the ravages of the night. Oh, occasionally you saw new shingling on a house, or a new roof, or a spanking new paint job, but mostly—smashed windows, junk overflowing on porches, a dead car on the front lawn—mostly the area was sliding into slow and certain death now, hanging on for another generation until the urban renewal monster came along and gobbled it up, decimating the Timecheck area so completely, all trace of its existence would be gone forever except for a few fading photographs in Grandma's photo album or the civic history section in the library.

She lived in one of the worst houses. According to the radio reports, the police had now identified her as Stella Czmek, age forty-eight, unmarried. The reports offered no information about what she'd been doing in the Pennyfeathers' back yard in the first place.

From a beauty shop on the corner came two fat black women. One had plump pink curlers in her hair, the other what appeared to be an almost comically long cigarette dangling from her mouth. Seeing what house I was standing in front of, they frowned at each other and whispered a few things. As they drew near me, the lady with the curlers nodded to the house where Stella Czmek lived and shook her head with a slow sadness.

"Hello," I said.

The woman with the cigarette nodded. "You any relation to Stella?" she asked.

"No. I'm afraid not."

"You heard what happened to her, didn't you?"

"I sure did. Terrible. You knew her, then?"

The lady in the pink curlers had a very pretty face buried in excess flesh. "Not real well."

"She didn't like black people much," her friend said.

"Especially us," said the woman in curlers.

"Why not you especially?"

"Oh," she said, "'cuz one day we was walking past her porch and she flipped her cigarette just so it'd about hit Dolores here. Right on purpose."

"Absolutely on purpose," Dolores said.

"So I told her, right then and there, I said, 'Lady, in case you think you're any better than we are, you just take a look at this house you live in.'"

No doubt about her point. In a long row of dirty gray houses in various stages of falling apart, Stella Czmek's had been one of the grimiest, rust stains like blood running down the filthy white shingles around the small porch.

"What'd she say to that?" I said.

"Called us 'nigger trash,'" said Dolores.

"Bitch," said her friend.

"That was about it, huh?" I said.

"Till about two weeks later, when she got that car."

"Oh, yeah," said Dolores. "You should've seen that car."

"Big?" I said.

"Big ain't the word for it." Dolores giggled. "Try humongous. Right, Esther?"

"Cadillac?" I asked.

"Lincoln," Esther said. "You could sit in the front seat and on this little panel you had controls to do everything."

"Lock all the doors, roll up all the windows," Dolores said.

"Everything."

"It was her car?"

"That's what she said."

"She had money, then?"

Inevitably, Dolores looked at Esther. A tiny frown appeared in the corner of her mouth. She looked back at me. "Are you the police?"

"Nope."

"A friend of hers?"

"Not that, either." I took out my wallet and showed it to them.

Dolores was positively ecstatic. "Just like Mike Hammer on TV!"

Esther pulled the license I was holding toward her. "I'll be damned. I never seen no private eye's license before. This for real?"

"For real."

"The cops was here all morning," Dolores said. "Asked everybody in the neighborhood stuff about her."

"Didn't get much, though," Esther said. "Either people didn't know her or they seen what she was like when she was drunk and they didn't want to know her. And that goes for white and black people the same."

"She drank a lot?"

"Oh, my, did she drink," Esther said, giggling again. "I mean, I maybe shouldn't be sayin' this about her, her just dyin' and all, but she was the worst drunkard on the block. And believe me, there's some champion winos on the block. Some *champions*. See that little grocery store down there?"

I looked down the block. A shabby little place of smashed windows and 6-PK Beer $1.99 signs stood on a corner across the street from the beauty parlor.

"Four times a day," Esther said.

"Four times a day?" I asked.

"That's how many times she'd make a trip to that store."

"She drank beer in the quarts. She'd get two a trip. Plus cigarettes if she needed 'em," Dolores said.

"She have any friends?"

Dolores nodded to the house next door. "Mr. Bainbridge, he talked to her sometimes." She rolled her eyes. "In his line of work, of course."

"What's he do?"

"Well, what he does and what he thinks he does is two different things."

"Oh?"

"What he does is work at the post office sortin' mail. But what he thinks he does is minister to our needs." Dolores laughed. "He got hisself some degree from some bible college in Texas and ever since then he walks around thinkin' his shit don't stink. Excuse my French."

"So he was trying to save her soul?"

"Tryin'," Esther said sardonically.

"What time does Mr. Bainbridge get home?"

"Usually about three-thirty. But he's home right now. Seen him 'bout an hour ago peekin' out from behind that curtain right up there. He was watchin' the police."

"Wonder why he's home," I said, hoping one of them would volunteer an answer.

"Beats me," Dolores said.

"You gettin' cold?" Esther asked her. "I'm gettin' cold and I'm headin' inside."

"Real nice meetin' you," Dolores said.

"Likewise," I said, and gave each of them one of my business cards.

"You a private detective. I just can't get over it."

I smiled and watched them walk down to the end of the block. They waved to each other and went into separate houses, the grave dignity of the womanhood sad counterpoint to the wry girlishness of their laughter.

When I looked up, I saw a pair of eyes behind thick glasses peering from behind burlap curtains and out of morning gloom. The eyes behind the heavy lenses stared down at me from the second floor. As soon as we made eye contact, the curtain flapped shut.

The two-story house had been painted chocolate brown many decades ago. The brown showed everything—dust, mud, rust, even the white undercoating where the shutters over the front window had been torn out and now hung loose. On the porch were stacks of aged newspapers, yellowed and winey with the odor of mildew. Over the doorbell was a small cracked decal of the American flag. Another decal, this one on the small glass pane of the door itself, said, This House Protected by Jesus and Smith & Wesson.

I rang the bell and leaned forward to make certain it rang. It didn't. Inside I heard the noises of an old house settling, and then quick, sharp footsteps on the staircase. I peered into shadow so deep it was virtually like nighttime. All the curtains were drawn.

He opened the door so abruptly, I took a step back, sensing he might attack me.

He was skinny, tall, with an almost grotesquely large Adam's apple, short-trimmed gray hair, pasty white skin, eyeglasses so thick they seemed comic, and blue eyes that spoke of turmoil, grief, and abiding madness. He was probably a few years younger than me. In his plaid work shirt and baggy jeans and house slippers, he looked like the sort of melancholy psychotic you saw roaming the halls of state mental institutions just after electroshock treatment, the pain and sorrow only briefly dulled by riding the lightning.

"I saw you talking to those nigger women," he said. It was an accusation.

I had my wallet ready and showed him my license.

"What's this?"

"Private detective."

He glared at me. "Private detective?"

"Yes."

"About what?"

"I'm trying to find out some things about the Czmek woman."

"Why?"

He used his short, pointed questions the way a boxer uses jabs—to keep his opponent off balance.

"I'm just trying to find out some things about her."

"For who?"

"I'm afraid I can't say."

"You came to the wrong place."

"You didn't know her very well?"

"No."

I stared at him and sighed. "Mr. Bainbridge, all I want is—"

"It isn't 'Mr.'"

"No?"

"No, it's 'Reverend.'"

"Oh. Excuse me. Reverend."

"Inside I have a degree that says I'm a reverend."

"I see."

"But don't think I'm gonna help you just because you call me by the right name."

"All I want is—"

"I know what you want."

"You do?"

"It's obvious."

"It is?"

"You want to know if we ever fornicated."

"I do?"

"That's what those nigger women were telling you."

"Oh?"

"Don't play innocent."

"That doesn't happen to be what they said."

"I don't believe that. They used to spread stories about Stella and me all the time."

Just by referring to her as "Stella" he confirmed what Dolores and Esther had told me.

"How's your ministry doing?"

"What?"

"Your ministry. How's it doing?"

"I suppose you're really interested."

"I am. You said you were a minister. Seems a logical question to ask, how your ministry is doing."

"You know darn well what they did to me."

"They?"

"The people down on E Avenue. At The Church of Jesus Praised."

"I'm afraid I don't."

"Sure you do. That's another lie those two nigger women love to tell."

"About The Church of Jesus Praised?"

He nodded. "'Bout that teenage girl and how I was supposed to've been peekin' in that hole and all. They just said that to get rid of me 'cause I wasn't afraid to say they was preachin' the Devil's gospel." He leaned forward, as if church members might be standing behind me on the porch. His blue eyes glanced about with birdlike speed. "Reverend Cahill is the Antichrist."

"Really?"

He pulled back into the doorway and nodded. "That's why they put that hole in the wall. So I'd look inside just out of idle curiosity. I didn't know no fourteen-year-old girl was goin' to the bathroom in there."

"And as soon as you peeked in that hole—"

"They landed on me. They was just waitin'." Bitterness curled his lower lip. "'Course, they told the police that I put the hole in the wall."

"And the police believed them?"

"They're part of it."

"Part of what?"

"Part of the Antichrist's plan. Who do the police protect today?"

"I guess I'm not sure."

He swelled his chest up slightly and fixed me with a long bony finger out of which he probably imagined a death ray was firing. "Today the police protect niggers and drug dealers and queers. Those are the people who will run this country once the Antichrist has taken over."

"I see."

He eyed me carefully. "You're not a believer, are you?" He was back to making accusations.

"Not in the way you mean."

"You go to church?"

"Sometimes I go to mass. Not very often, I'm afraid."

"Mass," he said, chewing the word as if somebody had just put a turd in his mouth. "You know about the pope?"

I sighed. "This the one about how he has sex with nuns all the time or the one about how he's secretly Jewish?"

"Sarcasm is the Devil's device."

"Look, Reverend," I said, tiring of his madness and no longer able to sustain my pity. He'd be better off shot dead, I thought, despite all my Christian training. His grief was beyond help and his viciousness was dangerous. "I'd just like to ask you some questions about Stella Czmek."

"All I'll say is that she was my friend."

At least this was an improvement over pretending he scarcely knew her.

"Did she come into some money?"

"What's that supposed to mean?"

"I'm told she suddenly started driving around in an expensive new car."

He glared down the street to where Dolores and Esther lived. "Can't keep their mouths shut, can they?"

"You know where she got the car?"

"No."

From the wallet I took a twenty. Before coming over here, I'd driven into Merchants Bank out on Mt. Vernon Road, deposited the check Carolyn Pennyfeather had given me, and taken five crisp twenties from the automatic teller machine.

One advantage a licensed investigator has over a cop is that he can bribe people. In the kind of world we live in, that's one hell of an advantage.

I held the twenty out to him. He looked snake-charmed by the sight of the bill. "I'd like you to take this."

"Why?"

"Call it a contribution to your ministry."

"I ain't gonna tell you nothin' about Stella."

"Here. Please."

I could see him weakening. In a way, it was almost disgusting.

"You ever ride in that car of hers?"

"What if I did? We never fornicated, no matter what those nigger women said."

"It have a nice radio?"

"Very nice."

"I'll bet those nice plump seats were comfortable."

"Real comfortable."

"And those electric windows."

He grinned and I saw the boy in him. The boy looked just as screwed up as the man. "They was fun to do."

"Who do you think gave her the car?"

"Oh, no."

"Pardon?"

"Oh, no. That's what you want, ain't it?"

"What is it I want?"

"That fella's name. The one who come to see Stella sometimes."

"Well, I certainly wouldn't mind if you—"

"Oh, no." He pushed his hand up, almost knocking the twenty from my fingers. "You just go on, git out of here."

"But Reverend—"

"You just git and git fast."

He slammed the door as abruptly as he'd opened it, the sound booming off the snowy gray morning.

At least I'd learned that Stella Czmek had had a friend who was worth trying to track down.

Chapter 13

On First Avenue, near St. Patrick's, I found a drive-up phone and pulled up. For my quarter I got to talk to a female voice who identified herself as the cleaning woman and who told me that none of the Pennyfeathers were home. I asked if she could tell me where they'd gone. She sounded reluctant. "Some things came up," she said.

"I'm a friend of the family's."

"Oh."

"So you'd be doing both them and me a favor by telling me where they went."

"I really don't think I should say anything." She paused again. "They went—" She stopped again. "I'd like to hang up now, if you don't mind."

She didn't wait for an answer.

Sitting in the car, the wind cold through the open window, I took what was left of the phone book (it appeared that some deranged beast had taken out all its anger on it) and looked through the yellow pages for the number of David Pennyfeather's law office.

After the receptionist identified the place, I said, "I'd like to speak to David Pennyfeather, please."

"I'm afraid he's unavailable right now."

"Is he in?"

Hesitation. "Yes."

"Thank you."

Because his office was only six blocks away, in the center of the downtown area, I decided it was worth driving over. I made one more phone call and left.

Following the recession of the early Eighties, Cedar Rapids decided to impose its will on an unfriendly economy. Despite factory closings, long free-food lines, and some bad national publicity, the city gambled on its own future by turning the downtown into a model of refurbishment. Buildings that appeared to be on the verge of desertion were torn up and rebuilt with a ferocity of purpose that unsettled a good deal of the electorate until they finally saw the transformation completed—tall, gleaming buildings; skywalks; rebuilt offices that bore no resemblance to their former crumbling selves. It used to be easy to stand on the corner of Second Avenue and Third Street, say, and imagine how, only a few decades earlier, farm wagons used to roll into town on Saturday mornings bearing sweet little girls in braids and grinning little boys with wide eyes. Cedar Rapids was then a center for all the surrounding farm towns, but now it was a center for much more—national and international business alike. The restoration had been successful in all respects, as the bumper-to-bumper Mercedes-Benzes and all the fast-walking yuppies proved. The blueplate luncheon at the Butterfly used to cost $1.25. Now you could easily drop twenty times that in several of the more fashionable spots. Now it was almost hard to imagine that farm wagons had ever rolled down these streets.

David Pennyfeather's office was on the third floor of a building that had once been a department store. Not that you could tell.

I rode up on the elevator with two young women who carried briefcases and smoked cigarettes with an urgency that said they weren't able to indulge upstairs. They were mysterious creatures to me—attractive without doubt, but aggressive in the way men were aggressive, angry and curt, sarcastic and bitter. I had no doubt that they were a lot tougher than the men from whom they still probably had to take orders.

A massive wooden door meant to impress gave the Trotter, Styles and Pennyfeather law offices the air of a fortress under siege. I put my hand on a doorknob that seemed far too frail to open such a formidable door, and pulled.

Everything was mahogany and leather except the carpet and drapes, which were a sedate red the color of dried blood. In a wooden alcove, bent over a computer screen, was a spiritual sister of the two women in the elevator. Her auburn hair caught in a soft chignon, her knit dress an impeccable and dazzling white, the receptionist seemed to know vast and consequential secrets I couldn't even guess at intelligently.

Disappointment registered quickly in her brown eyes. She probably didn't see many clients dressed in car coats, white shirts, and chinos. "May I help you?"

"I called a few minutes ago about seeing David Pennyfeather."

"I'm afraid he's still busy."

"Would you tell him Mr. Walsh is here? I was at his parents' home last night. He'll probably remember me."

She let her irritation show. I was doing two things wrong. One, I wasn't taking her hint that I should just leave. Two, I was taking her away from her work at the computer screen.

She stood up. "If you'll have a seat over there, I'll go speak with him."

"Thank you."

She nodded and left the reception area. If her body wasn't perfect, it sure came close, tall and lean in a worked-at sort of way. One thing I've got to give my sons' generation. They take care of themselves. Physically, anyway.

First I looked through *Forbes*, and then I looked through a two-day-old *Wall Street Journal*. I had no idea what I was reading. Mostly, I looked for cartoons. *The New Yorker* was a lot more fun to skim through.

I sat in a fat leather chair long enough that one of my legs started to go to sleep. I was stamping my foot, trying to get some circulation going again, when the receptionist came back.

Standing over me, she said, "He can give you a few minutes."

"I appreciate it."

"He's very busy." She was scolding me, angry that he'd agreed to see me at all.

"Thanks again."

She led me down a carpeted hall. Behind various closed doors I heard the rumble of male voices being earnest. On the walls were Grant Wood reproductions.

When I was young, I could never understand why Wood painted the way he had. One day when Sharon and I were on a picnic, though, I stood on a hill just outside of Anamosa and looked down at the blue vein of creek and the green roll of hill and the gathered brown of forest and then I saw it, saw just what Wood must have seen, and ever since, all other nature paintings have seemed slightly wrong to me. He got it right and he was the only one.

David Pennyfeather was waiting for me. He wore a three-piece gray suit and black horn-rim glasses. For all his size, he looked like a mean boardroom version of his mother. He was perched on the edge of his large mahogany desk. His office looked just like the reception area, only smaller.

I put my hand out. He shook it without enthusiasm and broke quickly. "Why don't you close the door, Mr. Walsh."

"All right."

I went and closed it and came back. I glanced down at a chair. He held up his hand. "You won't be here long enough to sit down, so don't bother." He put his hand out palm up. "I'd like the $500 back that Carolyn gave you."

"Isn't that between Carolyn and me?"

"Hardly. Carolyn, much as I love her and much as I respect her intelligence, can be very naive."

"Have you ever considered the fact that I may be trying to help her?"

"To be honest, no. You're a retired cop who runs a nowhere apartment house. I checked you out, Walsh. Personally."

"Did you check far enough to see that I'm a licensed private investigator?"

"If I wanted to hire an investigator, Walsh, I'd hire one of the reputable ones. There's a Pinkerton office as close as Des Moines. For just one example."

"You seem to forget. You didn't hire me. Your sister did."

"Well, I'm just helping her out. Actually, you saved me a trip by coming up here. I talked to Carolyn this morning and she expressed some misgivings about hiring you. I told her I'd take care of it."

"I don't believe that."

"I don't give a damn what you do or don't believe, Walsh." He narrowed his eyes into a practiced gaze. He got up from the desk and pushed half a foot toward me. I had no doubt he was a tough man. He was bigger and younger, and I wasn't stupid. "You were the man who arrested my father. The whole idea of hiring you is ludicrous."

"Your mother doesn't seem to think so."

"My mother's been so hurt and confused she no longer knows what to think."

"So you'll do her thinking for her?"

"That's right, Walsh. That's right."

He went back around his desk and sat down. "We're through now." He put his head down. Apparently my audience had ended.

"Where's your father?"

"Did you hear me? We've finished talking." He kept his head down.

"When I called, the cleaning woman said that something had happened. She wouldn't tell me what."

"It's none of your business."

"Maybe I could help. You've got a nice mother and a nice sister. I've even started to like your father."

"The same man you helped put in prison for twelve years, even though he was innocent?" He let his anger go. It was considerable. He looked miserable now, young suddenly, and frustrated. "Just get the hell out of here, all right?"

I decided to have one last go at it. "You didn't advise him to hide, did you?"

He said nothing.

"That's the sense I got from the maid. That your mother had taken your father someplace. That wouldn't be smart. You know the police are going to want to talk to him."

He sat back. His gaze softened somewhat. "How would you react? You just get out of prison and all of a sudden they're threatening to take you back again. And both times you were innocent."

"Running isn't going to help."

He put his head down again. "They're not running. They're just trying to figure out what to do." He looked up. "Now, goodbye. Do you understand? Goodbye."

I put my hand on the door and let myself out.

Twenty minutes later, parked on Second Avenue, I watched as David Pennyfeather came quickly out of his building. He wore a gray overcoat and a black fedora. He moved without pause.

I followed him to the Second Avenue parking ramp. I waited below. It took five minutes before he appeared again in a new blue Volvo sedan.

He was upset enough that he nearly rear-ended a truck stopped at a light. He was also angry enough that he started leaning on his horn, as if the truck driver was at fault. The driver gave him the hi-sign and then spent the rest of the red light shaking his head about the condition of the human species in general today.

David Pennyfeather moved straight down Second Avenue and across the bridge, at the end of which he took a left.

After another near-accident, this time with a white-haired old woman in a big battered Buick, he clamped both hands on the wheel and began driving with real determination.

Ten minutes later we were on a gravel road that led to the interstate.

We were going out of town somewhere.

Chapter 14

Snow was more obvious in the hills where the horses ran, large white patches of it over the land brown with winter, and on the roofs of the farm houses that hugged the land sloping up to the timberline. Even on overcast days the land holds a severe beauty, milk cows plodding the fallow fields along the fencing, farmers tossing handfuls of yellow feeder corn to hogs like nuggets of gold, the fat lone snowman in the front yard with a green John Deere cap tilted across its eyes of coal, clean winter wind whipping in the bare black trees on the edge of a hill.

David Pennyfeather took the Amana exit, going west as soon as he reached the arterial highway, a two-lane strip of blacktop that skirted the original Amana colonies where the black-clad locals had until a few decades ago rolled back and forth to town in heavy farm wagons and buggies.

I hung back a quarter mile, afraid that he might get suspicious. At a sandy road veering sharply off the highway, he took an abrupt hard right. He must have known the road reasonably well because he didn't slow down at all, taking the first turn around a stand of firs at sixty miles per hour.

When I reached the same spot a few minutes later, I saw that below this road ran another, a narrow, angling devil that led deep into a forest of pines and high red clay cliffs. If he suspected I was following him, he could easily pull off the road, stop his car, and wait for me in a blind.

I had no choice but to go ahead.

Ten minutes later, coming to a stop on the edge of a clay cliff, I saw finally where he was headed.

Below lay a cabin on the edge of the river. In summer, when it was surrounded by blooming trees, you would not be able to see the place. Even now it was hidden behind a windbreak of pines. I'd sighted it only because I'd seen the blue of his Volvo flashing on the other side of the trees as he pulled up to the cabin.

I backed my car off the road, locking everything up, and got out. From here I'd have to do everything on foot.

The first thing I checked was the cliff. It was a sheer drop and I didn't think I could make it down that way. At my age you minimize your risks.

I took the road, which was little more than a winding dirt path that allowed for one car to pass. Arced across the gray sky was a silken pheasant enjoying itself now that hunting season was over. Just around the bend that pitched down to the cabin a fox glanced up from its feast of a dead squirrel, eyeing me cautiously but not threatened enough to move. My feet crunching tiny pieces of ice, I finished the rest of the walk with my collar turned up, a pair of green earmuffs riding my head. My nose felt like an ice cube.

The cabin was a large and fancy affair, built of logs to give it a rustic look but enhanced with housing shingles on the roof, a small satellite dish, and a screened-in porch large enough to seat at least a dozen people comfortably. In addition to the blue Volvo there was a new Cadillac Seville, in dark papal colors, and a small silver Porsche. There was no point in trying to sneak up and eavesdrop. The best way in was the most obvious way. I went up to the screened-in porch and opened the door, walked across a floor covered with dark green indoor-outdoor carpeting, and stepped over to the front door. There was a large black gas grill on the far side of the porch. You could still smell the summer's burgers.

I knocked.

Instantly, you could hear voices cease their talking, and *shush*ing sounds being made as they tried to figure out who was on the other side of the door.

Moments later, David Pennyfeather appeared.

"What the hell are you doing here?" he asked when he saw me.

I looked beyond him to where his mother and father stood in the center of a large room with a beamed ceiling, next to a fireplace crackling with pleasantly smoking logs, a tall stack of which lay next to me near the front door.

"I wondered if I could speak with you a minute, Mrs. Pennyfeather," I said, ignoring David entirely.

He shoved me hard enough to push me halfway back across the porch.

His mother and father shouted for him to stop. They came running. Carolyn, taller than anybody in the family except David, seemed to appear from nowhere and grabbed David's shoulder. "Stop it!" she shouted. "Right now, David! Do you understand?"

"He followed me!" David said.

George Pennyfeather, small and quiet, said, "Let him come in, David. He's only trying to help."

David Pennyfeather took three threatening steps onto the porch. I could see now how bad his temper was. He was having a difficult time getting control of himself. From the weary pleas of his family, it was also easy to understand that they'd had to deal with his anger for many years.

Carolyn Pennyfeather pushed herself ahead of him on the porch. She slammed her hands flat-palmed against his chest. For the first few seconds he managed to push her back but then she dug in with surprising strength and slowed him down considerably. "You stop it, now, do you understand? Do you understand?" She might have been talking to a dog she could no longer control.

Knowing there was no way I could hold my own in a fight with him, I'd picked up a log, wielding it as impressively as possible. He didn't even seem to notice.

"Why the hell did you follow me?" he said. He was still angry, but he was no longer acting irrationally.

Carolyn, still between us, said, "Let's invite him in and sit down and talk. All right, David? All right?"

You could see him collapse inside his expensive gray suit. Miserably, he said, "He's your problem, then, Carolyn. And you deal with him."

She looked back at me anxiously and said, "I will, David. I will. Now you go back in there and sit down. And right now. Right now."

He glared at me once more and went back inside.

Chapter 15

"I hope that's warm enough," Lisa Pennyfeather said fifteen minutes later.

"It's fine," I said.

"I hope I didn't put too much lemon in it."

"I'm sure it'll be just right."

Carolyn laughed, her gentle, beautiful face regal and sad. "This is what I call Mother's 'hostess anxiety.' She can never relax whenever anybody outside the family is in the room. She just can't sit still making sure everybody and everything's taken care of properly."

"She exaggerates," Lisa Pennyfeather said fondly, putting her small hand on Carolyn's shoulder.

"Probably not by much, though," I said. "And speaking of that, why *don't* you sit down?"

"Well," said Lisa Pennyfeather, looking at her husband and son on the plump plaid couch. "Well, I guess I should, shouldn't I?"

She sat down and lighted one of her improbable Luckies.

Rough-sawn cedar boards gave the cabin's interior the proper pioneer feel. Whittled-down ends gave all the boards an old-fashioned pegged look. Old brass and wrought-iron trim finished the motif. Shaggy throw rugs, wicker stands overflowing with magazines and board games, and a good deal of aged but comfortable furniture made me wish I lived here.

"This is a very nice place," I said.

"We all like it," Carolyn said. "Except David." She sat on the arm of the armchair David filled. She poked him playfully. "You never have liked this place, have you? Not even when we were kids." She looked at me and smiled. "He really is just as crabby as he seems, Mr. Walsh."

After a few minutes of seeming relaxed, David appeared uncomfortable again. Not angry; melancholy. There was a sense of real gloom about him as soon as she'd mentioned the cabin.

George Pennyfeather, cleaning his eyeglasses with his tie, said, "I'm still very happy that Paul—Heckart—made us a present of this place that time. His interior decoration business had really taken off at that point, and he was feeling generous."

"It was on our wedding anniversary," Lisa Pennyfeather said to me. "He came over to our house with a cake and candles and then just handed us the keys. He used to let us use it all the time—and then he just gave it to us."

David, still seeming uncomfortable with the drift of the conversation, said, "This is all nice and fine to sit here sipping our tea. But it still doesn't answer the question of what he's doing here in the first place."

"David," George said. "You don't need to be rude."

Prison had neither toughened him nor coarsened him, not in any obvious ways, anyway. He sat there in his yellow shirt and blue cardigan and tan slacks and gray slip-on Hush Puppies as quiet and polite as a seventh-grade English teacher during the principal's visit to class. But of course all this could be deceptive. Many murderers are essentially shy people forced by their own desperation—perhaps by their very shyness—to strike back at a world that has always subtly punished them for not being more demonstrative.

"All right, since my family insists on courtesy, Mr. Walsh, why don't we just let you tell us why you came out here?" David said.

"To help."

"Sure," David said.

"David," Carolyn said. "There's no reason to talk like that." She nodded to me. "Anyway, as I told you, I hired Mr. Walsh."

David glowered. "Well, I unhired him."

"What?" Carolyn said.

"After you told me what you'd done, I took the liberty of phoning your bank and stopping payment on the check."

Her cheeks were tinted with anger. "You had no right to do that. No right at all."

He backed down some. "I'm sorry if I made you angry. I was only trying to help."

I said, "I wonder if you'd go for a walk with me." I was speaking to George.

He glanced at his wife. "Uh, well, of course."

"I'm sure you two have things to talk about," Lisa said. "And by the time you get back, I'll have some sandwiches fixed for you."

"See what I mean about 'hostess anxiety,' Mr. Walsh?" Carolyn smiled.

I smiled too. "She's got it pretty bad. No doubt about that."

"The worst part was the medical care. Or lack of it. I suffer from asthma, Mr. Walsh."

"I hear it's pretty bad. The care, I mean."

"Sometimes I'd have to wait days. And even then you don't always get to see a doctor. You see a nurse and if you come at the end of the day, it's even worse. She's worn-out or crabby and she makes you wish you hadn't come in the first place."

We were walking along the river. Out in the center, tugged by the currents below the choppy dark gray water, a rowboat was being pulled downstream. A tall man in green rubber fishing gear sat with one oar in the water, letting himself be dragged downstream until he found a suitable place to cast. On the far shore the birches looked almost pure white.

A dog trotted along behind us. George Pennyfeather had already said the mutt didn't belong to him. It resembled some odd combination of Husky and Collie. He'd come up every few feet and lick my hand. His tongue was warm and familiar. I thought of our boys growing up, how they'd loved dogs. Now, neither one of them liked pets. They had wives who valued clean houses over companionship.

"I don't imagine any of it was much fun, prison."

"I became religious. That helped a great deal."

I shrugged. "I suppose I would, too."

"The worst part was missing Lisa. That was the absolute worst part. I missed the children, of course, too. But Lisa—well, I've always been one of those men who needed a mother as well as a wife. And Lisa was always willing to be both."

We walked up a narrowing trail. He went ahead. He spoke to me over his shoulder. "Passing the time is the hardest part. I didn't get involved in any of the politics and I learned not to make myself available to anybody for anything. That's the fastest way to get used in prison—sexually or any other way. To make yourself available in some way." He turned and glanced ahead at the leaf-covered hill we were cresting. Then he smiled back at me. "It's a good thing I was the meek CPA type. It prepared me for surviving prison. I knew how to keep my mouth shut."

When we reached the top of the hill we stood looking down at the water bashing the rocky cliff we stood on.

I said, "Lisa still insists you were innocent."

He looked at me almost apologetically. "I know this will probably hurt your feelings, Mr. Walsh, but I was and am innocent. Just as I'm innocent of killing the Czmek woman, though my lawyer was informed that the police will charge me with her murder sometime today."

"That's why you came out here?"

"Yes."

"Running?"

"Not exactly." He tilted his head to stare down at the hard smashing water. "I just wanted some time with my family. If we'd stayed home there would have been reporters and neighbors and relatives. You know."

"Last night you said you didn't know the Czmek woman."

"Yes."

"Carolyn tells a different story."

"I know."

"I doubt she's lying."

"No," he said. "No, she's not. I'm the one who's lying."

"I see."

"I don't think you do, Mr. Walsh."

"No?"

"No. You see, once I said I knew the Czmek woman, then there would be nobody else to suspect of the murder except me. I didn't want to help the police any more than I needed to. No offense."

"Carolyn followed you."

"Yes, she told me."

"Would you tell me why you saw the Czmek woman?"

"I'm afraid I don't know."

"What?"

"I really don't. Know, I mean."

"But Carolyn—"

"Oh, I understand why she thinks what she does. If you'd followed me that day you'd have had the same impression she did. Meeting this strange woman in the park. Arguing with her. And this only a few days after I left prison." He shook his trim little head. No matter how old he got, he would always look like the precocious eight-year-old who knew how to act around grown-ups. "But I'd never seen the Czmek woman before."

"Then why did you meet her?"

"Because she called me and told me she could supply me with the evidence I needed to prove myself innocent of killing Karl."

"Did she say what this evidence was?"

"No."

"Or where she got it?"

"No."

"She wanted money?"

He smiled. "Oh, of course."

"How much?"

"Ten thousand dollars. Cash."

"Did you bring it that day?"

He raised his head to follow the flight of blackbirds against the gray sky. They were headed south. Far behind the others was a tiny fluttering bird that threatened to drop from the sky.

From here you couldn't tell if it had been injured in some way or if the freezing November air currents were simply too much for it. I looked away in case it fell from the sky. I felt helpless enough already with Faith. I didn't need some little bird to remind me again of how powerless we are to help one another.

"Oh, yes, I brought it that day. Wouldn't you if you'd been given a chance to prove you were innocent?"

"Yes, I guess I would."

"Fortunately, Lisa and I come from very wealthy families. Within reason, money's never been a problem for us, or for Lisa while I was in prison."

"So you gave it to her?"

"No. There wasn't time."

"Not time?"

He shook his head.

"She saw somebody and got scared."

"Where?"

"I'm not sure. In the park, I think. Near us. She got very frightened. She said she'd call me later and just took off."

"You didn't get any kind of look at this person who frightened her?"

"None."

"Did she have time to show you any of the evidence she was going to offer you?"

"I'm afraid not."

"So then she just took off?"

"Yes."

"How long did you stay there?"

"Ten minutes. I was stunned. I'd gotten my hopes so high. So had Lisa. We'd let ourselves believe that everything was going to be all right and then—that's why Lisa hired you right after this. To help us."

"Did you see the woman again?"

"No," he said.

"Or hear from her?"

"No. The next time I saw her was in the back yard."

"Did you try to contact her?"

"No."

"How about your family?"

"My family?"

"Did any of them try to reach her?"

He turned to me, disturbed. "What is it you're trying to suggest here, Mr. Walsh?"

"I'm merely looking at all the angles."

"All what angles?"

"The police could certainly make the case that one of your family, disappointed that the Czmek woman didn't come through with the evidence, got angry and killed her."

"They don't even know about her."

"Lisa did. And Carolyn took her name from the car."

"No, it's not possible."

"Then that would leave you."

He sighed. "Yes, I suppose it would. And I'll tell you something."

"What?"

"If they're going to blame any of the Pennyfeathers, I would prefer it be me."

"That's very honorable, but the police will keep looking until they get the right one."

He smiled again, showing for the first time a vague bitterness. "The way you kept looking into my case, Mr. Walsh?" I said nothing. There was nothing to say.

"Are you getting cold, Mr. Walsh?"

"Yes."

"Then why don't we go back. Did you find out what you wanted?"

"Yes."

"It was the Czmek woman you wanted to talk to me about?"

"Right. And turning yourself in."

"I knew you'd come to that."

"It's the best thing for you, Mr. Pennyfeather. Staying out here at the cabin sounds very nice, but it's certainly not going to look very good for you."

"I suppose not. It's just—" He shook off the thought. "I seem to have developed this aversion to correctional institutions. I'm not even sure I could enter the police department without making a total fool of myself. Every night since I've been home, I've had nightmares about being locked up again. The noise. The smells. The violence. They're terrible nightmares, Mr. Walsh."

"I'll be glad to go to the station with you. If you think that would help."

"Oh, that's all right. I appreciate the offer, though."

I watched the dog who'd tagged along lift his leg and send a seemingly endless stream of yellow urine into the grasping roots of a giant oak tree. Steam rose.

I said, looking back at George Pennyfeather, "I meant that. About me going with you to the station."

"Oh, I'm sure you did."

"You just tell me when."

He stared at me. "Are you going to keep working for my wife and daughter?"

"If you'd like me to."

"I would indeed."

"Then I will."

"What if you find out that you put the wrong man in prison?"

I stared back at him. "I'm not sure how I'd handle that. There really wouldn't be any way to say I was sorry."

He laughed softly and then put a small hand against my arm. "Carolyn said she trusted you, and by God if I don't, too, Mr. Walsh. Now that's a big surprise."

We walked back to the cabin.

Chapter 16

Early in the afternoon I ate lunch in my car, Hardees being the culprit. I sat between a panel truck belonging to a plumber and a motorcycle belonging to a guy my age who still obviously remembered Marlon Brando and *The Wild One*. About this time, I assumed, George Pennyfeather would be in his lawyer's office and they would be phoning the police, arranging a time to go over to the police station. While it was not certain that he would be arrested, it was certain that the police wanted to talk to him. After being a good citizen and tossing my crumpled bag into the depository Hardees had prepared for me, I wheeled my car across the street to a drive-up phone. I let it ring twelve times before giving up. Faith and Hoyt had gone someplace. My hand tightened. I could almost feel her bed-warmth in my fingers. Faith, Faith....

Most of my background checks begin at the credit bureau, and for a simple reason. In assessing a person's credit, the bureau collects all sorts of peripheral information. While legislators have debated the legality of the bureau's gathering this information, it is nonetheless just the sort of material you need when you're checking somebody out. You get a lifetime's worth of employers, any pertinent spousal information, and a pretty good sense of how the person has been doing economically. (I've always thought that smart drug czars, for instance, would purposely allow themselves to have a bad credit rating. But then "smart" and "drug czar" are two concepts that usually are mutually exclusive.)

The bureau was busy this afternoon. A neatly dressed woman (big floppy ties were in vogue this season) argued with a clerk about certain things that had been left in her file. A lawyer I recognized from the courthouse gravely pointed out some file items to a very anxious-looking client, the lawyer whispering a bit too loud the phrase, "Chapter 11," as in bankruptcy. A young couple, cheery and confident and enviably in love, chattered amiably with a clerk about their intentions to buy a little house up in the West Highlands area, and therefore needing a Xerox of their record to take to the realtor and to the bank.

I got the Stella Czmek file by convincing the manager that if I didn't get it a client of mine would be in great and abiding trouble. He let me see the file. He was used to my melodramas.

She had been born in 1941, graduated from St. Wenceslaus High School in 1959, worked for ten years at Cherry-Burrell in the shipping department, attended Hamilton Business College at night where she learned secretarial skills including dictation, and had then gone to work for a man named Jerry Vandersee, who operated an import-export business out of the Executive Plaza building. Originally, for the duration of her employment at Cherry-Burrell, her credit rating had been terrible. People's Bank had been forced to reclaim a 1965 Mustang it had loaned her the money to buy; Standard Appliance had sued her for money owed on an Admiral TV console, an Admiral refrigerator, and a Tappan gas range. A revolving charge account she'd had at Armstrongs had been cut off after six consecutive months of nonpayment. She was evicted twice from apartments on First Avenue West for being in arrears on her rent. After finishing her courses at Hamilton, and after joining Vandersee's International Import-Export, her life seemed to improve—not right away and not as if she'd won the lottery, but over the first year with Vandersee you saw steady improvement in her rating. She'd rented a small house up near St. Patrick's, started a modest savings account at Merchants Bank, and paid $500 cash down on a 1964 Plymouth. At this time she married a man named Stan Papajohn, who was then employed by Wilson Packing Company in the hog kill. Four months after the marriage, they moved to a house on Edgewood Road, N.W., where they soon bought a motorboat and successfully applied for credit cards at Killians and Younkers department stores. This was in 1973. The marriage lasted eight years, during which time the Papajohns saw their financial status become very, very good. There was even money for a small lake cottage up on the Coralville Reservoir. After the divorce, things didn't seem to go so well for either of them. Stan Papajohn lost his job when Wilson was sold; Stella Papajohn (who had gone back to calling herself Stella Czmek) was unemployed for nearly two years after the death of her employer, Mr. Vandersee. Nowhere in her file was any mention of children. Apparently broke, Stella Czmek slid back to her old way of life. There were several credit complaints dating from 1982 to 1986. A 1985 Ford Fairlane was repossessed by Farmer's State Bank in Marion. An eviction from an apartment in the Calder Arms led her in 1987 to her last address on Ellis Boulevard.

From a pay phone in the lobby, I called Stan Papajohn. A somewhat harassed-sounding woman answered as a baby cried in the background.

"Mr. Papajohn, please."

"Who's this?"

"My name is Walsh."

"Who you with?"

"Uh, with myself. I have a small investigative agency."

"Investigative agency?" She cupped the phone and shouted at the squalling infant to god dammit shut up. "What kind of investigative agency?"

"I do background checks."

"What're those?"

"Employers hire me to make certain that potential employees are who they say they are."

"Oh." She obviously had no idea of what I was talking about.

"Is Stan there, Mrs. Papajohn?"

"We ain't married."

"I see."

"So I'm Kitty Malloy, not Kitty Papajohn."

"Right. What time does he get home?"

"Why?"

"I'd like to talk to him a few minutes."

"About what?"

Always tell the truth, particularly if there are no other options. "I'd like to ask him a few questions about his ex-wife."

"Why don't you ask me?"

"You knew her?"

"No, but Stan and his brother Jimmy told me all about her. A real ball-buster, take my word for it. She wanted to wear the pants in the family, if you know what I mean."

"Did you ever meet her?"

"Just once."

"When was that?"

"Say, you know she's dead, right?"

"Right."

"Does this have anything to do with that?"

Once again, having no choice. I nobly told the truth. "Yes. I'm working for somebody who's involved in the case."

"Oh."

"You said you met her once."

"Right. She came over here one night, real drunk and abusive and demanding to see Stan. I didn't have no choice but to let him go with her. They went down to the Cedar View."

"The tavern?"

"Right."

"Do you know why she wanted him?"

There was a pause. "You'll take this wrong, if I tell you."

"I'll try not to."

"I don't think he told me the truth. Stan, I mean. And he never did that before. Lied, I mean."

"You're saying you don't know why she wanted him?"

"Right. Oh, he came up with some cock-and-bull story about her needing a loan, but she was always the one with the money, anyway."

"I see."

"She had some inheritance or something."

"That's what she told Mr. Papajohn?"

"Right."

The kid started crying again and once again she cupped the phone and said god dammit Ricky shut up.

"What time does Mr. Papajohn get off work?"

"Three, if he don't work overtime."

"I'd like to leave a message."

"Lemme get a pencil, Mr. Walsh."

The kid was crying. She was saying shut up god dammit as she hung up.

Chapter 17

He was good, but he wasn't that good. He knew how to kind of hang back without exactly hanging back and he knew how to look real interested in other things when we both got stopped at the same red light out on 19th Street. But as soon as I even suspected he was following me, I started taking rights and lefts, out through the plantation-style homes along Blake, and then past the elegant houses sweeping up to Cottage Grove. You've never seen a wooded residential area any lovelier. I was going a long way out of my way and he was going with me.

I swung over to Clark Road then, and finally to Mt. Vernon Road where I quickly pulled into a self-serve car wash. If I'd done my work right, he was going to come screaming down the street any minute now, wondering just what the hell had happened to me.

He came along in one minute and forty-six seconds and boy did he look pissed.

While he was at the stop sign, looking so hard left and so hard right I thought he was going to give himself whiplash, I strolled over to his new metallic green Chevrolet and knocked on the driver's window.

He turned toward me so fast, you might have guessed he'd been shot.

The first thing he did was roll down the window. "Just what the hell do you want?"

"Directions."

"Huh?"

"Why don't you pull over into the 7-Eleven drive there and you can tell me where you're headed."

"Now why would I want to tell you something like that?"

"Because you've been following me for the past hour and I just thought that maybe you knew where we were going. I don't seem to."

"Get lost."

He started to roll up the window. I put my .38 right in his face.

"Hey," he said. "You pulled a gun on me."

"That seems to be the case, doesn't it?"

"What the hell are you doing?" He sounded hysterical.

"Pull over there. And don't try to move too fast. I want to walk right along with you."

"Do you have any idea how many municipal laws you're breaking?"

"Probably a lot of them."

"God," he said, still in the throes of disbelief.

I walked right along with him. I pushed my body close enough to the car that nobody could see the .38 unless they were looking straight in.

He didn't seem to be so much scared as irritated. He just kept shaking his big, bald head. He had shaved it. Apparently he still remembered when Telly Savalas was doing all right with the ladies. He was probably in his early fifties, but the aviator shades and the brown leather bombardier and the white turtleneck sweater were meant to suggest a sixth decade given over to beer-belly macho.

He pulled into the 7-Eleven lot on the far side where I instructed him. I told him to shut off the engine and hand over the keys.

"You're really pushing it, pal," he said. But he gave me the keys.

I walked around the car and got into the back seat. The car still smelled new.

"I'm going to have your ass busted so hard, you won't believe it," he said. He had a way of whining that spoiled his angry words.

"Who hired you?"

"I have no idea what you're talking about."

"Who hired you?" I asked again.

"I guess you're just going to have to shoot me, pal. I don't have a clue about what's going on here."

"Let me see your billfold."

"Why don't I just give you the cash? Let me keep the other stuff. Sentimental value, you know?"

"Billfold," I said.

"You muggers are getting a lot bolder, I've got to say that for you. Walking right up to my car in broad daylight."

He gave me his billfold. It was some kind of crushed black leather. I looked inside. It was right there waiting for me.

"The Conroy Detective Agency," I said.

"So?"

"You just out for a nice drive today, Conroy?"

"So what if I was?"

I dropped the wallet on the front seat. "Now let's see your log."

"My what?"

"Your log."

"I don't know what a log is."

"Right." I pushed the gun against the back of his sleek skull. "The log."

"Huh?"

"Open the glove compartment."

"Why?"

"You know why, Conroy."

"You sonofabitch."

So he opened the glove compartment and took out his log and handed it to me. It was nothing more than a small thirty-five cent spiral tablet. It had a sketchy drawing on the corner of a freckle-faced kid with a mortarboard on. As I took it, Conroy said again, "You sonofabitch."

Most investigators keep logs. It's the best way to document your driving and your expenses, not only for the client but also for the IRS boys.

Conroy stared at me in the rearview as I looked over his morning's entries.

"You jerk," he said.

"I thought I was a sonofabitch."

"You're both."

"Well, that's some kind of distinction, anyway." I handed him his log back.

"Who's at 2987 A Avenue?"

"I'm sure I don't know."

"That's the address you've got written down here."

"Then it must have been by accident."

"Uh-huh. How about the other address, on Mount Vernon Road?"

"Another accident."

"You know, Conroy, when I saw you wearing those shades on a day this overcast, I said to myself, nobody could be that dumb. It must be a disguise. He's disguising the fact that he's actually very bright and in control of the situation."

"Very funny."

"But you know what I found out? You're even dumber than you look, Conroy, and that's an accomplishment, believe me."

"Can I go now?"

"You know how easy it will be for me to find out who hired you now that I've got these addresses?"

"I wish I knew what you were talking about, pal."

Now I was the one who was getting irritated. "We're probably going to meet again, my friend. And next time it won't be half as pleasant as this little routine. You understand?"

"I'm peeing my pants I'm so scared."

I glared at him and sighed. I was the one with the gun and he had me right where he wanted me.

I got out of the car. After I'd walked around to the driver's window, I tossed the keys into the front seat.

"We through now?" he said.

It was one of those times when I wished I had something smart to say, a capper to his line. But nothing came. I walked across the street to the car wash and got into my car.

Conroy took off.

Chapter 18

At a drive-up phone, I called my apartment. Faith answered on the second ring.

"How're you doing?" I asked.

"I was doing pretty good until I turned on the TV. Guess what my favorite soap opera is about today."

"I don't know."

"You can't guess?" She sounded wound pretty tight.

"Faith, I'm afraid I can't guess. I'm sorry."

"Well, what am I worried about? What am I going through? I turn on the TV set, thinking my favorite soap opera will help me get my mind off what's happening to me—and guess what it's about? I mean, don't guess; that was rhetorical. I'll *tell* you what it's about. It's about Beth dying. She just learned today that she's got this terminal illness." She sounded about to cry.

"It's just a terrible coincidence is all. Turn it off and watch something else."

"It isn't a coincidence. Don't you see that?"

"Then what is it?"

"A sign."

"A sign?"

"Sure, it's a sign. It's telling me that I'm going to die."

"Oh, honey, why do you do this crap to yourself? Go play with Hoyt or just watch something else."

"Don't start patronizing me. Just because you don't believe in astrology and stuff."

"It isn't a sign," I said. "I promise."

She didn't say anything for a while. A truck rumbled by.

"Where are you?" she said, sounding notably calmer.

"Drive-up phone on Mount Vernon Road."

"When are you coming home?"

"Now, I'm not sure."

"'Now'? You mean you were sure but now you're not?"

"I was headed home when somebody started following me."

"Somebody?"

"A private investigator named Conroy."

"This sounds like a movie."

"Well, it's true. And now I've got to check out a couple of addresses I took from him."

"'Took'? What's that mean?"

"Nothing important. I'll explain when I get home."

She was silent again. "You really don't think it's a sign?"

"I really don't."

"It's just a coincidence?"

"One time I had a real sore throat and I went to the doctor and he told me I'd better go to a specialist and have it checked. It scared the hell out of me. That same afternoon, I went to this used bookstore where I always go and I bought a detective novel, figured that would get my mind off it, a book called *Blowback*. Guess what it was about?"

"What?"

"This private eye who has to have his throat examined because he may have cancer."

"You're kidding."

"Swear to God."

"You're not just saying this to make me feel better?"

"It really happened."

"And you didn't see it as a sign?"

"No, I just saw it as a terrible coincidence."

"God, I really would have freaked. I really would have."

"Now please just go watch something else, okay? I love you, Faith, and I want you to relax. Do you understand?"

"Thanks. Really. Thanks. You're such a good man. You really are. I don't deserve anybody as good as you. I really don't."

"That's me," I said. "A real prize."

We kissed into our respective receivers and hung up.

Chapter 19

The first address on Conroy's log was a white bungalow on A Avenue N.E., over in what realtors like to call transitional neighborhoods. Not too long ago you would have seen Packards and Chryslers sitting in the drives and also along the curbing. Now the cars ran to ten-year-old heaps whose rusty bumpers proclaimed how they'd visited shrines such as Graceland or Grand Ole Opry or Six Flags in Nebraska. Women of many races—white, black, oriental—dragged reluctant kids along the sidewalk, threatening to spank them or worse, while on the porches, despite the temperature, sad-eyed men without shaves or hope sat sucking on cigarettes and quarts of 3.2 beer. They were waiting for something that had long ago passed them by, and probably without them even knowing it.

The porch tilted when I stepped on it. As I approached the door, I heard whispers inside the front window, and I saw a young girl jump behind a couch. She was playing, probably at her mother's instructions, a game of hide-and-seek, the same sort she'd play when a bill collector came to call. I didn't like the feeling that I was ruining the life of a four-year-old.

I knocked confidently, as if I didn't have anything at all to hide, as if I was the most reasonable and gentle man who'd ever come to call.

This time I saw a woman in her mid-thirties pop up from behind an overstuffed chair and then pop back down. There was something familiar about her, though at the moment I wasn't sure why.

I knocked once more and while I waited moved over a few steps to the rusty black mailbox that was hanging at an angle to the door, held in place by a single nail.

Through a slot in the lid I could see the white edge of an envelope. Quietly, I lifted the lid and took the envelope out. As I'd hoped, it was mail coming in, not going out.

Her name was Kathy Stacek. I knew instantly why she'd looked familiar a moment ago. Kathy Stacek had played a key role in convicting George Pennyfeather of murdering Karl Jankov. She was the witness who testified that she'd seen George at the scene of the crime, and probably carrying a gun.

I put the envelope back, and just as I turned to go back to the door I heard the porch creak and I saw the two of them moving toward me. Obviously they'd been inside. They'd come out the back door and around front.

"What do you want?" the red-headed one said.

They were dressed similarly but not identically. Both big men gone to early-thirties beer fat, they wore chafed black leather jackets, T-shirts, faded and grubby jeans, and motorcycle boots bulked at the toes with steel reinforcement. The redhead had more scars than the blond-haired guy. Both of them looked in need of jobs, shaves, baths, and dental work.

"I was hoping to speak with Kathy," I said.

"Kathy don't want to speak with you," the redhead said.

"You mind if she tells me that herself?"

By now they were on the porch. I'd expected an argument, some macho banter back and forth, but they surprised me by getting down to business right away.

The redhead got me by the shoulder and slammed me face first into the front door. I could taste the dry dust drifting up from the rusty screen. He got my arm behind me and bent it sharp and fast.

"Hey, Christ, Johnny," said his buddy. "Take it easy. This guy's gotta be sixty years old."

"Who the hell are you?" Johnny said, and gave my arm another sharp twist that again pushed my head into the screen door.

"My name's Walsh," I said. "I'm a private investigator."

"What the hell you doin' here?"

More pressure on my arm. I could feel the pain all the way up into my shoulder.

"I saw this address in a log."

"What log?"

"Belonging to another private investigator. Conroy."

"That's who that sonofabitch was this morning," Johnny said to his pal. "I told you, Eugene. I told you he was some kind of cop or something."

Apparently, Johnny was of the opinion that he could get back at Conroy by hurting me. I looked down the street. Nobody seemed to be paying any attention to a white-haired guy pushed up against the door while two bikers had sullen fun with him, that white-haired guy being me of course. I watched a small kid Hoyt's age in a red snowsuit. He sat perched on a small mound of dirty city snow. He was, of course, eating the snow.

Johnny surprised me. He let me go.

I spent the first thirty seconds just rubbing my wrist and forearm.

"You leave her alone, you hear me?"

"Who?" I said.

"You mess with her," Eugene said, "and Johnny's really going to lose it." He chucked me under the chin. I didn't know when, but someday I was going to pay him back for that. "He didn't do jack-shit to you today—not compared to what he could do. You dig?"

I said, "Do you know a man named Pennyfeather?" Johnny and Eugene glanced at each other.

"You really want a good one, don't you?" Johnny said.

"Then I take it you do know Pennyfeather?"

"Pops," Johnny said, and in a curious way he spoke out of pity and not anger, "I can really be a bad guy. Now why don't you go get in your car and get out of here?" He nodded to my arm, which I was still rubbing. "I'm sorry if I overdid it. I've just got this temper, all right?"

In the window now I saw the four-year-old girl, wearing dirty pink pajamas, pressing her sweet dirty face against the pane, watching me.

I said, "Why don't you tell the police everything you know? They're going to be here sooner or later."

"Just get out of here, pal, and that's my last warning."

"He's getting pissed again," Eugene said. "Usually he isn't this nice."

I sighed, rubbed my hand again, and started off the porch.

The little girl watched me as I started down the stairs. She looked sadder than any child her age ever should.

Chapter 20

Before checking out the second address in Conroy's log, I went to Donutland and had two cups of coffee and a donut. The sweet-faced waitress kept looking at my hands and how they still shook. It's nice to tell yourself that in your prime you could have handled punks like the two at Kathy Stacek's place, but the fact was that I'd never been especially tough. When I lost my temper I was liable to pick up something and hit you with it, but I'd never been gifted with quick or terrible fists. Even back in my detective days, I'd always fought only as a last resort. So now I shook from lost pride and animal fear and great useless rage.

I sat for a while looking around at the other people in the small shop on Mt. Vernon Road. They talked in little groups or sat staring off alone just as I did. This was one of winter's first overcast days and it was taking its toll.

The second address was a new Drive-Mart farther out Mt. Vernon Road. There were six pumps on the drive and an overhang to protect customers from the worst of the elements. Inside, the mini-grocery store had the air of a long-ago corner store. There would be everything from baby food to cigarettes to toilet paper; the only thing there wouldn't be was an immigrant Irish or Jewish owner, the way Costello's or Mendlebaum's used to.

"You know what used to be here?" I asked the girl behind the counter.

"A lot."

"A lot?"

"Vacant lot. I know because I used to live in this neighborhood and I always played baseball with my brothers here."

"Oh."

She grinned. She had bright blue eyes and soft bottle-blonde hair and that peculiar vulnerability that accrues to young girls with dental braces. "It's weird when you think about it."

"What's weird?"

"Oh, you know, you play baseball on this vacant lot when you're growing up and then you move away and then fourteen years later you move back and work in a store that's built on the same vacant lot. It's just kind of weird, you know, how things happen over the years."

I smiled. "That's pretty smart, what you just said."

"Aw."

"Really." I gave her a small wave and walked out.

There was a pay phone on the corner. I walked over to it, a hard winter wind pushing me faster.

I phoned a friend of mine named Sweeney.

"Can you hold on?"

"Sure."

"It may take a little while."

"That's fine."

Whenever I need to find out something about real estate, I call Sweeney. He works in the courthouse. He's about my age and he's a Democrat the way other people are Hare Krishnas. FDR was the Father, JFK the Son, and Jimmy Carter the Holy Ghost. The first two I might be able to buy, but Carter I never could stand. Maybe it was that psychotic smile.

Usually, Sweeney can find the previous owner of a given address in under five minutes.

This time, it took him eight. "Marvin Scribbins. Owned it for fifteen years. 1971-1986."

"He sold it?"

"Ummm. To a developer who put up some kind of Dairy Queen deal. Insty-Freeze. Lead balloon."

"Huh?"

"Lead balloon. You know, 'sank like a lead balloon.'"

"Oh, yeah."

"Then they sold it to the corporation that owns the Drive-Marts."

"Anything on Marvin Scribbins?"

He riffled some papers. "Just the usual stuff. No forwarding, if that's what you're looking for."

"So he could still be here in Cedar Rapids?"

"I suppose."

"Well, I'll check it out. Thanks."

He said, "I didn't see you at the Jefferson-Jackson Day dinner this year."

"Busy, I guess."

"The party really needs your help, Walsh. It needs everybody's help."

"I'm going to pitch in. I promise."

He laughed. "I don't know why I put up with this stuff."

"You know something? Neither do I."

He laughed again and hung up.

Chapter 21

Marvin Scribbins was listed as living out in the hills east of Marion where the newer rich were building homes in the middle of timberland. A maid answered and told me that Mr. Scribbins was out of town on a business trip until tomorrow. I left my name and number.

In the East Side Maidrite I had a maidrite with mustard and pickles and a bottle of Hamm's, the mid-afternoon meal I started eating in my fifties, one of the ways I keep my energy up. Finished, I smoked two cigarettes, one-third of my daily allotment. They tasted better than they had any right to.

In the car again, snow beginning to splatter on the windshield, I drove down First Avenue past the crumbling houses that only thirty years ago had been the special province of the upper middle class, down past Coe College and the refurbished buildings that looked sleek and formidable even in the afternoon gloom, and on down to the beginnings of the business district.

Paul Heckart's building was a prim three-story brick that had recently been sandblasted. With its tinted and sealed windows, it appeared almost brand new. Inside, everything *was* brand new—bright wallcoverings, carpeting, doors, even the office furnishings. The effect of all this was apparently good on the workers. Everybody moved around quickly, desk to desk, floor to floor, and when they spoke to one another it was with the kind of pleasantness that can't be faked. There was a good working atmosphere here.

Paul Heckart's office was on the third floor.

While I waited for him in a reception area, I walked around and looked at the large photographs of the office furnishings the Heckart Company designed and built. The stuff was gorgeous and not quite real. You just didn't think anybody could be that creative with something as mundane as desks and chairs and tables, even wastebaskets that did not in any way resemble wastebaskets. No wonder Paul Heckart and his brother were two of the most successful men in the city.

"Hello," Paul Heckart said.

In the daylight, he appeared bigger than he had last night, a long-striding man who was probably most at home on the golf course, tanned, white-haired, firm-jawed, and with a grip that shamed mine. Adjusting his regimental-striped tie inside his three-piece blue suit, he said, seeming worried, "Has something happened, Mr. Walsh?"

"Not that I know of. I just wondered if I could talk to you."

"Of course," he said. "Of course you can."

To the fetching young receptionist with the Katharine Hepburn auburn hair and the wry Myrna Loy gaze, he said, "Trish, we'll be in my conference room."

"Should I interrupt?"

"Not unless it's really an emergency."

She nodded, and he led me down a hall that was just as sumptuous as the rest of the layout.

The conference room was very conservative: mahogany furnishings and wall trimmings with dark blue carpeting that made you feel, at first, as if you were walking into quicksand. From the large window in the east wall you could see all of downtown, the Teleconnect building looming especially large only a few blocks away.

He poured us each a cup of coffee from a silver server that probably cost half as much as my car. When we were seated across the conference table from each other, he said, "Now, how may I help you, Mr. Walsh?"

"I thought that maybe you could tell me a few things about the Pennyfeather family. I can't quite bring them into focus."

"I'm not sure what you mean." He looked, for the first time, vaguely uncomfortable. Before I could explain further, he said, "Before we start, there's something I'd better tell you."

"All right."

"I'm the closest friend they've got, and in turn they're my closest friends. The entire family. I'm sorry if I looked a little apprehensive there—when you asked me to talk about them—but I just couldn't bring myself to say anything negative about them."

"I'm not asking for anything negative, Mr. Heckart. I'm just trying to find out what happened twelve years ago so I can learn something more about last night."

"You think they're connected?"

"Possibly, probably."

"What would you like me to tell you?"

"About the family relationship, for one thing. I don't think I've ever seen a family that close-knit before."

He smiled. "They're like a TV family, aren't they?"

"Do you spend as much time together as they seem to?"

"Yes, unfortunately, they do, and I'm afraid that's why neither David nor Carolyn is married any longer. Their respective spouses just couldn't handle that kind of closeness."

"Oh?"

"Have you ever been around a family whose only reality is themselves?"

I shrugged. "I suppose; I guess I'm not sure."

"Well, no matter how often or cordially they try to include you, you can easily develop the sense that because you're not a blood part of them somehow you just don't belong. Again, this isn't anything the family does consciously. But as an outsider, you certainly could get that impression."

"Were the Pennyfeathers like this even before George went away to prison?"

"Oh, my, yes. They've always been like that. First George and Lisa and then the kids." He shook his Roman senator head. "That's what was so ludicrous about the charge that Karl Jankov and Lisa Pennyfeather were having an affair. She was so completely wrapped up in her family that it just never could have happened."

"'Never' is a pretty strong word."

"But in this case it's the appropriate word."

"So you don't think that George killed Jankov?"

"No offense, Mr. Walsh, I know you were the detective in charge of the case, and I know that with that Stacek girl's testimony the obvious suspect was George—but he didn't do it. I'm sure of it."

I sipped some coffee. It was very good. "Could we talk about him? Jankov?"

"Of course. If you'd like."

"During the trial, I got the impression he'd been your right-hand man, that anything that needed doing in the company, he'd do for you."

"That's a fair impression, I suppose."

"Did you like him as a person?"

"To be honest, no."

"Why not?"

"With Karl you always saw all the gears working. He never did anything that didn't advance his career or put himself in a good light. He was like this little animal that needed constant attention and reward. As valuable as he was, his toadying made me uncomfortable."

"But he was an effective vice president for you?"

"Very. We enjoyed a great period of growth during his tenure here."

"Did he ever make a pass at Lisa Pennyfeather?"

"Probably." He laughed. "For Karl there were two kinds of rewards. A pat on the head from the boss and the approval of women who came from a higher social class than he had. Karl was a poor boy who'd been gifted with great cunning and energy—if not exactly brains—and very good looks. He appealed especially to women who wanted some excitement in their lives." He poured us more coffee. "On any given day, that would describe about half the women at the country club. That was Karl's 'circuit,' if you will." He chuckled. "He did a lot of 'recruiting' out there."

"Do you think it could have been one of those women who killed him?"

"No, I don't, Mr. Walsh. I know who killed him."

The certainty in his voice surprised me. "You do?"

"Of course. His wife, Terri."

"Why would she kill him?"

"Terri was—and still is, I'd assume—very much like Karl. Graced with cunning and energy, and very much upwardly mobile. She came from the same kind of background. Terri had one problem that Karl didn't, however."

"What's that?"

"Jealousy. In those days, anyway, she was pathologically jealous. If she hadn't disrupted the work day so much around here, I might even have felt sorry for her."

"She made scenes?"

"Scenes?" He made a sour face. "Try slapping Karl right in his office with a client present. Or interrupting him with phone calls during key presentations. Or waiting out in his car for him with a revolver she fired into the roof. The county attorney could have brought this out at the trial, but he was interested only in

George. George made for bigger headlines."

Just then there was a discreet knock on the door. I was assuming it would be the receptionist. Instead, it was Heckart's brother, Richard. He came in without saying anything. He wore a brown suit cut a little more fashionably than Paul's, and black horn-rims that lent him the air of a man intellectually intent. As he came over to me, he said to his brother, "When you get a chance, go down to the lab and look at my design for the new desk. I think I really hit it this time."

Paul laughed. "You remember my brother, Richard, Mr. Walsh. He was just trying to tell you in his subtle way that he's really the brains of our company. He does all the major design work. All I am is a glorified peddler."

Without being asked, Richard sat down and poured himself some coffee. "I heard you were up here, Mr. Walsh. I thought I'd just come up and say hello."

Heard I was up here? Who had told him? And why?

"My brother likes to know everything that's going on," Paul Heckart laughed. "It's from his army days. He was a colonel, and he never got over his taste for being in command—even though technically, I'm older and the one that my father left in command." An uneasy melancholy filled his gaze. "Dad died while Richard was in Korea. He went very slowly." He offered me a social smile. "It's funny, I can always get that way about Dad."

Richard Heckart said, "You're confusing Mr. Walsh here, Paul. He probably thinks we don't get along. And we do."

"Just as long as I do everything you tell me to, little brother," Paul Heckart said. He spoke with cold authority. There was nothing ironic in his voice. He was quite serious.

"Your brother was just telling me about Jankov," I said, uncomfortable with the tension between them.

"Ah, Mr. Jankov," Richard Heckart said. He shook his head with quick and pointed disgust. "I never cared for him. I can't even say I'm sorry that he was murdered." He stared at me. "I keep forgetting that you're the detective who arrested poor George."

I nodded.

"It's damned funny how these things turn out," he said, rueful as always. Last night I'd had the impression that he might be less skilled socially than his brother. What I'd missed was the fact that they simply represented two different styles— the senatorial gloss of his brother, his own barely disguised contempt for most subjects and most people. He'd probably made a fine colonel. "Your representing George now, I mean."

"I'm just trying to help out a little."

"And of course you wouldn't think of taking any money for it."

"Richard, for Christ's sake," Paul Heckart said.

"I'm not sure it's a good idea any of us talk to you, Mr. Walsh. Frankly, given your ties to the local *gendarmes*, I wouldn't be surprised if you told them everything you found out." Richard Heckart smiled as he spoke. "I wouldn't think that at all unfair of you, either, as far as that goes. A man who was a detective as long as you—naturally your first loyalty is to the force."

"It wasn't the 'force,' Mr. Heckart. I was with the Linn County Sheriff's Department."

"Whatever. You know what I'm talking about."

Flushing now, his right hand curved into an impressive fist, Paul Heckart said, "You seem to be forgetting something, brother."

"And what would that be, brother?"

"That Mr. Walsh came to see me. And that what the two of us talk about is none of your goddamn business."

Ironically, the tension eased after Paul Heckart swore. The animosity was plain and open now, and it was always better this way than hiding behind masks and bitchiness.

"You'd like me to leave?" Richard said. There was a tartness to him that was neither appealing nor amusing.

"Please," Paul said, "so we may finish our conversation."

Richard was on his feet now. He looked at me. He smiled again. "Would you like me to tell you what Paul will tell you about me as soon as I leave the room?"

Now, I was the one with red in my cheeks. I dropped my gaze. My palms were gummy with sweat. This was like having Sister Mary Frances make me stand in front of the fourth-grade class that time and apologize for writing the word "shit" on the blackboard.

"He will say," Richard Heckart went on, "that I'm just overprotective of both him and the company, that I'm as reclusive as the Pennyfeathers, and that the reason I hated Jankov was quite simple—he had an affair with my wife. It took me a long time to get over it. A long time. It wasn't good for my wife, me, or our children. We spent thousands of dollars seeing a marriage counselor before we had any kind of home life again."

"None of this came out during the trial," I said.

Paul Heckart said, "For just the reason I hear in your voice—because if it had, Richard would have been a prime suspect. And I knew for certain that Richard had had nothing to do with Jankov's murder."

"How could you know that?" I asked.

"Because during the established time of death, Richard was with me out on my boat. It was just a small craft, one I generally keep moored out at Ellis. I use it sometimes for fishing trips. We went to a lake home owned by a friend named Delaney. Usually, we would have gone to our own cabin, but I'd given that to the Pennyfeathers."

"I see."

Richard said, "The cabin's been in the family for three generations, Mr. Walsh." He looked directly at his brother. "We've all taken guests up there. Paul used to take George fishing, and sometimes he'd take young David for a weekend every once in a while. Is there something about the cabin that interests you?"

Something had changed his attitude. He was no longer bitchy; he wanted to understand my curiosity, and that meant good behavior.

"I just thought it might look awfully convenient to a county attorney—a prime suspect with such a good alibi. A respected brother and a cabin in the woods."

"Meaning what, Mr. Walsh?" Richard asked.

I decided to rattle him some. "Meaning that it might have looked contrived. Your alibi. To anybody of a suspicious nature."

"And is that your nature, Mr. Walsh? Suspicious?"

"I suppose."

"Well, whether you believe it or not—and I don't give a damn if you do—I was with Paul that whole evening."

"That's true, Mr. Walsh," Paul said.

"I wasn't making any accusations," I said to Richard Heckart. "I was only making a comment."

"I'll accept it at that, then." He surprised me by putting out his hand. He had the steely family grip. "I'm sorry if this got nasty. I'm naturally upset over what's happened with poor George. You can understand that."

"Of course," I said, and in fact I supposed I could. Richard Heckart nodded goodbye to his brother and left. He closed the door quietly.

"Well," Paul Heckart said, "I don't know about you, but that isn't something I'd care to go through again."

I laughed. "I've been through a lot worse."

He frowned. "He's just very afraid we'll let Dad down."

"How would you do that?"

"By letting something get beyond our control. That's the military man in Richard. He wants to control everything. He always looked at this mess with Jankov as something that could ultimately hurt the company. That's why he gets so angry about it, though he'd never admit it. We were raised to believe that the business our great-grandfather started several generations ago was something to be kept in impeccable condition—like a shrine of some sort. I'm afraid Richard got a little too much of that instilled in him. He tends to get feisty and arrogant any time he perceives the company is threatened."

"You really were with him the night of Jankov's murder?"

"You think he's lying to you, Mr. Walsh?"

"That isn't exactly an answer."

"Well, here is an exact answer, Mr. Walsh. Yes, my brother was with me all the time that night."

"Fine. I'll accept that then."

He laughed. "Now we're getting into it, aren't we?"

"Nothing major, Mr. Heckart. You've been very helpful, and I appreciate it."

"I just hope you or the police can find the person who killed that poor woman last night. Have the authorities learned much about her yet?"

"Not much."

"In the gazebo. It seems such a waste."

"It generally is, Mr. Heckart. Murder."

I tugged up the collar of my car coat. I put out my hand.

We shook. I walked to the door.

"If you think of anything about the Jankov case that you think is useful, please call me."

"Why don't you try Terri Jankov? As I told you, she would be my first suspect."

"Maybe I will. Well, thanks again."

At the door, he said, "Please don't judge either my brother or me on our little disagreement this afternoon."

"I won't."

"We're just concerned for George."

"Of course."

"But I really would look up Terri. She tried to kill him a few times before somebody actually did kill him."

"Something else that didn't come out at the trial."

"I'm not sure anybody took her attempts very seriously. Sometimes murder attempts—especially between lovers—are like suicide attempts. Really just calling out for attention."

"I suppose."

"I hope you'll look her up."

I smiled. "After all you've told me about her, I guess I don't have much choice, do I?"

Chapter 22

On the other side of the door you could hear Barry Manilow complaining about how various people had done him wrong and he was getting tired of it. That was a modest joke between Faith and me, anyway—she says that Tony Bennett (who I like) always sounds drunk, and I say that Manilow (who she likes) is always complaining. About the only singer we like in common is Elvis Presley. When you had two teenagers, you learned to like Elvis. You didn't have much choice.

When she opened my door, she put a shushing finger to her lips. "Hoyt's asleep."

I nodded and went in and noticed immediately how hard she'd been working all day. Everything had been dusted, set right, picked up, polished. The place looked great.

There was even a frilly white apron tied around her lovely hips. She'd once told me she considered aprons the ultimate symbol of a woman's subjugation. She must have changed her mind.

She came up and kissed me gently on the lips and said, in a half-whisper, "Do you suppose we could make love? I mean, is this the right time to ask you?"

I smiled. "I guess we could find out."

"Could I ask you something, though?"

"Sure."

"Don't touch my breasts. I think I'll just leave this blouse on if you don't mind."

"Fine, hon. Fine."

There are a lot of different reasons to make love and lust is generally the least of them. When I was in Italy in the final months of the war, I slept once a day with an Italian woman because I was convinced these would be my last hours and I needed to do something human and profound. I made love out of fear—fear that nothing made any sense and that I had to make some small connection between myself and another person before I faced oblivion. When Sharon was dying, I made love to comfort her. She was facing oblivion, too, and though her religious faith was greater than mine, I saw in the nooks and crannies of her final days the fear of extinction that comes to all animals, probably even those of the lower orders if we only knew how to understand them properly. When I met Faith, I made love to heal myself. The first time we went to bed I could scarcely get an erection. There had been too much loneliness and loss in my life for anything as positive as desire. But gradually it happened and soon enough I heard myself laughing as we tumbled into bed one night, and things were fine ever after. Faith had no idea what she'd given me; no idea. And now it was my turn to repay her.

In the gray dusk, the smell of roast beef cooking in red wine filling the apartment, we made slow gentle love on the couch, with the sound off and Bullwinkle making broad pantomime gestures to Rocket J. Squirrel, and Hoyt snoring sleep from his tiny pink mouth in the bedroom.

Several times my hand went instinctively to her breast, then at the last minute drew back.

Afterward there were none of the frail, insecure questions lovers usually ask to be reassured that they have given pleasure to their mates. We were way beyond ego; way beyond.

She lay on top of me, her head on my chest. When she spoke, she raised her small head a bit and spoke off to the side, as if addressing a ghostly presence.

"I'm sorry about not letting you touch my breasts."

"I understand, Faith. Hell."

Silence. Her head back down.

I said, "We're going to be celebrating tomorrow. You'll see. After the mammogram."

Silence.

I stroked her fine, soft hair. When she started to cry, shaking there on my body like a sad little girl, I held her tight as I thought wise, and said nothing.

Late afternoon became full night, headlights playing off the north wall as cars sped out the avenue swishing through the wet snow, and you could hear in the silence a TV set in one apartment, laughter in another, an old man's lonely curse in yet another.

"Why don't we go lie down with Hoyt?" she said.

We stood up, dressed; I went into the bedroom while she headed for the bathroom. I lay next to Hoyt, giving him one finger to grasp while he slept. You could hear her peeing and then the toilet flushing and then the basin water running. She came in and lay on the other side of Hoyt, the bedsprings squeaking slightly. It was darker in this room. When headlights came they played against the window wet with snow, the melting liquid briefly the color of gold in the splash of lights. From the closet came the faint odor of mothballs; from the bureau the faint scent of Old Spice. Hoyt let out with a considerable fart. We were desperate for something to laugh about and this was it. She reached over Hoyt's head and took my hand. She was asleep in a few minutes.

After we woke up, we went into the kitchen. She set dinner on the table.

"You want me to go with you?" I asked.

"I go back and forth."

"I'd be happy to."

"I thought you were working for the Pennyfeathers."

"I am. But I'd take time off."

"How's it going?"

"I'm not sure."

"You still think Pennyfeather killed that man?"

"Yes."

"You think he killed the woman last night?"

"I'm not sure."

She sighed, put her head down. She'd gone to the trouble of a candlelight dinner, and now she wasn't eating.

"You going to get Marcia to babysit?"

"Ummm. If she can, anyway. Guess I'd better talk to her before she goes out to Rockwell tonight." She paused. "Why would he kill her?"

"Pennyfeather?"

"Ummm."

"I'm not sure. You really interested in it?"

"I don't want to talk about—my situation anymore. I'm sick of it. That's the trouble with being sick—it makes you the focus of everything, and you get tired of your ego long before you get tired of the illness. You know?"

"Yeah."

"So what happens if Pennyfeather didn't kill that man?"

"His name was Jankov and I'm not sure what happens if Pennyfeather turns up innocent."

"It's a possibility?"

"I suppose."

"Do you have any other suspects?"

"Not really, though there are several people who seem to have some peculiar bearing on the case."

"Such as?"

The phone rang. Immediately Hoyt began crying. She got up and went into the bedroom. I went into the kitchen to the wall phone. "Hello."

"Is this Mr. Walsh?"

"Yes."

"Hi. This is Dolores."

The name and voice sounded familiar but I couldn't quite place them.

"This morning. Out in front of Stella Czmek's place."

"Oh. Right. Dolores. How are you?"

"I'm fine. But I'm not sure Bainbridge is."

"No?"

"No."

"What's wrong?"

"I was walkin' to the store and I saw somebody go in there. Then when I was walkin' back I heard somebody scream. I'm sure it was Bainbridge."

"You're at home now?"

"Yeah."

"Can you see Bainbridge's house from where you are?"

"No. But I can go out on the porch."

"All right. You know what kind of car his visitor was driving?"

"Some kind of green car."

I thought of Conroy, the private investigator. "Could it be a Chevrolet?"

"Could be. They kind of all look alike these days."

"You'll go check?"

"Be right back."

Faith came carrying Hoyt. She brought him over and leaned him into me. He gave me a small warm wet kiss on my cheek.

Dolores came back. "Car's gone. No lights on in Bainbridge's. You comin' over?"

"Thought I might, yes."

"See you in a little bit, then."

"Thanks, Dolores. Thanks very much."

I had just turned to hang up the phone when Faith said, "I won't mind."

"You won't?"

"No, I like to see you working. You seem more—complete, I guess."

"I suppose you're right. But—"

"I'll be fine. Really."

I leaned over to Hoyt and chucked him under the chin.

"You take good care of her, you hear?"

He gave me a small solid punch on my forehead.

"I could be back late."

"That's all right. I'll probably pick up a little and watch some movie on TV and doze off."

"There's a movie called *The Gunfighter* on cable."

"A western?"

"Yeah. Oh, I forgot."

"I'm sure they're good. I just don't appreciate them, I guess."

"This one's a little different." Then I thought of how he dies in the end. "But I don't think you'll like it." I went over and picked up the *TV Guide*. "You're in luck."

"What?"

"They're showing one of those colorized deals of *Casablanca* tonight."

"I love *Casablanca*."

"That's what I figured," I said.

I kissed her, I kissed Hoyt, and I left.

Chapter 23

By the time I reached Ellis Boulevard the snow was coming down in earnest, cars spinning back wheels at stoplights and sliding forward in little unwanted bursts of power, people leaning over windshields and scooping off handfuls of cold numbing white stuff after having forgotten to buy gloves and scrapers, tiny old people walking with sad comic caution down slippery sidewalks.

There were no lights in Mr. Bainbridge's.

I was on the sidewalk about ten seconds when Dolores appeared, bundled up in a large red coat. She grinned. "My kids still don't think you're really a private detective."

I smiled. "Did you get a look at the man in the car?"

"Not really."

"About how long ago do you think he left?"

"Twenty, twenty-five minutes."

"And you haven't seen Bainbridge on the street?"

"No."

"Maybe he just went to sleep."

"Not Bainbridge. He always watchin' that religious channel on the TV and keeps the sound up real loud, especially when they playin' music. Man, does he like loud music."

"Why don't I go up to the door?"

"Go ahead, but it won't get you nothin'."

"There's a positive attitude."

Her laughing behind me, I went up to the door. Through the small glass of the door window, I looked inside. Nothing. No light; no sign of life. I knocked. It was like tossing a coin down a very deep well. It got lost before it touched bottom.

"Tol' ya," Dolores said.

I turned around. "I appreciate all the confidence you have in me."

"You sure are a smart-ass."

I turned back to the door and knocked again. Two cars of teenagers went by. Several generations of Cedar Rapids kids had driven down Ellis Boulevard, all in search of the same elusive things. Pretty soon they'd have beer bellies and mean factory foremen and then it would be their own kids who went looking for all those lovely things young people make fools of themselves over. You could hear their radios now; you could smell their underage beers.

"You scared to try the side door?" Dolores said.

"You'd be great during a burglary. You could stand down on the sidewalk and shout out instructions to me."

She started laughing again.

So of course I went around the side of the house, sticking to the smashed concrete walkway, sort of bobbing up and down for a dark useless look inside the side windows.

I pounded on the side door with the authority of a cop effecting a bust. And got, for my trouble, the same response I'd gotten from the front door.

Dolores came around to the side of the house. "You want inside?"

"I don't have a key."

"The way I've got in mind, you won't need a key."

"Really?"

"Really, Mr. Private Eye."

"Why're you being so helpful?"

"Because this will make a great story at my Amway party next week."

"I see."

"I hope you find him dead."

"Bainbridge?"

"You got it. First, 'cause I'd like to see him dead, the way he feels about black people. Second, 'cause it would make my story better."

"Well, I sure hope I can oblige you, Dolores, and find a corpse inside."

"You ever actually find one before?" Now she didn't seem quite so certain she wanted me to find Bainbridge dead.

"Couple of times, when I was with the Sheriff's Department."

"It scare you?"

"Didn't scare me but I've never forgotten them. One was a two-year-old that the mother had walked off and left. He died when the gas started leaking."

"You believe in the death penalty?"

"Yep."

"So do I, for shit like that anyway. How about the other one?"

"Old man who'd fallen down and hit his head on the edge of the coffee table. The fall induced a stroke. It was two weeks before they found him."

"Musta stunk."

"You wouldn't have believed it."

She said, "I shouldn't a said that."

"Said what?"

"About Bainbridge."

"Oh."

"I don't really wish he was dead."

"I know."

"It's just how he carries on about black people."

"I understand. I really do."

"So maybe we better check him out. For his own sake."

"Good idea."

"Let me lead you around back."

She got ahead of me on the walk in her big red coat. The darkness took some of the color from the material. But nothing could take the confidence from her stride.

In the rear were two slanting doors leading to a cellar. I hadn't seen one of these in thirty years. She went over and opened one of the doors. It made a *scraw*ing, rusty-hinged sound as she pulled it back. She said, "This is as far as I go. I got to get back home. One of my kids is sick."

"I certainly appreciate this."

"I really shouldn't a said that about him."

"It's nice to know you're guilty about it."

"You bein' a smart-ass again?"

"No, knowing you're feeling guilty means you didn't really mean it in the first place."

She laughed. "You're a strange man, Walsh. Just like my husband."

"Thanks for helping." I put my hand out and we shook.

She waved goodbye and said, "I'll be going down the alley here," and then she was gone.

Up from the cellar came the dank smells of mildew and dampness. The place appeared to be deep as a pit.

I put a tentative foot through the slanting doorway. I half-expected a monster to grab it and eat it.

My foot found a step; my other foot found another step. I started my descent, using my Zippo, best as I could, as a frail torch here in the gloom.

The mildew smell got overpowering. The dampness at once seeped through my clothes and began brushing at my flesh like something wraithlike and unclean.

The wooden stairs were warped. Twice I nearly tripped and fell forward. Quickly enough, my Zippo went out.

By the time I reached the floor of the cellar, darkness had sealed me inside. Behind me the open cellar door showed only the faintest evidence of night sky. It was as if somebody had closed the door.

Ahead of me I heard the *whoof* of a furnace catching wind. Keeping my hand ahead of me like an antenna, I moved down a dirt floor path between cardboard boxes that had been piled high on either side. Around a corner, I saw the blue glow of a gas jet. I walked over to the furnace, feeling as exultant as the prehistoric man who had discovered fire.

From the plump belly of the furnace came warmth and enough light to see the outline of rickety wooden stairs rising at an angle to the upstairs of the house.

I went up the stairs carefully, afraid they would literally disintegrate beneath me. The wooden steps were rank with the smell of mildew. The rot had seeped into the deepest fiber of the wood.

At the top I found a door and tried the knob. Unlocked. I put my head against the door and listened, hearing nothing but the groaning noises old houses make.

I opened the door and went inside.

During my time as a detective, I had seen many houses where lonely old people had died. Invariably, I'd found at least some evidence of the pack-rat mentality. I'm not sure what it's all about. Perhaps it's as simple as this—amassing things is a way of building a fortress against the outside world, a variation on the idea that some fat people have that their fatness forms a protective wall around them, inside of which they are secure. Whatever the impulse, a surprising number of the elderly follow up on it. You find houses and apartments packed with newspapers, canned goods, a jungle of ancient furniture, clothes, anything that a human being can bring inside.

Bainbridge's house was not much different except for one thing: The rows and rows of packing crates that filled each room were far more orderly than you usually encountered. In fact, my first impression was that the place was a warehouse of sorts. After looking through my third room on the first floor, that was still my impression.

Enough dirty electric light came through the windows to guide me through the first floor. I saw all the things I'd expected to find—lumpy, dumpy furnishings; wallspace packed with paintings of Christ, the sort that depict him as Elvis Presley's religious older brother; the smells of cigarettes and cold pizza boxes and cough medicine and liniment for tired bones; and a glowing TV set in a small room that looked like one of those forlorn little nooks you see in VA hospitals, where you spend half an hour with the carnage of a man hacking his way through the final stages of lung cancer. An empty Pepsi bottle lay overturned on a coffee table that had only three legs, like a maimed dog, and several ashtrays with gnarled butts.

On the tube a TV minister was bowing his head to pray for people. I hoped he was including me. I couldn't be sure because the sound was off.

The only thing I knew for sure was that Bainbridge wasn't on the first floor. I had even checked all the closets.

Above me stretched a staircase that rose toward and then vanished into utter darkness. I tried the light switch. Nothing; no light on the staircase. I listened for the reassuring sounds of traffic on Ellis. I started up the stairs. Long ago they had been carpeted; now the carpeting was barely a nub, and the stairs made more noise than an old man with asthma. Decades-old dust filled my nose and mouth; I coughed.

I was two steps across the landing at the top of the stairs when I stumbled over something. It might have been one of those comic pratfalls we all take from time to time, arms flailing, mouth yawped open without any dignity whatsoever, head aimed directly for the floor. But this was different because as I started to fall, my foot kicked into something that I recognized immediately as a human body. I didn't have much doubt about who it belonged to.

I landed on all fours, which saved me a headache anyway. I crawled over to Bainbridge and tried to see him, but it was too dark. I stood up and started groping around for a light switch. I found one in the bathroom, the smell of which was acrid. I soon enough discovered why. Either Bainbridge didn't believe in flushing or the toilet didn't work properly. Cupping a hand over my nose to kill the smell, I wobbled back to Bainbridge.

On his forehead you could see a faint red indentation where somebody had hit him, probably with a fist. At his age, in his condition, it hadn't taken much to knock him out.

I went into the bathroom, cupping my nose again, and soaked one towel in cold water, grabbed another that was dry, and started back to him. Then I stopped. Though the bathroom was small, it was packed tight with the same kind of crates that filled the first floor. Here, in the light, I saw that the crates had a company name printed on them: Vandersee Import-Export.

I thought of Stella Czmek and how her fortunes had improved so abruptly and mysteriously once she'd gone to work for Vandersee. Then I remembered that Vandersee had died a few years ago. Now I was curious about how he'd died.

Bainbridge had started to moan by the time I knelt next to him again and began to daub his face with cold water.

"Bainbridge?"

Moaning.

"Bainbridge? Who hit you?"

Moaning.

"Bainbridge. I want to help you. Tell me what happened here tonight."

Still moaning, but now the tiny mad eyes beginning to open and peer up at me; the eyes of a predatory bird.

"Bainbridge. Was it Conroy who was here tonight? A private detective named Conroy?"

He spoke then, and for all his pictures of Jesus, for all his Biblical talk of sin and salvation, his words were most inappropriate. He said, "You go to hell."

Chapter 24

"How long did you know Stella Czmek?"

"Not long."

"How long would that be?"

"Couple years."

"Bullshit."

"They let you in here, didn't they?"

" 'They'?"

"Those nigger women."

"I'm asking you about Stella Czmek."

"I don't know anything about her."

"That's why you've got a houseful of crates from Vandersee's."

"She just stored the stuff here. Gave me money for it."

"What's in the boxes?"

"Don't know. Never looked."

"You really expect me to believe that?"

"I don't have to answer your questions."

I decided to roll the dice. "Why don't you call the police?"

"What?"

"You heard me. Call the police."

"I'll call them when I feel like it."

"You're afraid to call them."

"That's a lie."

"Because of what's in those boxes, that's why."

"You leave them boxes alone."

We sat in his bedroom upstairs. I had stretched him out on the bed and put the wet towel across his forehead. I sat on a straight-back chair across the room. He stared at the ceiling. Above him was another painting of Jesus, a velvet painting. In this one Jesus appeared to be scowling. I could understand why.

In the street below traffic *shoosh*ed along the damp boulevard. Somewhere nearby a dog barked. Bainbridge's breathing was very loud. He didn't sound so good.

I had a cigarette going. My lungs probably didn't sound so good, either. I said, "Who was here tonight?"

"Nobody."

"You knocked yourself out?"

"I tripped."

"Right. Was it Conroy?"

The way he blinked, I could tell he knew who I was talking about. "I don't know no Conroy."

"He drives a new green Chevrolet. It was seen parked along the side street about an hour ago."

"Those nigger women again."

"What does Conroy want from you?"

"Nothing."

"Why did he come here?"

"He didn't come here."

"What's in the boxes?"

"Vases."

"Anything else?"

"Just vases."

"From where?"

"Hong Kong."

"Why would she want all those vases stored here?"

"You'd have to ask her."

"You just stay on the bed."

"Where you going?"

"Going to start looking through the boxes."

"Bullshit."

"You've got some mouth for a reverend."

"You leave them boxes alone."

He started to get up. I pushed him down harder than I needed to. He cracked his head on the metal bedpost. He said another word reverends aren't supposed to say.

I said, "Why don't you call the police?"

"You leave me alone."

"Why not, Bainbridge? Why not call the police?"

"You bastard. I'm an old man."

"In case you hadn't noticed, so am I."

"Who the hell you work for, anyway?"

I pointed to the bed. "You stay there. You hear me?"

Twenty minutes later I'd gone through ten of the packing crates on the second floor. Vases were what he'd promised, and vases were what I found. Vases. Cheap blue ones and cheap purple ones and cheap yellow ones, each with raised dragon figures, each with a somewhat lopsided mouth in which to put cut flowers.

For my trouble I had received a bruised thumb, having never been much good with a hammer, a body slick with sweat, and the growing suspicion that my suspicions were unfounded. Maybe Stella Czmek had taken on Vandersee inventory as a favor to Vandersee, or with an eye to setting up her own import-export business. Or just because she plain liked vases.

Whatever, there seemed to be no sinister intent in storing them here.

I changed my mind as soon as I found the open crate on the bottom of a pile. The first thing I checked for was some small difference between it and the other boxes and I found it without much trouble at all, a small rubber-stamp black star along the bottom of the crate. The second thing I checked on was the inside of the box, which was where I found two more eyesore purple vases, and an indentation in the bottom of the box where some sort of book had lain. At least I assumed it had been a book. That's what it looked like under the dull glow of the flashlight I'd borrowed from Bainbridge's bathroom.

I spent the next twenty minutes checking all the other boxes, upstairs and downstairs, for sight of the black star again. It was not to be found.

I took the empty box back to Bainbridge's bedroom.

He lay propped up against the back of the bed now. He had his Bible spread out on his lap. From somewhere he'd produced a pair of ancient wire-rim glasses. He probably played Scrooge in the local KKK chapter's version of *A Christmas Carol.*

"What does this black star mean?"

"Wouldn't know."

"Look at it."

"Don't need to look at it. Don't know what it means."

"Look at it."

He sighed and swung his head around. You could still see where he'd been smacked hard in the forehead. He looked enfeebled. I wished I could feel sorry for him but I couldn't.

"Don't have no idea what it is."

"This is what Conroy wanted, isn't it? He's the one who opened this box tonight, isn't he?"

"Don't know no Conroy."

"What was in the book?"

"What book?"

"There's an indentation on the bottom of the box. That means that when this was shipped from Hong Kong, somebody hid some sort of contraband in the bottom of the box."

He went back to his Bible. "Wouldn't know about anything like that."

I grabbed him by the shirt and yanked him around. I slapped him once hard across the mouth.

His Bible dropped on the floor. He put his face down on the bed and started sobbing. He sounded sick and crazy.

"What the hell's going on here, Bainbridge, and what does Conroy have to do with this?"

He waved me off, apparently afraid I was going to hurt him some more.

I went over and sat in the straight-back chair and lighted a cigarette and stared down at the boulevard and the traffic lost behind the white wavering sheet of snow. The smells and creaks and ravaged condition of the old house had begun to weigh on me.

And so had Bainbridge.

Angry, not knowing what else to do, I went over to his bureau and began looking through the drawers. They were empty except for pieces of newspaper that dated back to 1948. It was like opening a time capsule, one of the newspaper ads advertising Harry James at Danceland. Sharon and I might well have been there, her in a corsage for our occasional night out, me in my new Wembley tie, eager to foxtrot.

The memories calmed me down.

I went back to the chair. "I want you to tell me about Conroy."

"I don't know about him."

"You're lying."

"You going to hit me again?"

He looked so old and frail, I couldn't even bluff.

"No."

He was relieved. "You shouldn't ought to hit somebody like me that way."

"I didn't hit you. I slapped you."

"Still and all."

"Conroy. What the hell's he got to do with all this?"

"I can't tell you. I'm afraid."

"Tomorrow I'm going to have the police come and question you."

He shook his head. "Then I'll be gone." He lifted his Bible. "The Lord will protect me from people like you."

Conroy had scared him, and now I was just wasting my time here. I stood up and said, "If you hear from Conroy, tell him I'm looking for him."

He stared up at me with his birdy eyes. A terrible grin exposed his dentures. "You think he'll care? You really think he's afraid of you?"

He was starting to enjoy himself again. It was time for me to leave. Before I saw Conroy, there were a few other answers I needed.

Chapter 25

Terri Jankov turned out to be in the book. She lived in one of the new apartment complexes out near Mt. Vernon. I'd thought of calling and then decided it would be too easy for her to say no. Turning me down in person might be more difficult for her.

On the way out, I counted three cars that had skidded off the road and ended up in the ditch, and two big city trucks hissing sand from their rear ends. For once the TV weathermen had been correct. A major storm was about to hit Cedar Rapids.

Terri Jankov's parking lot ran to new sports cars, presumably for the single people, and fine expensive new station wagons. I knew just how expensive because on a day when I'd had nothing better to do, I'd spent several hours pricing them.

In the snowy darkness, the lights of the various apartments looked snug and warm. In a window here and there you could see the tiny faces of children staring out at the approaching storm. You could just hear them praying that the weather would get bad enough for school to be canceled.

I was careful going up the steps. I had to be. They hadn't been sanded or shoveled, which was surprising in a place this expensive. You'd think all these yuppies would get collectively pissed off about such terrible service.

You had to be rung past the vestibule, which ended my plans for sneaking up on the poor unsuspecting widow of Karl Jankov.

I rang the bell.

"Yes?"

"Mrs. Jankov, my name is Walsh. I'm working for George Pennyfeather."

"My God."

"Pardon me?"

"I said 'My God.' You've got to be some sort of cop, don't you?"

"Yes."

She laughed a cigarette-and-whiskey laugh obvious even over the small tinny speaker. "I admire your nerve."

"My nerve?"

"You want to come in and ask me questions that may help the man who murdered my husband. Isn't that right?"

"Basically, I suppose."

"Oh, this is delicious. It really is." I hadn't realized till then how drunk she was. "By all means, come up, Mr. Walsh. I'll buzz you in. You come straight up the stairs and take a right. I'm down at the end of the hall, next to the large window."

"Thank you."

"Oh, the pleasure's all mine. The snow had started to make me feel cooped-up and restless. You'll be much more interesting than TV."

When you manage an apartment building yourself, you tend to notice how other such buildings are maintained. This one was enviable. Not only was the blue hallway carpeting fairly new, it was kept up. The faint tangy smell of cleaning solvent rose to my nostrils. The walls had been painted no more than a few months ago, and the trim was without any scarring. I was impressed.

The first thing I noticed about her was her size. She had to be sixty or seventy pounds overweight, a fact she tried to conceal by wearing a dark silk robe that hung from her shoulders without exactly touching any other part of her body. She wore festive red slippers and festive red nail polish and festive red lipstick, which contrasted with the dyed jet-black color of her hair. Even from here you could smell her perfume, heavy enough to sting the senses momentarily but not in any way unpleasant. But however much the rest of her had deteriorated, the beauty of her face had remained intact, almost eerily so, like a doll's head that had been stuck on the wrong body, a sculpted face with high cheekbones and a gorgeous slash of a nose and a wry erotic mouth with the tiny white teeth of a little girl showing in the flash of her smile.

She put out a hand heavy with rings. If even half of the rings contained real diamonds, I was impressed.

"May I fix you a drink?"

"Coffee would be fine."

Her dark eyes conveyed disappointment. She rattled her highball in my direction. "I hate to drink alcohol alone. It always makes me feel sinful." She showed me her little girl's teeth. "But then feeling sinful isn't the worst feeling in the world, now, is it?"

I followed her inside. It was like stepping into a showroom. A Victorian sofa, with matching period chairs, dominated a living room impeccably appointed with what appeared to be a genuine Persian rug, a large round mahogany coffee table, and lacy curtains that trapped the soft pink light emanating from a small pink lamp in the corner. It was a room meant to impress, and it did.

"Cream?"

"Black is fine."

"Some cake, perhaps?"

"No, thanks."

She laughed. "Looking at me, you'd never think that I liked sweets, now would you?"

She spoke in the tone of all people who hate themselves for their weaknesses.

"I think I'll just stick to coffee, thanks."

Apparently, she didn't like my answer. She stared at me as if appraising a dog she might consider buying, and said, "How old a man are you, Mr. Walsh?"

It was meant to put me in my place, and to establish her superiority. She might be fat but she was not old, her question said. She might be drunk but even sauced she had more bitchy wit than I did. We had one thing in common. She didn't like herself, and I didn't like her, either.

She disappeared then, smiling unpleasantly, as if a small victory in an endless war had just been won, leaving me to park one cheek on the edge of her sofa. I almost felt as if I were violating it in some way. Next to me lay a hardcover book that had been left open approximately in the middle. A new chapter heading read: "Getting Control of Your Impulses."

I was scanning the first few paragraphs when she returned. She bore the pewter mug on the pewter saucer and sat them down on the coffee table with a model's contrived and precarious grace.

"Do you suppose that will help?"

"Pardon me?" I said.

"I saw you were looking at the book. Do you suppose it will work for me?"

She enjoyed making you despise her. I suppose she hoped that somebody would despise her almost as much as she despised herself.

"I couldn't say."

"You're uncomfortable, aren't you?"

I shrugged.

"You'd rather sit here and pretend that I'm not fat at all, wouldn't you?"

"I really came to talk about your ex-husband."

"He's the reason I'm fat."

"I see."

"No, I'm afraid you don't, Mr. Walsh."

"I'm trying to understand why George Pennyfeather would have killed him."

"You think I don't remember you, but I do, Mr. Walsh. You were the detective in charge of the case."

"That's right."

"And now you're working for George?"

"Yes."

She laughed. It was a sexual laugh, bawdy in the way fat women are sometimes bawdy. But there was no enjoyment or freedom in it. It was still nasty. That never quite seemed to leave her, that nastiness, no matter what she did.

"Why do you think your husband was murdered?"

"You don't think it was the reason given in court? That little Lisa Pennyfeather was considering having an affair with Karl, and that little George Pennyfeather couldn't handle it?"

"Do you think that was the reason?"

"If that was what was decided in court, then that must be the reason, don't you think, Mr. Walsh?" She spoke in broad ironic tones. She even batted her eyelashes at me.

"Then, I take it, you don't believe that?"

Her mouth drew tight. "With Karl, you could never be sure. Things were almost never what they seemed." Rancor narrowed her eyes; her tiny teeth took on a feral sharpness now.

"Did he ever mention anything that made you suspect any other reason for his death?"

Her bawdy laugh again. "You certainly didn't find out much about Karl, did you? There were dozens of people who would have been happy to kill him.

Dozens. Literally. And I'm not just talking about angry husbands. I'm also talk-ing about all the people at the office he'd stepped on. There were a number of them, too."

"Such as?"

"Such as dear sweet Richard Heckart." She smiled again. "Don't you just love men who devote their entire lives to interior decoration?"

"Richard didn't like him?"

"Of course Richard didn't like him. The only two people who had any real power in that company were Paul and Karl."

"How did Karl get so much power?"

"Would you like a cigarette? I've been noticing your pack in your shirt. And maybe you could give me one—I don't inhale them but they do slow down my need for—food."

I got out two cigarettes, giving her one. I almost hated lighting it for her. It was like lighting another man's cigarette.

"Karl was so indispensable that he took over the number two spot, even though it would ordinarily have gone to Richard Heckart?"

"You don't understand, dear. Karl was a kiss-ass. That and his looks were his only talents. Believe me, he certainly wasn't very bright and he certainly wasn't very good in bed. But he had this earnest boyish quality that men seemed to trust and women found very appealing." She smiled. "And he looked wonderful in a three-piece suit."

"So he kissed Paul Heckart's ass?"

"Shamelessly."

"What form did it take?"

"Oh, there was the makeover."

"I don't understand what that means."

"Well, in female terms, it means you take a very drab girl and with makeup and the right clothes, you turn her into a fox. You see?"

"All right."

"And that's one of the things he did for Paul, who was strictly brown shoes when Karl met him. Paul was this sort of chubby, sweaty guy who spent a lot of time serving on church committees and giving money to his wife's various Junior League activities. But Karl changed him."

"How?"

"Well, dear, you could start with the hair. Paul always used to get one of those bowl jobs—literally, it looked as if his barber had put a bowl on his head and just sheared off the bottom half."

"That was Karl's idea?"

"That, and the Savile Row suits and the sports car and the business trips to Los Angeles and New York. Karl introduced Paul to a variety of things, if you know what I'm trying to say here."

"Sex?"

She smiled. "Yes, if you can imagine poor Paul actually getting an erection, I'm sure there was sex."

"How did Paul's marriage fare?"

"Oh, Nedra Heckart loathed Karl. Absolutely loathed him."

"Did she ever try to get him fired?"

"Many times."

"It apparently didn't work."

"No, but it did succeed in bringing Nedra and sweet brother Richard together. They'd never been close until they joined forces against the dreaded Karl."

"So that was the basis of their relationship, Karl and Paul Heckart's, that he introduced Paul to a different lifestyle."

"That and some kind of power game."

"What kind of power game?"

"I was never sure." She paused. She took a heavy drag off the cigarette. She inhaled it. "Karl didn't confide in me much the last few years of our marriage. We were both unfaithful, it was the seventies and that sort of thing was very much in vogue at the time, but Karl never learned that it's possible to give your body without giving your soul. He always convinced himself that he was in love with these skinny little bitches." She exhaled now, her wrath formidable. "Anyway, something was going on between Karl and Richard Heckart."

"Richard? I thought he and Karl didn't get along."

"They didn't. That's what was so surprising. One night, Richard came over very late. I was up in bed, exhausted from a trip I'd taken to a fat farm. At first, I thought it was just some kind of weird, late-night social call. But then I heard them argue and Richard did something most uncharacteristic."

She wanted to play this out like a Saturday afternoon serial, with me asking questions, her teasing me. I played my part and asked, "What did he do?"

She laughed. "He beat the hell out of my husband."

"That night?"

"Yes. There was a great row. Things got thrown around and smashed. And Karl got a black eye. He was mortified. He felt it ruined his looks, of course."

"That may shoot your theory."

"What theory?"

"About Richard. The way you portray him."

"Oh, no need to defend Richard. He is what he is."

We were back into her parlor games. There were better ways to spend an evening than with a fat, bitter woman who hated herself far more than you could ever hate her, anyway.

"You never found out what the disagreement was about?"

"No. And I really didn't worry about it. I was becoming very successful in insurance, and it was obvious Karl and I were through. I'd humiliated myself enough for him. There's a limit to everything, don't you think, Mr. Walsh?"

"What did Karl do about Richard coming over here?"

"Oh, he told Paul, of course, and Paul and Richard had this terrible argument. And Richard had even less power afterwards."

I could see the alcohol begin to drain her. You reach a point where it really is a depressant, and she'd reached that point now.

I stood up.

"You're hurrying off?"

"I appreciate the time."

She tried to stand up. With her weight and the booze, she was a pathetic sight. I wondered if she knew just how pathetic. No amount of expensive clothes, no amount of clever patter, could disguise it.

"You don't need to get up," I said.

"Are you implying that I can't get up?" she said.

I said good night and let myself out.

Chapter 26

In the old days, back just before the big war, this part of Third Avenue west was a kind of small melting pot unto itself. You found Italians running fruit stands, Irishmen running taverns, blacks running small auto repairs out of concrete garages that opened onto alleys, and you found the sidewalks alive with children of virtually every color and description. On Friday nights you'd put on a necktie after a long day working at the plant and go see one of the big bands downtown, and you'd find yourself surrounded by people living up somewhat to their ethnic stereotypes, particularly where my people, the Irish, and the bottle were concerned.

Now there was no evidence that any such neighborhood had ever existed. It had been uprooted and knocked down, hauled away and burned out, replanted and paved over. The neighborhood and the people and the colors and the smells and the hopes and the fears of those days when Bing Crosby had been the sentimental and Duke Ellington the dark dream—they might have been a fantasy, and inside my head only. Carlucci, my Brooklyn friend with whom I'd served in the war, said one drunken night, "You know, Walsh, when I die it all goes with me—everything. Did you ever think it didn't exist in the first place? You ever think of stuff like that?"

And he'd been right, I thought, as I wheeled my car into the curb, deep in the heart of a neighborhood that had vanished as utterly as any lost tribe. When you die, everything goes with you because it's all just a part of your mind anyway.

Two three-story office buildings lay behind a shifting sheet of snow, the tops of them lost in shadow and flakes so large they formed a kind of fog. They bore the same address as Conroy's name in the phone book. I'd also written down the home address.

One lone car sat on the wide, empty asphalt lot, a new green Chevrolet even lonelier looking in the light of the mercury vapor.

I tried the front door of one of the buildings and had no luck at all. Behind the pane rose a staircase quickly lost in gloom.

I went around to the back. The wind was powerful enough to nearly knock me over at one point, so that I had to bow my head and walk into the freezing snow at an angle. My footprints on the ground made me think of being lost in the arctic someplace—the only prints that had ever disturbed the snow here.

The back door was identical to the front door, but instead of a staircase seen through the darkness, there were two small elevators, side by side, and ready to go.

I walked back fifty feet to look up at the windows. I had to shade my eyes to see through the shifting white wall.

No lights anywhere in the building.

I wondered where Conroy had gone.

Deciding to check his car, I once again headed across the empty, howling lot. There being no windbreak, I had to do the best I could.

By now, Conroy's Chevrolet was heavily covered with wet snow. He would have to scrape off his front and back windshields before going anywhere.

I leaned over and started the process myself, wiping snow off the passenger window.

It wasn't long before I saw him. He was sitting up very straight, as if he had the key in the ignition and was about to go someplace. At first, I had the odd notion that he might merely have been asleep. Apparently, he'd had a long day and was most likely tired.

But then as my eyes adjusted to the interior of the car, I saw the blood that soaked the side of his head, and saw the splashed particles of brain and bone dripping down the window across from him. It looked as if somebody had vomited up a particularly gruesome meal.

I started to put my hand to the door but then I stopped. This was not something I would want to be involved with anyway, and besides, whoever had killed him had undoubtedly took from his person whatever it was he or she had been looking for.

I put my hand back in my pocket.

I stood for a time letting the wind and snow cut my face. The coldness felt reassuring somehow. Conroy wouldn't be feeling any coldness now. Or ever again. I felt lucky. Whatever else, I was alive.

I began to wonder how long it would be before the police discovered his body here. Moments later, I left.

Chapter 27

"You a friend of his?"

"I work for him."

"You do?"

"Part time. I'm a former policeman."

"You are?"

"Yep."

"Cedar Rapids?"

"Yep."

For the first time the apartment manager showed some vague belief in my story. A stubby man in a flannel shirt and baggy jeans and new leatherette slippers, he rubbed at a stubbled chin and said, "So he sent you back here to get something?"

"Right." I chuckled. "Except he forgot to give me the key."

"He don't usually forget stuff."

"No?"

"As a matter of fact, Conroy's got one hell of a memory."

Behind him, in a recliner, his wife sprawled in a robe. It was late enough for her to have a face shiny with cream and a head grotesque with curlers. She avoided looking at me, just kept staring straight ahead at the TV where somebody on one of the nighttime soap operas was just learning that he had an illegitimate son somewhere in the jungles of Ecuador.

"Boy, this is a toughie."

"I know it is, Mr. Haversham."

"It's just his temper."

"Tell me about it."

"I let you in there and you aren't who you say you are and—" He gripped the back of his neck and shook his head.

"Boy."

"'Boy,' is right. I wish I could help you."

He looked back at the recliner. "Hon, you been listenin' to this?"

She just waved him away. She was watching TV.

"The missus don't get involved unless she has to."

"I understand."

He stared me up and down again. "Well, you sure look honest enough."

"I appreciate that."

"And you swear to me that you're working with Frank? I mean, I know he hires 'backup' from time to time."

"And this is one of those times."

"Boy."

"I'm really in kind of a hurry and all, Mr. Haversham."

"So he's waiting for you back there at the stakeout?"

"Right."

"Boy." He clapped his hand to the back of his neck again. "Well," he said. He said it expansively, the way people do when they've given into something against their better judgment.

It was the sort of apartment old men go to die in. Everything had the feel of long use, of being passed down from transient to transient, one set of despairs to another.

There was a wicker rocking chair, the seat of which had long ago come unraveled, and there were faded photographs describing other eras entirely, Conroy in what appeared to be Vietnam, Conroy pointing to a door that had his name on it with "Detective Agency" just beneath, Conroy with a sad-eyed child who had to be his own glimpsed on a terrible Saturday-with-Daddy before the stepfather or new boyfriend came to claim him, Conroy as part of a five-man bowling team high on Schlitz and new silk shirts.

The room smelled of Lysol, cigarette smoke, beer, garbage that needed carrying out, and cold wind coming in through a window that had been smashed.

I went over, past a couch that was still folded out into a bed, and checked the window. It had been cracked so a hand could reach in and open the lock. My feet jangled on shards of glass. The window had been recently cracked, perhaps tonight.

What made me curious was that nothing bad been tossed. The bureau drawers were tidy, the bookcases with paperbacks running to Jackie Collins and Sidney Sheldon untouched, and the one large walk-in closet a model of neatness.

Nobody would have broken in unless they'd been looking for something. The orderliness implied that they'd found it, and without much trouble.

I went into the bathroom, needing to. After I finished, I washed my hands and dried them on a faded yellow towel on the rack. The nub was gone, and so was most of the "Holiday Inn" logo. As I put the towel back, I saw that the door of the long, narrow built-in storage closet was open an inch or so.

The scent of baby powder came to me as I pulled the door slowly open. I sneezed.

The first four shelves contained about what you'd expect. Bic razors new and old, a tube of Vitalis, Old Spice deodorant stick, combs, a Norelco electric shaver that apparently didn't work, an empty red box that had contained Trojans, and several wads of toilet paper that had been used to apply cordovan shoe polish.

I found the dark brown photo album on the bottom shelf.

As soon as I lifted it, I knew immediately what had made the indentation in the bottom of the Vandersee Import-Export crate back at Bainbridge's house.

The photo album was the identical shape and size.

I flipped through the album quickly. All the cellophane windows were empty. You could see, again from impressions left on the sheet, that the book had once held photographic slides.

I knelt down, my old knees cracking as I did so, and began groping around on the bottom shelf, hoping that a slide had fallen out from the book.

Within moments, way in the back, the smell of baby powder even stronger here, my fingers touched the cold plastic edge of a slide.

I was just retrieving it when I heard the apartment door open and Mr. Haversham say, "He told me a bare-faced lie, officers. A bare-faced lie."

A cautious male voice said, "We'd like you to come out here, Mr. Walsh, and spend a little time explaining some things. Do you understand?"

"Oh, yes," I said, pushing myself up from my haunches. "I understand."

Chapter 28

Twenty minutes later, Detective Gaute and I sat in Conroy's living room, him with a pipe, me with a cigarette. Mr. Haversham appeared every few minutes to glare at me for deceiving him.

Detective Gaute said, "Why are you so interested in Conroy?"

"He was following me."

"When?"

"Today."

"Do you know why he was following you?"

"Not exactly."

"Do you know who he was working for?"

"No."

"Did you confront him about following you?"

"Yes."

"What happened?"

"Nothing much. I used my old service revolver to threaten him."

"I'm glad you told me that."

"Why?"

"Because Conroy told his secretary all about it this afternoon, and tonight she told us."

"I see."

"There could possibly be charges against you."

"I know."

"You might even be a suspect in his murder. Especially since you lied to Haversham to get in here. What were you looking for?"

"If I knew who hired him, I'd probably be able to tell you."

"His secretary didn't know, either. That's the weird thing. She said he'd been in a strange mood for the past week, ever since he started on this thing."

"What's his background?"

"Reasonably straight. Did a lot of defense attorney stuff. Didn't go into the divorce racket so much. Like I say, pretty clean." He said, "So what'd you find up here?"

"Huh?"

"You should see yourself. You look like a little kid who just got caught doing something he wasn't supposed to." Gaute laughed. "Really, Walsh. You should see yourself."

"I didn't find anything."

"Right."

"I didn't."

"We'll have to search you."

"You won't find anything."

Gaute made a face. I wondered if it was over me or if his stomach had suddenly acted up. "Walsh, you used to be a cop. You know what a murder investigation's like. A fellow needs all the help he can get." He turned to nod at a uniformed officer who had just come through the door. Gaute's easygoing manner worked against his blunt boxer's profile.

He turned back to me. "I know what you're going through."

"You do?"

"Yeah. You're starting to feel guilty."

"I am?"

"Sure."

"About what?"

"About George Pennyfeather. Those people have got you convinced that you arrested the wrong man twelve years ago."

"Maybe I did."

"So you're being a nice guy and trying to prove that he's innocent."

"Maybe you're right."

"But he's not."

"No?"

"No. He killed Karl Jankov and he killed the Czmek woman, too."

"Why would he kill the Czmek woman?"

"Because she was blackmailing him."

"For what? He'd already gone to prison."

"She was blackmailing him for something else."

"Such as?"

"We're not sure yet. But we do know the Pennyfeather family paid her once a month. A check for a thousand dollars."

I tried not to act interested. "Really?"

"Really, Walsh. A check for a thousand dollars a month all the time Pennyfeather was in prison."

"And you can prove it?"

"Without any problem. We've got the bank records."

"So who killed Conroy?"

He shrugged. "We may be looking at two different cases here. It's at least a possibility. A man in Conroy's line of work makes a lot of enemies."

"You really believe that?"

He smiled. "Right now the only thing I believe is that George Pennyfeather killed the Czmek woman and that his family was paying her blackmail money." He leaned back in the chair and said, "They haven't been very good friends of yours, Walsh. They haven't told you the truth. If I was you, I'd be mad."

"I am mad."

"Then I'd quit trying to help them and tell me everything you've found out."

"Right now, that isn't much."

The photographic slide I'd put down my sock had tilted and was now leaning awkwardly against my ankle. I was thinking of telling Gaute about the slide when another uniformed man came through the door and said, "The lab crew's finishing up with Conroy's car."

Gaute got up, drawing his overcoat around him. "I'd better get back there."

Gaute said, "You feel like talking, you know how to get ahold of me."

"I appreciate the way you've handled this."

"You're not off the hook yet."

"I know."

"And I'd really tell the Pennyfeathers where to get off. They've got you running around and they won't even tell you what's going on."

"I plan to talk to them tonight."

On the way down the stairs, I saw Mr. Haversham peeking out his door. When he saw me, he scowled and closed the door.

I stopped at his door and knocked. He opened it too quickly. His wife still sat behind him, staring at the TV.

"What?" he said.

"I'm sorry I lied to you."

"I'll bet you are."

"I am. That's why I'm apologizing."

He whipped his head to the left and said, "Honey, he's apologizing."

She said, not taking her eyes from the screen, "I heard."

Back to me, he said, "She's really disappointed."

"Oh."

"She tries to trust everybody, but it's things like this that really get her down."

She let out a mean little laugh just as one wrestler threw another to the canvas and proceeded to step on his throat. "I try to shelter her from the world," Mr. Haversham said. "But it doesn't always work."

"I don't imagine it's an easy job," I said, and left.

I drove three blocks very quickly, pulling over to a side street curb beneath a streetlamp that was almost lost in the relentless snow. Down at the far end of the block, I could see another sanding truck headed in my direction. With yellow lights mounted on the top of the cab, it looked like a ferocious metal insect.

I held the slide up to the light and immediately felt sick.

Before I looked at it a second time, I lighted a cigarette and put my head back and closed my eyes. During my years as a county detective, I'd come up against this sort of thing two or three times. In a way, there was nothing worse, not even the butchery some people visit upon one another.

I held the slide up again and took a closer look, and then I opened the glove compartment and tossed it inside. I didn't want to handle it again. Ever.

The sanding truck made a furious grinding noise as it shot splashing yellow light through the falling snow. The two men inside the cab were as bundled up as little kids headed off for school on a cold day. One of them waved to me.

After what I'd just seen, I wasn't too sure I felt like waving back.

Chapter 29

I found a phone booth in the back of a tavern and called Faith. She asked if I could call back in a few minutes—her mother had suddenly gotten extremely upset over Faith's condition and had been calling every ten minutes and Faith wanted, gently, to put a stop to it.

While I waited I got a bottle of Hamm's and a glass and sat in the phone booth blowing blue smoke rings at the TV set over the bar where ESPN was running a tribute to Ali. In just a few minutes you got to see him go from a very young man, and maybe the best boxer who ever lived, to this shambling clown in very serious condition during his last fight with Larry Holmes. It was very depressing.

When I phoned Faith again, she said, "You sound down."

"Oh, no. Things are going fine."

"You're helping Pennyfeather?"

"Ummm-hmmm. How're you?"

"I took two tranks and I'm a little spacey. Right now I feel that there's nothing to worry about."

"I'm sure you're right."

"God, I wish I had these tranks all the time. I borrowed them from Marcia." She paused. "Oh, this woman called."

"This woman?"

"Kathy Stacek."

"Really. That's interesting. Did she leave a number?"

"Yes." She gave me the number and I wrote it down.

"You going to bed?"

"Thought I'd watch your favorite show on the couch."

"That's got to be Carson."

"Right. I know how much you hate him."

"He's stayed too long."

"When're you coming home?"

"I've got to drop by the Pennyfeathers', then I'll be along."

"You're lying."

"Huh?"

"Things aren't going well at all."

"No. Really."

"God, don't you think I can read you by now? Something's wrong. Your voice always gets tight when something's wrong. So what is it?"

I thought of the slide. "Some real twisted stuff."

"Such as?"

"Child porn."

"Oh, God."

I told her about being at Bainbridge's tonight and then Conroy's murder and then finding the slide in his apartment, the one with the naked six- or seven-year-old girl standing in the clearing of a woods.

"Who does it belong to?"

"Maybe Conroy," I said.

"You think he was into it?"

"I'm not sure."

"How does this involve the Pennyfeathers?"

"I'm not sure it does. Though from what Gaute says, they were definitely paying this Czmek woman a thousand dollars a month."

"And you have no idea what for?"

"No idea at all."

"You should come home."

"Why?"

"You sound real depressed and now I'm getting depressed again."

"I shouldn't have called. I was just being selfish."

"We're supposed to rely on each other, remember?"

"I suppose."

"Just come on home, all right?"

"Soon as I stop at the Pennyfeathers'."

"I'm sorry this is turning out to be such a sewer."

"Yeah, so am I."

It took two beers and three cigarettes before Kathy Stacek's line quit giving me one of those mean-spirited little busy signals.

I said, "Kathy Stacek, please."

"Speaking."

"My name's Walsh. You called this evening?"

"Yes, Mr. Walsh. I just wanted to ask you to leave me alone."

It was the way she said it that struck me as odd. There was no emotion in her voice. "I'm sorry the boys roughed you up this morning, but they were just trying to protect me."

"Protect you from what?"

"From being dragged back into it all over again."

"Into what?"

"The trial. The Pennyfeathers. The attorneys. The police. It wasn't any fun, believe me. When I was on the stand, the defense attorney tried to prove that I was an unfit mother and a hooker and everything. I'm not very well educated and I don't have much money but I do have my pride, Mr. Walsh. I've never forgiven the Pennyfeathers for the way they had me treated."

"I'm afraid that's pretty standard procedure."

"I don't care. It's not standard procedure where I come from."

"All I really wanted to know was if your story was the same?"

"What you're really asking is, was I lying?"

"I suppose so, yes."

"No, I wasn't, Mr. Walsh. I saw what I said I saw. George Pennyfeather coming out of the cabin where they later found the body. I couldn't be sure but it looked as if he had a gun in his hand. At the trial I didn't say he *did* have a gun in his hand. I said I *thought* he might have. If I was a dishonest person, Mr. Walsh, I would have gone ahead and told the judge and jury that I saw the gun for sure."

"You're right. You would have."

"I don't want to go through it all again."

"I don't blame you."

"I still have nightmares about sitting there in the witness box and the things the county attorney said about me."

"I'm sorry again."

"I saw what I saw, Mr. Walsh."

"All right."

She hung up.

Chapter 30

The Pennyfeather house looked like a melancholy painting, the snow surrounding it blue from the night sky, the yellow glow from its windows soft and sentimental. A wisp of smoke struggled up from the brick chimney, gray against the full circle of silver moon. The people who lived inside should be sipping hot cider and singing Christmas songs in fetchingly off-key voices, hugging one another in vast reassurance that the world was, after all, a good, true, and knowable place, and that nobody was more deserving of this knowledge than they were.

I sat in my car at the curb, the lights out, trying to calm down. They had deceived me—George and Lisa Pennyfeather for sure, but perhaps even David and Carolyn as well.

The snow was crisp beneath my feet, new snow falling softly now to blanket it. As I drew closer to the front window, shivering slightly in the chill, I saw that the festivities I'd imagined were just that—imaginary. They sat in the front room, paying no attention whatsoever to the blazing fire or the soft New Age music that came from the stereo. It could hardly be described as a holiday celebration.

My knock had the resonance of a club falling against the door, something unyielding and final, and the way the voices fell inside, I could tell it struck them the same way, too.

There were quick whispers as to who would answer, and then the scuffle of two feet across thick carpet, and then Carolyn in silhouette stood in the doorway, light from inside flowing around her like golden waves.

"I'm afraid we're busy, Mr. Walsh."

"I'm coming in, Carolyn." I knew how angry I sounded.

"Even if we don't want you to?"

This was the first time they'd pulled class on me and obviously she thought it was going to work, but before she could say anything else I pushed gently past her, and into the warmth of the living room.

David nearly jumped to his feet. "Didn't you hear what Carolyn said?"

I had the impression he was on the verge of punching me.

"Please, Mr. Walsh," Lisa said. "We're spending the night with just our family. And anyway, you've spent a lot of our money and not turned up all that much." You hear this in a lot in cases—clients who begin to blame you for their misfortunes.

"Where's George?"

"He's upstairs lying down."

"I want him down here."

"And I want you out of here," David said, coming at me. I was angry enough that I didn't care, was willing to be beaten for the pleasure of one punch at his arrogant, sullen face. Carolyn threw her arms around David, breaking his stride, stopping him from coming at me.

"Aren't things crazy enough; do we really need this, too?" Carolyn said. She spoke quietly, but the sadness in her voice was overwhelming. David relented. He called me a few names but he went over and sat on the edge of the couch and scowled in the direction of the fireplace.

"Would you like to come up and have a drink, Mr. Walsh? We have a very nice study upstairs."

George Pennyfeather had come into the room without anybody noticing. In a rust-colored cardigan, white shirt, and dark slacks, he stood in the archway as if he were the host at a small, friendly get-together. He looked a little happier now that he was out on bail.

"I imagine you'd like to talk to me," he said. "We really shouldn't bother my family with all this. Not when it's between you and me." He raised a glass of what appeared to be whiskey. "I imagine you're here about the Czmek woman, and Conroy, aren't you?"

My curiosity overcame my anger. I looked around at the family—Lisa and Carolyn spent, David still volatile—and sighed. In my mind it had all been so simple—barge in here, demand the truth, and get it. But if I got the truth at all, the process would be far more circuitous, and it would involve hurting somebody at least emotionally, and perhaps physically.

"Would you like something to drink?"

"A beer would be nice."

"Why don't I get it, Dad?" Carolyn said, and left for the kitchen.

Lisa, nervous, said, "It's cold out, isn't it?"

We were going to stand here and pretend that her husband hadn't only days ago been released from prison, and that two murders hadn't taken place in less than three days.

We were going to talk about the weather.

"Yes, and it seems to be getting colder," I said, doing my part.

"Dave Towne on Channel 9 said the snow is going to continue all night," she said.

"Oh, for Christ's sake, Mother," David said, getting up from the couch, and making another fist of his hand. "You don't need to stand there and be nice to this slimeball. You shouldn't have hired him in the first place."

Lisa Pennyfeather dropped her gaze, looking ashamed at her son's words.

"David just gets excited," George Pennyfeather said. "I'm sure he didn't mean anything by that."

"No," I said, hoping I sounded properly ironic. "In some countries, 'slimeball' is actually a term of endearment." Nobody laughed.

Carolyn came back with the beer. Raised to be the proper hostess, she had put on the bottom of my glass one of those bright red little tug-on coasters made of cotton with elastic at the top. The beer had a two-inch head, which meant that out in the kitchen half a bottle was going shamefully to waste. But now probably wasn't the time to raise that subject.

"We'll be upstairs," George Pennyfeather said unnecessarily, as if there might have been somewhere else we were going.

I followed him up the winding, carpeted staircase and down a hallway covered with handsomely framed photographs of Carolyn and David at various ages. In one photograph, Paul Heckart stood with his arm around David, who was probably then ten or so.

We went past darkened bedrooms, a bright and enormous blue-tiled bathroom, and finally into a den that was one of those shaggy, book-messy places with soft leather furnishings and throw rugs and a barking walrus of an old TV console. This would be a great place to watch George Raft movies and dream of the old days.

A gooseneck lamp propped on the corner of a small mahogany table provided soft, shadowy light. George pointed to the leather armchair and I sat down. He took the couch.

"The first thing I should tell you is that I didn't know this Conroy fellow, no matter what the police say." He shook his head. "There was a news bulletin on TV."

"You told me you didn't know the Czmek woman, either."

"Well, that one I lied about. I was afraid of getting involved, and going back to prison."

"But of course you're not lying about this one?"

"I don't blame you for being angry."

"Let's concentrate on Stella Czmek."

"All right."

"How did you know her?"

"You won't believe this."

"Just tell me, George."

"I had an affair with her."

We all build up false images of one another. The stupid jock; the happy fat person. Then suddenly we're confronted with a piece of evidence that completely obliterates all our expectations. That was how I felt now, sitting here with a small, gentle man who rarely spoke more than was necessary and who gave the impression of being lost in all respects. I had attributed to him intelligence but not cunning, industriousness but not ambition, and loyalty. If any man was loyal, it would be George Pennyfeather here. If any man was true-blue—

"You did?"

"You're surprised?"

I cleared my throat. "Well—"

"I'm not the type, I know."

"It's not that—"

"Oh, it is; and that's probably why I did it. I've never been particularly secure about my relationships with women, anyway. You know, here I was pretty old and I'd never kissed anybody but my wife." He shook his head. "I don't know which is more embarrassing now—the fact that I was so stupid or the fact that I very deeply hurt my wife."

"You told her?"

"Yes. I—I wish I could say I did it by way of being honest but what really happened was that I had no choice. Karl had been murdered and Stella—Stella wanted money to be quiet. I had to tell Lisa about her. How she was blackmailing me for having an affair with her." He frowned. "It was a pretty crazy time in my life. I'd also found out some things about Richard Heckart."

I sighed. "What things?"

"I'd been working late one night—this was before the rumor started that Lisa was having an affair—and I saw Richard Heckart leaving the office late. He accidentally slammed a metal case he was carrying against the elevator door and a few things fell out."

"What things?"

"Slides."

"Photographic slides?"

"Yes."

"What did the slides show?"

"Is it really necessary to go into that?"

"Yes."

He put down his drink and stared off into the darkness. "It would have killed Paul, finding out the sort of thing his younger brother was into. They're from a very old family, you know."

"You still haven't told me what the slides showed."

"You're a bright man, Mr. Walsh. I'm sure you've got some idea."

"I need you to tell me exactly what was on the slides."

"Pornography, of course."

"What kind?"

He hesitated. He looked embarrassed. "It makes me feel dirty to say." He paused again. "Children."

"I see."

"I'd never seen anything like it. Small children, boys and girls, five or perhaps six years old. Doing—" He dropped his gaze again. "Nothing ever disgusted me in the way that did. I—I even thought of confronting Richard—slapping him or something. I felt so bad for those children—"

"So Richard didn't know you knew."

"No, not directly."

"Not directly?"

"I mailed him an anonymous letter just before I went into prison."

"And the letter said what?"

"Oh, about what you'd expect. I'm afraid I was awfully outraged and sanctimonious. The man is obviously mentally ill and probably didn't need to hear—"

"What did the letter say you were going to do?"

"Nothing, really. Just that I was aware of what he was doing and that he should stop or he would be turned over to the police."

"But you had no way of knowing if he stopped or not?"

"No."

I finished my mostly-foam beer and set it down. "Did you ever think that those slides might have had something to do with Karl's death?"

"No, and you'd have to show me very hard evidence to prove they did. I know who murdered Karl. It's just that neither my lawyers nor the investigators they hired were ever able to prove it."

"You think it could have been Terri Jankov?"

"Absolutely. If you'd met her—"

"I did meet her. Unfortunately."

"I can tell that Terri hasn't changed much just by your tone of voice." He leaned forward in the cone of light. He looked very old suddenly. "All those years in prison, I had such fantasies of what I'd do to her when I got out. How I'd make her confess. How my family's name would be cleared."

"Did you see her when you got out?"

"Yes. And—she laughed at me. She called me names and laughed at me and said that I just hadn't been able to face the truth that Lisa and Karl had been lovers."

"I'm sorry to let you down, George, but I don't think she's the person we're looking for."

He sat back wearily, out of the light.

"How did you meet Stella Czmek?"

"At a party."

"Whose party?"

"One of Paul's, actually. For all I know, they may have been lovers, too." He raised his glass. Ice cubes clinked. "The woman you saw in the gazebo the other night wasn't the Stella Czmek I had an affair with."

"No?"

"No. That Stella was—well, never svelte, but she really took care of herself and she was... quite knowledgeable in bed, if that's not too stuffy a way to put it."

"How long did your affair last?"

"Nearly a year."

"It ended before Karl's murder?"

"A few weeks before."

"What ended it?"

He smiled unhappily. "My natural timid soul and my good Wasp guilt. I just couldn't go on telling Lisa that I loved her while all the time—"

"So she began to blackmail you."

"Yes, right after I told her we'd have to split up. One night I'd been drinking and I told her all about the slides and—The day she told me she was going to black-mail me, I saw a whole new person. It's like those science fiction movies where you suddenly see the monster that's beneath the human exterior."

"You didn't have any doubt she was serious?"

"None."

"And so Lisa began paying the money while you were in prison?"

"Correct."

"Do you have any idea why Stella Czmek came over here the other night?"

"None."

"She'd been paid for the month?"

"Yes, but the way she went through money—"

I nodded, pushed myself to my feet. Abruptly, I was tired. I thought of Faith and Hoyt, of the warm bed with them on such a cold night.

"I got the impression you were going to quit helping us, Mr. Walsh."

"I was going to."

"You've changed your mind?"

"Let's just say I've put off making a decision."

He got to his feet and led the way out of the den and down the hall. At the front door, Carolyn said, "David asked me to apologize."

I touched her elbow. "I appreciate the words, but somehow I doubt David said them."

"If he weren't under so much stress, he would have apologized," Lisa Pennyfeather said. "That's what Carolyn meant to say."

They were a nice family. I just didn't know if there was anything I could do for them.

"Tomorrow may be a bad day," George Pennyfeather said.

In his mild way, he was asking me, and rather desperately it seemed, for help.

"Let's see what I can turn up," I said, and left as quickly as I could.

Chapter 31

She had reversed the usual sleeping arrangements tonight. Hoyt was packed with pillows on the couch and she was in on the bed. A note in pencil and large letters said, "Sleeping pills."

In my underwear, I slid under the covers next to her. She was warm and damp with sweat. Sleeping pills always bring on flu-like symptoms with her, but at least she sleeps.

I smoked three cigarettes. I wondered how I was going to approach Richard Heckart in the morning. I also wondered how I was going to get hold of Stan Papajohn, Stella Czmek's ex-husband, and Marvin Scribbins, the man who'd owned the lot Conroy had listed in his log.

I thought about these things as long and as hard as I could because I knew that the moment I quit playing with them, I'd have to start thinking about the woman next to me, and all that she meant to me, and what lay ahead for her tomorrow.

I tried some more of my failed prayers, not even getting the words right, but trying to address something, anything, that was alive and aware and powerful out there in the cosmic darkness, pleading her case and hoping for the best.

I put out my last cigarette and snuggled up next to her as close as I could, the lines of my body lightly touching the lines of her body, so as not to wake her.

I went to sleep with the fresh smell of her hair filling my senses.

"You want me to go with you?" I asked.

"I'm sure you're busy."

"You know better than that."

"You'd really go?"

"Of course I would."

"That's all I need, then."

"What is?"

"Knowing that you'd really go. Now you don't have to."

"You're not making a lot of sense."

"It's just knowing you love me."

"You knew that already."

"Yes, but now you're willing to demonstrate it. You know?"

"I see, I guess."

"Could we just lie here a minute and not say anything?"

"Sure."

So we did.

Against the curtains pressed gray dawning light. She'd awakened at 5:20 and I'd snapped alert, too, afraid something was wrong.

She'd slept in her bra and panties. She lay still, the smooth jut of her hip against mine. There are times when lust is not only impractical but immoral. Even given what she was facing this morning, I wanted to make love.

I moved away from her, over to the edge of the bed.

"What's wrong?" she asked.

"Nothing."

"Why'd you roll away?"

"I was just getting warm under the covers."

"Oh."

I didn't say anything for a time.

"Were you getting horny?"

"No," I said.

"Really?"

"Really."

"Oh."

I said, "Why did you ask?"

"Oh, no reason especially."

"Oh."

"Well, sort of a reason I guess."

"What was that?"

"Well, because I was getting a little horny myself."

"I see."

"So you weren't horny?"

"No, I was horny but I didn't want to impose."

"I wish you would. Impose, I mean."

"Really? You're sure?"

"I'm not this delicate little flower."

"I just meant—"

"I know. With the mammogram coming up and all. But maybe it'll help calm me down. My heart's racing." She took my hand and put it to her chest. "Feel that?"

"Yeah. It's really racing."

It was sweet, the way we made love. It had never been so gentle there in the warm tangle of sheets and covers.

Afterward, she said, "My mother's going to be over at Mercy."

"Oh."

"I'd invite you, but—"

"I know."

"I wish she liked you better."

"So do I."

"I guess it's because you're about the same age."

"To be fair to your mother, I'm a few years older than she is."

"Yeah, I guess that's true."

"And if I were your mother, I'd have the same reservations about me that she does."

"But she won't even get to know you."

"Maybe someday she will."

"So you understand why I don't want you to go along?"

"Sure."

Just then Hoyt started crying. When he hears us talking, he always wonders why he can't be included.

I went out and got him. His diaper needed changing so I changed it and then I brought him in and laid back down and put him between us.

She picked him up and played airplane, suspending him above her. He put his arms out, the way he usually does, like wings. She jiggled him around and he laughed with his pink little mouth and his merry blue eyes.

When she was finished, she put him down between us. I rolled over on my side and put my finger in his small damp hand. He liked to grip my finger and tug it right and left, the way he will someday when he's a wrestler or a fullback.

"I hope I know."

"What?" I said.

"I hope I know right on the spot this morning."

"What did they tell you?"

"Well, this real nice woman, this Kay Jackson I told you about?"

"Right."

"She said that sometimes the mammogram can pick up on certain characteristics and tell right away if the lump is malignant. It's the waiting and the worrying that's the worst part."

"I said some prayers for you."

"Really?"

"Uh-huh."

"That's really sweet."

"So now you know you'll be all right."

She laughed. "I guess so. I mean, when even a heathen like you starts to pray—" She stopped and leaned over Hoyt and gave me a chaste kiss on the nose. "I shouldn't have called you a heathen."

I said, "Call me anything you want."

When I looked at her then, I could see that her eyes were starting to fill.

She got up quickly and went into the bathroom, closing the door and running the water. She sometimes does this as a way of disguising the fact that she's going to the bathroom. Apparently she's under the impression that I still believe she doesn't have to go to the toilet.

After a few minutes, the shower started running. I wondered if she were crying in there, standing under the blast of the water.

I said another prayer. I still wasn't sure it mattered one way or the other. But I had to do something.

Then I went and got Hoyt's food. It wasn't often he got breakfast in bed.

Chapter 32

Irma Ozmanski said, "You going over to Big Boy?"

"I hadn't thought of it. Why, would you like something?"

"Well, I don't want you to make a special trip."

"I suppose I could do with a donut."

"You sure?"

"Sure. What would you like, Irma?"

But before she gave her order, she wanted some praise for what she'd done to the office. I didn't blame her. After she'd pushed furniture around, dusted, hung bright new drapes, and lugged out maybe two dozen cardboard boxes with files we neither needed nor wanted, the office looked as good as Don and I always said it should.

She said, "I know I kinda get people down."

"Nonsense, Irma."

"I can be pretty pushy."

"You?"

"No sense you being nice, Walsh. You know what I'm like and I know what I'm like." Her pudgy hand swept the office.

"But this is the only home I've got left so— So I just want you to know I'm gonna shape up. You understand?"

"I understand."

"And I hope that someday you even let me help you out on a case. When you're married to a cop as long as I was, you just naturally pick things up."

"Right."

"So anytime you want me to do anything more than just sort of be a secretary, you let me know, all right?"

"All right."

"I won't put any pressure on you."

"Right."

"It'll be up to you. When I start being your assistant."

"Right."

"Glazed would be great. Two of them."

"Glazed. Got it."

When I walked back through the door ten minutes later, she was holding the telephone receiver and saying, "There's a call for you."

I immediately thought of Faith. "A woman?"

"No. A man."

"Oh."

I handed her the sack. Grease had stained the bottom. I took the receiver, wound the cord around the desk, and sat down.

"Hello?"

"Mr. Walsh, my name is Marvin Scribbins. I'm returning your call from yesterday."

"Oh, yes, thanks for calling back."

"Quite all right. How may I help you?"

"I'm a private investigator."

"Yes, that's what the woman said."

"I'm doing some background work for a client and I wondered if you could help me with a few things."

For the first time he sounded slightly hesitant. It meant nothing. People are automatically hesitant about talking to investigators of any kind. They feel that all questions are trick questions and that they will inevitably give the wrong answer.

"I'll help you if I can."

I asked him if he knew Conroy.

"No, I don't believe so. But that name—Wait a minute. Wasn't he killed last night?"

"Yes."

"Just what kind of investigation is this, Mr. Walsh?"

"It's not directly involved with the murder, Mr. Scribbins."

"You're sure?"

"Yes."

"All right, then. You have another question?"

"You used to own property out on Mount Vernon Road, correct?"

"Right. In fact, I owned two or three different parcels of land out there. Which one did you have in mind?"

"The one where the Drive-Mart is today."

"Oh. Right. What about it?"

"Somebody tried to buy that land?"

"Yes."

"Could you give me the name?"

He hesitated. "I guess there's no reason not to. Jerry Vandersee was his name. Unfortunately for me, the deal fell through. He'd been going to spend a lot of money but then his partner backed out at the last minute."

"His partner?"

"Yes, it was one of those things where two men put up equal amounts of capital. Only his partner lost interest and found some other investment."

"Do you remember this partner's name?"

"I think so. I deal with so many names—"

I waited.

He said, "Heckart."

I tried to conceal my surprise. "H-e-c-k-a-r-t?"

"Correct."

"Do you remember his first name?"

"Oh, let's see; Robert—no; Richard—yes; Richard Heckart."

Behind him a phone rang.

"You sound like a busy man, Mr. Scribbins."

"You know how it is when you just get back from a business trip."

"I'll let you go."

"I hope I was some help."

"A great deal. Thanks, Mr. Scribbins."

He sounded pleased I wasn't going to ask him any more questions.

I knew it was too early for Faith to be back. But I called my place anyway. It was like making some sort of inexplicable contact with her. There was no answer. I closed my eyes and tried to imagine what she was doing, saying. I felt my control go. On the steering wheel, my fingers trembled.

Chapter 33

Richard Heckart looked cross as always, like one of those mean, prim male schoolteachers we all remember from our childhood. Not effeminate, just fussy and without any evidence of humor or joy.

When he came out to the reception area, he gave a miserable little shake of his head, as if I'd interrupted him while he was in the process of finding the secret to star travel.

"Yes, Mr. Walsh?"

"I'd like to speak with you, if that's possible."

He indicated the couch across from me. He pulled himself up inside his tan three-piece suit. "I'll sit over there."

"This has to be private, I'm afraid."

He saw how the receptionist was pretending to read her computer screen while actually listening quite openly to our conversation.

He said, "Trish, is the small conference room open?"

"Yes, it is."

"We'll be in there, then." As I stood up, he said, "Would you like some coffee?"

"No, thanks." Given what I was about to say to him, I didn't think it would be right to accept his hospitality.

The small conference room, different from the one we'd been in yesterday, was done in leather and mahogany, like an old-fashioned den. One large window looked down on the rear of Armstrong's department store. Steam whipped out of huge heating ducts. While he waited for Trish to bring him his coffee, I stared down at the people hurrying along the sidewalks. Everybody looked cold as they bent into the wind.

Trish closed the door. I went over and sat down across from Richard Heckart at a small teak conference table.

"What can I do for you today, Mr. Walsh?"

I wasted no time. From inside the pocket of my sport coat, I took the photographic slide. I set it on the polished surface of the table and pushed it across to him.

"I'm supposed to look at this?"

"Please," I said.

"I take it I'm not going to like what I see?"

From the way his voice had begun to tighten, I knew he had guessed what the slide was.

"Just hold it up and look at it, if you would."

"And what if I wouldn't like to?"

"I guess I can't force you."

"I don't like playing games."

The slide rested maybe three or four inches from his left hand, the one with the fat gold wedding band. He had perfectly manicured nails and perfectly shaped fingers. He would not look at the slide, nor would those perfect fingers touch it.

"You know what's on that slide, don't you?"

"How would I know that?"

"Because you were working with a man named Vandersee and because slides like these were his real business."

"I've never heard of any Vandersee."

"Well, a businessman named Marvin Scribbins is willing to testify that you and Vandersee were business partners who tried to buy a parcel of land from him a few years ago. I'd say that qualifies as knowing Vandersee."

His eyes dropped to the slide. His hand opened and seemed about to reach for it but then closed again and lay still.

"You're afraid to touch it, aren't you?"

He said nothing.

"You know what kind of filth is on there and you're ashamed and I can't say I blame you. That's the lowest kind of exploitation there is."

He said nothing.

"You and Vandersee were selling child pornography—maybe even taking your own photographs—and exporting them, weren't you?"

His jaw muscles had started to clench and unclench. Still, he said nothing.

I reached over and picked up the slide. "Did you ever wonder what happened to this poor little girl, you bastard? What kind of life she had after you and Vandersee were done with her?"

He said, quite simply, "What do you plan to do about all this?"

I don't know what I'd been expecting—some mixture of shock and remorse, I suppose. Certainly nothing as cold as his question.

"Go to the police, of course."

"What if you're wrong?"

"Wrong about what?"

"Wrong about what seems to be going on here."

"You still claim you didn't know Vandersee?"

He paused and glanced down at his perfect fingers. His right hand reached over and touched his wedding ring. He kept his head down. "What if I told you that I did know Vandersee?"

"That would be a good beginning. Then I'd like you to tell me what Vandersee and you had to do with the murder of Karl Jankov and Stella Czmek and a private investigator named Conroy."

He raised his eyes. Our eyes met. He looked grim. "You think I killed them?"

"I think it's a distinct possibility."

"Why would I kill them?"

"Because they knew what you and Vandersee were into. Jankov and the Czmek woman could have been blackmailing you."

"That's a pretty fancy theory."

"You may not find it interesting, but I'm sure the police would."

He stared at me and shook his head. There was an air of sorrow about him now, but I sensed that the grief was for himself rather than the little girl in the slide or any of the people who'd been murdered. "I'm not the person you want."

"No? Then who is?"

"I'm not sure."

"I don't believe you."

He stared at the table again. He seemed to be in some kind of reverie.

"Did you and Vandersee take the slides yourselves?"

"No," he said. "Vandersee bought them from overseas. A man in Hong Kong."

"What did he do with them?"

"Sold them. He had a list of men who bought slides like these. They're all over the country. And they're willing to pay whatever the traffic demands."

"The slides came in the import boxes?"

"Right. In false bottoms."

"Customs never caught on?"

"Vandersee never gave them much chance. He only needed one or two shipments a year, which meant that the odds were in his favor."

"He made a lot of money?"

"Hundreds of thousands a year."

"He duplicated the slides?"

"He duplicated them endlessly."

"Where did you fit in?"

"It doesn't matter, now, does it, Mr. Walsh?" His blue eyes had turned almost silver with tears. "There's nothing I can do about what happened."

"Did you kill Jankov?"

"No."

"Did you kill Czmek or Conroy?"

"No."

"Then who did?"

"As I told you, I'm not sure."

"And as I told you, that's the part I don't believe."

He said, "I never thought anybody would find out." He was going into a reverie again. It was ten in the morning in downtown Cedar Rapids and it was eerie.

He reached across the desk and picked up the slide I'd set down. He didn't glance at it. Instead he put it in the palm of his right hand and then closed the right hand with the sudden ferocity of an animal striking its prey. His strength was impressive. He crushed the slide and tossed it, twisted, back on the table.

"Wouldn't it be nice if things were just what they seemed?" he said. "Wouldn't it be nice if I were the pervert everybody has always thought I was?"

I wasn't sure what he was talking about; I just sensed that this was one of the few times he was being honest.

He said, "Things didn't turn out as I'd planned, Mr. Walsh."

"I hope you're going to explain that."

"Not now."

I sighed, slumped back in my chair. "Maybe it would be better for you if you told me everything."

"I can't. Not without—certain preparations."

"Then you're willing to let me go to the police?"

His smile was morbid. "How could I stop you?"

"By telling me everything."

"I—can't do that. Not now, anyway."

"You know who the killer is, don't you?"

"I have a good idea."

"The police are going to assume it's you."

"People have been making assumptions about me all my life. You pay a price for that."

I nodded to the twisted slide. "That's no excuse to get involved in that kind of thing."

"Someday you may know the truth, Mr. Walsh."

I couldn't tell if he was being deliberately misleading or if he was trying to say something through a kind of code.

"Would you give me till four this afternoon before going to the police?"

"Why?"

"By then I'll be able to tell you some things."

"Such as what?"

"Such as who the killer is, perhaps."

"And why they were killed?"

"Yes." He said, "You want to clear George, don't you?"

"If he isn't the killer, I do."

"Then give me till four and I'll have some information for you."

"All right. Are you going to call me at four or should I call you?"

"I'll call you."

"Try my home number first."

"All right."

I said, "I hope you know what you're doing."

The death-mask smile was back. "So do I, Mr. Walsh. So do I."

Chapter 34

She'd burned something—toast, most likely—and my apartment smelled of it now. She'd left the TV on. Donahue in his dramatic way was about to probe a woman's face with his microphone. In the bathroom I found a pink plastic bottle of talc overturned. The damp bathmat was covered with white powder that looked vaguely like heroin. She was scared and so was I.

In the living room I picked up the phone and dialed Faith's apartment across the street.

"Hello."

"Marcia?"

"Yes."

"Walsh."

"Oh. Hi."

"How's Hoyt?"

"Kind of grumpy today, actually."

"Give him a kiss for me."

She laughed. "I was thinking of giving him something else."

"I'm sure he's picking up our moods."

"Oh, you mean Faith's test."

"Right. You heard anything?"

"Huh-uh. Not a word."

"Well, if she should happen to call tell her I'm back at my apartment for a while."

"Okay. You want to say goodbye to Hoyt? I just picked him up."

Hoyt made a few wet babbling noises. I puckered up and gave him a noisy telephone kiss.

"Bye," Marcia said.

I was just taking my cup of Folger's Instant from the microwave when I saw the gray ghost of the mailman cross right-to-left behind the curtain. Cup in hand, I went into the hallway and got my mail. The only thing interesting was a letter from my friend Salvadore Carlucci who I'd served in Italy with during World War II and who, like me, was a retired cop turned investigator.

Lately, Carlucci's letters were more like small essays as he reminisced about our days in the war. "Remember when you could room and board—and I mean six good meals—for a whole weekend outside Fort Dix... for just $10.85? Remember the time we saw Betty Grable perform in New York? Remember the kid from Oklahoma with trench mouth so bad all he could do was cry? Remember how we used to pack dead men on mules and send them down the long, winding mountain roads so the Red Cross people could attend to them?"

As I sat there, my coffee going cold, I began to think back and in doing so realized how many different people I'd been in my life. In the war I'd been forced to be the kind of cold, ruthless man I later learned to despise. Later, as a detective, I'd developed a real sympathy for the plight of most people in trouble—a sympathy based, I suppose, on the belief that each of us at heart is scared and alone.

I was just debating sticking my coffee back into the microwave when the phone rang. Assuming it would be Faith, I jumped for it.

"Mr. Walsh?"

"Yes."

"My name is Stan Papajohn."

"I appreciate the call," I said.

"I'm told you were asking about Stella."

"Yes."

"I guess I'd like to know why."

"I'm an investigator, Mr. Papajohn. I'm working for a client."

"That doesn't tell me much."

"I'm trying to figure out your ex-wife's relationship with her former employer, a Mr. Vandersee."

"Are you trying to be smart?"

"No. Why?"

"If you know anything about Stella then you know just what kind of relationship it was."

"I see."

"They were honeys."

"Do you mind talking about it?"

He hesitated. "I guess not. I suppose this has to do with her murder?"

"Yes."

"Then you must be working for George Pennyfeather."

"You know George?"

"Not really. But he came over here one night."

"He did? When?"

"Back before he killed Jankov."

"Do you know what he wanted?"

He laughed. "Whatever it was, he wanted it pretty bad."

"Oh?"

"That's right. He slapped Stella."

"George Pennyfeather?"

"Yep. Stella said he was a real wimp. But he slapped her anyway."

I didn't tell him about George's relationship with Papajohn's late wife. "Did she know Karl Jankov?"

"The same way she knew Vandersee."

"They were lovers?"

"Yup. Bitch. That was the kind of woman she was."

"Is that why you got a divorce?"

"That and the way the bill collectors were comin' around."

"I thought she was doing very well in those days."

"She was but got in too deep."

"Do you know exactly how she and Vandersee made their money?"

"Import-export as far as I knew."

"Nothing else?"

He hesitated again. "To be honest, I always knew there was somethin' else but I never could figure out what it was. I think that's how they made their real money."

"You didn't ever get any real sense of it?"

"Not really."

"Do you know a man named Heckart?"

"Yup. He brought Stella home one night."

"Richard Heckart?"

"No. His name was Paul Heckart."

"What?"

"Yup. I wrote down his license number and checked it the next day. Paul Heckart. Those were the days when I was still trying' to keep track of who she was seein' on the side. After a while, it got to be too much trouble."

"You're sure it was Paul Heckart?"

"Sure. Who's this Richard Heckart anyway?"

I was about to answer when I heard the key in the door and before I could turn around, she was crossing the threshold.

Given the look on her face, I didn't need to ask how it had gone. She moved quickly through the living room and into the bedroom. She closed the door quietly. Moments later she started crying.

"Mr. Walsh?"

"Yes."

"You all right?"

"I guess so, Mr. Papajohn. Thanks for your time."

"Well, sure. Is that it?"

"For now, anyway. Thanks again."

I hung up. I couldn't ever recall my apartment being this silent. Her tears were a scourge on the air.

I went to the door and knocked with one knuckle.

She just kept on crying. I turned the knob and went in.

Chapter 35

In the rooms of the dying there is a silence the ocean floor could not equal. In the rooms of the dying there is the first faint roar of the nothingness that awaits us all.

I sat on the chair next to the bed and smoked two cigarettes. I knew better than to say anything.

She lay across the bed, arms out crucifixion-style. She wore a blue two-piece suit wrinkled now from sitting. On the backs of her knees you could see where her hose had chafed. There was a spot of mud on the heel of her right blue pump. On her left pump there was a small tear in the leather.

After a time she quit crying. She drew into herself physically, putting one hand to her nose, the other against the back of her head. She kicked her pumps off. They were loud hitting the floor. She drew her knees up, hose scraping, so that she was in a semi-fetal position. The only sound she made was sniffling.

I got up and lighted another cigarette and went to the window and looked out at the parking lot. I'm not sure I saw anything. I couldn't quite focus.

She said, "I'm sorry."

I turned around and walked to her. "Why would you be sorry?"

"Because I'm not stronger."

I sat down on the bed. The springs squawked. I took her hand.

She said, "I wish you'd quit."

I felt a speech coming on. I put out the cigarette.

"I'm afraid if I start telling you about it, I'll start crying again."

"I like it when you cry."

"You do?"

"Yeah, that way you can't talk."

She smiled and snuffled at the same time. "I do talk too much sometimes, don't I?"

"We all do."

"They did a biopsy."

"Oh."

"The mammogram—well, it was inconclusive, but there are certain characteristics they look for and—well, they found a few of those characteristics. It could be malignant."

"But then again it may not be."

"See, that's why I wish I were stronger. Like my college roommate Sandy."

"She'd handle this pretty well, huh?"

"She wouldn't even worry about it. She'd just go on with her life until they called her. I'll just sit by the phone waiting for the results. I won't be able to think of anything else."

"Then I guess I'll have to break down and take you to a movie. Maybe it's time we take Hoyt."

"Oh, God, you know what babies are like in theaters and churches. I love Hoyt, but I wouldn't want to inflict him on anybody."

"I had a nice time this morning. Making love."

"What if they find something?"

"If you read the brochures carefully, Faith, you know that you've got pretty good odds with breast cancer."

"If they caught it soon enough."

"You don't seem to even consider the alternative."

"What alternative?"

"That the biopsy will show you're fine."

"But I've been through two tests now and neither one of them was fine."

"That isn't exactly true, hon. The first test just showed that you had to have a second test and the second test showed that you needed to have a third test."

"Did you ever have to go through something like this?"

"With my colon."

"Really?"

"Ten years ago. I just went in for one of those tests where they give you a barium enema and something showed up on the screen. I knew something was wrong because they wouldn't let me leave the hospital and they just kept calling me back for more X-rays. Everybody in the waiting room knew something was wrong, too. I was embarrassed; I hate being watched by people. But every time I'd be called back, the people waiting would get more and more fascinated with me. They started shaking their heads and looking very grim. One couple even started whispering about me. They seemed sad, as if they were convinced I wasn't going to make it. I was there all morning and then I went home and lay down and I was very scared and I called my doctor. He was busy, his nurse said, and he'd get back to me. I asked her if she'd call Mercy and get the results. She said they usually didn't do that, that the hospital just mailed the X-rays over. But she relented finally and agreed to check it out. So I waited and when the phone rang two hours later, I got it on the first ring, and I said, 'Did they find something?' and the doctor said, 'Yes, they found something. We're not sure what it is yet, but there's a shadow on the X-ray.' And from there things moved fast. Even though the doctor explained that the shadow might be nothing more than a piece of stool that hadn't gotten washed out by the enema, they sent me to see a surgeon and he took out this piece of white paper and proceeded to draw my colon and show me exactly what he would have to do with it, where he'd be cutting and what he'd be looking for. Maybe I would have felt better if Sharon had been in better health. I was worried about both of us—who'd take care of us if we were both sick? I started to put everything in order. I called my insurance man, and I double-checked on the burial plot that I'd paid for in advance, and I patched things up with my youngest son because we'd had an argument a few months earlier, and then I just waited. My doctor said they'd want to give me the barium test again just as a precaution. So this time I wanted to get cleaned out as well as possible, and I went to the hospital and I was there for two hours and just as I was getting dressed, the radiologist who had taken the X-rays came in and said, 'I know what they thought you had,' and he smiled. 'But you don't have it. The X-ray is clear.'"

"God, you must have really been happy."

"All I could think of was those old movies where the man in the electric chair gets a last-minute reprieve."

I took her hand and brought it to my cheek and closed my eyes. "It's going to be like that for you. They're not going to find anything."

She lay down on her back and stared at me. "I'm glad nothing was wrong with you."

"Thanks."

"You're the only nice man I've ever had a relationship with."

"Oh, there must have been at least one or two others who were nice."

"Not the way you are."

"Well, that's very flattering."

"You know what I'm afraid of?"

"What?"

"I mean, besides dying?"

"Huh-uh. What?"

"That if they have to remove the breast, things won't be the same between us."

"Oh, God, you've got to know better than that."

"All my life I've managed to get by on my looks. You know that?"

"I know that."

"But if they took my breast—"

"They're not going to take your breast."

"But *if* they did—"

"If they did—"

"Then people would start feeling sorry for me and that would be terrible. It really would."

"They're not going to take your breast."

"You'd start feeling sorry for me."

"No, I wouldn't."

"Yes, you would. At least a little."

"Maybe a smidgen."

"And then our relationship would change. I wouldn't be this appealing young woman to you anymore, I'd be this—thing of pity."

"That's kind of tough to imagine, kiddo. You being a thing of pity, I mean."

"But it could happen. And you know it."

"Everything's going to be fine."

And she started crying again, so hard her entire body shook, and she put her arms out to me the way a child would, and I took her inside my arms and I held her tighter than I ever had, stroking her hair and feeling her soft warm tears on my face, and her trembling body pressed against mine.

Gently, I eased her back down on the bed and got a pillow under her head and took the extra cover from the end of the bed and spread it over her.

"Shouldn't I see Hoyt?" she said.

"Why don't you try to take a nap first? You're exhausted. Then you can see Hoyt."

"He really is your son, you know that now, don't you?"

"Yes; yes, I know that now," I said.

I went out and closed the door. I went into the living room and sat on the edge of the recliner. I smoked a cigarette with almost suicidal need. Her tears were still wet on my face. My hands were shaking.

Next to me, the phone went off like an explosion. I picked it up. A woman's voice said, "You better get down here."

"Where?"

"The office."

"What's wrong, Irma?"

"There's a guy."

"A guy?"

"Yeah, and he's—" I hadn't realized till then how rattled she was.

"There's a guy, Irma, and he's what?"

"He's dying."

"What?"

"He's dying. He opened the door and asked for you and then he fell on the floor."

"Call an ambulance."

"He won't let me."

"How can he stop you?"

"He's got a gun pointed at me. He made me call you. He wants you to come down here right away."

"Did he give you his name?"

"Huh-uh."

"I'll be right there."

I went in to kiss Faith goodbye. She slept. She was as warm as a slumbering child. I tiptoed back out, got my shoes and heavy winter jacket on, and headed downtown.

Chapter 36

All I could find was a no-parking zone, so I took it, knowing I'd most likely have to pay a $15 fine.

I climbed the stairs to my office, not wanting to wait for the elevator. When you do something like that at my age, and while you haven't completely given up smoking, you pay for it.

I arrived at my office door panting and sweating.

I pushed open the door. Irma, her thumb in her mouth, paced back and forth in front of the inner office. Seeing me, she jerked her thumb from her lips, as if I'd caught her doing something disgusting, which perhaps I had.

"Where is he?"

"In there." She indicated the inner office.

"Have you called an ambulance yet?"

"I thought you'd want to talk to him first."

I nodded a thank you and went on inside.

In the drab daylight, the place looked more like a museum than ever. The aged furnishings, the painted steam heat register in the corner, the linoleum floor—it was like stepping inside a time capsule.

He sat in the plump leather chair angled to the side of the coffee table. On his white shirt inside his tan suit you could see a wide patch of blood. He was pale and sweating, and when he spoke, you could almost hear his dry lips crack from fever. "You took a while."

"I got here as soon as I could."

"I didn't mean to scare the old lady."

I smiled. "Takes more than that to scare her."

"I'm not the guy you're looking for."

"Why don't you let me call an ambulance?"

"I want to tell you something first."

"No, first we call an ambulance."

I turned away from him and walked back to the door. In the silence my footsteps made squeaking noises on the old floor. Back when this place was new, men were probably still wearing spats.

He said, "Don't you see the gun I've got in my hand?"

"I see it."

"I told you I didn't want you to call an ambulance for me just yet."

I glanced back at him. "I guess you'll have to shoot me."

I opened the door and said to Irma, "Dial 911. Get an ambulance here as fast as you can."

She nodded.

After closing the door, I walked back to the desk and took the chair across from him. He was going quickly. His breathing was coming in small spasms and he didn't have enough strength to hold on to his weapon any more. It dropped from his hand to the floor. I was afraid it might discharge.

"You want to know something funny?"

"What?" I said.

"I'm the straight one. Paul, he—"

Richard Heckart's head twisted to the side abruptly, as if an invisible hand had slapped it. He lay like that a long moment and then angled his face back to me. "I just wanted you to know what really happened."

"You can tell me later. Maybe you'd better rest now."

"I just couldn't let Paul bring down the whole company. Our father's reputation. That's why I got involved with Vandersee and those slides. I wanted to force Vandersee to stop before people found out what he and Paul were doing."

Since he wanted to talk, I thought I might try to take advantage of it. "Who shot you?"

"I'm not sure. I was in my garage—"

"Could it have been Paul?"

"It could have been." He started to say something else and then stopped. His whole body had begun to twitch. During the Fifties I'd had a Collie who'd died of a lung disease. I'd held him there at the last as my two boys looked on, held him tight so they wouldn't see him tremble and get frightened. Richard Heckart was going into that phase now. "Could you get me a glass of water?"

"You bet."

I went to the door and asked Irma to get a glass of water quick, but when I turned around I said over my shoulder, "Forget it, Irma."

"What?"

"Forget it. I don't think he's going to need it."

Down the street I could hear the whoop and wail of the ambulance. On television, detectives always know when somebody's dead. In life they rarely do. Once, I threw a sheet over the face of a guy struck by a car, sure he was dead. He reached up with a big bear paw of a hand and ripped the sheet from his face, understandably angry with my mistake.

But instinctively I sensed that Richard Heckart had passed on. In the war I'd known a kid from Des Moines who always studied the bodies of people recently killed. While he would never admit it, I always suspected that he sat there and watched the corpses to see if he could find any evidence that souls did indeed migrate. Maybe now, as I stood over Richard Heckart, I was looking for the same thing. Maybe, given Faith's possible condition, I needed reassurance that we had souls to begin with, and that after our bodies died they did indeed go someplace more peaceful.

"He was a nice-looking man," Irma said, coming up and standing beside me. "I wish he would've let me call an ambulance earlier."

"I'm not sure he wanted to live all that badly."

"How come?"

"Oh, people made a lot of unfair judgments about him—and I think he was also tired of protecting somebody."

"Who?"

"His brother."

"What'd his brother do?"

"Well, for starters, I think he killed Karl Jankov."

"I thought George Pennyfeather—"

That's when the male-and-female ambulance team came trotting through the door, intense and singular in their white uniforms and air of urgency.

They went over to Richard Heckart and started all their procedures.

I leaned in to Irma and said, "I've got some things I've got to do."

"You be back today?"

"Probably not."

"What if somebody calls?"

"Just tell them I'll be back tomorrow."

"You okay?"

I laughed. "Do I look okay?"

She patted me on the shoulder. "Tomorrow I'll go over to Big Boy for the donuts. How's that?"

"Sounds more than fair."

"You going to look up Paul Heckart?"

"I guess that sounds like as good an idea as any."

"You think you're ever going to let me be your assistant?"

"Sure. Someday."

"I'd be a good one."

I then did something I never thought I ever would or even could. I brought my lips to Irma's forehead and kissed her. "I'll talk to you tomorrow," I said, and left.

She looked as surprised as I felt.

Chapter 37

The receptionist at Paul Heckart's office was sipping coffee and glancing at a *Cosmo* she had skillfully tucked beneath a wide swath of papers. Presumably she hadn't heard about Richard Heckart's death or she wouldn't be her usual indifferent self.

"Good morning," she said, then frowned slightly. "Do you have an appointment?"

"No. But I'd like you to buzz Paul if you would and tell him that I need to see him on a very urgent matter."

"I'm afraid that without an appointment—"

"He'll want to see me. Believe me."

I kept my voice level but I sounded more serious than most people she met at this desk.

She covered up *Cosmo* completely and then picked up the receiver from the small bank of phone buttons. She touched an expert red-tipped finger to a certain button and waited, tapping that same red-tipped finger against the desk. Finally, she said, "Humphf."

"What?"

"He doesn't seem to be in his office. Would you like me to page him?"

"Please."

"All right." She paged. The sound was like that of a hospital, discreet but imposing nonetheless. "Paul Heckart. Please call the receptionist. Paul Heckart. Please call the receptionist." To me, "It should just be a minute. Would you like to sit down?"

"No thanks."

Seeming vaguely insulted, she said, "Would you mind if I got back to my work, then?"

"Not at all."

I wondered if that would be *Cosmo* or the stack of papers.

After a minute, I said, "Would you mind paging him again?"

She glanced up. "Sometimes he gets busy and it's hard for him to get to the phone right away. If you'd just be a little patient—" Just then a pleasant-looking woman in her forties appeared.

She wore a gray suit that gave her the formidable look of a country-club matron who had once been a babe.

"Oh, Helen," the receptionist said. "Have you seen Paul in the past twenty minutes or so?"

Helen looked at me and then back at the receptionist. "Yes, I did. About fifteen minutes ago."

"Where was he?"

"In the small conference room in the back, but I think he went down the back stairs. He had a topcoat and valise with him."

"The back stairs lead to the parking garage?" I said.

She did not seem happy with me. There was an order to the universe and I was upsetting it. "Yes, why?"

"Thank you."

I got out of there before they could say anything.

The parking garage was a big gray concrete tomb, cold and shadowy on a day like this one. Car engines sounded like fighter planes echoing off the walls; the air was tart with the smell of exhaust fumes.

The parking place that said Paul Heckart in black-on-white letters was empty. At an outdoor phone, I called the Pennyfeathers. Lisa answered.

"Is George there?"

"Not right now. He's gone somewhere for a few hours."

"I'd like to know where."

She started to sound worried. "What's wrong?"

"I'm not sure yet. But I really need to get a hold of George."

"Would you mind telling me why?"

"It would be better right now if I didn't have to explain, Lisa. When I've got more time and more answers, I will. I promise. Now, would you tell me where George went?"

"The cabin."

"Where we were the other day?"

"Yes."

"Why did he go out there?"

"Well, he hadn't planned on it or anything but Paul came over and asked if he'd just ride along. Paul said he needed to check the cabin for a leaky roof. He still uses it from time to time, even though he officially gave it to us a long time ago."

"Thank you."

"You really sound in a hurry."

"I am. A little bit, anyway."

"Well, I hope everything's all right."

"I'm sure it will be."

I left town just as crews began putting up Christmas decorations on Third Avenue. The brightness of the ornaments gave the gray day a lift. Cedar Rapids is very pretty at Christmastime especially, the timbered hills surrounding it snow-topped and serene. The downtown decorations just make it all the more gorgeous.

Unfortunately, right now I didn't have time to think about anything pleasant at all. I wondered if Paul Heckart planned to kill George Pennyfeather the way he had the others.

Chapter 38

Snow had made the rutted cabin road even trickier to navigate. My car jostled left and right as if its springs were being tested. The windshield wipers, one of which needed new rubber, thwacked through the accumulating snow. The heater roared ineffectually at the seventeen-degree temperature. I found it a good idea to keep my black leather gloves on inside.

Finding the shelf I'd used the other day, I pulled the car over and got out. From here I could see down through the heavy forest and the whipping snow to the cabin and the lone blue Buick Regal parked there.

Huddling into my coat, my nose and cheeks already numb with cold, I started angling my way down the road.

In all, it took fifteen minutes to reach the small horseshoe-shaped clearing to the west of the cabin. Kneeling behind the thick trunk of an elm, I tried to see into the side windows ten yards away. But the only sign of life was the fragile curl of gray smoke from the chimney and my own silver breath. A vast silence lay on the cold day.

As I trotted across the clearing to the cabin, my feet crunching through patches of ice on the dead brown grass, I took out my .38 and gripped it tight into the curve of my hand.

I went around back. A screen door opened onto a small porch where three garbage cans and a tarpaulin-covered lawnmower stood. My weight on the porch wood was sufficient to make it creak as loud as the cry of a bird. I paused, my whole system charged with anxiety, certain that I'd been heard.

After a long minute, I took another step up onto the porch, leaning across so my hand could grab the doorknob and give it a turn. I wasn't really surprised that it was locked.

Backing off the porch, fixing my .38 tight into my hand again, I started around the side of the cabin, walking on my haunches because the windows were low and otherwise I would be easily spotted. I had gone perhaps ten feet hunched down this way when a voice behind me said, "I have a rifle, Mr. Walsh, and I'm fully prepared to use it. Please set your gun down carefully and turn around."

In one way the words had an almost comic effect. You hear them so often on television and so seldom in life—in my case, never once had I heard them in more than thirty years of law enforcement. But I didn't doubt their seriousness. There was a heat in them, a desperation, and I knew enough to take them seriously.

I squatted and set my gun on a patch of browned clover. Knees cracking, I stood up, turned around, and faced Paul Heckart.

Ever dapper, he wore a gray herringbone suit and a startling white shirt and a red necktie. A black fedora rested at a jaunty angle on his silver head, and a black topcoat complemented perfectly the gray of the suit. In his black-gloved hands he held a Remington, the stock an expensive mahogany, the blue steel oiled expertly. He looked like the world's most fashionable assassin.

He came closer, though not by much. We stood five feet apart. "I wish you hadn't come out here," he said.

"After your brother was killed, there wasn't any place else to go."

He couldn't have faked it, that look of surprise and remorse.

He said, shaking for the first time and not from the cold, "Richard is dead?"

"Yes. He died in my office."

His face resembled that of an animal that is just beginning to experience intolerable pain. His features could not settle on an expression but remained fluid in their grief. "Jesus, all he ever tried to do was help."

"You and Vandersee and Stella Czmek were involved in importing child pornography and Richard found out and tried to get you out of it by closing down the whole operation. Right?"

"Yes," he said, but he didn't give the impression he was listening very carefully.

"And you killed Karl Jankov because he learned what you were involved in and started blackmailing you along with Stella Czmek."

"That's where you're wrong," he said. "I didn't kill anybody."

"Well, somebody killed Jankov and Stella Czmek and Conroy and Richard."

"It wasn't me." He was beginning to fold under the pressure. I had the sense that a part of him wanted to hand the Remington over to me and put me in charge. He raised his head. He looked terrible. "I know what you think of me and my—compulsions. The children, and what happened, and all. But I didn't kill anybody. I swear."

"Is George inside?"

"Yes. Why?"

"I want to talk to him about Conroy."

"What about Conroy?"

"Who was he working for?"

"For Richard."

"What?"

"That's how Richard found out that I was involved with—the slides."

"This was when?"

"Years ago."

"And he was still working for Richard when he was killed?"

"Yes."

"Why?"

"Because Richard was afraid that I was still caught up in it all. Conroy would follow me around and—"

"There's something wrong here."

"What are you talking about?"

"All these deaths. There's somebody on a rampage. You just don't kill this many people without—"

The rifle shot was a high, hard sound on the drab, frozen day. At first, I reacted instinctively, not even trying to determine the direction of the shot. I simply dove for the crusted earth, banging my chin on the ground as I did so, stars forming on the sudden temporary darkness inside my eyes. As I struggled to shake my senses clear again, I heard the second shot, this one accompanied almost instantly by a small animal sob, the sound of an entity abruptly dying. There was the unyielding noise of a body hitting the ground, joined again by the gasp and sob of death, and then, as the echo of the gunshot died, there was once more the frozen silence.

The bullet had gone in the back of his head and ruined utterly his swank black fedora, just as it had ruined his forehead where the bullet had exited, leaving only a raw red hole, like something from the inside out, that I did not care to look at for long.

There was nothing to be done for him now. I hurried inside the cabin.

Chapter 39

My first impression was that he was dead, George Pennyfeather. He had been lashed to a straight-back chair with plastic-covered clothesline, and the side of his head smashed in with something of reasonable size and heft. As I bent down to untie his hands, I saw tossed away by the coffee table a piece of alloy that was probably a decorator paperweight of some kind. One corner of it was a gelatinous red, with hair covering the mucus-like blood.

As the clothesline came off, he groaned a few words that were unintelligible. His eyes rolled white and then closed again.

A small man, he was easy enough to get to the couch, where I helped him lie down. From the sink I grabbed a towel that I soaked in warm water, placing it carefully across his forehead. In one of the kitchen cabinets I found a half-filled fifth of Old Grand-Dad. I poured him a strong shot of it and brought it back to him.

Swallowing, he coughed, and when he coughed you could see the effects of the pain work like lightning across his head. He cursed, which I'd never heard him do before, and he stared at me with what seemed to be a mixture of gratitude and anger.

"Paul's dead," I said. "Somebody shot him."

I'd fixed him so finally in my mind as this weak, soft-spoken little man that his anger was all the more startling. "I should have known what happened and shot him myself a long time ago," he said. His fury gave him momentary strength.

"I don't know what you're talking about."

He tried to sit up. The pain from his head wound paralyzed him at midpoint, just after he'd tried to put his feet down on the floor. "Sonofabitch," he said.

"Just sit back. I'll get you some more whiskey."

He watched me for a long moment, as if trying to literally read my mind, and then he said, in the soft, almost plaintive voice I usually associated with him, "Maybe he'll come back and kill me, too. I deserve it."

"Who'll come back and kill you?"

"My son, David."

"David killed Paul?"

"Yes."

"But why?"

"Because they all knew what had happened and nobody did anything about."

"The child pornography, you mean?"

"That and what Paul had done to him."

"I still don't understand."

He waved his empty glass at me. I stepped over to the cupboard and got him more whiskey. Some of it spilled on my hand. The tart, inviting smell made me want some. I knew I'd better put it off till later.

After taking a long drink, he said, "Do you remember Lisa and me telling you that Paul—our good family friend—used to take David on fishing trips up here?"

"Yes."

He didn't get to the real subject, at first. He was more interested in punishing himself. "You know, I should never have had a son. I had nothing to teach a son. I was just this mousy little man who was fortunate enough to inherit a small amount of money and to marry into an even larger amount of money." He stared over at the fireplace. It was dead inside and smelled of ashes. "He told me what happened. That's why he insisted I drive out here with him. So he could tell me everything. I went berserk and he tied me up."

"You're talking about Paul?"

"Yes. He came over to the house this morning. He looked almost crazy. I guess all these years finally wore him down."

"Why did he want to come out here?"

"Because this is where it happened, I suppose."

"Where what happened?"

His jaw set. His fingers tightened on the glass until his knuckles were white. "Where he molested David when David was ten years old. Paul said he couldn't take the guilt any longer. And he said he knows who the killer is. He feels responsible for that, too."

He started crying. They were quiet tears, nothing dramatic, but you could tell the toll they took by the way the glass dropped from his hand, as if he had no more strength to hold it. "I didn't know till this morning," he said. "I didn't know."

I went over and poured a drink for myself in a coffee cup. It tasted much better than I'd wanted it to. I had a second.

Pennyfeather held the towel to his wound. His eyes were closed. He didn't open them when he spoke. "Looking back now, I can see all the hints David tried to give me over the years. How angry he'd get about Paul for no reason. How he'd tell me that he hated Paul and wished I'd get another job. And so he paid us back, starting with Jankov."

"Why Jankov?"

"Because when Jankov found out what Paul had done, he started blackmailing Paul. David decided to kill everybody who knew but who did nothing about it. There's this great—rage—over what happened to him."

"He let you go to prison."

He opened his eyes. "He was punishing me. And I deserved it. He'd reached out to me for help and I hadn't been bright enough to read the signs."

"So everybody who died knew what Paul had done to David?"

"Yes. We were all—in one way or another, we were all accomplices. Jankov and Stella Czmek tried to cash in on what had happened to David—and Paul and Richard had tried to cover it up." He drank some more whiskey. "He's never gotten over it. I know that now. It—changed him forever. He was always so worried about being manly and now I know why." He gazed off in the direction where Paul

Heckart lay in the snow. "I only wish I'd had the chance to kill Paul myself. I would have done it." He looked back at me. "I really would have. If I'd known."

"I believe you."

"Now we'd better find David."

I took the last of my whiskey so reverently you would have thought it was altar wine. "I'm going alone."

"He's my son."

"He's apt to be calmer if I'm alone."

"I don't want him to die."

"I don't either."

"You think you can convince him to give himself up?"

"I can try."

He started crying again, those soft tears of failure and regret that burn like acid inside the mind forever.

I buttoned my coat, tugged on my gloves, put my .38 in my right hand, and set off.

Chapter 40

The first shot tore a piece of elm bark off two feet to my right and came less than a minute after I left the cabin. Falling to my left, behind a chunk of granite boulder, I saw David up near the timberline. Even from here, he gave the impression of being frantic. He turned, stumbled, and continued his way up into the hills.

I gave him half a minute and then I went after him, weaving my way at an angle up the slope, keeping low and always looking for a glimpse of his blue sleeveless down jacket.

Within five minutes, the cold started to get bad again. I could feel my sinuses begin to plug up and my eyes to tear. By now, I stalked him along the crest of a cove, the river far below gray and cold. I had no idea where he was going and I doubt he did, either.

Spotting him, I dropped to my knee, slammed my hands into the cup-and-saucer for firing, and was seconds away from a warning shot when a deer appeared along the trail above me, blocking my shot. Any other time, the tawny-colored creature, beautiful even on this drab, overcast day, would have been worth approaching just to pet. Today she was an annoyance. I threw a rock to scatter her and then started weaving upslope again, thinking I was closing in on him now.

At the top of the hill, he let go three shots that put me flat on the ground, behind a rusted-out garbage can used by picnickers in the summer. There was a pavilion twenty yards away and it was from there, hiding behind tables that had been upended and tied together for the winter months, that he did his firing.

Knowing this was the only chance I'd have, I rolled back down the hill a few feet, got up on my haunches, and started running as hard as I could in that uncomfortable position, angling for the backside of the pavilion.

I was halfway there when I heard the shout. Then there were two shouts, one of them belonging to David. The other I was still not sure of.

Out of breath now, I fell to my knees behind the green chemical toilet the state park folks had planted here in the woods. I had a good view of the tables David hid behind, and an opportunity to wound him if he showed himself at all.

The second shout came again, and when I turned and saw whose voice it was, my stomach tightened and a chill sweat covered my upper body.

Carolyn Pennyfeather, dressed in a blue down jacket and Levi's like her brother, came up over the top of the hill, waving and shouting.

"Please, David; please just come back to the cabin and talk to me."

"You know better than that, Carolyn. You know what's going to happen to me."

"Please," she said. "Please, David."

All the time she talked, she moved wide in an easterly course so that she would eventually emerge directly in front of him. Her gloved hands were spread wide, as if she wanted to take him to her, and even from here I could hear the tears in her voice.

The pavilion had a pitched roof and railings painted silver. In the back was a big kitchen. In the summer there would be Japanese lanterns of red and blue and green strung here and caught in the soft breeze, and young couples on fire with love and lust, and grandkids parked on the knees of grandpas and grandmas. There would have been square dancing and beer kegs exploding with foam and the clang of horseshoes in progress. But now, in that terrible death that comes each autumn, there was just the cold and the dead, stripped trees and low, flat coffin-lid of sky.

He fired at her and it startled me. He didn't mean to kill her, of course, but that he fired at all meant that he was much more frightened and unbalanced than I'd imagined.

She just stood there, listening to the crack of rifleshot and the crackle of echo a few moments later. It scared her and you could see on the soft lines of her lovely face the first inkling that this was not the brother David she knew and loved. This was a stranger.

"She's trying to help you, David," I called as I came out from behind the green toilet.

I waited for his shot, and when it came I ducked and dropped to one knee.

She started running toward the pavilion. This time he didn't fire but let her come all the way under the roof, her footsteps slapping hollowly on the concrete floor.

I saw him lean out from behind the tables. She grabbed him by the head and shoulders and yanked him into her arms. She began sobbing immediately.

She gave me just the moment I needed, and I moved quickly, running hard up to the pavilion, edging closer along David's blind side and getting my .38 directly in line with his head.

I let them hold each other until David, too, started crying, and then I said, "Please give me your rifle, David. Now."

He started to get angry, to whirl away from her and put his weapon on me, but she blocked him, falling toward him so that he could not fire.

"Please, David; please. He's just trying to help."

From there, it was little trouble getting his rifle, turning him toward the river, starting him down the hill. I said nothing, just let Carolyn hold his arm and hug him as they moved downslope between the hardwoods.

"You know what they're going to do to me." David kept saying over and over. "I'll never get out of prison. Never."

"David, just try and calm down. Please."

"You don't understand, Carolyn. None of you ever did. Ever."

When the cabin came into sight, Lisa and George Pennyfeather stood in the front yard, staring upslope at us. Lisa looked as if she wanted to wave, one of those cheery flags of social-greeting poise she was so good at producing, but then her hand faltered when she saw my .38 trained on David's back, and she started crying and put her head on George's shoulder.

The worst part of arresting anybody in a domestic situation is the grief and anger of the other family members. The screams and epithets get shrill, and the threats frightening. Today, I saw something even more terrible, though—family members who blamed not you but themselves.

They fell onto David like supplicants, the three of them, enchaining him inside their arms, all of them crying and saying things that made no sense but yet made perfect sense if you understood the circumstances.

I put the .38 away and leaned against George Pennyfeather's car and smoked a cigarette and rubbed at my nose to get some feeling back into it. I wanted it to be spring and I wanted David Pennyfeather to have the opportunity for a decent life that Paul Heckart had denied him. I wanted the sun to shine and the quack of strutting ducks to be heard on the shoreline and the laughter of swimmers in the blue river to be sprinkled like gold dust on the day. I wanted Faith to be all right.

I was lost to my own thoughts when it happened, and it happened so quickly nobody could do anything about it.

He broke from them with great and overpowering force and ran to the edge of the woods, all the time tugging something from inside his blue down jacket. I saw what was about to happen, but there was no way I could stop it. He raised the gun to his face and set it against his temple. Then, in obscene slow motion, the gun fired. David's head jerked away just as the gun kicked in his hand. The roar was incredible and seemed to echo for many minutes.

David died later that evening, after telling his mother and sister what had gone on. He had killed Jankov because Jankov had one day made a remark about what had taken place between Paul Heckart and David. And David was only too happy to let his father go to prison for the murder. David, in his blind rage, held his father responsible for Paul Heckart's molesting him. Paul had been, after all, his father's friend.

For twelve years David had been in psychotherapy. Curiously, he never told the therapist about Paul Heckart... but David did manage to sublimate his anger. Then when his father was freed from prison, David began killing everyone associated with Paul Heckart and the porno ring. He killed Conroy, the private detective, because Conroy was about to go to the press with everything he'd found out. A PI who breaks a porno ring involving prominent citizens will find himself inundated with new clients.

George Pennyfeather sat in his living room listening to all this as if Carolyn were relating it in a language other than English. He didn't seem to quite understand—until, without warning, he began sobbing. They sat on either side of him, his wife and his daughter, taking turns holding him and rocking him gently the way they would an infant.

"Oh, Jesus, Jesus Christ," he said, a small man with a small sorrowful voice. There didn't seem much else to say.

Chapter 41

Six Days Later

Faith was in the recovery room for half an hour. Afterward, they brought her down to her room in the elevator. They let me and her parents ride along. In her room, the nurse fluffed the pillows and began arranging the various vases of flowers Faith had received, and made sure Faith was carefully set into bed. Only occasionally would she speak, and rarely was it more than a moan or some broken meaningless word, the voodoo effects of the anesthesia.

In the window the day was harsh gray, winter.

On either side of her bed stood her parents, her mother holding one of Faith's hands, her father the other. I caught myself thinking how old they looked, and then I remembered that I was older than them.

Not even by noon was she speaking coherently. Her father said, "Would you like to get a cup of coffee?"

It was the first time in four meetings he'd ever said a single word to me. I felt like a seventeen-year-old who'd lucked into something pretty big.

In the cafeteria, her father lit a Camel. When he brought it away from his mouth with a farm-tanned, liver-spotted hand, he said, "I don't know what you got in mind for my daughter."

"Neither do I, to be honest."

"She sure seems to like you."

"I like her." I paused. I tried to say I loved her. I couldn't quite. Not to him.

"She seems to trust you, too. You'd think a girl with her looks would've had better luck with men than she has."

For a time he didn't say anything at all. I watched nurses and interns carry sensible lunches on bright plastic trays to small Formica tables.

He said, "That doctor said he thinks they got it all."

"They got it early. That's the important thing."

He said, "You be all right watchin' Hoyt for a few days? Otherwise, we'll be glad to take him."

"I'll be fine."

He had another cigarette and said, "You wanna go back up? I told the missus she could come down and have lunch when we got back."

"Why don't you go on ahead? I need to make a phone call." I walked him to the elevators and then walked over to the phone booth.

"How's she doing?" I asked George Pennyfeather a few minutes later.

"Better. Not great but better."

"How's her mother doing?"

"Lisa's a very strong person. Look how she held the family together when I was in prison."

Yesterday Carolyn had had what the family doctor called "a breakdown." She had been heavily sedated since David's funeral two days earlier. Even with the drugs, she'd slumped into a deeper depression.

"We should have known," George Pennyfeather said. "We should have guessed. What Paul did to him, I mean."

It was something he would be saying for the rest of his life.

Around five-thirty, just as Dan Rather came on the set mounted high on the wall across from Faith's bed, her parents said they were going downstairs to the cafeteria for dinner. I said fine, I'd stay here. We'd spent the afternoon sitting in chairs around the bed, snapping to attention each time she so much as moved. They were not yet what you'd call friendly, but they were no longer hostile, either.

When they were gone, I stood up and went to her. I picked up her hand. Her eyes didn't open. I held her hand all the time I said my shabby little prayer. It wasn't just for her, my prayer, it was for that more abstract unit called "us," Hoyt and her and me, and what lay ahead.

It was dark then, and you could see the street lights burning faintly in the fog of an early December evening.

I turned back to the bed. Her eyes, open now, stared at the ceiling as if she did not quite comprehend where she was. I leaned in and kissed her on the forehead.

"Why don't you see if you can get Hoyt on the phone?" she said. "Marcia can hold the receiver to his mouth and he can babble or something."

So I got Hoyt on the phone and he did babble. And at the end, Marcia said, "So how's she doing?"

"She's doing fine," I said, and hung up.

In the darkness, in the silence, the TV set having been turned off, she said, "It's not going to be easy for me. Even if I'm all right physically, psychologically it's going to be tough."

"I know."

"I keep wanting to—touch myself up there—but I—I'm afraid."

"I love you, Faith."

I was afraid I was going to start crying. She must have sensed this because she saved me just then. "How's it going with my parents?"

"Pretty good."

"You look like you're about fifteen when you're around them. Tripping all over yourself."

"I've got evil designs on their innocent young daughter."

She reached out through the rails of her hospital bed and squeezed my hand. "I don't want to start crying and I don't want you to start crying, you understand?"

"I understand perfectly," I said but then of course that's exactly what we did, both of us, started crying.

"I thought you were tougher than that," she said as she pulled me closer for a kiss.

"Oh, no," I said, barely able to speak, "I'm not tougher than that at all."

THE END

Ed Gorman Bibliography

Mystery/Thriller/Horror

Novels

Shadow Games (1993)
Cold Blue Midnight (1995)
Black River Falls (1996)
Cage of Night (1996)
Runner in the Dark (1996)
Shadow Games (1996)
Night Kills (1999)
The Poker Club (1999)
Daughter of Darkness (1998)
The Silver Scream (1998)
Rituals (2002)
The Midnight Room (2009)

Series

Jack Dwyer

Rough Cut (1985)
New Improved Murder (1985)
Murder Straight Up (1986)
Murder in the Wings (1986)
The Autumn Dead (1987)
A Cry of Shadows (1990)
The Dwyer Trilogy (1994) (includes
    The Autumn Dead, A Cry of Shad-
    ows, and the short story "Eye of the
    Beholder")

Tobin

Murder in the Aisle (1987)
Several Deaths Later (1988)

Jack Walsh

The Night Remembers (1991)

Robert Payne

Blood Moon (1994; UK title Blood
    Red Moon; reprinted as Dead
    Cold, 2014)
Hawk Moon (1995)
Harlot's Moon (1998)
Voodoo Moon (2000)

Sam McCain

The Day the Music Died (1999)
Will You Still Love Me Tomorrow
    (2000)
Wake Up Little Susie (2001)
Save the Last Dance for Me (2002)
Everybody's Somebody's Fool (2004)
Breaking Up Is Hard To Do (2004)
Fools Rush In (2007)
Ticket to Ride (2010)
Bad Moon Rising (2011)
Riders on the Storm (2014)

Dev Conrad

Sleeping Dogs (2008)
Stranglehold (2010)
Blindside (2011)
Flashpoint (2013)
Elimination (2015)

As E.J. Gorman

The Marilyn Tapes (1995)
The First Lady (1995)
Senatorial Privilege (1999)

As Daniel Ransom

Toys in the Attic (1986)
The Forsaken (1988)
The Babysitter (1989)
Nightmare Child (1990)
The Serpent's Kiss (1992)
The Long Midnight (1992)
The Zone Soldiers (1996)

Westerns

Novels

Graves' Retreat (1989)
Two Guns to Yuma (1989 as by Jake
    Foster; reprinted as by Gorman,
    2005)
Night of Shadows (1990)
Wolf Moon (1993)
The Sharpshooter (1993)
Trouble Man (1998)
Ride into Yesterday (1999)
Storm Riders (1999)
Lawless (2000)
Desperadoes (2001)
Ghost Town (2001)
Vendetta (2002)
Gun Truth (2003)
Relentless (2003)
Lynched (2003)
Branded (2004)
Shoot First (2006)

Series

Cavalry Man

Cavalry Man: Killing Machine
    (2005)
Cavalry Man: Powder Keg (2006)
Cavalry Man: Doom Weapon (2007)

Leo Guild

Guild (1987)
What the Dead Men Say (1990)
Death Ground (1990)
Blood Game (1991)
Dark Trail (1991)

Dev Mallory

Bad Money (2005)
Fast Track (2006; with Bill Crider)

Collections

Prisoners: And Other Stories (1988)
Dark Whispers: And Other Stories
    (1988)
Best Western Stories of Ed Gorman
    (1992)
Prisoners and Other Stories (1992)
Cages (1995)
Moonchasers: And Other Stories
    (1995)
The Collected Ed Gorman, Vol. 1:
    Out There in the Darkness (1997)
The Collected Ed Gorman, Vol. 2:
    The Moving Coffin (1997)
Famous Blue Raincoat (1999)
The Dark Fantastic (2001)
The Long Ride Back (2004)
Different Kinds of Dead and Other
    Tales (2005)
The End of It All: And Other Stories
    (2009)
Noir 13 (2010)
Scream Queen and Other Stories
    (2014)

Chapbooks

Out There in the Darkness (1995)

Graphic Novels

Trapped (1993; with Dean Koontz)

Novellas

Reason Why (1992)
Dirty Coppers (2012; with Richard T. Chizmar)
Cast in Dark Waters (2002; with Thomas Piccirilli)

Young Adult

Robin in I, Werewolf (1992; with Angelo Torres)
The Killer (1995 as by Chris North)
Night Screams (1996 as by Daniel Ransom)

Non fiction

The Dean Koontz Companion (1994; with Martin H Greenberg)
Speaking of Murder: Interviews With the Masters of Mystery and Suspense (1998)
"They're Here…" The Invasion of the Body Snatchers: A Tribute (1999; revised 2006; with Kevin McCarthy)
Speaking of Murder, Volume II: Interviews With the Masters of Mystery and

Edited Anthologies

Cat Crimes

Cat Crimes I (1991; with Martin H Greenberg)
Cat Crimes II: Masters of Mystery Present More Tales of the Cat (1992; with Martin H Greenberg)
Cat Crimes III (1992; with Martin H Greenberg)
Danger in DC: Cat Crimes in the Nation's Capital (1993)
Feline and Famous: Cat Crimes Goes Hollywood (1994; with Martin H. Greenberg)
Cat Crimes for the Holidays (1995; with Martin H Greenberg & Larry Segriff)
Cat Crimes Takes a Vacation (1995; with Martin H Greenberg)
Cat Crimes Through Time (1999; with Martin H Greenberg & Larry Segriff)

The Black Lizard: Anthology of Crime Fiction (1987)
The Second Black Lizard Anthology of Crime Fiction (1988)
Stalkers (1989; with Martin H Greenberg)
Under the Gun: Mystery Scene Presents the Best Suspense and Mystery, First Annual Collection (1990; with Martin H. Greenberg & Robert J. Randisi)
Invitation to Murder (1991; with Martin H. Greenberg)
Solved (1991; with Martin H Greenberg)
Dark Crimes 2: Modern Masters of Noir (1993)
Predators (1993; with Martin H Greenberg)

The Fine Art of Murder: The Mystery Reader's Indispensable Companion (1993)

The Year's 25 Finest Crime and Mystery Stories (1997; with Martin H. Greenberg & Joan Hess)

American Pulp (1997)

Love Kills (1997)

The Big Book of Noir (1998; with Martin H. Greenberg & Lee Server)

The Year's 25 Finest Crime and Mystery Stories: Seventh Annual Edition (1999; with Martin H. Greenberg)

Pure Pulp (1999; with Bill Pronzini)

Pulp Masters (2001; with Martin H. Greenberg)

Murder Most Feline: Cunning Tales of Cats and Crime (2001; with Martin H. Greenberg & Larry Segriff)

Guns of the West (2002; with Martin H. Greenberg)

The Blue and the Gray Undercover (2002)

Kittens, Cats and Crime (2003; with Carol Gorman)

The Deadly Bride: And 19 of the Year's Finest Crime and Mystery Stories (2006; with Martin H. Greenberg)

Prisoner of Memory (2008; with Martin H. Greenberg)

Between the Dark and the Daylight: And 27 More of the Best Crime and Mystery Stories of the Year (2009; with Martin H. Greenberg)

On Dangerous Ground: Stories of Western Noir (2011; with Martin H. Greenberg & Dave Zeltserman)

The Interrogator: And Other Criminally Good Fiction (2012; with Martin H. Greenberg)